THE GARDEN
OF MONSTERS

Lorenza Pieri

THE GARDEN
OF MONSTERS

*Translated from the Italian
by Liesl Schillinger*

Europa
editions

Europa Editions
8 Blackstock Mews
London N4 2BT
www.europaeditions.co.uk

Translation by Liesl Schillinger
Original title: *Il giardino dei mostri*
Translation copyright 2020 by Europa Editions

A catalogue record for this title is available from the British Library
ISBN 978-1-78770-221-9

Pieri, Lorenza
The Garden of Monsters

Book design and cover illustration by Emanuele Ragnisco
www.mekkanografici.com

Prepress by Grafica Punto Print – Rome

Printed and bound in Great Britain by Clays Ltd, Elcograf S.p.A

CONTENTS

0. THE FOOL - 13

1. THE MAGICIAN - 17

2. THE HIGH PRIESTESS - 31

3. THE EMPRESS - 51

4. THE EMPEROR - 65

5. THE HIEROPHANT - 77

6. THE LOVERS - 89

7. THE CHARIOT - 105

8. JUSTICE - 117

9. THE HERMIT - 129

10. THE WHEEL OF FORTUNE - 143

11. STRENGTH - 155

12. THE HANGED MAN - 167

13. DEATH - 173

14. TEMPERANCE - 197

15. THE DEVIL - 215

16. THE TOWER - 243

17. THE STAR - 253

18. THE MOON - 267

19. THE SUN - 287

20. JUDGMENT - 299

21. THE WORLD - 317

ACKNOWLEDGMENTS - 345

ABOUT THE AUTHOR - 347

In memory of Paolo

THE GARDEN
OF MONSTERS

0. THE FOOL
Energy. Origin. Liberating Force.

Nobody thought any more about what this region had been like only a few decades before. A putrid swamp, an inhospitable locale infested with malaria, where you could be felled by mosquitoes, or wracked by sweats from atrocious fevers and bad water. All that was left of that world were heartbreaking folk songs about lost loved ones, voyages of no return, and birds whose feathers fell out simply from flying overhead. The hills and the ancient trees were the same; and as always, the nearness of the sea converted the light into a substance that made everything glisten.

Once death had been vanquished, beauty remained.

The area and its surroundings had been transformed into places that were pleasing in every season. There was the autumn sun on the leaves of the oaks, the horseback rides along the beach before lunch, the fine wine, the countryside with its olive trees and orderly vineyards, their ever-changing colors as nuanced as renaissance frescoes. There were beaches of gray sand, darkened by the water, which was nevertheless clear and clean; there was the village with the tower, the crows, the medieval wall, and the little square; the sublime food, the placid animals, the farmhouses that were ugly, but still could be bought cheaply. There was the proximity of Rome, and something in the air, at the end of the eighties, that promised a change for the better. Money had arrived, the lifeblood and the poison of everything that would come after. But before it had created a trap too large to be seen by those who found themselves caught within it, the money that arrived was a good sign, as cheerful and shameless as the decade in which it circulated so freely.

Yet the region would remain a place that everybody swore at. That everybody cursed, with epithets like *fucking Maremma*, *stinking Maremma*. Maremma.

In those years, great changes were brought about by the arrival of newcomers, and by what went on between the local people and the tourists; between the noble families that owned the estates and the families who had obtained the "land they labored on" from the agricultural reforms of the postwar era. State-owned farmhouses were bought and renovated one after the other by rich families, who used the land to provide themselves with lawns, patio furniture, dog runs. Stables were transformed into dining rooms, watering troughs into swimming pools, feed lots covered to make room for benches and dancing after parties.

Changes of ownership and inexorable waves of colonization; the arrival not only of people, but of personalities. Then, at a certain point, someone who was completely different arrived, someone from far away, strange, a foreigner, running away from her life, her obsessions, her illness. An artist. A genius. The joker in the deck, the wild card that can represent every other card without identifying with any one of them.

By a series of accidents, a hillside in this area was ideally suited to the artist's intentions, a place where she could create a world of her own. A magical and colorful garden, an unusual and extraordinary refuge. She stayed there a long time, but not forever. For the time it took to build twenty-two gigantic sculptures that embodied the Major Arcana of the tarot deck; to transform that hillside, and the lives of several people, for all time; to assert a presence on the natural environment with generosity and imagination. To leave a gift to the world. An enigmatic gift that would inhabit an eternal present. A gift that gave life to a story which could only be told there, in that time, and in that space. Where the encounter had taken place; where the magic was transacted.

1. THE MAGICIAN
Shrewdness. Beginning. Choice.

S auro had quickly understood the potential of his land. He was a man who knew how to harvest signals from the wind and turn them into profit. The first test of his intuition had become a kind of turning point for his own life, and not only for his. The demand for summer houses had grown in recent years, and he'd thought that, with a little bit of work, he might be able to rent out the second farmhouse, the stone one, which up to now had been used as a tool shed. It was in a quiet, rather isolated spot, but it wasn't far from the sea and the village, and it had a view that wasn't bad. His own house was nearby, with an olive grove, and horses to rent out for riding, an activity that was taking off pretty well. At that time, he was the only one offering that in the area. Farm stays—later there would be dozens of them—were only just beginning to come into fashion. The notion that the countryside was a place where you might happily spend an enjoyable vacation was already fairly popular, and the idea that you could exchange work in the fields for hospitality was in circulation. But that was something that never came to pass, at least not in these parts. The farmhouse had no electric light or heating, but Sauro had cleaned it well and installed a generator. It had floors of worn terracotta; a few tiles were missing, but the color was pretty, and most important, they were the same ones as when the house was built, in the 19th century. As soon as he saw them, he realized they would go over better than the geometrically-shaped majolica tiles his wife had wanted for the renovation. He was surprised, but had stored up the information. He understood that using the adjectives "antique" and "original" in place of "old" and "broken" would work in his favor. Similarly, inside the enormous fireplace that dominated the central wall of the living room, he installed a bench made of two old railway ties, which made everything reek of tar whenever you built a fire. It was suffused with carcinogenic oil, but those were years when people were more or less indifferent to the toxicity of things, as long they looked "natural," felt like "old-time" solutions. In the kitchen he'd avoided replacing the cracked granite sink, which had only cold running water, and had left the dark-green, flaking wooden window frames, with their paper-thin glass, exactly as they were, even though he recognized the great advantage of the anodized aluminum window frames in his own house. On the wall, he'd hung horseshoes and big rusty keys that no longer opened any door, though his wife had wanted to put up framed prints of Impressionist paintings that she'd bought in Grosseto. He'd told her that his clients went crazy for old iron. She'd let him do it his way, as always.

The garden out back, which had been overgrown with briars and weeds for years, was put in order; and he hung a hammock between the two surviving trees, an oak and an ailing plum. And finally, in a stroke of genius, he invented a story for the stone house. He dredged up a tale he'd been told when he was little by his father, Settimio, who had been drunk at the time, in a time and place when habitual excessive drinking wasn't considered a problem, it was something normal—even grounds for boasting about your stamina when you joined the others to work the land. Settimio took bottles out of the family wine cellar and hid them in that farmhouse, turning it into a kind of warehouse. To keep Sauro away from it, he'd told him that it was the place where, at the end of the 19th century, the police had captured and killed the bandit Tiburzi, who'd been taken by surprise in this peasant dwelling, along with his accomplice Fioravanti. He'd added that Tiburzi's ghost appeared on certain autumn nights, sometimes accompanied by rifle shots. Sauro remembered that, as a child, whenever he heard hunters shooting before dawn, he'd always thought it was Tiburzi, come back from the dead. Even after he found out that the house where they'd captured the outlaw was some-where else, he didn't stop hearing phantom shots. Tiburzi was a true legend, hailed as a kind of local Robin Hood. He'd been a fugitive for twenty-four years, with a huge price on his head. It was never clear whether he was a good guy or a bad guy; probably a little of both. Stories about him painted him as a kind of a vigilante, who avenged the wrongs done to the peas-antry by the landowners; rather like a mobster who demands protection money. But he'd always retained a heroic aura. Sauro made the most of that. A photo of the bandit hung in every local restaurant, always the same one, taken at the time of his death: tied to a post, a shotgun between his lifeless hands, his sightless eyes half closed.

The first person who came to visit the house was an extremely elegant brunette, who had a Northern accent but said she lived in Rome, and that she'd been coming to the area for years, though Sauro had never seen her. Sauro thought the farmhouse wasn't up to her standards, but he revised his opin-ion as he watched the movement of the woman's eyebrows in front of the enormous fireplace. More information emerged: he learned that she was a university professor, and that she was looking for a place to spend the summer with her *companion*, as she called him, and her son, but also wanted a guest room for friends. Space wasn't lacking, but everything else was.

Sauro took a Toscano cigar from his jacket, slipped it halfway into his mouth to dampen it, cut it in half with a cigar cutter that he always kept on him, and lit the moistened part with a lighter. It made a flame at the tip that he blew out with one breath. This operation took no longer than ten seconds, but the woman had not remained indifferent as she watched this work of lips and hands.

Right there, in front of the fence beyond which the dense woods began, Sauro started telling the story of Tiburzi. He lied, saying that this was *definitely* the last place he'd been seen alive.

The woman's face lit up.

Fiddling with his cigar, he upped the ante: "And of course, you know the story about his grave?"

"No, what is it?"

"When Tiburzi died, the priest didn't want to bury him in the cemetery because he was a criminal. But the people of the village insisted he was a good man, and ought to be buried in the churchyard. And so, to make everyone happy, they buried him half inside the graveyard and half out. If you go to the village and visit the cemetery, you'll see that there's still a half column marking the old entrance. The body of Tiburzi supposedly lies beneath it: the legs inside, the head and shoulders outside. But the ghost comes here; and sometimes you can hear him shooting in the night. But not in the summer, just in hunting season, don't worry."

They smiled at one another.

"How beautiful. I love ghost stories," the brunette said, turning to leave. "I'll tell my companion about it, and I'll call you back as soon as possible. Be sure not to give the place to anyone else in the meantime. I think this farmhouse would be perfect for us."

The story had worked; the tale had cast its magic on four broken windows and an uneven floor. When Settimio found out how much Sauro had asked in rent for the farmhouse, he shook his head, let out a brief profanity that ended in a burst of laughter which seemed to come straight from his cirrhotic liver, and exclaimed, "People are such assholes!"

By nightfall the woman already had brought a check for the deposit. A whole month, with no discount, which Miriam, incredulous, rushed to deposit in the bank the next morning, confessing in a loud voice to her friend at the Credito Cooperativo, who was standing by the teller window, "If I had that kind of money, no way in hell would I spend it on a vacation in this pigsty of a shack, with no light, with the wind coming in everywhere. I'd book a nice luxury cruise and get out of here. Who can understand this?" Then she said goodbye, laughing.

Sauro, without truly understanding it, had understood everything.

Sauro, also known as "the King." A nickname he'd earned playing cards at the bar—one afternoon, thirty years ago, he'd won with a king, three games in a row. "Another king!" the others at the table had shouted. "Unbelievable! What are you doing, shitting them out?"

No merit, no honor, attached to this "King;" no noble lineage; just card luck, and the prideful instinct to instantly take the title as his due. Besides, his friends had ridiculous nicknames, too, which either derived from their physical flaws or had been handed down for generations, like Poorboy, Tightass, Thief, or the more modern Bootlicker and Wuss. He even started calling himself "the King" because he thought the nickname fit him like a glove. When he came knocking at somebody's door, he would announce himself like this: "I'm Sauro, the King." At first he was teased, got insults like, "Get lost, go away," and "Yeah, and I'm the Pope," but he didn't give up until the mother of his girlfriend at the time, Adriana, had said to him solicitously, upon opening the door of her house, "I'll call the Queen for you."

Everyone thought he and Adriana would get married early: their families had known each other forever, they were a very compatible couple, they even resembled each other physically. They seemed destined to spend their lives together and to reproduce an infinite succession of black-eyed beauties with ultra-long eyelashes.

Adriana had a first cousin her age whom she really liked, Miriam, who was sort of a blonde version of herself, with blue eyes. Miriam worked as a saleswoman in an optician's boutique in the nearest big city. When Adriana wanted to buy Sauro a pair of sunglasses for his birthday, they went to the boutique and spent an amusing afternoon there. Miriam made him try on dozens of models, and when he finally managed to choose a pair, he said, "I don't know how it happened; you two have put a spell on me." The two cousins smiled approvingly at the image of Sauro reflected in the mirror: he truly was handsome and nice, and beyond that, he was completely aware of the game they were playing. But then, a few days after his twenty-third birthday, Sauro deliberately broke the arm of his sunglasses so he could go back to Miriam and ask her to fix them, so he could go back again two days later to pick up the glasses right before closing time; and, with the boutique empty and almost all the lights turned out, kiss her on the lips and take possession of her heart for always.

A period of secrecy lasted several months, but even though Sauro and Miriam tried to be seen together as little as possible in the company of others, every exchange of glances between them was like a lightning bolt that lit up the room. Adriana figured it out on the afternoon of Saint Stephen's Day, when the whole family was gathered at their aunt and uncle's house, playing cards and eating *panforte*. She seethed with hatred for them. She demanded that every single one of their relatives break ties with Sauro and all of the Biaginis, and she ordered her parents and siblings to stop talking to Miriam.

Not long after, she got herself pregnant by a neighbor who had pursued her for ages, a country boy of few words and little land, who worked as a farmer for a countess in the area. They got married before her belly was showing, and all in all, given that it was a revenge marriage, it was less disastrous than it might have been. Giovanna was born, a beautiful girl, even if, according to Adriana, she looked too much like Miriam, with the features of her mother's side of the family, and the fair coloring of her father's side. Two boys would follow, Antonio and Massimo, who grew up in the gardens of the estate where their parents worked but were strictly kept away from the horses, because Adriana didn't want them to end up being cowboys one day, like someone she didn't even want to name.

Miriam quit her job at the glasses boutique and moved to the village, where Sauro had a tiny apartment inside the walls, and started working at the grocery store there. She felt very bad for Adriana, and loved her very much, but she would have given up anything in the world for Sauro, whatever the consequences. Nothing could stop her from getting married in the village and from being shamelessly, radiantly happy, even if half the family wasn't invited and her mother cried the entire time over having a daughter who'd stolen another woman's man, and a cheating son-in-law who'd made her niece and her sister miserable, which could bode nothing good. Miriam, whose father was dead, was walked down the aisle by her future father-in-law, Settimio, who for once was happy with *his* Sauro, on whom he had never before bestowed a possessive adjective, or any adjective that was not derogatory. Settimio was so happy that he offered to pay for a lavish wedding feast, at which he became so drunk with joy and devotion that he ended up passing out during the last toast.

When she became pregnant with Saverio, at the end of the 1960s, Miriam stopped working at the grocery. From that time on, there was very little money, and prospects were very uncertain for her and Sauro. Things only got worse four years later, when she got pregnant again. But they were young and, on the whole, lighthearted, with the heedlessness of youth—especially her, because she never thought about the future. Her life revolved around the daily chance of going to the seaside. If, after she'd made lunch and done the dishes, Sauro was free to go to the beach with her and their son to get some *fresh air*, all her ambitions were satisfied.

When Annamaria was born, it was a year of true hardship. Fruit flies had cut the olive harvest in half in the family's groves, and Sauro was forced to go out looking for piecework, which he'd never done before. Miriam kept house and looked after the children. She was often tired, but she was never anxious, because she felt so confident that Sauro would always find a solution.

One morning, a big wooden box was delivered to her. This frightened her, because Adriana had sent it, and Miriam expected anything that came from her cousin to be tainted with hatred. On first glance, she thought it resembled a child's coffin, and was afraid it might contain an evil gift, like the curses that bad fairies hurl at innocent babies when they don't get invited to royal christenings. In any event, she was too curious to resist, and so, overcoming her fear, she opened the box: it was full of little outfits, handmade coverlets, socks and tiny caps, crocheted baby clothes, finely embroidered bed linen, little pajamas, everything in pink. A marvelous, elegant, brand-new trousseau for her baby. At the bottom of the box was a letter from Adriana: "All of this comes from the countess. She also has a little girl, and too many things she can't use because the baby grew so fast. She is a very generous lady and has taught me a nobility of soul that you will never possess. Nonetheless, I know that you are in need, and that things aren't going well for you and Sauro, so here are some gifts for your little girl. I send you my congratulations. Don't thank me, it's all the countess's doing."

Miriam pulled everything out of the box and made the sign of the cross before putting each item from the layette into the wardrobe. Even though she was superstitious, these things were too beautiful not to be used. She dressed little Annamaria all in pink. In the ensuing days, she had a pretty photograph taken of the girl, with the little cap, the eyelet lace dress, the crocheted cardigan, and the embroidered baby blanket. After having a few copies printed, she sent one to the countess with a thank-you note. The note had to be forwarded, because the countess never spent any time in the country after summer was over, so Adriana would send on her mail, after first steaming open the letters to read them for herself. She took care of the countess's home as if she lived there herself, to such an extent that she felt herself mistress of the house. On the morning that the letter appeared in the sunny dining room, alongside a vase of roses from the garden, freshly cut, Adriana was at ease in the role of a noblewoman. As she twirled a silver teaspoon in a porcelain cup, she looked at the photo of the daughter of the King and her cousin, dressed in all the pink lace she could wear at one time, and she winced in compassion for that little girl with the low forehead, and those two paupers for parents, not admitting to herself that she hadn't stopped being jealous.

The letter was opened by the countess in Saint Moritz. She looked distractedly at the photograph without fully understanding who the little girl might be. She recognized the cardigan but felt no sense of connection to the child's features, not even a distant one. She threw it in with the mail that required no response, which was to be thrown away. She did so many acts of charity that she could hardly be expected to remember them all. She had an appointment for tea with her cousin Marella and one of her friends, an American artist who'd come to the mountains to recover after a hospital stay. Her name was Niki de Saint Phalle; her father was a New York banker with roots in the French nobility, and her mother was a rich American who'd grown up in France. She had met her many years before in Paris, and, as often happens in certain exclusive social circles, she had met her later in New York, and now in the Alps. Niki had told her about her pneumonia, about the pulmonary defect she was born with, and about the asthma that plagued her incessantly in that period, partly because she used synthetic materials to make her sculptures, materials her doctors had advised her not to handle.

It was on that afternoon that the artist confided to Marella her dream of building a magical garden of colored statues so enormous that you could walk through them. To Marella this sounded like a splendid idea, she would discuss it with her brothers. Perhaps it would be possible to use some of their land in Tuscany, right by her cousin's estates. "What a coincidence, I just opened a letter that came from there," the countess said. That was the beginning of a long and laborious dream. Nobody could have expected that the life of the artist and the life of the child festooned in pink would intersect.

* * *

In the summer of 1988, in a farmhouse not much different from the one Sauro had rented out as the "house of Tiburzi," and not far away from it, a photo shoot took place that provoked a great deal of controversy. The subject of the shoot was the secretary of the Italian Communist Party, which was in crisis at the time. This was an era when political compromises were becoming harsher and harsher, and the label "communist" was becoming harder for many people to bear with pride. It no longer evoked the idea of progress as much as it conjured a far-away, practically unreal past, which perhaps never had existed as it had come to be portrayed, but was associated with repressive forms of government. Times had changed across the globe, and communists were beginning to feel the need to compensate for the strange and precarious present with private comforts that were made public. And so it was that the recently-married secretary of the Italian Communist Party allowed himself to be interviewed and photographed kissing his bride under a beautiful blue summer sky, amid the boughs of the olive grove of the farmhouse, which was instantly rebaptized the "love dacha."

The photographs, which were initially published in a magazine affiliated with the main national Leftist daily paper, *L'Unità*, had unexpected resonance. For weeks, nothing else was discussed in the newspapers, on the radio, or at local party meetings. At *Unità* festivals, polls were conducted to determine whether this public display of affection in broad daylight was welcome to the base or not. A shocking majority said yes.

In very little time, Sauro saw his workload double. On the day when journalists and photographers from a different newspaper showed up at his place, looking to do another shoot on "love dachas" in the area, he realized that something was happening right beneath his cowboy boots, amid the peeling walls of the so-called Tiburzi farmhouse. That night he introduced himself to his tenants, walking up to the door holding a horse by the bridle, bearing a basket of apricots and a bottle of a local red, Morellino di Scansano. Sauro had always known how to make gestures that would be appreciated. When the brunette's *companion* opened the door, he handed him the basket and said, "Of all the places you could have chosen to bring your ideology to die, you had to come here? Now, besides being guilty of the death of Tiburzi, this house will also have the death of communism on its conscience. It seems to me this farmhouse hasn't brought much good to the people. When you leave, I'm bringing in the priest to bless it. I don't want the other ghosts in this place to go on a rampage." The comrade started laughing and invited him in. He tied up his horse and said he wouldn't stay long. He didn't leave until late into the night, after having eaten and drunk.

"Sauro's a funny name for someone who deals with horses," the professor told him, when she led him to the door.

"Why's that?" he said. "Because it means 'chestnut?' It makes life easier, like when you call a black cat Blackie—it's easy to remember. As they say, your name is your destiny."

"*Nomen omen.*"

"I'm not sure what you mean, but, yes, Sauro is a man's name, and a name for animals, and for a hair color, and it's also who I am. Anyway, at home, all of us have names that start with an 'S': my father Settimio; me, Sauro; my son Saverio. If I ever have a grandson, I'd like him to be called Silvio."

Even though he'd finished high school, because his mother was a communist and had wanted Sauro to learn all the words that the ruling class knew, he was aware that the battlefield of knowledge was one on which he would never prevail. In any case, being a cowboy didn't call for intellectual refinement; and Sauro knew that conforming to people's expectations had always served him well. Secretly, he was convinced that know-it-alls understood nothing about real life, and that they were easily fooled, especially if you let them think they were smarter than you.

The professor laughed. Sauro lingered, hesitating, on the threshold. Outside, the song of crickets, which had replaced the keening of the cicadas, seemed to remind him how much time had passed.

"It's a shame you're with that prick, otherwise I would kiss you."

She shrugged, raised her chin, her eyes, as if to say: "Oh yeah?" But she wouldn't have objected at all. She thought over his words. She remembered watching him mouth the cigar the first time they met.

Sauro untied his horse, which followed him like a dog. In

fifty steps he was home. He took off its harness and led the horse to the stable. He came in through the front door—the key was still in the lock. He tossed his boots, pants, and jackets into a corner of the entryway, then fell into bed beside Miriam, who'd been asleep for a while, and had given up waiting for him a while before that.

2. THE HIGH PRIESTESS
Purity. Knowledge. Gestation.

T wo beautiful girls, when they become allies, know that they're invincible. They identify each other, check each other out, maybe at school, in a class, or at the same summer camp. They can choose to compete with each other, and end up getting hurt. But they know that the other option is more advantageous for both of them. If they become friends, they won't have to be afraid of anyone, they'll be protected by a bulletproof shield of desire, impervious even to envy.

When Annamaria saw Lisa for the first time, Lisa was with her best friend, Flaminia.

Their names spoke volumes: Lisa, Flaminia—the play of soft, silken syllables, like their long, wavy hair. And "Flaminia" carried history, geography, a semantic connation with it; it evoked the Roman Empire, a consul's road that led straight to the riches of the north.

But her name was just "Annamaria," all run-together, and she was ashamed of it. She thought everyone in her family had horrendous names, and that hers was no exception. A double name, lately fallen out of use, composed of two old names, suitable for grandmothers, maybe. On their own, they still could sound acceptable, even elegant—Anna, Maria; but put one after the other they were less alluring, almost out of place among the Lavinias, Ginevras, and Isabellas (not to mention the goddesses—the exotic Olympias, Athenas, Petras).

Not identifying with your own name was the first step to insecurity. Besides, Annamaria was the daughter of Sauro the cowboy, and she'd grown up in the country, which hadn't helped her either. Also, the nickname they gave her was ugly. She was called Annamarì, truncated like a verb in dialect. The moment someone turned to her, even before they'd given her the order or the reminder that usually followed, she was at a total socio-economic disadvantage.

Lisa's father was in parliament and was named Filippo. Filippo Sanfilippi, the life of a saint, summed up on his identity card.

Sauro had brought the two girls over to Annamaria and told her, "We're going to the seaside today, they're coming with you, Annamarì, OK? I think it's a great idea. You're all about the same age, make friends. Ride Pallino and Seta. Stay in a group and don't fool around. No galloping unless I say so."

The girls looked at each other without shaking hands. Annamaria smiled and said, "Nice to meet you. I'll go saddle the horses."

The other two stayed silent, leaning against the fence. They were dressed in beige riding breeches, black leather boots and English ascots, and held velvet-covered caps in their hands.

Annamaria was wearing jeans, rubber boots, and a faded sweatshirt of her brother's, not even the right size. She'd gotten a perm, as the fashion of the time required, a trend that had arrived in their region just late enough for it to be over, and which had made the thick black hair she'd inherited from her father all frizzy. If it had just been the hair, she would have been all right. But Sauro's dominant genes had given both of his children sturdy frames, crooked legs, a hooked nose, and bushy eyebrows. It had only worked out well for the boy. Saverio was nineteen, and having added height to his inheritance, plus his mother's blue eyes, he was striking and cocky. In Annamaria—whose eyes were brown—the same things that made her brother attractive created a jarring effect: she was stocky and clumsy, she walked like a man, she hunched over as if she were trying to hide herself. When she was little, she'd had trouble with balance, she learned to walk late, and she often stumbled. Even now that she was bigger, every time she climbed a staircase she had to concentrate on where to put her feet, step after step.

Nobody ever said she was pretty. Smart, maybe, and nice—which she really was, she had a better sense of humor than anyone else in her family—and strong. At the most, they might say that a certain dress, or hairstyle, looked good on her. But pretty? No, never. Only Miriam, her mother, had ever said that to her, and only once.

Annamaria still remembered it. It was the day of her first communion. Miriam, with her shapely legs, generous bosom, and the face of an Etruscan princess, her eyes as blue as the sky on a July morning, had said it to her while she was standing in front of the mirror with sagging shoulders, stuffed into the white dress of a child bride, in which she couldn't have felt more awkward, wearing a circlet of little flowers that snagged her hair, which had been done in a wave with a bouffant puff in front that exposed the dark down at her hairline. "Raise those shoulders, show how pretty you are, Annamarì." She raised them. But she knew her mother was lying. She could see her mother in the mirror behind her, in a silk dress with shoulder pads that attracted the eyes. *She* was beautiful. And the compliment she'd received fell apart, like a lie, in the reflection of the two of them.

Make friends, Sauro had said. Of course, because that's how friendship begins, with someone commanding you to do it, as if it were a job.

Annamaria came out of the barn three times, leading out a variety of horses. Samba, a pureblooded Arabian, black, gorgeous and high-strung; Seta, a gentle chestnut; and Pallino, a calm old gray.

"How do you want your horse saddled?" asked Annamaria. "Maremma-style or English?"

Lisa shrugged. "I don't know, but don't give me that gray."

Flaminia said, "English-style, obviously. I'll take the black one."

"No, the black one's mine; my father told me to give you Seta and Pallino, it's those two."

"So, you only do what *your daddy* tells you, then?" said Flaminia.

Annamaria was offended. She wanted to mount Samba and take off at a gallop on her own, leaving those two bitches to her father. Instead, she answered calmly, smiling, "No, it's just that you won't be able to mount Samba. She gives strangers a hard time."

"And who told you that? You realize that we do know how to ride. We also ride in Rome," Lisa retorted.

"She knows me. She goes crazy with strangers," Annamaria repeated. "I would let you take her, but if you get thrown, what happens when my father hears about it?" She failed to add, "If it were up to me, you could take her and go to hell."

"Oh well, in that case, God knows we wouldn't want to piss off *your daddy*," said Flaminia, turning toward Lisa, laughing.

Annamaria didn't answer and started saddling the horses. She pulled the cinch straps tight and adjusted the stirrups to the right height, listening to the girls all the while. Tiburzi, the stable mutt, wagged his tail at their feet.

"This ride sucks. I don't want to go," Flaminia complained.

"Tell me about it," Lisa replied.

"I'm not getting up on this gray donkey."

"Me neither."

"What a shit horse. Are you sure it's not a donkey?"

"I think it's *her grandpa*."

They burst out laughing.

Annamaria adjusted the bridles and watched the girls,

feeling a kind of regret that she had fastened the girth belts securely.

"We're ready. Should I help you up?"

"Who do you take us for?" Flaminia responded, nimbly placing her foot in the stirrup of the chestnut horse.

Lisa complained, "So I'm stuck with the donkey. Thanks a million, Flami."

Annamaria was burning with rage: "He's one of the best horses in the stable, he's intelligent and good-natured, he eats a little too much, but he never gives any trouble."

"Fine, but aesthetically, he's disgusting."

"Morally, you two are much worse," Annamaria thought as she helped Lisa mount. She was so light that it would have taken only one hearty push to send her flying over to the other side. She couldn't stand having to do this work for these hateful girls who talked cruelly about Pallino. And yet, she felt pleasure when Lisa's hand gripped her shoulder for a moment—it was as if her hand wasn't doing it only to boost herself up, but was making an affectionate gesture. Lisa was thanking her. For Annamaria, that was enough to make her feel better.

She mounted Samba and ordered the girls to follow her. Lisa and Flaminia rode at a gentle pace, staying side by side so they could chat. From the head of the trio, Annamaria heard laughter every now and then, and automatically turned around, signalling with her head that they needed to catch up, sure that they were laughing at her. Of course they were laughing at her. The adults were ahead of them, five in all, with Sauro in the lead. They were riding at a faster pace, smoking, in their autumnal velvet.

Tiburzi ran alongside Annamaria. He knew he could run anywhere he wanted in the foothills, but once he got to the Via Aurelia, he would have to turn around. The highway was dangerous, and the dog was forbidden to go near it. They would have to cross it with the horses, a quick but risky operation. The group of adults waited for the girls. Cars zoomed in both directions. Even if the traffic wasn't as bad as in the summertime, they had to be very cautious all the same, keeping in mind that they were riding animals who lacked accelerators or brakes. That's what Annamaria's father told the clients.

Sauro installed himself at the head of the group and asked everyone to draw in their reins. It was only a minute until the moment came when there was enough distance between a car that had just passed and a truck that was approaching from the other direction, still pretty far off. "Now!" he shouted.

Everyone struck their horses on the flanks, and with a pounding of hooves on the asphalt, they were on the other side of the Aurelia in a few seconds. Everyone except for Lisa and Pallino. Last in line when the others crossed, he'd started eating the grass on the border of the road, and even when Lisa pulled with all her might on the bridle, he'd kept on placidly munching. The girl was terrified, she couldn't make him move, and was afraid that if she hit him too hard on the flank, Pallino might take off at the wrong time, maybe throwing himself in front of a car. On the other side of the road, Lisa's father was shouting at her to stay where she was, her mother for her to get off the horse. She had started to cry.

Sauro raised a hand to silence everyone, but it was Annamaria who, at great speed, re-crossed the road and went to Lisa, who had dismounted in the meantime, and was sobbing with fright.

Annamaria dismounted Samba, took the reins from Lisa's hands and brought the horse into order with a light tug and a guttural command. Then, holding both the horses, she asked Lisa to remount.

"I don't want to."

"There's no need to be afraid. I'll lead you now."

"But I *am* afraid, I don't want to get back on, that horse is an asshole, and I want to go home." The tears were welling up, her hands trembled.

"Come on, Lisa, you can do it. I'll help you get back on."

"What an incredible nightmare! I hate horseback riding, my parents always make me do it."

"It's a beautiful thing, and you're learning well."

"Yeah right. Beautiful for an Amazon, maybe. Otherwise, it's a shitshow."

On the other side of the road everyone was watching and waiting. Flaminia called out, "Come on, Lisa! Come on donkey!"

Sauro gestured to the girl to move. Lisa stayed put.

"I'm not moving."

"They're waiting for you; don't be afraid, I'll help you."

"*Don't be afraid.* Quit talking like you're giving directions to a horse. If I'm afraid of doing something, is that going to change my mind?" She drew her hand across her face and put one foot on the stirrup. "Fuck off," she said under her breath.

Annamaria crouched down and held her hands with the palms open, supporting the soles of the girl's boots. Settling herself on the saddle, Lisa lightly squeezed her shoulder again with her fingers. Annamaria smiled, and nimbly remounted her black horse. Holding Pallino's bridle, she led them across the road at the right moment, like a dog on a leash.

The group applauded. Lisa turned red in the face. Going up to her mother, she said to her in a low voice, "This is the last time, I swear to God—and to hell with you if you bring me to a horse ever again!"

Flaminia came up to her:

"She gave you that donkey, the bitch. You see how right I was? A stubborn donkey."

"Definitely. A chickenshit donkey. But this is the last time, right?"

The ride continued under the October sun. Once they were on the beach, the riders instantly broke into a gallop with the sun's glare in their faces, the outline of the headland edging the bay on one side of them, a lone fisherman on the other. It was not ideal terrain for horses, they got tired, their hooves sinking into the dry sand, but it was perfect for giving a person a sense of well-being: riding on horseback along the beach, without a track to follow, with no branches to dodge, no hurdles. The joy of racing along the shoreline, exhilarated by the muscles and the hooves, the tangled manes. Some of the riders from Rome wore spurs, which goes against the cowboy code; they struck the flanks of their beasts hard with their heels, spurring them to run towards nothing, in the breeze that smelled of salt and sweaty horsehair.

Once she'd arrived at the sand dune, Lisa got off her horse and tied it to the fence, took off her boots and went to put her feet in the water. The other two girls had a quick run but returned to her right afterwards. Lisa had a way of quietly attracting attention. She liked to be alone, but always found herself with someone who wanted to be with her.

Flaminia looked at Lisa's bare feet.

"Wow, what hideous big toes. Put them away, they're scaring me."

"It's pointe shoes that did this to them, stupid."

"Could be, but even if it was the wizard Merlin himself who made them that way, they're incredibly ugly."

Lisa shrugged her shoulders and dug her feet into the sand.

Annamaria watched them in silence. Who knew how many ugly things they saw in her?

"Speaking of which," said Lisa, turning to Annamaria, "I saw that you worked with the animals and the sheep. Could you get me a little bit of lambswool? It's perfect for putting in pointe shoes to cushion your toes."

"Actually, I don't work with sheep. But I can ask my neighbor."

"You'd be doing me a favor. Do you know which discos are open these days?"

"Maybe the Bella Bimba, and for sure the New Line."

"No, no, not those shitholes packed with hicks from Viterbo—I mean like King's, or the Strega in the Argentario."

Annamaria turned red. She was ugly, a hick who tended sheep and went to the wrong discos, on the rare occasions when she went at all, and always at the worst time, too—Sunday afternoons.

"I don't know, you'd better ask my brother."

"*Your daddy, your brother*," interrupted Flaminia. "Without them, apparently, you wouldn't do anything, wouldn't decide anything, wouldn't know anything. Let me borrow your horse, because mine's an old nag; I want to have a proper run."

Annamaria hesitated.

"That is, should I ask *your daddy* for permission?"

"No, take her, but be careful, she's high-strung."

"Honey, who do you think you're talking to? I've been riding at the Acqua Santa hippodrome twice a week since I was seven. I have an Arabian in Rome named Caffeine."

Flaminia shortened the stirrups on the saddle to switch it to English-style. Annamaria, following her with her eyes, saw Samba startle from a sharp flick of the riding crop, and clenched her jaw. Not the riding crop, no. She had asked her father not to let anyone use them, it wasn't necessary. But he let his clients do what they wanted, spurs, whips, English saddles made by artisans in Suffolk that had initials engraved on them; he let them smoke while they were riding and exhaust the horses by making them run on the sand. Whatever made them happy. The horses were there for anyone to ride, and many of them were owned by the cowboys; Sauro boarded them in the country, fed them, took care of them and kept them ready for use, in exchange for a boarding fee.

Annamaria averted her gaze to avoid seeing Flaminia make Samba jump a stray tree trunk that the tide had thrown up. "If she hurts him, I will kill her," she thought.

Lisa still seemed spooked. She kept her eyes lowered, and her feet under the sand.

"Is Flaminia always like this?" asked Annamaria.

"Like what?"

"Umm . . . pretty mean. Or, I don't know, maybe I'm wrong."

"You're wrong, she's incredibly nice, and a lot of fun. Every now and then, I guess, she talks back a little like that, but all girls do that sometimes, right?"

"All? Not me, I always try not to offend anyone."

"It's true, you're nice. Maybe too nice. You seem a little drippy."

Lisa smiled at her, and Annamaria was sure of one thing: Flaminia was a bitch, but Lisa was only a bitch when she was with her, which meant it was better to get her on her own.

"You really don't like riding horses?"

"No, I'm terrible, and horses hate me."

"Horses don't hate you, you just have to learn to make them respect you."

"Besides, it's dangerous, and if I hurt myself that's not a good thing."

"That's not a good thing for anyone."

"Yes, but I study classical dance. If I break a leg or a shoulder, it's over, get it? That's all that matters to me."

Annamaria picked up a concave remnant of a plastic shovel and brought it to her ear.

"You can hear the sea in this, try it. 'Hello, Sea?'" She started laughing. "Actually, I've been told that the sound you hear is your own blood flowing," Annamaria added, proud of her comment.

"In your case, that's practically the same thing."

Annamaria looked into Lisa's eyes, not understanding if this was meant as an insult or a compliment. Did she mean that I have the sea inside me, or that I've got saltwater instead of blood? She decided to take it as positive. Then she got distracted by Lisa's eyes; they were an unusual color, green but also yellow, like the eyes of a cat.

"What would you say to the two of us heading home? If we take the underpass it will make the trip a little longer, but we can avoid crossing the Aurelia. That way we won't have to wait for these guys. We can meet up with them later at the horse yard for lunch."

Lisa welcomed the idea enthusiastically and sent her off to tell the others. Annamaria spoke with her father, who had nothing against it, then hurried to sneak off before Flaminia, who had split from the rest of the group and was off galloping with Samba, could intercept them.

Annamaria took Pallino and managed to make him work up a bit of a trot toward Lisa and Seta. The return took much longer than the journey out, and she didn't want to be late. It took them forty minutes to get off the beach. Then they had to walk along the edge of the highway, one behind the other. Cars passed, and tractors, then Antonio, one of Annamaria's cousins, on his souped-up Caballero motorcycle. He knew he shouldn't make loud noises when animals were nearby, but he revved his engine and gunned the motor when he passed them anyway, raising an arm in greeting. Lisa's horse shied to one side, but she managed to restrain him with a timid jerk on the reins. Once back in step, she relaxed. Her back was slightly slumped, her legs were limp, her feet were jammed in the stirrup, and her arms were too far forward. It was clear that the horse was moving forward without paying attention to her presence. But Annamaria didn't give Lisa any advice. She watched her from behind, her perfect ass in her tight pants, her slender thighs, the long hair that escaped from her cap in light-brown tendrils, perfectly streaked in different shades. She couldn't think of a single reason why anyone wouldn't want to be her.

Once they were out of the underpass, Annamaria took the lead; they would have to take shortcuts if they were going to arrive in time to have lunch with the others. They cut through a sheep meadow. On their left, in the middle of the woods, they saw a bizarre construction that radiated glittering light and transformed the appearance of the whole landscape. It was as if a UFO had landed in a field. A giant hand covered in mirrors emerged through the trees, halfway up the hillside. As they got closer, they could make out a kind of mask in front of the hand, composed of the same sparkling material; and a sky-blue reflection glinted from the mirrors, hinting at the presence of another giant figure.

Lisa flicked the horse on his flank and rode up to Annamaria. "Would you mind if we went and had a look?"

"At what, at the Monsters?"

"They're not called 'Monsters,' but basically, yes, at the garden."

"But it's closed. And it's private property."

"I know, but it's the property of the Italian kings. And it just so happens that I know them very well."

"The kings of Italy? We haven't had a monarchy since the Second World War."

"Bravo for your knowledge of history. But it's a figure of speech. There's still a king of Italy."

"And who might that be?"

"Agnelli."

"Why? Do the Agnellis live here?"

"You should know. They're never here, but this is one of their family properties. I've come here a thousand times."

"Well yeah, so have I," Annamaria hastened to add.

"There's a picture of me when I was little, on the scaffolding of the big monster, a kind of sphinx. I have a cousin who works there, named Giovanna. We don't see a lot of each other, but she's the daughter of my mother's cousin."

"I personally know the artist who makes them. And they're not monsters or sphinxes. They're figures from the tarot. Let's go look."

"You always win," Annamaria whispered.

They led the horses along the gently rising dirt road that led to the grounds and found themselves in front of a locked gate and a high chain-link fence.

Lisa suggested they climb over it.

"But wouldn't that be dangerous? There will be guards, dogs . . ."

"What are you talking about? There's no need for that here. The Agnellis have an understanding with the Sardinian shepherds: nobody will touch them. It's funny, when you think about it, that the word 'agnelli' literally means 'lambs' in our language."

"Shepherds, lambs . . . they've got everything under control," said Annamaria, making Lisa smile. Then she added, "Still, you can't just walk onto private property like that."

"You're so annoying. I bet you want to ask permission from *your daddy*."

"Knock it off, you're just trying to bug me. I bet you don't know how to climb over the gate, either, and you might sprain your ankles, which would be bad news for a ballerina."

Annamaria tied the horses to the branch of a tree and hoisted herself up onto the gate. Once she was straddling it, she said to Lisa, who was looking up at her from below, "Now we'll see if you'll do it."

Lisa preferred to clamber up by holding onto the posts of the metallic structure, sticking her feet in the holes in the chain-link fence. She was strong, extremely agile, and light. She was over the fence in an instant.

They went down a short path in the bushes that, after a rising curve bordered with myrtle and evergreens, opened onto a sort of quarry that contained the magic garden.

They found themselves beholding an enormous face covered in blue ceramic tiles. One eye was as dark as a deep, black hole; another one was red, smaller, higher up, like a porthole. The nose was enormous and flat. The mouth was wide open and covered in a mosaic of tiles of different shades of blue. A grey cement ladder descended from the mouth, ending in a gigantic basin paved in irregular shards. On the left side of the visage, a serpent clad in ultramarine ceramic tiles, white and green, snaked back toward the hillside before reaching the side of the open mouth. The snake's mouth was open too, and one of its eyes had a red iris. Behind the face rose an enormous mask, almost entirely covered in mirrors, shielding the enormous hand that could be seen from the road, sparkling with mirrored glass. There was not a single right angle; only soft, feminine, disturbing forms emerged from the oaks and the cork trees. They seemed like beings that had sprung from the earth like gigantic poison mushrooms, in toxic, unnatural colors, in the middle of the woods, after a night of enchanted rain.

Lisa came to a halt and stood stiffly, the tips of her feet pointing in, as if she were facing a strict dance mistress.

"Oh my god, the last time I saw these, they were all just cement and iron; I didn't think they would end up like this," said Annamaria.

Lisa brought a finger to her mouth to hush her. They remained motionless, in silence, for a few minutes, enthralled by the figures and their glinting. At some stage, they heard a noise in the brush to their right, a rustle of leaves. Lisa screamed and grabbed Annamaria's arm.

"Oh my god, a wild boar!"

"Calm down. It's a person."

"Help. Maybe it's a hunter and he'll shoot us."

"Mother of God, you are such a coward."

A tall young man burst out of the bushes. He had a receding hairline and a long beard with auburn highlights, and he was wearing jeans and a strange collarless jacket, something you never saw in the country.

"What are you two doing here? How did you get in?"

From the accent, he didn't seem Roman or Tuscan. Maybe he was a Frenchman who'd learned Italian very well. He rolled his R's.

"I'm Filippo Sanfilippi's daughter," said Lisa.

He shrugged. "OK. How did you get in?"

Annamaria interrupted, "We climbed over, we're leaving right now."

"When there's a locked gate with a 'private property' sign above it, what do you think that means?"

Annamaria played her card. "My cousin works here, and she's always telling me to come by and look at it. Her name is Giovanna. I'm the daughter of Sauro, the man with the horses."

"Oh, the daughter of the King."

"The King? I think you've made a mistake—the king of Italy is somebody else," Annamaria said, searching for confirmation from Lisa.

"Every village has its kings," the boy responded. "Nevertheless, you should go. I doubt Giovanna asked you to come by on a Sunday and climb over the locked gate. And your family connections don't authorize you to break and enter."

"You're right, we're leaving at once. We're so sorry," said Annamaria.

"It's just that we like the art so much. This place is incredible. We wanted to see it. We rode for miles and miles to get here, we were at Macchiatonda beach . . ."

"You can stay ten minutes, no more. In total silence. The artist is present," he said, pointing to the sphinx. "And she doesn't want to be disturbed. Take a tour and don't touch anything. I'll wait for you here."

The girls thanked him, and with quick steps went up the path that led to the enormous blue face, which, once they'd passed it, they saw could be climbed by azure steps that led to the top, to the mirrored mask. On the right rose another giant cement monster, with seven snake heads. On one flank it had a hole, inside which was placed a stylized statue of colored metal, of a man hanging upside down by one foot. A few steps away from that was an enormous female figure, who was in the process of being dressed, in stripes of white and black tiles. The woman was holding her breasts, which were made of wire and resembled two enormous platters, with an iron scale resting on them that turned each breast into a platform on which something could be weighed. A door opened inside her skirt, barred by a gate. The skirts contained a little room, with a rusted machine in the back, a sheep's skull tied to a hubcap. In front of that stood a much bigger structure, a kind of uneven plaza, supported by scaffolding, encircled by an arcade of low, slanted cement columns, on which shapes and numbers were painted, like an unsolved rebus. The columns supported a walkway with a parapet that looked like it was made of children's modeling clay, from which you could look down onto the plaza from on high. The parapet also passed through rocket trails, continuing on under a crooked bell tower to another tower that also was covered in mirrors. They stopped there and looked around them. Reflections of thousands of Lisas and Annamarias surrounded them, observing them from every side. Annamaria was enchanted and horrified by all the fragments of herself flickering into Lisa's eyes.

"How totally amazing," said Lisa. "It scares you!"

"Good God."

"Do you know who the guard is?"

Annamaria shrugged without averting her gaze from the reflections of Lisa. Bits of eyes, of hair, of eyebrow, cheeks.

"He's the son of the king."

"That's strange; my brother is different, and younger."

"Idiot, he's the son of the real king."

"My father's the real king too, he's said so himself. And anyway, how do you know?"

"I told you, my family comes here all the time, we know their aunts and uncles."

"This couldn't have gone any better. We were received by the prince, in his magic kingdom."

"He's a weird guy."

Lisa let out a yell into the mirrored grotto, so she could hear the echo.

"Stop it. He said we shouldn't make noise!"

"Um . . . we've awoken the Sphinx. Now we'll be eaten. Let's get out of here."

They were excited. Lisa took Annamaria's hand. "Before we go, we have to see her."

"You said it wasn't a Sphinx."

"I know, it's a tarot card, but I don't remember which, maybe it's the Empress. She lives inside."

"She who?" asked Annamaria.

"The artist."

It was one of the largest sculptures. A crouching creature, half woman, half animal. Gigantic and fluid, with enormous breasts, and with two portholes instead of nipples, in between which a door opened. Behind, hair softly covered the back and hindquarters. Above that was a sort of terrace you could walk up onto. The sculpture was surrounded by scaffolding and didn't have any colors yet. Lisa and Annamaria walked up quickly onto the terrace and, from there, looked out onto the landscape: the sea they'd come from, the alternating stripes of green olive groves and brown-and-green fields, the nuclear power station of Montalto di Castro.

"I heard that she wanted to build the giant hand so it would point towards Montalto, to shut the power station down. Maybe it will work."

"Could be, could be—fucking Maremma. I'm terrified. In the days after Chernobyl, I didn't leave the house. You?"

"My mother's an activist, she's opposed to the power station. She holds a protest on the Via Aurelia with some other people from around here once a month. She always asks me to go with her, she says it's a civic duty, for the future of the environment and young people . . . what a pain. Whether it's the power station or the bomb, what can anyone do about it? We're all going to die. I like my father's idea better, building a nuclear fallout shelter."

"Seriously?"

"My father never jokes about things like that," Lisa replied.

"I saw *The Day After*. I'd rather expose myself to radiation immediately than live in a fallout shelter."

"But what if it's just for a while, then you can come out and escape to a place that isn't contaminated?"

"Yeah? And where would that be? There wouldn't be any place that wasn't contaminated."

"But maybe there would be, and then your life would have been spared."

"All right, go ahead, do what you want. Lucky you, to have the money to build a fallout shelter."

As they were talking, they had made their way down and found themselves behind the sculpture, at one side. There was a locked door between the animal's thighs. Nearby was a small chapel, shaped like a colossal pumpkin, its entrance barred with a rope. Inside, the ceiling was covered with a puzzle of colored mirrors, concentric circles, planets, stars, and flowers shaped like hearts. At the center was a small altar that had a ceramic bas-relief stretched across it, depicting a black Madonna with a green child. Two photographs were set out beneath it like ex-voto offerings. Annamaria made the sign of the cross.

Lisa looked at her funny. Then she let out a short scream, so she could hear her voice echo in the little chapel. Annamaria nudged her. "We were told to keep quiet!"

A voice reached them from behind: "Who are you? What are you doing here?"

They had woken the Sphinx.

Annamaria looked at the woman and lowered her eyes.

Lisa assumed the ballet dancer's first position, with her long neck and straight back, and responded promptly: "We are the daughters of the king, and we love art."

It was the right answer.

3. THE EMPRESS
Motherhood. Creativity. Seduction.

S he was serious. She was dressed in a padded floral jacket with a faux fur collar, and soft trousers of damask silk with an emerald-green and black pattern. Dark-blond bangs emerged from a shapeless red velvet cap, a kind of oversized beret, but you couldn't really focus on all of that, because her blue eyes were so intense that you couldn't help quickly averting your gaze. Annamaria had never seen anyone dressed like that. In truth, she had never seen such a magnetic woman.

She looked them over. She rebuked them with a raised eyebrow and a curl of her lip that said, "You can't stay here." But that was just for a moment, and then she quickly responded to Lisa in a strange accent, "I am the Empress, and the mother of this place. You may come see my home if you wish, but then you must leave—I am expecting visitors."

Annamaria apologized for them both and thanked her for showing kindness to strangers.

The Empress set off. They entered through the door on the back of the big statue shaped like a Sphinx. On the outside it was covered in cement; inside, it was an actual home. But it looked like no other home. The walls and ceilings formed sinuous waves; they seemed to have been molded from some malleable material, which also had been used to make the fireplace, the bench, a column. Everything was entirely covered in a mosaic of mirrors, including the cover of the gas stove, located inside of one of the Sphinx's breasts, whose porthole window was the nipple. You climbed ten mirrored steps into the other, larger breast to reach the bedroom. The bathroom, a small grotto built in the round, held a red bathtub bordered in blue majolica tiles that joined together, climbing to form a massive, vertical snake from whose open mouth, red and pointed downward, the shower's water fell.

The girls moved slowly through the space, looking around at the thousands of fragments of their bodies reflected in the glittering light that came from every direction. The dining table, surrounded by metal and ceramic chairs, was also covered in mirrored glass. Overhead hung a chandelier shaped like a bicycle crankset; rusted pieces of iron, a chain, an animal skull, colored bulbs. The whole scene was reflected, fragmented, on the ceiling.

To the right of the entrance stood a sculpture of mirrors and ceramic tiles, a kind of cart pulled by two half-horses, one of them gold, the other black. Rusted metal wheels. A black and white canopy framed a queen with wide hips, dressed in blue, with breasts painted like targets, a yellow crown with three convex spikes on it, a red scepter.

"This represents the Chariot, the seventh card of the tarot," said the Empress. "It's the card of triumph over your enemies, the card of victory; but it also warns you that you must be careful, because it is precisely in the moment of triumph that one becomes, *comme on dit, vulnérable.*"

"Vulnerable," Lisa translated.

"Exactly. Do you speak French?"

"A little."

"*Et toi, petite?*" she said, turning to Annamaria.

"No, she doesn't," Lisa answered. "She speaks the language of the Maremma."

Annamaria felt her cheeks flush. Then she broke in, "I am Giovanna's cousin. Excuse us again for bothering you."

"Ah, Giovanna—without her I'd be lost. What a marvelous woman. I didn't know she had a cousin who was an art lover."

"We don't see each other very often. Pardon me for asking, but do you live in here all the time?"

"Stop apologizing so much! It's not right for girls to always be apologizing."

"You're right, sorry."

All three of them started laughing. Annamaria was purple.

"Yes, I live in here all the time. It's my refuge, my enchanted house."

"But isn't it a little . . . well, strange . . . ?"

"It's the only way I can track the growth of my creations. It's a little cold in winter, but it's a womb. And then, someone always comes along and finds me. There are many of us working here."

"But the light, all the reflections? Doesn't it ever make you dizzy?"

"I have other problems with my head, but it's not the mirrors that bother me. I'm used to them, in any case." She smiled. She had the perfect nose for that smile, and teeth, and jaw.

"I really have to tell you, Ma'am, you are truly beautiful."

"Thank you, you two also are beautiful, and very young."

"No, we are not beautiful. Lisa maybe, but not me."

"Why do you say that?"

"Because I know it, I can see it for myself."

The artist made them sit down.

"It is not at all true that you are ugly. People have so many *bêtises* in their heads at your age, but at my age, I can tell you with certainty: beauty can be helpful, but it does not shield you from pain. And that also holds true for art: my feminist performances were probably well-received because I was beautiful. I suspect that if I'd been ugly, they would have said I was frustrated, that I made my "shooting paintings" with masculine symbols in them because I resented men, because men didn't want me. At least they couldn't accuse me of that. But then there's the flip side of the coin. If you're beautiful, you're always struggling to be taken seriously. People don't look at what you do—it's taken for granted that anything you happen to do, you've done because some man fell in love with you and let you do it, they don't give you any credit. In any case, the two of you said that you like art. Which artists in particular?"

Annamaria was happy that the speech about beauty had been cut short by this question; as for the rest of it, she appreciated it up to a point: this divine apparition could not have the faintest idea what it meant, at fifteen, to be ugly, insignificant, and invisible.

Lisa said she liked Roberto Matta, and that her father knew him well. The artist knew him well, too; she often went to see him because he lived nearby, in Tarquinia. But she had met him years before in New York City, where he had lived in exile.

Annamaria felt left out again. She had never heard the name of this "Matta."

"And you?" asked the lady. Out of nervousness, she couldn't even remember Botticelli. "Um, I'm not sure, I like what you do, I like this place." Her cheeks were still flushed, she felt even more awkward.

The door opened, and a tall boy came in, speaking Spanish. The artist replied to him in French and asked the girls to leave, because now they had things to do. It was if they suddenly didn't exist anymore.

Once they were outside, Lisa spoke to Annamaria mockingly: "You were such an idiot, you acted like a stupid child: '*I'm sorry, I'm sorry, Ma'am,*' '*You are beautiful,*' '*I like everything you do . . .*' What's wrong with you, are you five years old?" Then, looking at her Swatch, she started to run. "Shit, it's two o'clock! My mother will be so worried." She left the Monsters behind her and ran towards the gate. There was no sign of the skinny guy who had greeted them.

"I can get you there quickly if we go at a gallop," Annamaria said.

"I really can't fall."

"So, hold on tight to the reins, and grip the horse's mane in front of the saddle." Annamaria helped Lisa mount, and showed her how to hold on. "You've got muscles; squeeze this damn saddle like . . . like you wanted to stay a virgin forever."

"I'm not a virgin anymore."

"It was just a figure of speech."

"You?"

"Mind your own business and hold on tight."

"Ha, ha, little virgin, I knew it."

Annamaria gave a quick kick to her horse's flanks, and it set off at a smooth trot.

Behind her, Lisa held on but bounced in the saddle; she couldn't find the rhythm. Too bad she's a ballerina, Annamaria thought. It would have taken very little to make her fall. A sudden swerve, a run through the rough, or just taking off at a gallop, leaving her behind to chase after her with no control. But she didn't do that.

They cut through an area of scrubland, and by the time they arrived everyone was already at the table. Over the preceding years, her father had transformed the saddlery into a kind of dining room, with tables, benches and an illegal fireplace. At the beginning, they only served salami and cheese, bread and wine. Later, for the better clients, the ones who'd become friends, he'd asked Miriam to cook something, and she would carry in big pots of *acquacotta* soup, and stewed wild boar and beans in tomato sauce, kept warm on an electric hot plate. At the end of the meal she served cake and biscotti, "because if you're going to eat, you might as well go the whole hog," she had told her husband. In this way, the saddlery had become a kind of illicit trattoria, which Sauro described as "informal;" but which became so in-demand that telephone calls started coming in for reservations for "horse rides followed by lunch," and the place was fully booked for months in advance. First, Sauro had raised the prices, and then, at Filippo Sanfilippi's suggestion, he'd decided to transform it into a true, proper restaurant. Sanfilippi had insisted on being a partner—he'd invested money in expanding the property, installing an industrial kitchen and an accessible bathroom, and getting everything into good shape. Sauro had had to get the licenses taken care of—nothing could have been easier, he was friends with everyone in town—and to convince Miriam to become the official cook—which also was easily done. Miriam had always done everything he asked her to do.

"Let's give her a small salary," Sanfilippi had said, "because women always like to be paid; nothing makes them feel more emancipated than a little cash. So, pretend like she's the boss, and give her your share. It'll work out for you financially; you'll have the power and the land, the country girls who'll help her out, your daughter will serve tables, and . . . you're golden." He said it with a smile, sure of himself, in the manner of someone who's always giving you a wink.

The restaurant project had gone off without a hitch. The incorporation of the company with Miriam, the licenses, the jobs, the country girls. In the course of six months, everything was ready. Saverio, Sauro's son, was the only obstacle. He was contrarian as a matter of principle ("Your partner is a member of the Roman Parliament? I don't know what you're thinking, you'll end up totally screwed, Babbo"); egotistical ("Mamma won't take care of us anymore"); misanthropic ("just picture the people who'll come, we'll always have cretins underfoot"); and lazy ("I won't help you"). Sauro was not remotely put out: he responded to every protest from Saverio with one single, unchanging sentence: "If you don't like what we're doing, find another job, like you should, anyway, and get out of here, you're a grownup."

Upon their arrival at the Saddlery, Lisa and Annamaria

were scolded good-naturedly, everyone was relieved to see them safe and sound, and above all, not to have to leave the table to go look for them, given that they were more than an hour late. Flaminia was the angriest. Getting up from the corner where she was eating, next to Lisa's mother, she went over to the girls.

"You two are absolute bitches. You stranded me and went off to do your own stupid thing without telling me anything. Anyway, I know who the moron behind this was," she said, turning to look at Annamaria, "but you, Lisa! I'm only here because you invited me to this shitty weekend on horseback. You and me are over. Over, do you understand? I've already asked your mother to take me to the train this afternoon. I wouldn't stay here tonight if you paid me. You loser bitch who starts crying when a horse stops to eat. Go to hell, get lost." And she went out of the restaurant, slamming the door. Lisa went out after her, mortified. When Annamaria tried to follow her, Lisa gestured rudely for her to go away. Annamaria went back in and sat down beside her father, who quickly had the pasta brought to her that they'd kept warm for the girls.

"So, what did the two of you end up doing, if I may ask?" said Sauro, without removing his cigar from his mouth.

"We stopped to see the Monsters. We also met the artist. Just think—she lives there; she built a house inside one of the sculptures. It's a crazy place, Babbo, the rooms are all covered in mirrors, and she's fantastic, we talked, she was so nice."

"Annamarì, how did you get in?"

She hated it when he called her that.

"Uh, it's not important, we . . . we ran into a guy who knew you. A skinny guy who was tall, who had a beard, and Swiss 'Rs'."

"Ran into . . . You climbed over the fence. It must have been Edoardo."

"I think so, Lisa told me he was someone important, and that they know him."

Sanfilippi interrupted to confirm. "Yes, we're friends with Edo."

"But we weren't with him, we met the artist."

Sanfilippi continued, "I can't stand her. And that place looks to me like a giant pile of shit, pardon my French."

Gianmaria Molteni, an ever-present fixture in their circle, concurred. He was a wealthy art history professor and critic who was becoming something of a celebrity, thanks to television.

"Actually, she doesn't strike me as very talented. She wanted to remake Gaudí's Parc Güell in Barcelona, to give it the appeal of the Park of the Monsters in Bomarzo. But it doesn't seem to me that the synthesis has worked out for her. Sadly, she's done it at the expense of a marvelous hillside in our region. Wishful thinking combined with gigantism are the evils of the wannabes of contemporary art. And honestly—it was bad enough when they were just iron and cement, but now they've been completely covered in those horrendous mirrors. Those primary colors . . . The poetry of our Mediterranean landscape has been disfigured by the clay figurines of a retarded little girl."

Filippo's wife, Giulia, disagreed mildly. This was the way she always argued with people who knew more than she did, almost excusing herself for having an opinion, searching with false modesty for someone else to affirm the correctness of her point of view. With more ignorant people, however, she acted the opposite way: speaking in pedantic tones, with ill-concealed arrogance.

"I don't consider myself an expert on contemporary art . . . but I think it's a brave and interesting effort. As for the aesthetics of it . . . I don't know, but the idea of the mirrors is pretty, they reflect the light, and those sculptures gleaming in the woods exert their own fascination. I don't have much imagination, so I can't picture how it will look when it's finished. Genni, who's a close friend of the artist, showed me sketches of how it's supposed to look, it looked good to me . . . But if Gianmaria says it's in bad taste, I'll take his word for it. Regardless, she seems like a special person."

"She really is a special person," Annamaria said. "And besides that, she's beautiful, the Garden is amazing, and the house of mirrors is the coolest place I've ever seen."

"Cool, hey? Certainly, for you two, if something's cool it's automatically beautiful. But that's a little reductive, don't you think?"

Annamaria clammed up. As usual, the right comeback only came to her an hour later.

Miriam interrupted; she was leaning against the doorframe of the kitchen in her white apron, a cap on her head, her face pretty but shiny, like any cook's after three hours at the stove.

"She really must be a special lady, but you know what she did, right? She abandoned her children so she could become an artist. I don't know . . . maybe she's brilliant, but that's something even a dog wouldn't do, I mean . . ."

"Oh my god," Giulia retorted. "'Abandoned.' The reality of the situation is that she and her husband separated, and he took the children. She sees them regularly. I know that she also sees her grandchildren. I would hold off on calling her a monster. For once, it's the mother who left the house, and the children stayed with their father," she said.

"Look, I know he was a great guy. Still, I can't understand how a woman could think of leaving her home to go play with paintbrushes. She must not be right in the head."

Annamaria wanted to get up, but she was trapped between her father and Giulia. Everyone's smoke was getting to her, she wasn't hungry anymore. She would have liked to scream that they didn't understand anything, that if all of them put together had half the courage and creativity that that woman possessed, then maybe they would be entitled to say half a word about her. But how dare this bunch of lazy, conceited drunks criticize the work or the life of an artist? She wasn't even able to formulate the thought. It gave her stomach cramps to hear the adults attack the Empress. She hated them.

Her father came to her aid, the way he knew how to do, with his coarse pragmatism.

"I don't understand a fucking thing, but let a moron speak: that monstrosity brings loads of people to these parts. Annamaria is right, it's cool. And she truly is a beautiful woman."

"But what does her being beautiful have to do with anything, Sauro?" Giulia countered. "You men judge women only on that basis. We're talking here about a work of art. And it's not like, since she's beautiful, her work will automatically be beautiful. That's just the typical masculine way of judging women and what they do."

"What's it got to do with masculine? I love women; I like them much more than I like men," Sauro replied.

With that, a ruckus erupted that settled the mood. People laughed, and the conversation downshifted to a calmer register, to sexism, over glasses of red wine that never remained empty. Sauro was banging Giulia, which everyone knew, except their respective spouses.

Annamaria saw Lisa, who was coming back inside. Serious, her eyes puffy from crying. Annamaria crawled under the table to get out, and went up to her.

"Do you want something to eat?"

"I'm not hungry."

"The tagliatelle is good."

"Tagliatelle makes you fat."

"You're incredibly thin."

"Exactly. I want to stay that way."

"Did you fight with Flaminia?"

"Yes. She wants to get out of here, and she says we're not friends anymore. You landed me in shit."

"I landed you in shit? Me? I saved your life, when you were stranded at the Via Aurelia!" Annamaria said, giggling.

"It's not funny. It was your idea for us to go off on our own."

"You could have said no."

"I hate horseback riding. You're the only person who understood that, but you landed me in shit all the same."

"I thought that at least you might thank me. Instead, now it's totally my fault that your friend is a bitch."

"She's not a bitch. She was left all alone. You could have called her."

"You could have called her, given that she's your friend."

"I wasn't being very logical. I was afraid. Also, I didn't think we'd be so late."

"But you're the one who wanted to go into the Garden."

"That's not true at all, you were the first to climb over."

"Do you want me to go talk to her? I'll take the blame."

"I already blamed you, thanks. Now she'll hate you most of all."

"It's mutual. You can both go to hell."

This time it was Annamaria who went out, slamming the door.

"What's going on?" Sauro asked, looking at his wife.

"She's fifteen, Sa'. She's fifteen." Miriam fanned away the smoke and went back into the kitchen.

Nobody followed Annamaria. Lisa and Giulia started talking in low voices.

Flaminia was outside. Annamaria passed her by without saying a word and walked into the barn. Tiburzi came up to her, tail wagging. After a fight, there's nothing better than an affectionate dog to reinforce your negative thoughts about the entire human race. And your self-pity. Annamaria bent down to let him rejoice and lick her cheeks. She thought it was horrible that her own home had become a place where you felt ill at ease around everyone except a mutt like Tiburzi.

Then she went to Samba. She was still sweaty. She brought her some fodder and rubbed her down. She always felt a sensation of great relaxation when she energetically groomed a horse's coat. She could tell that it made the horse happy, and it felt as if the animal's sense of well-being transferred to her, like a vapor.

In the course of ten minutes, her anger faded. She decided to go home and study her Latin for the next day. She wanted to take advantage of the empty house to recite her lessons out loud. As she walked past the restaurant, she heard the voices and laughter of the men. Their alcohol-fueled bluster had devolved into innocuous fake fights.

In the driveway she saw the Sanfilippis' BMW. Giulia was in the driver's seat and Flaminia was in front. Lisa was getting into the back seat. When she saw Annamaria she ran up to her.

"Sorry about before. And the visit to the Garden really was an amazing adventure. We did the right thing, getting away from everybody. Maybe one of these days I'll call you from Rome."

Annamaria smiled at her. "Give me your address, maybe I'll write to you."

"Write to me? But why? I come back almost every weekend."

"It doesn't matter, give me your address."

"Piazza dei Quiriti, 68. Do you want me to write it down?"

"No, no, I'll remember it. I remember Quiriti, I remember 68."

They hurriedly said goodbye to each other.

The rumble of the car starting broke the silence of the

gathering autumn dusk. While it wasn't a sad sound in itself, it felt out of place to her. Annamaria heard all the dissonance that surrounded her, even if she couldn't clearly identify its origin or intensity. There had been no harmony on this autumn Sunday. There had been beauty and anger, magnificent discoveries for the eyes, and petty cruelties for the ears. Symphonies spoiled by offstage sounds. A bitchy girl with unexpected flashes of kindness.

She hurried home, losing the rhythm of her gait for a moment, thrown forward by her torso. She just wanted to get there before it got cold out. It was true: they'd done the right thing, getting away from everybody.

4. THE EMPEROR
Power. Stability. Father.

Saverio went out late in the morning without saying where he was going. For a long time he hadn't considered that necessary anymore, and besides, it was something he didn't know himself, for the most part. When he'd gotten his driver's license, after qualifying as a chemical lab technician, he'd rewarded himself with a blue Peugeot 205 with a 1.6 liter engine, a supermini. Driving had practically become his raison d'être. He burned up the miles every day without any precise destination, just for the sake of being at the wheel. He left the house and drove into the village, from the village to the sea, from the sea to Orbetello, from Orbetello to Albinia, from Albinia to Porto Santo Stefano, from Porto Santo Stefano to Talamone, and sometimes to Grosseto, or Forte dei Marmi. One Saturday afternoon, with a friend from the gym, he drove all the way to Monte Carlo to gamble at the casino. They returned at dawn the next day, nobody the wiser. His love for driving was wedded to a passion for speed. Toward the end of the eighties, a blue fireball could be seen hurtling up and down the Via Aurelia. It was Saverio, who knew by heart all the spots where the highway police might lurk, and, who, incredibly, had managed never once to get a ticket.

He came home to shower, change clothes and go back out. When he noticed that Annamaria was home, he went to her room to give her a kiss on the head, as he often did, and to ask her for the millionth time if she had made that cassette of hit songs recorded from the radio. She said she hadn't had time, which he already knew. He gave her another kiss. He was in a good mood, and Annamaria was the only one in the family he showed affection to.

There had been a moment in their childhood when the four years and the gender difference that separated them had melted away, and the two of them had become each other's best friend, as well as brother and sister. It was when she was six, and he was almost eleven. It hadn't lasted long, maybe a couple of seasons, but that was the strong foundation on which their relationship was built. They had just moved from the apartment in the village into their grandfather's farmhouse when their father had started setting up the activities with the horses and the tourists. They had found themselves isolated, with no other kids to play with, and with a lot of time and space on their hands. Saverio, who had been exceptionally strong since he was little, treated Annamaria like a little doll: he would scoop her up and flip her in the air; grab her by the wrists and spin her round like an airplane; at the seaside, he would throw her into the water over and over. He would walk miles carrying her on his shoulders, and sometimes when he was distracted, or sitting down somewhere, she would suddenly leap at him so he would pick her up.

Most of the time they weren't cuddly with each other: their physical interaction could be rough, one of them plowing into the other, lifting the other off the ground, tugging at one another, and, most of all, wrestling—but almost never hurting each other; it was like the playful tussling of puppies, whose style of play has its own verb: romping.

Annamaria almost never complained. She put up with everything, as long as Saverio didn't truly hurt her. But even when he did, she didn't tell on him to their parents, even if she walked away from him in tears. She rode behind him on her bicycle, followed him to the fishpond in San Floriano, doing "dangerous things" out of their mother's sight.

She loved those secret adventures, jumping from the roof onto a haystack; tying her bike with its training wheels onto his BMX, which pulled her behind him at top speed on the asphalt; jumping off the swing when it was highest off the ground.

And then the horse. They'd both begun riding so early that they couldn't remember the first time. But it was only when they moved to the country that the covert escapades began, the memorable afternoons. There was one time that Annamaria would remember later as *their moment*.

Sauro had recently bought his son a two-year-old colt, which he had just barely tamed. His coat was very fair, almost blond. His name was Pinocchio. In spite of help from older, experienced cowboys, Sauro had a great deal of trouble getting the horse to take to the saddle, and riding him without being thrown. Training him was a difficult job: leading him around the wooden dummy in the riding arena hundreds of times with his lunging cavesson on, trying to harness him, which the young horse made difficult, rearing, squirming, and sinking to the ground. Sauro had to get him accustomed to bearing his weight little by little, climbing up onto the fence and mounting him, putting one foot on the saddle for a few seconds while another horseman held onto him.

The first to mount him after Sauro was Saverio. His father had told him that the horse was all his. They had gotten along from the start, Pinocchio hadn't kicked him. Besides, the boy's weight was negligible. Saverio felt like his lord and master, so much so that, right after the colt was tamed, he'd brought Annamaria into the stable and, without saying anything to anyone, saddled up Pinocchio, badly, with his childish strength. When he had touched the colt's underbelly, the horse had puffed out his stomach, and Saverio had barely managed to tighten the cinch on the saddle to the second hole.

Annamaria, who had brought carrots from the house to keep the horse on good behavior, got bitten, not very hard, but hard enough to make her tear up. Nonetheless, as Pinocchio drooled and chewed on his metal bit, her brother managed to adjust the curb chain under his chin so it wouldn't bother him too much. After half an hour had passed, the horse seemed to be harnessed and ready.

"Do you want to go for a ride?" Saverio had asked her. The little girl had said she was afraid, but if he held the bridle, she would ride around the horse yard. He lifted her onto the horse, then he tricked her. Quickly mounting, he pushed her forward against the padded edge of the saddle. He took the reins and told her to hold on tight to the mane. Then he kicked Pinocchio in the flank, who bucked and broke into a gallop. Saverio had no control over him, but he didn't care. The horse wasn't afraid, Saverio wasn't afraid, and Annamaria wasn't afraid either.

They galloped with the wind in their faces into the field where Porcu's sheep were grazing. Pinocchio ran straight into the middle of the flock, startling the sheep and terrifying the lambs, then headed off toward the distant scrub. Saverio and Annamaria started laughing and shouting with joy, they held on tight, their cheeks red and their hair tangled, and let loose a kind of battle cry, as if they were at war with those poor peaceful lambs, Sheeeeeee-ep, Sheeeeee-ep! They kept laughing as they held on and galloped, the happiness of the one passing through to the other and to the horse, through the saddle, through the sweat on his coat, through Saverio's hands that held the reins, through Annamaria's fingers that gripped Pinocchio's silky, thick mane.

That was their moment, the one in which the knot of their sibling bond was formed, knotted so tightly that it couldn't ever come undone. A unifying, pure love. The ride probably didn't last longer than ten minutes. Because of the horse's sweat, the saddle, which wasn't completely secured, began slipping to one side. Saverio tried to stop Pinocchio, pulling on the reins with all his strength, but the colt bucked, throwing them off the other side. They both fell to the ground, rolling many times. Full of dust and fear, they looked at each other for a few seconds to confirm that they were alive, and kept laughing and laughing, unable to stop. Pinocchio had stopped running not far off. He seemed to be waiting for them. Then, all of a sudden, Annamaria began to cry. She had realized that one of her wrists hurt terribly. Saverio ran to get the horse. He put the saddle back on as best he could. He put his little sister back in the saddle at once, because that's what you had to do after you fell, remount at once. He returned to the stable leading the horse on foot, holding it by the bridle, Annamaria concentrating wholly on not falling again. It was some time before they got there. Time in which they both kept silent. She wasn't angry at her brother, and even the pain didn't bother her very much. She was happy.

Sauro was in the stable yard when he saw them come back in.

"I took her on a gentle, easy-peasy little ride," Saverio told his father.

Annamaria dismounted on her own, in silence, using her good hand and keeping her eyes lowered. For a long moment, the children hoped their father would buy it. But when Sauro saw the horse all sweaty, the children's clothes stained with earth and grass, their messy hair, he understood that they had fallen. And when he saw Annamaria's crooked wrist, he gave Saverio a severe beating. Sauro was a big man, with hands that could inflict pain even when he meant to caress. Saverio was stiff with rage, red from the effort of not crying.

Annamaria interrupted: "Babbo, I asked him to do it, I asked him to do it."

She was aware that he wouldn't have done anything to her, that she would always be spared such blows. But Sauro knew that bad ideas always came from his firstborn, even if the little one took responsibility for them.

He raised his voice.

"When you two are alone with the horses you must never touch them, do you understand? How many times have I told you that?"

Annamaria kept quiet. Saverio remained rigid. They left Pinocchio to their father and returned home to ask their mother to take Annamaria to the emergency room, as Sauro had ordered them to do, in between curses.

Annamaria's wrist was broken. During the weeks when she had to wear a cast, Saverio helped his sister to bathe, to dress, to cut her meat, continually asking her if she needed help. He would never again in his life take such good care of another human being.

Lately, Saverio hardly thought about her at all. That afternoon he whistled in the shower. He put on clean, Americanino jeans, cowboy boots, a long-sleeved sweater with three buttons, and, over it, a bomber jacket, military green on the outside, orange inside. He wore his hair a little long in the back, spiky in front. He'd had a girlfriend for six months. Her name was Tamara. She was the daughter of a farmer who'd made his money by robbing graves with his father and brother. They had extensive experience: they could recognize land that had Etruscan tombs hidden beneath it from the way the wheat stalks grew; they knew how to tell the poor tombs—worthless to them because they contained no valuable objects—from the rich ones. The former they covered back up, or sometimes destroyed with a bulldozer. It was said that in the seventies they'd found a grave chamber that contained all the wife's jewels, intact; and that it may have been the proceeds of that sale that had paid for the family's two enormous farms. There was also talk of Swiss bank accounts.

Every time she saw them, Annamaria tried to decide if she believed the rumors or not. It seemed impossible to her that men who were incapable of producing a complete sentence could be experts in archaeology. She didn't understand that they possessed another set of skills, which were the exact opposite of an archaeologist's.

Tamara was universally desired, and hard-to-get. Sixteen years old, with light brown curls, doe's eyes, and so much money. After three months during which he only kissed her, Saverio had gotten irritated, and told her that if she wanted to stay with him, she had to prove her love. He had taken her virginity one May afternoon on a dune by the sea. He had worn pants stained with her blood for three days as a trophy.

Saverio was desired, too. Above all, for his independent spirit. He wouldn't sacrifice it for anyone, not even for Tamara, even if she officially declared herself his girlfriend. People were attracted to him without his needing to seduce anyone, and he took advantage of that. Besides, seduction, at this age and in this environment, was pointless. Some did it, some didn't. There were the beautiful and the ugly. The cool and the clods, as they said in the village. At a certain age, everyone started to pair off pretty randomly, if only to gain experience.

Saverio's sexual initiation, like that of the other adolescent boys in the area, had been achieved through a kind of collective abuse of a mentally retarded twenty-year-old who arranged a tryst with all of them in an abandoned farmhouse, to which a mattress, condoms, and tissues had been brought. She spread her legs and the boys took turns; she said to each one of them, "I love you. Not one of them responded" "Me too," even just pretending, which had been the only thing she'd wanted in return. In the village they made fun of her and treated her like an animal. When her ancient parents discovered what their daughter was up to, they sent her to a group home in the north; it wasn't clear if that was to protect her or to get rid of her.

In the countryside, the young boys were wild and feral. Only when they got a little older did judgment take over, and along with the desire to be superior to other people, and the goal of making an engagement that would be transformed almost automatically into marriage.

Saverio never had to deal with competition. He was the alpha male in every circle of his peers he happened to enter. Aside from that, there was his father. With him, there was no question of competition, but Saverio wasn't interested in that anyway—they were already caught up in an endless war on too many fronts. He preferred to relax at home, and he had a young lover in every hamlet of the Maremma.

He'd showered and gotten ready in a hurry so he could go out and take Tamara to the movies in Orbetello. Usually, when she was in the car, she took off her shoes and rested her feet on the dashboard, which infuriated him, but that evening he bore it in silence. She'd had an abortion the week before. It hadn't been difficult. Physically, she'd recovered at once; but she kept on crying, and Saverio wasn't well-equipped to console her, apart from saying that she shouldn't think of it as a child, but as a mistake of a few minutes' duration; that they hadn't killed anyone; and to promise her, without believing it, that they would have a child when they were older and ready to start a family. That seemed to calm her down, but then she started crying again. So, the only thing he could do was to distract her, to take her to movies to see stories about other people, so she would stop thinking about her own situation. He took her to see *Rain Man*. Afterwards, in the car, as they were driving back, she started crying again, and he said to her, "Tamà, I've had it with this. Think about what if the kid turned out to be retarded like *Rain Main*. It's better this way, right?"

"We could take him to the casino to count cards and we'd get rich."

"But in our case, it wouldn't turn out to be a retarded genius, we'd just get a retarded moron, like us. And anyway, you're already rich."

She started to laugh. Still driving, he put a hand on her leg; she took it and kissed it.

"We can always have other moronic children, right, Savè?"

"Whatever."

After the visit to the Garden with Lisa, Annamaria had thought for days about the meeting with the sculptor, and what it had been like being in that place and talking to her; and the strange effects produced by a world in which everything was so altered from normality. There were the disorienting perspectives produced by the reflections of the concave little mirrors; the things that were said about art, beauty, the power dynamic between men and women—things so different from everyday conversations about food, transportation, who was doing what for their grandfather, for the horses; the progress of the dogs and the chickens; and where were the keys? Physical contact with objects, the earth, the backpack, the silverware, the brown cabinets, and all the other inanimate colors of the furnishings of home. She remembered all the other times they'd visited the Garden, it was always her father who took her, because he was curious about what was going on there, and he liked to see his little girl's astonishment. He had fun with her, they told jokes in the car and laughed about everything, even about the way his daughter stumbled on the stairs, because there weren't any right angles to help you get your bearings.

Sauro had a weakness for Annamaria; it's easy to have one for little girls, especially when the older brother is a big, argumentative boy; but Annamaria knew how to be sweet to her father, how to awaken tenderness. She knew that for him, carrying her on his shoulders after she'd stumbled for the thousandth time was the most satisfying way for him to feel like "the King," because nobody else saw him the way she did. But there was more to it than that.

She sensed vaguely that there was a kind of anxiety in the tender looks her father gave her. She tried to reassure him by laughing and making him laugh, but the vague sensation remained that she was *his* princess, yes, but that this magic did not extend beyond his gaze, and that in some way he was aware of this at all times. Could it be that he was ashamed of her? He had taught her to ride horses early, because horses didn't stumble, he took her to see the Monsters. But he didn't introduce her to the countess. They greeted the cook, never the artist. He didn't treat her like a princess when anyone was around whom he wanted to impress.

At the Garden they would play with her favorite toy, the welding machine. Once, when she was about five, a blacksmith had come to repair the barn door, and she'd been enchanted by the experience: the flame that melted the metal, the welding helmet with the smoked visor that shielded the face, the fact that it was really dangerous, and you had to keep far back, because the fire that fixed the iron door could harm the eyes at the same time. It was Christmastime, and Annamaria had made a helmet for herself from the cardboard of a panettone box, into which she'd cut a window for the eyes. She went around the house in her rubber boots, wielding a gas lighter with a long barrel, and pretended to weld everything; doors, chairs, beds. They let her do it; her grandfather would suggest all kinds of things that needed welding: "Come here, Annamarì, the television is broken," and she would run up with her make-believe blowtorch to repair the set. At the Monsters, as Sauro called it, it was almost always Guido, the local mailman, who brandished the blowtorch, who always delivered the mail a few days late so he could help with the construction of the reinforced concrete scaffoldings. The last time she'd gone there with her father she'd been ten years old, and Guido had let her try it. She wasn't as drawn to it anymore, but Sauro was still into it. And it genuinely was fun. They'd climbed up the structure that had been erected, a kind of small castle with arcades that only recently had become recognizable as the figure of the Emperor in the tarot. On that occasion, Annamaria had been happy to be there, but she had not completely perceived the magic that permeated the place. It was just a strange building site filled with unsettling shapes made of reinforced concrete, a place where you went with your dad so he'd lift you up on his shoulders, and where you could weld things.

The other times, she hadn't met the artist, just the workmen: someone from the area, some stranger with an odd way about him, the cook from the estate, and also Giovanna, who was her second cousin, though they barely greeted each other. Annamaria knew there was bad blood with those relatives, though she wasn't clear on the reason. In the car she said to her father, "Doesn't it seem to you that Giovanna looks a whole lot like Mamma when she was young?" And he replied, "I thought that immediately when I saw her, my god she's beautiful—she's like my Miriam when she worked in the eyeglasses boutique." Annamaria was glad he thought the same thing she did, and made him retell the story of how he'd broken the arm of his Lozza sunglasses on purpose so he could see her again. A story that Sauro always told without mentioning the presence of Miriam's cousin Adriana, and the betrayal.

5. The Hierophant
Tradition. Guidance. Marriage.

Settimio was born a farmer and would always be a farmer. In those days it was an occupation that never began and never ended; there were no holidays or Sundays off, nobody got fired, no one retired, it was a permanent state, like being a parent, or having a congenital illness. Settimio said, "When you have the land and the land has you, that's forever." His father had been a sharecropper for the prince on estates that had belonged to the Papal State for centuries. He had managed to liberate himself, to buy his own acreage, thanks to his wife's inheritance. He had a farm in a valley, with wheat, olives and vineyards. A garden for his domestic needs, twenty Maremma cows that continually got lost in the fallow scrub, a pen for a couple of pigs. The horses only came later. He sold whatever he could, and firewood, too. They had enough to eat, but nothing more. Settimio, the seventh of eight siblings, had started working as a kid, which was normal, and he had never stopped. Three of his siblings had died of malaria; their mother died when he was so little that he couldn't remember her. It happened with the eighth child, an enormous boy, born breech, whose labor took so long that the local midwife was called in, far too late, and could not save her.

At that time, the countryside was not yet the poetical realm of fresh air, organic food, and artisanal honey that it would become many years later. It was exhaustion, hernias, and sweat, alarm clocks set before dawn, the stench of manure. It was a place where you were always dirty, tired, weathered by the sun, with calloused hands incapable of caresses. The farmsteads were not sunlit houses with sage-green sashed windows and vases of fresh flowers on the tables, but fly-filled ruins, cold in winter and hot in summer, with pails of dirty water, food hanging to dry in the rooms, and floors encrusted with mud.

His father had joined the fascist party and had made his children who were of age sign up, too. Without conviction, under duress. So that they could live together in peace, out of self-interest. They had sold six horses to the army for the Ethiopian campaign. During the Second World War, their widowed father had made sure that none of his sons was called up. Settimio would have liked to join the army. He was comfortable with rifles, he hunted wild boar. But he'd been told he was of no use to the king, or to the queen either, which frustrated him very much.

After he'd lost his wife, Settimio's father had strengthened his religious faith, which already had been strong. He made his children go to mass on Sunday, and, without discussion, they prayed every morning, and every night before the evening meal. He was devoted to Saint Anthony above all, to whom he prayed for grace, and for miracles for himself, his children, and the livestock. In the kitchen, next to the fireplace, he'd built a niche where he installed a terracotta statue of the saint, with a hollow underneath where he stowed money. His children had accepted, to different degrees, the transformation of their home into a kind of monastery where only work and prayer took place. Luigina became a nun so she could get away and stop having to take care of her little siblings. Settimio became a communist heretic, though he'd never managed to deny the existence of God, so the more he blasphemed the more he believed in Him—to such a point that, as he'd grown older, he'd taken to violently denouncing the amorality of atheists, and their total lack of values. But since they were all under their father's thumb, nobody dared dispute his decisions. In any case, he beat them so soundly when they disobeyed that they tried not to cross him. They all left home fairly early.

Settimio left when Alma entered his life.

She came from the mountainous province of Grosseto. She had been sent to the countryside to live with an aunt after her father, a miner, was killed in the Nazi-Fascist massacre in Niccioleta, on the road to Larderello, in June of '44, along with eighty-two other miners. When she arrived, she immediately became the main attraction of the surrounding area. She was exotic because she was new, and because of her mountain origins and her blond hair, which were completely unfamiliar to the farmers at the time. There was also her slenderness, definitely a defect, which suggested fragility and malnutrition, but which conferred an unusual grace upon her. Her aunt and her cousins always came to the Biaginis' farm for the grape harvest, and in September they brought Alma to help. The war wasn't over yet, so women and children had to do the hard work. Alma was sunburned and got exhausted when she cut the larger bunches of grapes. The most they could make her do was to carry the filled baskets. It was clear from the start that her job among the vines would be to go through and pluck out immature grapes, to carry drinks, and to help prepare food for the harvesters; but cooking wasn't her forte, either. In the course of two days, they discovered how she could be useful. Alma could sing beautifully, so they sent her to pass through the vine rows like a goldfinch. She knew arias from classical operas, popular songs, the folk ballads of Monte Amiata. There were songs about miners, wine, anarchy, but most of all, about love. The festival of the grape harvest took place only after the harvesting was finished and the first wine had been pressed; but with Alma it felt like it was celebrated every day.

Settimio fell in love with her even before he heard her sing. He had brought her an old apron and boots that had belonged to his dead mother, to wear in the vine rows. They were enormous on her; she started laughing. "They're fine!" she said, while he tried to tighten the cloth bow, which he didn't know how to do. It was an excuse to keep her close to him for an extra moment. Her hair smelled of ashes and baked apples. Settimio had no particular gifts. He was gruff, he couldn't dance, or make a woman laugh. But he was tall and sturdy, and his face somehow had a kind of somber beauty, with thick eyelashes and extremely dark eyes. He wanted this girl even though he was younger than her. He had never wanted anything so much in his whole life. She had told her cousin that she didn't want to get engaged or to get married, and she didn't want children either. Now that the war was over, she wanted to get out of here and go to America, to sing with colored women. That's how she put it. She had never seen a black person, and the longest journey she'd ever made was fifty miles, from a village in the mountains to a village between the hills and the sea, in the same province.

Settimio found out about her dream of becoming a singer. He decided he would wait her out, and sooner or later, make her change her mind. On Alma's birthday, he gave her a gramophone that played 78s, with money he had removed, a little at a time, from under the statue of Saint Anthony, and three records that had been recommended to him in a shop in Grosseto, where he rode on horseback (eight hours there and back): a fantasia of Vienna waltzes, "La Strada nel Bosco" by Gino Bechi, and *Rhapsody in Blue* by Gershwin. It was while she was listening to this last one that Alma discovered that her America was right there, in Settimio's arms. They married when she was twenty-four and he was twenty-two. Thanks to the land reforms that were initiated under fascism, and which continued even afterwards to reclaim the marshes, they obtained a farm and a piece of land from the Maremma Corporation in a few years, which they slowly enlarged. Their holdings would become the house, the land, and the annexes where Sauro was born, where he grew up, and where he later came to live with his own family. Alma and Settimio loved each other very much. To him, it felt like he had had nothing until the moment he met her.

What was he before Alma? A sad and angry farmer who spent his days exhausting himself. There was land; but with Alma he realized that there was also air, water, fire, and a fifth element that he hadn't even suspected, which was the sensation of completeness, something that filled him with joy when the rooster crowed early in the morning and woke him, and he saw Alma sleeping beside him, her mouth open; he on his side of the bed, she on hers, next to each other at the moment of greatest vulnerability. Settimio let her sleep. He would have liked to find his breakfast ready and his bread and wine packed for the fields, as it was for the other men, but he prepared them for himself.

It was Alma who turned Settimio into a communist, by telling him stories about the miners, about her beloved father. Settimio became a communist out of love, because he wanted so much to avenge his father-in-law, to repay Alma for her loss. He had always been indifferent to the world around him; now he began to care about politics. His sincere interest wasn't in a more just society, but in doing what Alma expected of him. When he brought home his Italian Communist Party card, when he went to party meetings, when he organized the first *Unità* festival, Alma glowed.

As long as she lived, Alma had given him everything he wanted without reservation, and with something he'd never known before: happiness. Everything Alma did, from working in the fields to keeping house, from ironing the clothes, running the hot iron across the cloth, to feeding the pigs, she did in song. And she smiled, so much, even though she had overlapping incisors, which other women might have been embarrassed to display so often. Yet she remained frail. Too thin, in an era when the dictates of beauty and health demanded that women be robust. She had trouble sustaining a pregnancy, and she had two miscarriages before she succeeded in carrying Sauro all the way to term. Sometimes she cried, but then she would start singing again, and smiling. Settimio had convinced her that if she prayed more, Saint Anthony could help her. She'd grown up in a family of anarchist miners and atheists, but she knew that when it came to women's affairs and household matters, it was necessary to turn to Mother Mary. Settimio told her no, Saint Anthony was the most powerful of all. It didn't take long to convince her—they always tried never to displease each other. And so she learned the prayers and she prayed, she even sang them; she gathered flowers for the saint, kissed Settimio, kissed him and hugged him, and he realized later how happy he was. He remained gruff, but he was content; he worked all day and returned at night to the arms of Alma, who cooked badly, and only on Sundays. Generally, bread, olives, and salami would appear on the table, but it didn't matter to him, because after the meal they would make love.

In the spring of '47, Settimio asked his sister Cettina, who was a seamstress, to sew new clothes for Alma, because, with her belly growing day by day, nothing fit her anymore. She had gained thirty pounds, and her bust had swelled, which made her proud. A photo of a pregnant Alma always leaned against the statue of Saint Anthony. In it she stood under an olive tree behind the house, her hands clasped under her belly, wearing a light dress with little buttons on it, fastened all the way up the front, and a broad smile that showed her crowded teeth. Annamaria, who had only ever heard her spoken of as a marvelous angel and a bearer of joy, prayed to her in times of crisis, prayed to the grandmother, Alma, whom she'd never known, and whose ready laugh she thought she'd inherited.

Sauro was already huge inside his mother's belly, and when

slender Alma gave birth to him, he took everything out of her, including her uterus. The night she went into labor they had to rush her to the hospital in an ambulance. As soon as he saw the obstetrician make a strange face, Settimio raced on horseback to the community center to telephone the Red Cross. In the hospital, they instantly transferred her to the operating room and left him alone, telling him nothing. On the ground floor there was a little chapel. Settimio spent the whole night there, praying that Alma would not die like his mother, and vowed to go to mass every Sunday, to resume being a devoted Christian, and to blaspheme no more. When day broke, he stood up carefully, his knees stiff, his spine practically paralyzed, and climbed the stairs with tremendous effort. Once he was on the next floor, he asked a nurse for news of his wife, and she showed him where she was. He opened the door of the room and found them in bed, his wife and his son, the little one sleeping on her chest, with a chubby, rosy face that looked bigger than hers, which was pale and drawn, with purplish eyelids, dark circles around the eyes, her skin yellowish from the blood loss of childbirth. But her chest rose regularly as she breathed in sleep. It was the most beautiful sight he'd ever seen. Two tears unexpectedly fell from Settimio's eyes. He wiped them away, and without even looking to see if there were others in the room, he went to a chair between the two beds, leaned his forehead on the mattress beside the living, breathing Alma and their child, and fell fast asleep.

Alma died six years later of pneumonia. The doctors said she had latent silicosis, contracted in childhood, from inhaling pyrite dust in the mines (every day until she was eighteen, she had brought in lunch to her father), and the pneumonia was more serious than they had anticipated. What little happiness Settimio had experienced while he lived at her side expired forever with the last, short breath Alma exhaled on an autumn day in 1953.

The first thing Settimio did was to smash the statue of Saint Anthony and resume blaspheming. Work still remained, then wine and politics, which, more than anything, was an excuse for venting his anger and frustration at everything that was going wrong in the world. But he took no interest in Sauro. That warred with his love for Alma. Even though both of them were children who had been prematurely deprived of a mother, even though the child was all that remained of her, he could not manage to love him. He could not bear that the boy had out-lived her. Having only been loved by Alma, Settimio had never learned that another form of affection might exist, like love between father and son.

He asked Cettina, his seamstress sister, to look after the child while he was working in the fields. He paid her, even though she was a loving aunt to whom the child was hopelessly attached. So much so that she refused to marry or to have chil-dren of her own, so as not to leave her nephew all alone. During the boy's adolescence, the relationship between father and son deteriorated even more. Sauro wanted to study, Settimio considered that a waste of time. Unlike Alma, who believed that learning brought emancipation, in his opinion books were only good for muddling ideas and for producing impractical men who behaved arrogantly to people less edu-cated than themselves. Aunt Cettina always defended him; she was the one who provided his school supplies and sewed his uniform. Sauro was permitted to study agriculture on the con-dition that he help his father with the horses. Every afternoon, before and after his lessons, he went to the stables, gave the horses their fodder, and cleaned up. A couple of times, espe-cially during night chores, he'd come across his father crumpled on the storeroom floor, drunk and overcome with sorrow. At such times he went away without letting himself be seen.

Settimio never showed tenderness or compassion in his interactions with Sauro. The older the boy grew, the less he forgave him for having inherited his mother's beautiful smile and crooked teeth, which revealed themselves beneath the young man's first moustache. He couldn't bear it that lips so similar to Alma's could not produce her voice, her laughter, and her song. Their orphan pasts had left both men incapable of showing affection to anyone but women, always loving them in a way that was connected to an infant's need for nurturance; to nostalgia for a mother whose loss, having come too soon, could never stop being mourned.

The night of Alma's death, another husband accompanied his wife to a hospital, in Nice. It was Harry Mathews, taking his wife Niki to see a psychiatrist. That afternoon, Niki had kicked her husband's lover and swallowed an entire box of sleeping pills that she'd been given that very morning by a doctor they knew, a gynecologist who had ignored the reason for the appointment—a request for a medical prescription for insomnia—and had subjected her to an uncomfortable, invasive visit. Niki was in such a distraught state that the sleeping pills had no effect. After discovering an arsenal of sharp objects under the mattress of their marital bed, Harry had hugged his wife close. He was frightened by her expression, he didn't know how to help her, and he told her he would do anything to make her better again. Leaving their young daughter Laura with the nanny, they went in the middle of the night to the office of a psychiatrist, Doctor Cossa. Upon entering, the first thing Niki did was open her purse and dump out all its contents on the table: knives, scissors, a small hammer. All the weapons she had at her disposal. The doctor thanked her, nodding, and asked to speak privately with Harry. He told him that she needed to be admitted to the hospital at once, but that there were no beds available. To get started, he gave her electroshock right there in the office, leaving her totally dazed and weak, then sent her home for a few days to wait for a bed to open up. Doctor Cossa advised Harry to remove all sharp objects from the house, and to make sure his wife was in the company of friends who would monitor her at all times, so she wouldn't try to commit suicide.

During this waiting period, Niki confessed to Harry that she'd been having an affair with the English lord who was married to Harry's lover. Even though he hadn't kept his own adultery hidden, Harry was hurt and upset to learn of his wife's. Years later, Niki would say that this was, in part, the origin of her anguish: although she had married a man who was open-minded, who called himself a feminist, and who even energetically performed many household chores—something that was extremely rare in those days, particularly for a man from a wealthy family—she had found herself in a situation similar to her parents', in which the man felt entitled to cheat with impunity, but would not tolerate his wife doing the same thing, and in fact considered it disgraceful. Harry was a modern man, but not modern enough.

By the time Harry and Niki moved from the United States to Paris, and from there to the south of France, something inside her was already broken. Discovering that her husband was cheating on her with an older woman had weighed on her, but perhaps worse still was being drawn into the unhealthy, destabilizing practice of partner-swapping, which had thrown her together with the English lord, a war veteran who was extremely cultured but death-obsessed, and two years older than her father. All they did was talk about death. It was a destructive relationship. At the outset, she was intellectually stimulated by speaking in two languages, listening to him recite by heart all the poems he'd memorized in school, long swathes of Shakespeare. But erotic tension knocked her off balance, unleashed harmful impulses. Niki began to tell him her suicidal fantasies. In that period, she was constantly trying to come up with a way to die that would leave no trace of the self behind, not even a feeling of guilt in others. She imagined lying down in the sea on an inflatable raft, letting herself be borne away by the current, then puncturing the raft once she was far enough away from shore. The lord found this idea very compelling, and even proposed other means of effecting the suicide. While for Harry and his lover everything was about attraction and seduction, Niki had been drawn to her lover by Eros and Thanatos. The fact that this man was older than her father had likely contributed to the reawakening of her suppressed memories—the anguish of incest, and a grown man's forbidden desire—which had traumatized her since she was a little girl.

Things began to get much worse. She felt she was losing control over her own thoughts, and later she would always say that the feeling of losing her mind, piece by piece, had been the most hideous, frightening, and painful experience of her life. Worse than any illness, worse than any physical pain. Years later, she would tell Giovanna that even arthritis—"such a funny word isn't it? A disease with "art" in its name," she'd said—which often left her unable to sleep or made her weep with pain, could not compare to the anguish that gripped her breast and never left her at that time, a continual internal scream that tormented her day and night. From her youth, she'd been able to control and conceal her fears and anxieties. But at this point, she was no longer capable of hiding anything.

She ended up back in the psychiatric hospital, a place surrounded by barbed wire, with metal bars in the windows. When she asked Harry what they were for, she heard him reply: to catch butterflies. She was so frightened that she found this answer comforting: maybe she had turned back into a child and needed to trust someone.

They subjected her to extremely violent treatments, including insulin therapy, which provoked intense convulsions, and ten more electroshock treatments, which produced such powerful spasms that she had to wear a mouthguard to keep her teeth from breaking during the jolts. Doctor Cossa, who was absent during those days, had left her in the hands of a less qualified assistant. Harry didn't know what to do, but deep down he didn't believe in substitutes. Each treatment made Niki lose memory, and this lack of control terrified them both. They were afraid she would never completely be herself again. They also used dream therapy, so she wouldn't remember the pain.

It was in that hospital prison that she was struck by the overwhelming desire to paint. In the first days, she had no materials with her, so she started making collages with leaves she found in the clinic's garden. At her request, Harry brought her drawing paper and colored pencils, which were probably her salvation. She drew open heads from which body parts emerged: a face covered in a constellation of eyes, with a question mark in the center of the forehead, and phrases like "Do I exist?" "Where did you put my knife?" "Pieces of my head." She drew mice around the border of a self-portrait that showed her lying on a bed like a corpse; the barred window with the sun behind it was surrounded by words that read "Are the mice inside me, or are they devouring me?" and "Today they gave me another electroshock. Will it help me?" and "Will the teeth of the mice tear me to pieces?" and "Harry is coming this afternoon. In a few hours. Will he bring Laura?" Whenever she could, she painted and drew. The doctors told her she should stay there for five years; instead, she was out in six weeks. She had found her cure: painting. From that moment on it was clear to her that artistic creation would save her. She would use her art to free herself from evil.

this purpose. Also, this time, I ordered a tea with lemon and bought a box of cookies because their pastries are always stale. You would never come here for breakfast or for a drink, that's why I come here to write, and only for that: none of the people I know would ever set foot in here, so I'm safe. Every now and then the owner of the bar, who's ancient and crabby, asks me, "Would the lady like something more?" He intends to be confrontational, he doesn't want me taking over the table without buying anything. I would like to tell him straight to his face, "Don't interrupt me, asshole, you should thank me—nobody ever sits in this shitty table near the bathrooms, much less a lady like me." Instead I'm nice, I order another tea, even though I won't drink it. In these few lines I've already summarized what I have to say for myself: I'm a woman above suspicion in a place above suspicion, who thinks things through, and never says anything that would compromise the public image of who she should be, what others expect of her, what she has become identified with. The cliché "be yourself" is so ridiculous. Nobody wants to let anyone see what they really are; we all hide behind whatever we want others to see in us. And so, here I am: a cultured lady, wealthy, elegant, the wife of a member of parliament, who's also a journalist, a feminist, and ecologist, not to mention financially independent. Of course, my father's rich. The pennies I get from the newspapers wouldn't even pay the Filipina who cooks, does the washing, and walks the dog for me. It's wonderful to be in my position, to be able to take part in environmental and democratic battles, ignoring all the potential contradictions; because even if we lose these battles nothing will change for me. Therefore, I don't want my life to change. I'm fine with my two houses, one in town, one in the country, and maybe a third in Kenya. I can permit myself to consume less because I already have all the essentials. I'm against exploitation because I have enough money to pay the taxes for my domestic help; I'm against nuclear energy because expensive bills aren't a problem;

I'm feminist because I can make my own decisions, even if my son has never held a broom in his hand, and has never seen his father do that, either—but what does it matter, since we have another woman who does it for us?

I came here today to write in my diary because for two weeks I've had a lover, and I need to talk about it. He's not the first, he won't be the last, even if at the moment all I can say is that I wish he were the only man in my life. Filippo still is having his affair with his stupid young assistant. I know he'll never leave me for her, and I'm fine with that. I know she represents no threat of any kind to our marriage. When I found out about it—I no longer remember clearly if it was three years ago or four—it felt worse. Filippo hadn't come across as someone who would go for younger women. He was always more into power; it seemed as if sex didn't matter much to him, but probably it just didn't matter to him with me; or maybe a young lover always serves as a trophy for a man who competes with other men. When I found the receipt from the hotel, a double room in both their names, a convention in Taormina about the future of the European Left, I had a physical reaction, my heart started beating furiously, and I had to run to the bathroom. I decided not to say anything, not to make pointless scenes. We are progressive, worldly people, we know that monogamy is an unnatural sacrifice, but we never had an open relationship. We are aware of the consequences of jealousy, and forcing a crisis would probably have quickly led us to a divorce that I knew I didn't want. I began to doubt myself, to feel old and undesirable. A terrible period ensued, which I vented about during that lone season of therapy. The diary came later. It came along with a new haircut and an unexpected suitor, Sandro, with whom I started flirting just because it made me feel pretty and admired, and I desperately needed that. But I was aware that it was an illusion. If he'd been seriously in love with me, I would have had to pretend that I felt more than I did, and I didn't want to do that. Besides, the situation seemed very dangerous to me, given that he was the brother of a family friend, and on top of that, worked at my newspaper. Too many connections and too many risks; if it had come to light, it would have been a disaster for both of us, and the game wasn't worth the candle, not for me. I told him that one night in June, on a terrace at the end of a birthday party. It was hard, because everything was perfect; the air was warm, stars in the sky, a full moon. There was jasmine in a vase that gave out a strong fragrance that I will always associate with a short, but very intense, pain. It was like an amusing game, brutally inter-rupted by a harsh nanny. Still, I was the one who hastened the end of something that had been peaceful, light, and painless, something that in a sense had brought me back to life. So much useless moralizing. In all probability, I wouldn't do it again today. Instead of filling my mouth with acid words and nervous cigarettes, I would return to that summer terrace, I would kiss Sandro with all the passion he deserved. Because now I've lost my wisdom, all of that marvelous self-control. I've become the lover of someone I never would have thought could appeal to me, and I've completely lost my mind. Two Fridays ago, as usual, before going to the country, I called Sauro, our factotum and friend, who looks after the horses, and who has been my hus-band's business partner for some time now (they opened a restaurant inside a barn), and asked him to turn the heating on at our place. We talked a little on the phone, and he understood that I was going out there alone, and that the rest of the family would be joining me a couple days later. That news put him in a good mood, and he said bluntly, all cheerily, "Great, so I'll wait for you at home, and I'll also turn on the fireplace, that way you'll find me nice and warm." I thought of making a somewhat crude comeback—he's not a refined person. But during the whole trip out I thought about it. I thought about him while I was driving; every mile I covered on the Aurelia seemed to increase my desire. I thought about his enormous hands and his shoulders. But just think, I said to myself, you have nothing in common with that boor. He probably doesn't even bathe, what a cowboy. I had a tape of De Gregori; I was listening to "The Man who Walks on Shards of Glass," and picturing him. I kept searching for excuses to justify such a base desire.

Once I was on the path to the house, walking through the tall, dark cypresses, I remember how much I hoped I wouldn't see his car, hoped I would find the house warm but empty. I would make myself an herbal tea, I would put on a record, lie down on the couch, and read. Instead, there he was. I was carrying my leather purse, and when I came in and saw him, my cheeks were already flushed, my legs were shaky, and I felt pathetic. He took my purse from me, he smelled of sandalwood. He was wearing an ironed shirt, a beige sweater, and velvet pants of the same color. I confess with shame that I thought to myself, "Hmm . . . he looks like one of us, he's dressed like Filippo." I can't say exactly what sort of bogus and random conversation we had before we did what we both immediately wanted to do, which was to leap into bed and make love as if we'd been abstinent for years. I, in effect, had been. Him? No. His reputation as a womanizer was known by all. The men who make love the best are the ones who do it the most; experience is an advantage that's often attained through infidelity. Sauro reawakened all my senses so powerfully, that, rather than a reawakening, I would call it a revelation. At my age, I'd almost thought I could do without it. Being with Filippo, who did not excite me as a person, who gave no thought to my body, had brought me to this pass: to seek pleasure in other things, in friendship, in food, in reading, in music. Sauro not only reminded me that I still had a body, I believe he brought me to discover something I hadn't known, which is that it's practically all I care about. There was something in the way he touched me and kissed me that instantly bewitched me. He is a coarse man, vulgar, ignorant, but his body is not. It is capable of singular delicacy. An ability to calculate the perfect touch, which I have never found in any other man. He has hands so big and strong that they could easily break my neck. And it's that restrained power, which knows how to transform itself into a well-judged caress at just the right moment, that made me crazy about him. That eroticism from which violence can flow, but which he never uses with me. Contrary to my imaginings, he's never brutal, he's never pushed my head between his legs (which is something all the others did), he's never done anything he wasn't sure I really wanted. And with him, I want so much to do everything, which has never happened before. Without any inhibition, guided only by desire, by the quest for a mutual pleasure that is supreme, unexpected, inescapable. As I write down this thought, I could almost weep from desire. Retracing our afternoons at the farmhouse, the time when we did it in the staff shed, the kisses he gave me beside the fountain when he made me come while I was standing, just like that, so fast, sticking one hand into my riding pants.

The tragedy is that he's aware of what I'm feeling, and he gloats over my weakness. He knows it, he takes advantage of it. I think he secretly laughs at me. I hate him for that. Sometimes he tortures me, rejecting me, he invents fake family obligations, kisses his wife on the neck in front of me, which he never did before we became lovers, and which I'm sure he never does if I'm not there to witness it. I thought I had power over him; at first I did. He was someone who worked for us; and at times I think I have more power over him, strengthened for once by my feminine force, which I can see reflected in his eyes, full of desire. I got back something I believed was lost; I feel pretty again. A few other men have picked up on it, but that's just a nuisance. I hate it that Filippo is noticing me again, I don't know what to do with his kisses now, now that I don't want my body to be touched by anyone but Sauro. That bastard has taken away all my power—over him, over myself. All I do is try to fight off the thought of him, which torments me, turning me on at the most ridiculous times of day, while I'm sitting in the dentist's chair, or inside this bar, as I write on a dirty table with the stench of piss and bleach piercing my nose. I'm consumed by remorse when I think how out of control this desire is. Not just because of Filippo, who's only getting back the horns he crowned me with so abundantly, these last years. But remorse for my own behavior; for letting myself go this way, which I never should have done. For giving him this power over me. And for everything that I'm now forced to do to hide what I'm feeling from myself and from everyone else. A mountain of lies that I can't keep up. Lies in my interactions with Filippo and my kids, so I can be alone with Sauro; lies in my interactions with Sauro, to keep him from knowing how important he is to me. I have to keep up a continual charade of disdain with him, be it in public or in private, which doesn't scratch his confidence one iota, maybe because of what my body tells him, or maybe he's too unsubtle and chauvinistic to think my opinion counts for anything. To him I'm a joke, to him I'm just a distraction like any other, like any of his lovers. What a paradox for me: I used to be someone who made men feel emasculated, because they were intimidated by my intelligence. And now my own lies shame me, because I can't ever admit except in these pages that I am hopelessly in love. That I think impossible thoughts, that I dream of running away with Sauro, that I want to kill any woman who comes near him, that just hearing his voice or his laughter makes me wet, that I fantasize that he will leave his wife and ask me to leave Filippo so we can be together forever and make love every day and kiss each other in broad daylight. Everything connected with him fills me with a paradoxical joy, with a bitter aftertaste, like the affection he feels for his daughter Annamaria, a girl as homely and neurotic as she is kind and intelligent, and so eager to be Lisa's friend. She's got a hidden sweetness that reminds me so much of her father, that generous virtue that they hide beneath layers of roughness. She is Sauro's

Niki had accepted. Jean had the power to make things happen. To get them started.

She had perceived that power the moment she entered his atelier on the Impasse Ronsin, five years before. She was still struck by a black artwork set against a backdrop of white gesso, a self-propelled hammer that smashed a bottle. "Why don't you add feathers?" she had said. He flashed an electric look of fury at her. Irritated, he left the room. Their first meeting had felt like a fight. Not long afterwards he had pasted feathers onto the bottle. They had become friends. When Niki moved to Paris, leaving her husband and children so she could dedicate herself body and soul to her own work, Jean and his wife Eva were her first points of reference. She became a close friend. She often accompanied him to visit scrap-iron dealers, choosing together the pieces he would work with in his atelier. They teased each other; she pointed out that he looked like a car mechanic; he that she was always inappropriately dressed when they went on their missions: a pale-pink ostrich feather boa, a velvet cap, an ivory faux-fur jacket—the likes of which the scrap dealer had never seen. Sometimes she picked up pieces for herself, too, mostly at the flea market. At the time, she had started working with found objects, incorporating them into her canvases.

It was the evening of October 29, 1960.

Beneath her shearling coat, Niki wore a dress of grey silk with long sleeves. She was beautiful. She always would be. This was thanks to her nose. Thanks to the perfect angle it created with the rest of her face. The slightly protruberant blue eyes, set between the ample forehead and striking cheekbones; the full lips with their teasing corners; the smooth, light-chestnut hair; the slender body—all of this made her captivating. Her allure was enhanced by her aristocratic bearing, which she'd never managed to erase; by her American-accented French and her French-accented English; by the clothes she wore; as if she'd never stepped out of the *Vogue* cover she'd posed in, wrapped in fur, at the age of twenty-two.

But she was truly beautiful because of her nose, which she feared was as big as her father's and those of her Saint Phalle uncles. And yet, this was the source of her grace, that prominent ridge of an enchanting coast.

Jean had turned up at the dinner with dirty hair, his fingers black and yellow from the workshop and from cigarettes. He wore a blue shirt covered in stains that exuded the smell of smoke from the coal he stole from the church across from the atelier. But Jean was never inappropriate or out of place. He was never afraid of anything, from changing his ideas to looking ridiculous, which meant he never was ridiculous. As soon as he saw her sit down, take off her fur coat and unwind the scarf from her neck, he knew he wanted her terribly. He knew he'd never seen a woman like her, had never desired any other woman so much. That entire meal, he never took his eyes off her, even for one moment, not even to turn to the waiter, or to light a cigarette. He ate ravenously, and he looked at her as she talked, as she smoked, as she reached to stroke her hair. She was never still.

She had no doubt that he liked her, but she was afraid. Afraid of him, of the power he might exert over her, which she could feel growing every time he came near. She was afraid because she was newly separated, and she didn't want to end up in another dependent relationship. But her greatest fear at that moment was that the look that lit up his face as he gazed at her might suddenly burn out.

He asked her what made her angriest. She admitted that she was full of anger, that she always had been, but that she'd never distinctly understood what she was angry about. She felt she had been born that way, furious. She told him about her mother, who had blamed her for a terrible period during her pregnancy, when she'd cried all the time because she'd found out that her husband had been unfaithful, and on top of that, they'd had to deal with the family bank's enormous losses in the crisis of 1929, give up their house on Fifth Avenue, and watch as, a few months after Niki's birth, Saint Phalle & Company shut down for good. Her mother had sent her to live with her grandparents in France, where she spent the first three years of her life. Maybe her mother's anger had been passed on to her through the umbilical cord.

She told him about her rebellions. "I always needed to disobey. They sent me to a girls' school run by nuns, the Convent of the Sacred Heart on 91st Street in Manhattan. We wore a bottle-green uniform with a matching kerchief and a beige shirt. Every year the nuns gave the best pupil in the school a red ribbon to put on her uniform. I really liked that red ribbon, but I didn't have good enough grades to earn it. So, I bought one and put it on my uniform. Of course, it bothered me that I hadn't earned it, but I liked that red bow so much, it pleased me aesthetically, its contrast with the dark green, and that was the motivation I gave the nuns when they ordered me to cut it off and punished me for my impertinence. I just had been taken with the idea that I wanted a colorful accessory! I had no great abilities. I just needed to break the rules. In my new school, Brearley, they liked me better because it was an institution that highly encouraged creativity in girls. I met some of my best friends in the world there, like Jackie Matisse. She only drew horses, I only drew trees; Sylvia Obolensky, who was also one of us, and became an artist later, she only drew maps. And it was remembering what the three of us were like when we were little girls that made me think about how important obsession was to becoming an artist. Anyway, at the entrance to the school there were copies of Greek statues that had had vine leaves attached to them to cover the genitals. One day I took some brilliant red varnish and colored all the leaves.

The effect on those plaster leaves was gorgeous, but they didn't take it well this time, either. It was 1944, I was fourteen. I was expelled for the second time."

Then she told him that the most recent time she'd been angry was when Joan Mitchell—who, by the way she didn't rate highly as a painter—had asked her which art school she'd gone to, and when she'd replied, "none," had dismissed her as "another wife-of-a-writer who paints." She had felt all her muscles tense, as if she were preparing to leap at her jugular.

They laughed. Beneath Jean's eyebrows, something caught fire every time she laughed.

"Jean, but it's the truth, I didn't go to any school, and I don't know how to draw."

He told her the most important thing she would ever hear in her life. As she listened, she sensed something powerful in his voice, and a thought came to her: Jean's words were not compliments, they expressed his genuine desire to encourage her not to obey expectations, not to betray herself. He was the first man, perhaps the first human being, who had invited her with all his force to totally believe in what she felt she was.

He said to her, "Niki, you don't have to know how to draw, you have to know how to dream. And that you know excellently how to do. Dreams are everything. Technique isn't nothing, but technique can be learned. You are an artist." And as he was saying this, he had stamped out his cigarette butt in the butter dish, creating an amalgam of blackish ashes in the melted fat. It was the kind of thing nobody had ever done at any table where Niki had dined up to this moment. Jean came from a world far removed from hers. The anarchy behind that distracted, disgusting action made her heart flip. She averted her eyes for a moment. She had found something that she had never had before. She leaned across the table, coming nearer to him, and with her thumbs, smoothed his bushy eyebrows. He took advantage of that to kiss her wrists.

They fell passionately, instantly in love. Long before they told each other so.

They talked about their friends. About Brancusi. They talked about projects they were working on. Niki talked to him about her children, about how much she missed them, and she talked to him about herself, about her pain, her anxiety, about the psychiatric clinic, about painting, which was the only medicine that had worked.

He listened to her.

"You don't have to justify yourself, Niki. You're looking for a reason to devote yourself to art? Be an artist. Do the only thing you can do."

"I'm also a mother, and, supposedly, a wife."

"You still will be."

"No, those are roles that require a kind of commitment that I'm in no condition to sustain."

"Nobody will die from that."

"Someone will suffer."

"Less than they would if you'd stayed with them, unhappy and angry."

"I don't know, you can't measure suffering. The consequences of the loss can't be foreseen. But I know what you're talking about. My mother's frustration destroyed her. Her unhappiness devoured me and my siblings. I didn't want to be like her."

"Mothers are unforgivable by definition. You will be another unforgivable mother. Even more unforgivable because you're an artist. You have to start dealing with that at once."

Niki fell silent. He had said it again. "You're an artist."

She started to draw on the tablecloth.

"See, I can never get the proportions right."

"Who cares about proportions? Are you trying to do geometry? There's something strong in your line, it comes from inside. You're angry, you're presumptuous, you're full of fantasy. You can become a great painter if you want, Niki. But that's your business. It doesn't depend on anyone else."

They wouldn't make love that night. They had drunk too much.

Jean had had a chocolate cake made for her with thirty candles. It was a struggle for her to blow them out; even then her lungs had limited capacity. He let out a sigh at the sight of her face illuminated by the candles, her lips in an O, her eyes lowered.

He smiled at her. "There will never be a more wonderful year than this one. I promise you."

He had no gift for her, but in truth, he had given her the most precious gift of all: he had told her what she was.

They walked together to the entry of the studio she had rented near Jean's atelier. They hugged. He gripped one of her hands hard, then touched her back but quickly broke off. "Good night, Niki."

She watched him go, he walked so well, he moved like a panther. His legs were walking farther away, hers were paralyzed with desire. She thought that she and Jean were the two bravest people she had ever known.

In his atelier, Jean found his wife Eva sleeping next to her young lover, separated and tragic like a botched Pietà. He noticed a big bag, already packed, next to them. He didn't remember quite where, but he knew they were going south the next day. He hurried up to the loft and threw himself onto the mattress of his insomnias.

Niki didn't sleep much either. The morning of the next day, unable to concentrate, she ruined a canvas. She decided to go out. She started walking toward the Impasse Ronsin. At that moment it was the only thing to do.

She found Jean assembling a creature made out of a carburetor with mechanical arms. The atelier was very cold. He was wearing the same shirt as the night before.

"I was waiting for you," he told her.

She looked at him and walked toward him. He rose and went to wash his hands. She followed him. Without giving him time to dry off, she used his shoulders to hoist herself up and sit on the stone sink he'd just used. She pulled him to her and kissed him on the mouth. She wrapped her legs around him.

They gripped each other tightly. He lifted her up without moving his lips from hers, then laid her down on the mattress. He was concerned above all with her pleasure, as if there were no other happiness than to see her enjoy herself. She watched him come and thought in that moment that he was the one, her love, her inspiration. She thought of something she would do in her paintings, but she would start that the next day—this day was only for making love. They didn't get up even when it was dark outside and the lights of Paris came in through the high windows of the atelier, even to turn on the heat. It was freezing, but they didn't notice, caught up in their bodies. They didn't speak anymore. Only Niki, at one point, had interrupted the silence: looking at the clock she had said, "How wonderful, it's only five o'clock." They had made their choice. They had all of life before them. They would never let each other go.

7. The Chariot
Action. Victory. Conquest.

Sauro and Sanfilippi's little restaurant had met with greater success than they themselves had anticipated. People came from the villas of Ansedonia, Porto Ercole, and Porto Santo Stefano to get there. The Saddlery was always so crowded that they'd had to expand the annex in great haste to create an extra room, and widen the deck, where small sofas were set out. At the end of the season they were all so worn out that they decided to open only on Saturdays and Sundays during the winter months. But if the director general of the state-run television network, RAI, wanted to bring friends by on a Thursday; if Gianmaria Molteni's wife, or the countess, wanted to throw a birthday party there on a Friday; if some director had friends from abroad he wanted to take out riding then bring by the restaurant to unwind on a weekday, you couldn't say, "Sorry, we're closed." In this way, Miriam and the kids had not managed to get a day off for six solid months.

The structure was just a glorified wooden shack with a thatched roof made of long, dried reeds from the marshes, which offered protection from the rain, and in theory also served the purpose of letting out the smoke from the fireplace in wintertime. In theory. In certain winds, the fireplace would not draw, and the Saddlery filled with dense smoke that rose about six feet from the floor, sometimes making it impossible to see anyone's face. Then, the two doors would be opened, and at that point, the smoke would disperse but the cold would come in. It was a place where in winter you could really suffer a lot, but that didn't hurt its popularity. Giulia Sanfilippi often complained to her husband about having to go there every weekend, disguising her happiness at seeing Sauro so soon. Conducting her clandestine romance under her husband's nose gave her an added pleasure, which was heightened by her ostentatious display of a kind of contempt for her lover's uncouthness. She called him "the cowboy," never "the King," and declared it was impossible to have a conversation with him of more than three sentences, omitting the fact that, in private, she kept him from finishing his sentences by covering his mouth with hers.

Miriam was always exhausted. Shut up in the kitchen. She continually got compliments from everyone for the food, but towards the end of August she came down with an illness that sent her to bed for two days. Talking with the local country doctor, to whom she was distantly related, she'd decided that this was no life, and that if she withdrew from the Saddlery, it would be good for her health and also for family harmony. Sanfilippi got alarmed, and, unbeknownst to Sauro, gave her a check for two million lire (which she accepted without blinking an eye, believing she legitimately deserved it), and promised her he'd find a capable cook as soon as possible to help her and occasionally fill in for her. "That way you can take yourself on a cruise with no worries," he told her, not knowing that she wouldn't even take herself willingly to the train station.

It was not Sanfilippi who convinced her to stay of course, but Sauro. He devoted an afternoon to her. He brought her medicine, bought her a fan, which he placed beside the bed. He turned it on and got into bed with her; they had been keeping different schedules for too long, living at a different pace. He fucked her with dedication. Afterwards they talked, and he showered her with promises. He told her that their success was all due to her, that she was the agent of change not only for their family, but for the village; that she had gained prestige and attracted a select breed of tourist, thanks to her legendary wild boar ragù, and that if he was "the King," she was the Queen. But she couldn't bear hearing herself given the nickname that had belonged to her cousin.

Sauro continued, saying that soon they would have enough money to hire a chef and would at last be able to live off the rent from the Tiburzi farmhouse and their other small ventures; the children were grown now and soon would be self-sufficient. "Remember, Miriam, when we didn't have a penny, and I couldn't even buy a pair of new socks, and I had to go out to do piecework? That won't happen anymore. You'll be able to buy all the clothes you want, and before long we'll also get a new car."

She always liked believing whatever he told her, she had never questioned any of his words. She gave in at once, and the next day she put her chef's hat and white apron back on. Miriam knew in her heart that her ragù was a marginal factor in the restaurant's success, but it didn't matter to her. What mattered to her was Sauro. It mattered to her not to lose him.

The attraction of the Saddlery was the combination of cowboy and deputy, Sauro Biagini and Fillippo Sanfilippi, stars of the Maremma nights. With Sauro at his side, Sanfilippi felt like Robinson Crusoe and Friday, but with a much larger audience, and in civilization, with money, and power. He counted on the contrast between them to magnify his own refinement, eloquence, skills. It was a studied and willing snobbery. Sauro kept up his role, knowing in turn how to work the imbalanced friendship to his own advantage. Sanfilippi saw him as Friday, but in reality, he was Lady Chatterley's lover. Women spread the cowboy's fame. It signaled a kind of proof of membership; if you hadn't gone to bed with him at least once, even if you didn't talk about it, even if you didn't brag about it, it was tacitly understood that you couldn't be a woman who mattered in the Saddlery circle.

One night, a group of people from Milan at a table with Giulia were talking about him, about what an incredible, generous, practical man he was, how rich he was in the country wisdom that makes pragmatism an intellectual gift. Giulia nodded, she wanted to add, "And he knows how to fuck!" But she held back, not out of modesty but out of fear that the other diners might respond with a sneer, "We know, we know."

After that season went so fantastically well, Sauro decided it wasn't enough anymore.

"We should do something else, something bigger," he kept saying.

He had a vision of the future, and of all the accumulated potential the season held; but the Saddlery remained a shack without enough seats at the table, with smoke in the winter, a rustic menu.

"Higher quality than this?" Sanfilippo said. "I brought you the crème de la crème of the Italian Left. Politicians, journalists, professors, artists, prominent businessmen. The best of the intelligentsia that's out there, along with a quantity of exquisite ass that has never before been seen in these parts."

Sauro remembered the first time he had heard the word "intelligentsia." He had asked himself, wasn't the word "intelligence?" Why did they always have to mangle everything, make it harder? Over time he had learned all the key expressions and enhanced his vocabulary, by trying to emulate the better clients. But they tended to prefer his free-form way of talking, which amused them, like when he called the horse that a descendant of a pope had baptized, in French, "Éperon" (spur), with the handier and less pretentious name, "Pepperoni."

He smiled at Filippo.

"I don't mean an increase in quality, but in quantity. We

have to expand, to grow. The potential is there. I also need to set aside some money; it's not like I've got a parliamentary salary and a millionaire wife. To keep it going, we've got to offer something new, shinier, and bigger. To stay on the crest of the wave, we've got to have the wave. We need to open something by the sea, a beautiful restaurant, with cotton tablecloths, not butcher's paper under the plates, and to hire a chef who knows how to cook fish. The first time, we'll take everyone on horseback rides. We'll also create a kind of stable on the beach near the changing rooms, with refreshments for the horses. Think of all the stuff: besides the parking for the cars, we'll offer a corner in the shade, fodder and water for the horses while they're all eating *spaghetti alle vongole* and drinking chilled white wine. Who's ever heard of anything like that? They don't even have it at Forte dei Marmi, or Monte Carlo, where those bastards have terrible parking problems, traffic and giant buildings, apartments, see what I'm saying? While we've got farmhouses, hills, the sea—and we ride to the restaurant on horseback, where we cook with oil from our own olive trees. We've got the best of everything there is in the world."

When confronted with an ambitious project, Sanfilippi never backed off, provided it wasn't political. They decided to invest all the money they'd earned from the Saddlery, along with another little portion from Sanfilippi, who had become a fifty-percent partner in the business with Miriam, then a mortgage, which they calculated would be paid back within three years, for the purchase of the beach hut where they usually went riding in the low season. The old owner knew he could demand an exorbitant sum and held out until they gave him what he wanted: many, many millions of lira.

In the summer of 1989, they inaugurated the Seaside Cowboy. The logo, designed by Flaminia Ranieri della Corte, who once again was Lisa Sanfilippi's best friend, after the incident that had made her so furious, was a seahorse being ridden by a cowboy in a ten-gallon hat and boots, with half a cigar in his mouth. An architect friend of the Sanfilippis who specialized in seaside villas had transformed the beach hut into an elegant structure of stone and wood, painted white and sky blue, with a pergola, and a walkway that went to the water's edge. "It was inspired by the structures on Martha's Vineyard, where rich, intellectual New Yorkers go, which is what you should aim to become, but with better, more authentic food, and more beautiful surroundings," the architect had said as she unrolled the blueprints for them. "We've already become what we want to be," Sanfilippi responded, even though he was pleased that she had interpreted their idea so well.

The opening was a memorable occasion, so much so that photos from the evening not only ended up in all the newspapers but were framed and hung on the inside of the place, as a memento of the first stone laid on the monument of their own personal mythology. And so it was that, for many years to come, the images remained frozen in time: of Sauro and Filippo, glasses raised, sweatily hugging each other, their shirts unbuttoned, cigars in hand, their faces contorted with laughter and alcohol; of the countess emerging from the nighttime sea in a lowcut white dress that clung to her and was almost seethrough—a photo that she herself had approved and had enlarged; of the night-time rowboat race whose teams included a government minister and a member of Parliament, the director of the national post office, a bank president, and Sauro the King at the oars, leading his crew to victory. There were many photos of exuberant, suntanned women, in colorful dresses and elaborate hairdos, photos in which the local women were entirely absent, except by accident, or, in the background, wearing white shirts and black pants of synthetic fabric, the unisex uniform of the waiters.

That night, too, Miriam was in the kitchen and Annamaria waited tables. They had needed more staff for the occasion, and Annamaria had asked her father if she could tell her cousin Giovanna about it. She would have liked to share the experience with her, and maybe later, a cigarette and tips. And then to ask her about the artist. To find out how she lived, what they were doing in the Garden. Sauro had responded, "Ask your mother," and Annamaria had understood that the issue wasn't resolved, and completely avoided bringing it up with her mother.

Nobody could object to hiring Antonella, the daughter of Porcu the shepherd, who was already twenty, and had experience in restaurants and also as a baker; and in the end she was the one who was assigned the task of making the cake. She created an enormous rectangle of sponge cake filled with crème Chantilly, which was what she did best. It was a pity that her design of the cowboy on the seahorse, piped onto the cake with melted chocolate from a pastry bag, had come out so badly, and looked like a kind of deformed, priapic satyr. In the kitchen, there was no end of joking about it; Antonella was miserable, and tried several times to redo it, scraping off the top layer of whipped cream, but everyone was in a rush, and the results looked worse every time, until finally the girl started crying. Miriam kicked her out of the bar and told her briskly: "Buck up, go on then, what does it matter? Who looks at the design, all that matters is that it tastes good," and got ready to take it outside. She carried it out with the help of Annamaria and two other waiters, and put it on the table behind where Sauro had been sitting in the meantime with the architect in his lap—who didn't bother returning to her own seat even when Miriam appeared. Sauro stood up, delicately shifting her aside, and called for applause for his wife. When the jokes began about the design, "The cowboy with the giant erection," "Ha ha, Sauro, is that you?" Miriam smiled and said, "I'll go get the knife," but nobody caught the irony, because everyone was too drunk to notice that she really had come back with a steak knife, not a cake knife, and had served cake onto the plates, stabbing at it as if she would disembowel anyone who came near her to grab their own piece.

* * *

Women with knives are afraid. They don't want to kill but rather defend themselves from someone, or even use the knife on themselves. Being armed doesn't automatically make them warriors. In her darkest moments, Niki always carried knives, box cutters, screwdrivers, hid them inside her purse, beneath her mattress. She bit her lower lip so hard, and so constantly, that a kind of second mouth opened beneath the first one, and she had to have an operation to stitch it back together. There was a powerful anger in her that could not be assuaged by electroshock, even after she left the clinic in Nice, in '53. Once she got home she felt weak, but she got better, and Harry embraced her, relieved that she'd been released so quickly, after she'd been diagnosed with schizophrenia that would require years of psychiatric confinement. Their little girl Laura helped her to assemble collages; they spent entire mornings in the park drawing on the ground with pastel crayons. It was on one of those days of her convalescence that Niki found a letter for her in the mailbox attached to the gate. She had just had breakfast. The light was very white, and the sky was oppressive. She took the mail into the house: there was a card, a bill, a newspaper, and a letter from her father that came from the Swiss region where he had retired with his wife, in a Puritan anti-communist community that went by the unsubtle name "Moral Rearmament." In the letter that André Marie Fal de Saint Phalle wrote to his daughter Niki, the

The letter from Doctor Cossa ended up in the wrong hands. Niki's mother read it. Sometimes fate is much stronger than intentions. There was no forgiveness; the time for forgiveness was past, and dormant wrath never entirely dies. It can be appeased perhaps. Vented. With other weapons besides knives. With guns. Staged in ferocious vendettas, on canvas.

Seven years later, in the full flush of her personal renaissance, when she left her first life behind to dedicate herself to art, distancing herself from her family and going alone to Paris, Niki began her experiments with sculpture. Once again, there was a liberating event that propelled her. Before she got together with Jean, she had found herself again in a toxic relationship with a lover she could not get rid of. She returned to her old habit of carrying a weapon in her purse, even if it wasn't loaded. It made her feel better. But she needed a stronger ritual. One day she asked that man for one of his shirts, and stuck it to a canvas, with a target in place of the head. She began to bombard the painting with darts, feeling lighter with every strike; it was a kind of voodoo ritual, not against a man, but against the ghost of him inside her. The execution succeeded. Jean Tinguely and Daniel Spoerri decided to exhibit the work in a show of the New Realists, a movement in which Niki began to take part, the only woman. The relief she felt each time she struck one of her works exhilarated her. She began affixing objects onto canvases, hiding sacks of dye beneath layers of white gesso, then shooting them so they would explode, making the canvases bleed with the dye. She confessed, "I feel wounded, and I want everything around me to bleed. The paintings have to bleed to atone for living beings. I don't want darts anymore, I have more rapid means. Rage! Fascination, vendetta, immense pleasure, black, white, red, magical blue! I shot my father, my brother, men, my mother, the Church, school, conventions, myself." Art for her was a way of settling scores with the monsters she had inside her, as if at a certain point she had begun to exhort herself: "Shoot, Niki, shoot. Create, destroy, be reborn. In this way you will find your place. The newspapers will do nothing but talk about you. Your apprenticeship is over. You have turned your bad luck into something good; in your abyss, you have found a source of inexhaustible energy. With your paint, you have annihilated fear."

8. Justice
Decision. Judgment. False Perfection.

Annamaria helped her parents full time every summer. Once school was over, it was taken for granted in the family that the girl would continue her duties as assistant horse trainer, assistant stable hand, kitchen helper, and assistant waitress. And she did it, with no thought of an eventual alternative, she was used to it, used to not having real vacations. It was after the millionth fight between Saverio and their father that she suddenly recognized the injustice. Paradoxically, it was her own brother, the lucky one, who opened her eyes.

Saverio had lashed out at their father when he found out about the opening of the Seaside Cowboy. "Dad, I truly don't know how you can fail to see that you're being shafted. Sanfilippi has saddled you with debts; your clients, who you even have the gall to call friends, just want to act like bosses, to be served, all those smiles and all that laughter, but who is it that cleans up the horse shit, who gets stuck in the kitchen? You, your wife, your daughter. It's bullshit. I pity you all for how important it makes you feel to carry off the dirty dishes of those fucking VIPs, and to have your picture taken with them. You're idiots; and you, Babbo, are the worst of all, because you're dragging Mamma and Annamaria into it, too."

Sauro no longer bothered to respond to him. Miriam weakly chided him, "Saverio, don't be disrespectful to your father."

"Look, he's the one that's disrespecting you, and you ignore it, you big dummy." A few years earlier, Sauro would have slapped him. Now, not only was Saverio too old for that, but Sauro had given up; it seemed futile to him to argue with this son who had never supported him, who had never admitted he was right, who had never valued him, he felt. And Saverio ought to have been able to see how well his businesses were doing. Sometimes Sauro thought his son put him down sheerly out of jealousy.

"Get out of here, Savè, before I kill you. Get out of the house, you're old enough by now. If there's anyone here who deserves to be criticized it's you, who jerks around, being cooked for, cleaned for, and never lifts a finger. We may be idiots, but you're a parasite on us idiots, and that doesn't make you better than us."

"Look, do you think I don't know it's time for me to clear out of here? I'm just sorry for Mamma, because now there'll be nobody left here to defend her, to truly love her."

Sauro had said calmly, "You don't know shit about what it means to love someone, Saverio." Upon those words, Saverio had gotten up and walked out, leaving Miriam in tears and Annamaria shifting the debate to herself.

"There's something I'd like to bring up. It's one thing if you don't get along with him. But why do I always have to help out with every task, while he's exempted? To what does he owe this privilege? Is it just because he was against opening the restaurant? Because he doesn't like your customers? Or because you guys fight? I think it's just leftover male chauvinism, like in Grandfather's times: Saverio is a boy, free to make his own decisions, I'm a girl, who has to obey. And I'm not all right with that."

Grandfather Settimio emerged from his alcoholic silence and backed up his granddaughter without fully grasping the nature of her declaration. "Bravo, Annamarì, your brother is a no-good slacker. Back in my day, you would have been happy to be a woman, that is, to stay at home—our father took us boys out into the fields every morning before dawn. I give it two days before you see Saverio at the door, ready to take the horses out on rides, and carry plates to the table."

The issue was resolved with an economic agreement: Annamaria would receive her first, small, salary, which didn't completely rectify the situation, but at least took a little of the sting out of her brother's preferential treatment.

Besides, Annamaria liked working there in the summertime. Her friends went on study trips, or on vacations with their parents, visiting grandparents in some little village in the mountains or somewhere by the sea. They had relatives too, in Monte Amiata. But she preferred to stay put—there was her mother who needed help, and above all, there was Lisa.

Lisa, a mystery that always seemed on the brink of unveiling itself. They'd been exchanging long letters for ages, and they also saw each other at least once a month, at the weekend. They wrote about school, Lisa wrote about her dancing, Annamaria about the horses, Lisa wrote about her boyfriend (a little), and Annamaria about a guy she liked, from a nearby village, who had long, blond hair, so everyone called him Sandy Marton, like the pop star, but he was too old and didn't know she existed.

Lisa wrote beautifully, with an abundance of detail, and so many insights that seemed brilliant to Annamaria. She relished the task of responding to the letters, she tried to bring out her best thoughts, she wanted to make Lisa laugh. Once she also sent her a little package with the lambswool she'd asked for the first time they met, to stuff into her pointe shoes. Annamaria couldn't hide the importance she gave to any request from her friend, how everything she said was imprinted on her memory. Lisa was undeniably gratified by this. After the launch of the Seaside Cowboy, she'd gone to Cuba with her mother for two weeks. Through his political contacts, her father had managed to get her admitted to a summer session of the Ballet Nacional de Cuba in Havana. She had written two long letters to Annamaria from there, which she had delivered by hand because she didn't trust the Cuban postal system, and had written things that maybe wouldn't have pleased the censors. "Censors?" Annamaria had asked. "Oh please, think what it would mean to censor every letter! Like, right now, people are being paid to waste their time reading a young girl's letters? I think you've seen too many spy movies."

"You're naïve, Annamaria. Living in this little corner of the country has given you an amazingly narrow outlook. The outside world is much more complicated than a stable."

That's how Lisa was. When she talked with her, she could be caustic, when she wrote to her she was thoughtful and generous. When they were together, sometimes she was warm, more often she was indifferent. Annamaria never felt confident when she was with her, and she liked that. She kept her letters in the hollow of the mended statue of Saint Anthony, which her grandfather had given her as a christening gift.

Dear Annamaria,

I got here five days ago and went to the ballet school for the second time. I've never had such exhausting lessons. It probably was the jet lag, which I still haven't recovered from, or the unbearable heat and humidity, and the fact that they don't have air conditioning, only fans, which feel like dragon's breath, I couldn't do the right steps, couldn't get in sync with the choreography, the simplest moves, too, I even messed up the bar exercises, and felt like crap. The others are all incredible, maybe they're used to the heat, but I think there's something more. Maybe dance is truly a way of life for these girls. But not the way it is for me, I mean, it's the thing I like doing best in the world (all the same, there are many, or at least several, alternatives I can consider, I've got the ability to choose), for them I think it's different, they dance as if it were a question of life or death. And maybe it is. If they become outstanding ballerinas, they will have the opportunity to travel, to leave this island, they can go to Paris or New York, something I've already done without the least worry. My father keeps on holding up Cuba as a perfect model of a society where the communist revolution has succeeded and is strenuously resisting American imperialism. But I'd like to see him living with as little to eat as they do, and such bad food (since my arrival I've had only chicken, fish and tomatoes at lunch and dinner, and bland bananas and coffee at breakfast, you don't know what I'd give for a spoonful of Nutella), and not owning a house, not having money, and most of all, not having the freedom to leave, to choose a different life for yourself. When I come home I'll tell him how they live in this land of the perfect revolution, where, yes, everyone can study and gets medical care for free, but gets arrested if they speak badly of Fidel Castro, the supermarkets are empty and above all, you can't leave, and if you do, you can't come back. So many women, even girls our age, readily sell their bodies to decrepit old Italian men who come here on vacation to smoke cigars and drink rum all day, and to tap tight asses on the beaches of Varadero for a couple bucks. I'm telling you, Annamaria: at the moment, I fail to see the beauty in this communist paradise. And he sent me and my mother here as if it were some fantastic reward, something he'd managed to obtain for me at enormous sacrifice. His grand prize, a unique experience at the communists' ballet school. If he'd sent me to La Scala, it would have cost him less, and it definitely would have been more fruitful for me. Meanwhile, he's back home, nice and cool in a linen shirt, eating lobster, drinking wine at your place and taking a trip to Porto Ercole (speaking of which, do you know that our boat is called "Granma," like the one Che Guevara and Fidel Castro came over on from Mexico to begin the revolution in Cuba? I found that out here—what a modest guy my dad is, no?) My mother is acting all positive, but you can tell that inside she's freaking out. She doesn't even have the might look like an activity for fragile, pampered girls who like wearing pink tulle, but in reality it's a ferocious discipline that demands muscles of steel, and nerves even stronger. To look like a butterfly on the stage, you have to execute a series of terribly difficult exercises, smiling the whole time; then there's the ordeal of the workouts, the physical pain of the constriction of the toes in the pointe shoes. There's a lot of silent suffering in classical dance that you can't even imagine. Then there's the competitiveness, the disapproval of the teacher if you don't do well, the constant judgments on your body, because there's always someone who has thinner thighs, more flexible arms, a longer neck, a more beautiful face. There are ballerinas who are gifted with an undeniable grace who dance in a way that shows they've got something inside them that's perfectly wedded to the music, but maybe their boobs are too big, or their ass is too low, and you know that they won't get anywhere and that it's extremely unfair. Classical dance is the antithesis of communism, we are not at all equal in front of the mirror or onstage, and it's funny that there would be such a prestigious school here. It's a cruel discipline, and every day I see, positioned in front of the mirror or lined up in the corner, a lovely group of graceful masochists who pirouette, one after the other, and sometimes it makes me weary, really so weary, to recognize myself as one of them. I'll pay a price for this weariness, I know. There's no such thing as a star who is lazy, or pleasure-seeking, and I get tired, and I want to have fun, and I miss Dario and pizza, and my brother Luca pisses me off every time he says to me, "A dancer like Carla Fracci is all right, but what you want to be is Maradona." He can go to hell. Anyway, with Alicia Alonso I saw myself in the mirror and saw myself through her eyes, even if the others didn't see me, and when she nodded after I did my diagonale, I was on cloud nine, I was terrific! Think what I've come to. Taking the approval of a blind woman as the maximum satisfaction possible.

Kisses and hugs, say hi to my crazy father, tell him he's never allowed to plan a vacation for me again.

Lisa

Annamaria had reread these letters dozens of times. And she'd remained enchanted. She knew Lisa had gotten an A in Italian class, but these didn't feel like things a young girl would write. In her everyday life, when she spoke, when she joked, she didn't seem capable of such profound, wise thoughts. Most of all, Annamaria was stunned to be the recipient of them. Lisa's mystery was deep, and she was aware that she was unable to give back as much as she received, that she couldn't reciprocate the beauty and the intelligence that came from her friend. Maybe Lisa had chosen her because she was a foil who made everyone feel superior.

That summer she had missed Lisa and yearned for other company, besides the usual village crowd. She was fed up to find herself back in the role of the clown that nobody took notice of unless they wanted a laugh. There came one moment in particular when she realized she no longer wanted to play that part.

The kids from the village of Scalo, which the Roman regulars nicknamed Squalor because of its hideous architecture, organized a bonfire every year on the beach between the lake and the sea that nearly all the kids in the area went to. There was an old tower that was inaccessible because it was part of a nature reserve, but they could get there from the shore, with a tractor that transported everything that was necessary: the grill, the wood, the meat, the guitars, the stereo, the tents, and most important, copious amounts of wine. It was the first time that her brother Saverio invited her, but she'd always heard delirious stories about this party which everyone called "Woodstock on the beach," and compared to a rave, but with white wine from Pitigliano instead of acid. The moment came

when the meal had ended, the fire from the bonfire had
nearly burnt out, the sleeping bags already hidden behind the
bushes and stuffed with couples, only a few holdouts lingered
around the embers, the guy with the guitar, the guy with the
acne, the girl who was too Catholic to get drunk or to randomly kiss anyone, and Annamaria, the joker, who at a certain point had sighed: "Here we are, the ones with the complexes, the ones they invited just for the soundtrack, the third
wheels." After the others had laughed, Annamaria had lain
down on the sand to watch the falling stars, had wished to be
prettier, to become better friends with Lisa, to close her eyes
and be kissed, and at that moment in the darkness, she would
have been fine with it being the guy with the acne, and she
turned her head sensually to expose her neck, but that was
when she realized she had tipped her head into the tray of
leftover sausages, and a layer of smelly, clotted animal fat had
gotten all over her hair. Once again everyone was laughing at
her. Then she rinsed her hair with beer, because the seawater
was too cold, "It's freezing!" she told anyone who advised
her to go for a swim. She laughed at herself at first, but at the
same time she felt awful, hopeless, because the others only
paid attention to her when she let them make her the butt of
their jokes. She sensed that this was now her destiny, which
she kept on reinforcing with self-deprecating jokes like,
"Before going to sleep I always apply two drops of Porchetta
No. 5," and "I wanted to sleep with someone in a sleeping
bag, and now I've got a whole wild boar to myself," and
"You can't believe how well this sausage balm untangles
knots, does anyone have any leftover potatoes I can use for
curlers?" and she laughed even as tears of mirth mingled
with self-pity rose in her eyes. "You're cracking us up,"
Annamarì," and she nodded. "Yeah, if only I'd done it on
purpose!"

It was after that night of the sausages, which she spent

without sleeping, listening to the sound of the waves and of the others snoring, throwing up, or making love, slapping mosquitoes at dawn as she waited to join the first group that went home, who would start up again with the barrage of jokes about the smell and the consistency of her hair, that she decided to stay away from the village kids for a while. It wasn't a decision born of long reflection. It happened that Giovanna was in the first group that went back, and sat next to her in the car. During the trip, sitting in the lace-covered seat, keeping her head strictly away from the headrest, Annamaria asked that cousin who resembled her mother as a young woman: "How long have you been working at the Garden of Monsters? And what's the artist like? I met her once, and I can't stop thinking about it. She's . . . crazy, she's . . . strange, she's fantastic . . . I'd like to know more about her, I'd like to see her again there sometime. Maybe with you . . ."

"Come whenever you want," Giovanna said, "I'd like that. There's a lot I can tell you about the Garden, and so many things I can show you. I can't introduce you to her now because she isn't here. She stays away the whole summer, from the time the olive trees bloom. Because of her troubles with her lungs . . . she has asthma, and when the olive trees are in flower it makes it much worse, but now that the pits have already formed in the olives, she'll soon be back. I'd be happy for you to know her, Niki's an exceptional person. What we're doing is marvelous, and maybe she'll read your tarot for you. I know there's a lot of talk about the Garden in the village, they say that she's crazy and that we're all on drugs, and that everyone who works with her are either stoners or fags or lunatics, but the truth is that we're all working so hard there to make something beautiful. She's such a superior human being that when she hears about what the country people say, she just says: Let them talk, they're people who've traveled too little. She's had a hard time the last few years, she's also got arthritis, the doctors keep telling her she should stop working, stop living on a building site. The last two years have been complicated, her anxiety attacks have returned. Particularly when she had to build the tarot figures for Death and the Devil. It's not like being an architect, you know. A project like this one dredges up everything that's inside her, her visions, her suffering. After eight years of solitude, devotion, and frenzy, she had to face her demons. Sometimes at night, when she was sleeping under a mosquito net, the insects that drew near seemed to her like demons. She went to see psychiatrists to confront these visions—one of them even hypnotized her. Fortunately, the work went better after that. Mitterrand came to see her last fall, he visited the Garden."

"Mitterrand, the president of France?"

"Yes, that's the one. They're friends. They might have been more than friends, too, who knows. She had dressed for the occasion, and I pointed out to her that she was wearing one red sock and one pink one. She said to me: "Do you really think Mitterrand cares about my socks!" But in the end, he did notice them, and made fun of her. When her husband Jean comes, however, she's impeccable. She puts on makeup, she dresses elegantly, she gets Alessandro, the hairdresser from Scalo, to come do her hair. That's how life is with her. It's unpredictable; highs and lows, some moments are exhilarating, others are incredibly difficult, but always full, full; there's not one instant wasted, not one instant that isn't devoted to art, in the fullest sense of the word."

That same afternoon, after three shampoos and an afternoon nap, Annamaria took the moped and went to see Giovanna, for just enough time to share a furtive cigarette in the shadow of a big dragon, which was held on an invisible leash by a girl made of reinforced concrete.

9. THE HERMIT
Solitude. Wisdom. Illumination

The dust that rose from the harvesters stung the eyes and made the heat feel even more unbearable. Saverio had closed the windows of the supermini and put the air conditioner on high. He'd also turned up the volume on the radio to the max because "I'm Not Scared" by Eighth Wonder was playing. The voice of Patsy Kensit singing "take these dogs away from me" had given him a slight erection, not because it meant anything, as far as he knew, but because he thought of her, languid and blonde, dressed in white, singing on the video he'd seen on DeeJay Television. He was driving above the speed limit, as usual. But these were his roads, and at this hour in the summer they were deserted. He liked to take the curves at maximum speed, counter-steering. This was dangerous, he knew, and he did it on purpose.

The curves on the way to Pescia were the most extreme, the narrowest, flanked on both sides by stone walls covered in scrub. You couldn't see a thing, you risked collision with every turn of the steering wheel. Saverio loved this type of adrenaline, which he felt explode in his chest and head as the car came off the bump of a curve with a smooth lunge and hurled itself toward a man with his back turned who was walking with his dog. He slammed on the brakes, closed his mouth and his eyes, pulled the hand brake with a squeal that was also a scream, which spread across the countryside, announcing a fatal accident. There was a thud, the clang of sheet metal, Saverio's head hit the window hard, then, abruptly, there was silence.

He understood that the car had been stopped by hitting something, and had shut itself down, along with the radio. "Fuck, fuck, no!" Saverio said, as he reopened his eyes. The whole thing hadn't lasted more than five seconds, but it didn't take more than another ten to realize that something had happened: had he killed a dog, or a man, or both? Or had he destroyed the car against a wall? Or had he crashed into a tree, was he dead himself?

As he waited for the dust to clear that had mingled with the dust thrown up by the harvesters, so that he could see which of the possible disasters had occurred, he registered that he was, at least, alive. And then, that the dog, a black and white husky, seemed to be all right, though he was panting visibly, probably just from the heat. Saverio cursed and thanked God in the same thought, then got out to assess the damage. His heart pounded frantically, his hands were shaking. But his first glance went to the car. A total disaster to the bodywork around the right headlight, crumpled by impact with an oak tree.

"You shouldn't drive so fast on these roads," the man told him calmly, standing still. He was young and very tall, with a broad forehead, his curly hair combed back behind in regular waves, a hooked nose, the family nose, a white linen shirt rolled up to the elbows, one hand on the dog's collar. He looked at Saverio a little vacantly. He'd spoken as if he hadn't just cheated death, almost without opening his mouth, faintly whistling his esses and rolling his "r"s.

Saverio began to shake more intensely. His first impulse had been to leap at the guy's throat and scream at him that he was the one, fucking Maremma who shouldn't have been walking in the middle of the road at that time of day in the summer, what in hell was he thinking; his second impulse had been to fall to his knees and start crying, praying in gratitude that the accident they'd escaped had not had more disastrous, unthinkable, clamorous consequences, unlike the bodies flattened by tractors that turned up in the headlines of the local papers every other day.

He limited himself to saying, "Excuse me, I wasn't expecting . . ."

The man lowered his eyelids slightly and said, "Do we know each other?"

Saverio stammered, "No, that is, yes, I know you, maybe, I might be mistaken. My name is Saverio, we might have seen each other once with my father . . . Sauro, the guy with the horses."

"Oh, the King."

Saverio nodded with a gesture of annoyance.

"Listen, it's really hot out, the car's only damaged in the front, what would you say to going to get a cold drink at the bar, and toasting the fact that we're not dead?"

"I don't mean to be rude, but I would prefer not to. I just wanted to go on a walk with my dog."

He gave the dog a pat.

"What's his name?" asked Saverio.

"I don't think this is a moment that calls for that," the tall guy responded.

"As you like. It's just that it's hard to believe you'd be walking along these roads like that. I don't mean to pry, but shouldn't you have an escort?"

"It's a little presumptuous to tell me what I should do, don't you think? Anyway, I don't want one."

"You're wrong to feel so safe, fucking Maremma, I nearly killed you. If that had happened, I would've had to feed you to the pigs to hide the evidence, then throw myself into the sea with a stone around my neck."

They laughed. The tall man said, still so quietly that he was barely audible, "There's nothing we can do about God's will; clearly it was not our time."

"Can I at least give you a ride?"

"I would rather walk, and it's less than a mile from here."

Saverio hated walking. And in this heat. His blue t-shirt, which had a surfing gorilla on it, was already soaked in sweat. He was wearing slip-ons. He had a bandanna in the pocket of his shorts. He tied it around his head to shield himself from the sun and put on his RayBan Aviators.

"I'd better accompany you."

"Suit yourself."

The tall, thin man, dressed in linen, wearing a long shirt and pants; the tan, muscular youth, dressed for the beach; and the sled dog with one black eye and one blue one walked together in the dust of harvest time.

"I think I've met your sister—she sneaked into the Tarot Garden once. You play fast and loose with the law, you children of the King," the tall man said.

"Oh, yes, the children of the King. What a cretin my sister is, a total princess."

"It's not nice to insult sisters; as a rule, they're the only ones who love us."

"Maybe. I love her, for sure. But it's only my mother who loves me. Mothers love you even when you suck."

"And your father?"

"My father hates me. Fathers only love females."

"Meaning?"

"Well, something's always expected of us guys; results, which they acknowledge only if we support them and imitate them. And if we don't agree with them, if we don't want to become exactly like them, if we think of things differently than they do, they can't accept it, they find a way to make us pay, to punish us, to make us feel inadequate. They're not like that with women."

The tall man looked at him and nodded. Saverio noticed that under his shirt he wore a long necklace of wooden beads. It was a hippie touch that he hadn't expected. He continued.

"Well, and then, my dad knows how to make money, he's got good business sense, and I don't. But I don't blame myself for that. Excuse me for venting. I suppose that, where you come from, that's not a problem," he added maliciously.

The tall man grew serious. "Of course it is, it's a problem everywhere. You can't imagine how important it is not only to have business sense, but to have the credentials to be deemed someone who has business sense. Even if you have an inheritance, you've got to have substance; and not as many people have that as you'd think."

"I don't want to overstep, but it seems to me that the mess that you and your friends have made isn't helping, is it? You ought to have been more careful."

"Yes, you are overstepping, you know nothing about me, and I already told you: if I were you, I'd avoid telling people you don't know what they should and shouldn't do. And I would appreciate it if you would show me the kindness of addressing me formally. We are strangers."

Saverio, who was already red and dripping with sweat, turned even redder. He was impulsive, incapable of his father's tact. He didn't understand where the line was between frankness and rudeness, which in certain environments was everything, was the difference that allowed you to be either accepted or rejected. That's why he couldn't stand his father's and Sanfilippi's versatility, because he knew he didn't have what it took to pull it off. He knew they thought he was a rube, and he couldn't stand the inferior position he occupied.

"I'm sorry, I didn't mean to overstep."

"A lot of newspapers just print lies, you ought to know that."

In the meantime, they had arrived in front of a big gate, which opened onto a long allée of cypresses. "Give my greetings to your father," the tall guy said.

"And give mine to yours," said Saverio, as a kind of joke.

The other replied, "I don't even know when I'll see him."

The dog had gone on in and had started running toward the house. The tall guy took two steps, then suddenly turned around.

"Do you have a dog?"

"Yes, a mutt called Tiburzi, I have no problem telling you his name."

"Do you take him out with you?"

"Usually he takes himself out, but sometimes he comes with me."

"And when you both return home, whom does your father greet first, you or the dog?"

"Neither of us."

The tall man smiled. He had a very sad expression. "We have much more in common than you might think."

"I assure you, all the same, that there is very, very little. Surely less than I would like," Saverio said, laughing.

"Don't believe it. Have a good afternoon, thanks for the company, and above all for your quick reflexes. If you'll allow me to make a recommendation: I would advise you to drive a little more slowly on these roads," he said, closing the gate in front of him.

Saverio turned around quickly, extremely agitated. He had dodged a tragedy, he had lost an opportunity to keep his mouth shut, and he had taken a walk that he would remember for the rest of his life. Especially many years later, on the day when, on the television news, he would recognize the tall man with the sad expression, who had thrown himself off an overpass on the Torino–Savona expressway.

But now his concern was the car—to pick up the supermini as soon as possible and find the money to repair it. The heat was atrocious, the cicadas were chirring nonstop. The stubble of burnt hay and the smell of smoke all around him increased the sensation of being inside an oven. Saverio was heading back to the car at a quick pace, now drenched in sweat. He swore under his breath when his sister pulled up alongside him on her moped.

"What are you doing here, Savè?"

"What are you doing here, more like it? Shouldn't you be at work at this hour?"

"I've got the night shift today. But what in hell are you doing on foot, all sweaty? Maremma—what a bump, have you seen your forehead?

Saverio touched it. "Shut up, go away, I nearly ran over a big shot who was here. Give me a lift to the bar, I need a drink."

Annamaria managed to get the moped going, with a bit of skidding because of her brother's weight, which almost made them fall off. "Well done, two near accidents in one hour, that must be a record. I deserve two drinks."

Annamaria put the kickstand down in front of the bar, on the big curve, where the old men playing cards looked them over without saying hello.

Saverio ordered a beer and Annamaria a Coke. While she stuck in a straw, she asked her brother, "Will you tell me what happened?"

He began as if he were in a trance, with no preamble, without taking a breath, the same way he usually talked to her, taking it for granted that his sister could immediately enter his train of thought when it was already in motion.

"What an asshole, I saved his life, but did he offer to give me a single lira, much less a Fiat, in thanks, or even a glass of water, when it's so hot out? It wasn't appropriate to let me in, it wasn't appropriate to tell me the name of his dog—you know, for some people, privacy is sacred. You'd think I was going to kidnap him and then ask for ransom for his shitty dog, which was made to pull a sled on the ice, and you bring him out to walk in the dust when it's a hundred degrees out? Do you think that just because you belong to the richest and most powerful family in Italy that everyone wants to get something from you, to blackmail you, to ask you for money? Fuck, if I wanted I could even press charges: it's your fault that my car is now a heap of metal, you were standing in the middle of the road, in the middle! And I, to avoid hitting you, got into a crash, stinking Maremma! And really, who do they think they are? They're horrible people, too, just like us. There's no such thing as generosity, even men who could afford to act justly do not. Then, there's the way they treat us, as if they aren't even the same species, with that tender pity, in a way that always makes you feel like you're in the wrong.

Saverio continued, mimicking: "If I were you, I would not permit myself;" "Let us address each other formally . . ." Like spending time with them is the greatest thing you could ask from life; a concession, an honor, like the Sanfilippis do with Babbo, acting all the time like they expect to be thanked for being served by him, by Mamma, by you. What a privilege to be permitted to clean up your filth, truly. They're terrible to us, but also to each other, I think. What good is it to be taught, to be educated and to have money, if in the end you're worse than the rednecks? If you're incapable of loving anyone, if you cheat on your wife, screw over your business partner, your brother, exploit the workers, greet your dog before your son. They're just like us."

"What do you mean, Saverio? I don't even know who you're talking about."

He continued without paying her any heed. "What do you have to do to become a better person? I certainly don't know who to look to as a role model, and now it's probably too late. I'm a piece of shit. Not that it matters if I say so myself, but there it is. Even poor Tamara, I'll have to marry her sooner or later. And if Babbo and Mamma love you more, maybe one reason is that you're nicer, you're more helpful. But I'm a man, it's not my fault, nobody teaches us men what to do to be liked. And then, we can't ever be accommodating. If we're accommodating, in the end, nobody will let us fuck them."

"Well, of course, that's always the sole objective."

"Anyway, that guy's also pathetic, I felt a little sorry for him. Then again, what's the point of that pity, he's loaded with dough, with villas, cars, vacations, and freedom, he can do whatever the fuck he wants in life, I mean, who could be luckier than him. But still, I don't know. He had this sadness in his eyes. And that thing he said, about how his father didn't love him, you know. Don't worry about it, it's enough that he gives you money. You're guaranteed to find some nice girl who loves you to death, you're so good-looking."

"Oh my god, you ran over Edoardo Agnelli?"

"No, no, well . . . sort of. I'm not totally sure, I think it was him. But who knows. He walked onto their estate. Anyway, it's a good thing I didn't kill him, with all his curls. It could have been worse, a lot, lot worse. We're lucky, the two of us. Tonight I'll light a candle to Our Lady of Providence, then I'll go to the hunters' bar and get drunk. Given my bad luck, driving by at the wrong time, I don't half deserve it, I'm goddamned lucky."

"Savè, you're losing your mind. You're talking about people you don't know anything about. You're doing crazy things, driving like a lunatic, and you're too quick to put the blame on everyone else. And if you don't stop going so fast, one of these days you really are going to get into trouble. I'm leaving now. And besides, I wish there were more high-class people like them around here."

"Before you go, kid, tell me what you were doing here at this time of day?"

"I went to see Giovanna. She shows me the Garden and tells me about what they're doing, she's nice to me."

Saverio kept sweating and wiping his face and neck with the bandanna. Up until that moment he'd had a wild look.

Annamaria knew this was how he normally looked, that her brother often could be mistaken for a coke fiend, when really, he'd always just been a moody guy, tense, hyper, and irritable. Suddenly his expression changed—it seemed to her that he finally was registering her presence.

"Hang on a second. Does Mamma know that you go there?"

"No."

"Why don't you tell her?"

"Because she wouldn't take it well. But I'm not doing any harm."

"If you're not doing any harm, why wouldn't she take it well?"

"Savè, my god, don't play dumb, everything that has to do with Aunt Adriana and Giovanna and all of that bothers Mamma, but that's ancient history, and it has nothing to do with us. Giovanna is incredibly nice to me, and I like what they're doing there at the Garden. Every time I go there, I feel like I'm not in the real world anymore, like I'm Alice in Wonderland."

"Watch out, kid, you don't know what they're smoking in there. Who knows what's going on. I can see the effects. You shouldn't go there anymore. I'm older than you, and I know Giovanna and her friends. They're weirdos, they're communists, drifters, and some of them are fags as well. And Giovanna doesn't seem all there to me, either. She goes out with that guy Rossano, who's insane."

Annamaria wanted to turn the table over on him. Her brother was so dense, so narrow-minded. Full of snap judgments, closed in by the walls of the village.

"Savè, let me put you straight. It just so happens that smoking is forbidden in the the Garden because the artist has respiratory problems. And besides, I'll go where I want."

"Even if I tell Mamma?"

"Even if I tell Tamara?"

"And what would you have to say to Tamara?"

"Everything I know about you."

"And what do you know?"

"A lot of things that Tamara would not want to hear."

"Come on, be nice and keep your mouth shut."

"Well, you too."

Saverio shrugged his beefy shoulders. His T-shirt did not have one dry inch on it. The cicadas continued droning in the motionless air.

The old people at the other table swore half-heartedly behind their menus without much energy.

"It's good for brothers and sisters to get along. To look after each other, right? Drive slow and don't act like an idiot. You pay for my Coke."

"If you like. You're the one with the job."

"What are you, a man, or a fag?"

She put on her helmet and gave him the finger. He smiled at her with the despairing air of someone who has no comeback.

As she drove to the Seaside Cowboy, Annamaria watched the road. She went more slowly than usual, feeling strange and uneasy at higher speeds. In the space of a few hours, everything that had happened to her had to do with driving too fast, and the coincidence had spooked her, it felt like a bad omen. A little before she had bumped into Saverio, Giovanna had told her an anecdote about Niki. She told her that she'd never seen her cry, which seemed very strange to her, for a person with Niki's sorrows and sensitivity. Once, she'd had the courage to ask her why that was, given that there often were weeping women in her illustrations, their tears drawn one by one, like pearls, dropping from their eyes onto their faces, turning into necklaces. Niki told her that she'd learned how not to cry when she was little, that even when faced with the harshest and most painful punishments (her mother hit her with the back of a hairbrush; her father had whipped her one time, after catching her smoking in secret) she'd kept everything inside, she didn't ever want to show that she was upset. Still, she regretted this very much, because she was holding back tears that were liberating, which had the power to cleanse the soul. She was convinced that the tears she suppressed had hardened into rocks inside her and were the source of her asthma. She could only cry when she watched romantic movies, and whenever she watched a movie, she nearly always hoped things would turn out badly so she could cry freely. She told Giovanna that she knew women's tears were a great weapon, especially against men, but that she was so incapable of using them that once, hoping to convince Tinguely to drive more slowly because she was terrified by his speeding, she'd brought an onion into the car to try to persuade him with tears, but he'd figured out the trick at once and made fun of her, without slowing down.

Giovanna added, "But now she drives like a maniac herself. When we drive to town together to go shopping, I have to hold onto the dashboard and beg her to slow down. I invent spots on the Aurelia where the police are hiding to make her afraid of getting speeding tickets, but it has no effect, she seems to be unable to drive unless she's going fast, as if she were in an airplane that would fall to earth if it slowed down. It must be an artist's thing. Either top speed or stock still; a life of adrenaline, or death."

Giovanna was talking, smiling, and putting things in order without ever stopping, as if she too had this mania in her blood. Annamaria watched her go about her activities in the Garden, tidying the interior of the Sphinx as if it was an ordinary house, washing glasses, putting them away in the kitchen that had no corners; sweeping leaves off the mirrored walk. To Annamaria, it all felt practically surreal, the reflection of the sun on the sculptures made the heat feel even more torrid; an odor emanated from the land here that was different from the air she breathed outside. As she headed to the gate to pick up her moped, strange thoughts came to her, setting her head spinning.

She'd said to Giovanna, "You seem to be in the crater of an active volcano, one that's filled with flowers."

"Is being inside this place turning you into an artist? Today a poet, tomorrow who knows. By all means, go crazy like all of us. Are you sure you want to come back?"

Annamaria had laughed and said it was just the heat that was making her longwinded. With Saverio, she didn't say a word about speed, or tell the anecdotes about Niki and Jean, who drove too fast, just like him. But as she drove her moped to the restaurant, she gripped the handlebars firmly and stepped lightly on the gas pedal, paying attention to every crossing; she didn't even pass the tractor that was ahead of her near the end of the Aurelia. She scanned every foot of the road, and knew that the fear that gripped her wasn't about getting into an accident, it was something more personal. Perhaps it was the need to keep her balance, not so much to prevent a fall as to remain steady; I am Annamaria, I am cautious and normal; only crazy people go too fast, and I don't want to be a crazy person.

She arrived late at the restaurant and told her mother that she'd fallen asleep after lunch, and that her grandfather hadn't woken her up.

The damage to the car was more serious than Saverio had anticipated. The entire body had to be redone on one side, but the hood was also compromised, and above all, the driveshaft had to be replaced. It wouldn't cost much less than buying another used car, but Saverio clung to his supermini as if it were his favorite horse. It was his symbol. Also, he liked being able to talk about the incredible accident he'd had.

He'd told Tamara, "Today on the way to Pescia I almost ran over an Agnelli."

She'd replied, "The important thing is that nothing happened to you; lambs like the Agnellis we roast on the spit."

He'd laughed and told her everything: "They may be lambs, but it would have been me on the skewer."

He didn't want to ask his dad for money, which meant he had to borrow some from Tamara, and then he asked some people at his gym in Albinia if he could become an instructor. He had no education in physical training, but he'd been one of the gym's most faithful members for years, and by now he was familiar with all the machines, he had all the workout programs down, and he knew what kind of repetitions, and how many of them, were recommended for building up different muscles. Over the last year, he'd practically become addicted to working out. He went to the gym five times a week, and his body now looked like a true bodybuilder's. The owner had entered him in a regional competition. He'd trained furiously and gone on a high-protein diet, with a little hormone therapy added in. Illegal substances circulated at the gym, passed off as food supplements. Andrea, the owner of MaremmaGym, who was also a bodybuilding pro, had persuaded him. He knew the right time to give them injections to ensure they wouldn't test positive for hormones in the drug checks. They'd gone in the car to Ponsacco, in the province of Pisa, arriving so early that they'd had to wait an hour for the gym to open. They'd attended all the workout sessions in the competition, watched the other participants' trials, checked out the size, muscular definition and tension of every bicep, quadricep, abdominal, and deltoid. There were enormous men, and there were women whose biceps were bigger than his. Saverio was almost on the verge of dropping out, but a girl from their gym, Sabrina, was participating just for fun; and also, Andrea told him that that once he'd slathered on dark walnut balm he would look like the others: massive and chiseled, with bulging muscles, perfect. "Savè, don't worry about it, you might even win."

The thing he liked best about the contest was when he and Sabrina were smearing walnut balm on each other. They laughed, their hands brown and oily, spreading the color uniformly across each other's backs, legs, and butts. When Saverio had reached Sabrina's glutes, he had lingered for a long time. Then he said into her ear, "You've got the most beautiful ass in the world, and I've got so much testosterone circulating in my system that I'm not going to make it to the competition, I might explode first." She'd started laughing and said, "Me too . . ." then had invited him to follow her into the bathroom. They'd fucked hastily, full of tension and excitement, and they'd both come very quickly, even if he suspected that she had pretended, but that didn't matter much to him. Their outfits had been stained by the dye, so they had to change and apply the walnut balm all over again, this time in a more relaxed way. Sabrina had placed second-to-last in her category, Saverio third. All the same, in the car on the drive back, though Andrea had showered them both with praise, they'd decided they wouldn't do competitions anymore, that, basically, they'd felt kind of ridiculous. "It's a meat market," Saverio had said. "I felt like a side of beef hanging from a butcher's hook." And Sabrina, who wasn't very bright, had added that she'd felt awkward, too; she wasn't meant for the spotlight. All the same, they'd kept on going to the gym, and fucking in the bathrooms whenever nobody was around. Saverio had gotten a few photos from the competition enlarged that made him look really massive, and had framed one of them, the one that showed off both his front biceps, his arms raised high with bunched fists, one leg forward, his foot turned at an angle to show off his quads. He'd given it to Tamara. In his own room, however, he'd put up the one that showed the crunch, in which he was slightly bent forward, displaying his washboard abs at maximum contraction. He looked handsome in that photo, a smile and sculpted abs, blue eyes, skin bronzed from the tanning bed and further darkened by the balm, with bulging muscles: all things that made him feel confident and irresistible to girls; but which his father's female friends took in with contemptuous looks that he refused to acknowledge in any way.

Andrea had accepted Saverio's proposal immediately and had hired him on a temporary contract. "Six months," he'd said. "You can sub for me this summer when I'm at Formentera, then we'll see. The gym is doing well, but I can't give you anything more definite. If you bring me new customers and promote the place, you'll see that we'll find a way to round things out."

His way of rounding things out proved to be an anabolic steroid trafficking scheme much larger than Saverio had suspected. He'd seen stuff circulate, Andrea had even given him some, but he hadn't known that this particular gym was a kind of distribution center for all of central Italy. It was Saverio's duty to go to Livorno and get supplies from a wholesaler. He wasn't supposed to bargain about prices or quantities. He always knew in advance how much Nandrolone or Deca Durabolin he was supposed to pick up, and how much to pay for it. In general, Andrea gave him the money, pre-counted, in an envelope. Saverio had imagined he would keep track of the girls in the gym, filling out forms with their workouts for legs, abs, and glutes; had pictured himself becoming a trainer and spending the rest of his days smearing walnut balm on sweaty backsides. But he found himself unable to go to the gym more than once a week and on Sunday, because the rest of the time he was always being asked to transport boxes of hormones in the trunk of his supermini.

Andrea had reassured him by saying it was legitimate work, but Saverio wasn't that dumb, he knew he was taking a risk, and he wanted to be paid well for taking it. He started earning money. After a few months, the director of the warehouse in Livorno asked him do another commission that had nothing to do with Andrea's gym circuit. There were amphetamines, methamphetamines, and barbiturates. He was told how and where to deliver them: to Grosseto; to a bar in the city center; to Pisa; to a lady's house in Talamone; he was paid in advance, his payments arrived punctually. In the course of a few months he'd paid back the money he owed Tamara twice over, he'd given her a small used Rolex, he'd had the car repaired (which helped him drive faster to make his deliveries), and he'd also announced to his family that he was finally going to live on his own. He found a tiny apartment with a mansard roof not far from the gym, which was convenient both for getting onto the Aurelia, and for going home to the country to see his family, especially Miriam, to whom he brought his laundry, which she returned to him impeccably ironed in a bag, always along with some food—jars of wild boar ragù and packages of pasta,

Tupperware containers of roast meat and potatoes that just needed reheating. Saverio protested, told her not to give him anything, that he needed to eat healthily, that what he really needed was fresh eggs for his diet of egg whites and grilled chicken, and that it suited him to eat out.

"It's ragù that ruined Annamaria, look how fat she is, Mà," he told her.

Miriam shushed him, offended. She felt guilty about her daughter, who had not turned out to be beautiful, and whom she wasn't able to keep thin, either.

Sauro was happy with Saverio's transformation. He didn't understand precisely what he'd done to get so much disposable income, but he trusted him. In those days, the old ways were changing quickly, and there were streams of easy money to be made. Sauro thought the fitness craze must fall into this category; in his mind, the gym's earnings were entirely legal— he thought his son wasn't dependent on Andrea but was a partner. He even started talking to him again. "Bravo, you can see that once you took my advice you landed on your feet, now nobody will bust your balls anymore," he said, slurring his words, with a cigar in his mouth, thumping him on his mighty shoulder. "Economic independence is the most important thing, and I'm happy you've found something you like doing, even if all those muscles, I have to tell you, look really disgusting, not to mention the women who go to the gym; all they're lacking is moustaches and beards. I don't see how you can go for them."

In his rare, sporadic bursts of lucidity, his grandfather Settimio said to him: "Listen, why don't you and all your giant friends come and shift the hay bales? You'll build muscles that way, you'll shift the bales and the boss will pay you. He'll pay you to exhaust yourself, whereas now you're the one who pays. You all seem to me like morons these days. You pay to lift weights? Fucking Maremma. He went off laughing about it, with one solitary tooth in his mouth because his dentures bothered him, wearing his brown pants with the belt buckled to the last hole, into which he'd tucked his dingy wool under-shirt. He kept laughing at his joke, cloaked in his own anachro-nism, inside the alcoholic fog that always made him remember how much better things used to be, when they were worse.

On one of the last nights that Saverio slept in his old bed-room before moving to the mansard-roofed apartment, he heard his parents arguing heatedly. It was very rare for the two of them to be at home at night after dinner. Saverio heard Miriam raising her voice: "We do everything, everything the way they want, and I don't think we've ever let them down— how long has it been since we took a day off? How long has it been since you and I went out somewhere for dinner? And maybe that's the problem at this point, it's clear that you don't give a shit about going out to dinner with me, you'd rather have *me* make dinner for you and your girlfriends. And that would be fine by me, if this could be considered your job. But the way things are going, it seems like your pal Sanfilippi treats us like his own personal chefs! This is the third time that he's invited twenty people to dinner and nobody paid! Twenty complete meals, with fish as the main course, three times over, do the math: that's three million lira; and three payments to Manuela. Manuela at least has to be paid, you know?"

His father's voice was less easy to make out, he heard only "part of the investment . . . anyway we're not short on money . . . an important factor . . . anyway, it's doing a lot to spread the name of the restaurant, the people always come back, we're lucky that Sanfilippi brings in all those prominent people."

Then an angry retort before a sharp slam of the bathroom door: "I don't give a damn about your important factors, I want us to earn well, otherwise you can stop counting on me. I'm not here to act like a servant, and it's time you woke up. You're called the king, but you act like a fool!"

Saverio had wanted to go over and hug his mother. He'd never heard her sound so clear-headed; he wanted to say to his father, "See? See? I'm not the only one who gets it. You're wasting time and money. I, on the other hand, don't do anything for free for anybody, and I don't have bosses, I will never let anyone exploit me. I didn't let you, my own father, do it when I was a minor, so you can be sure I'm not about to let anyone else do it now. They say you're the king of the village, but that makes me laugh, because in your head, you're a servant, Babbo." He turned over and lay flat on his bed, his arms outstretched, and felt a satisfied peace steal over him that instantly sent him to sleep.

Annamaria was in bed too, but she couldn't sleep. Her room was too far from her parents to hear them arguing, but she'd been disturbed by her grandfather's heavy snoring—he was separated from her by a drywall partition, a consequence of the time when Saverio had no longer wanted to share a bedroom with her. She'd ended up with a kind of closet carved out of her grandfather's room.

She thought about Giovanna's stories. She'd gone there again secretly that afternoon. There was only one more week before Niki would be back. Annamaria had made her tell her everything from the beginning, when she'd met her, how she'd become her personal assistant. Giovanna didn't hide the joy that her younger cousin's interest gave her. She was used to being criticized and putting up with insinuations of every kind about her work; her mother accepted it only because the countess had got the job for her, her father didn't want her to talk about it, she just had to do her job and bring home her pay without getting any crazy ideas, while the rest of the family warned her to watch out and to behave herself, and gossiped behind her back about all the absurd things people said about the Garden.

Annamaria understood that the absurd things were magical things, much more interesting and exotic than the boring things that happened in the unchanging life of the countryside, sometimes sad, sometimes mean-spirited. She thought about her maternal grandmother, whom Giovanna had visited more than she had, because she was a more proper granddaughter, whereas she only retained a vague memory of visits that were all the same, days spent looking at photos of dead people trapped under glass.

With her cousin she sat in the shade of an olive tree, drank sparkling water and smoked a cigarette, which could be done in Niki's absence. That afternoon Giovanna had told her how everything had started. When she was seventeen, she'd gone one summer to work for the countess. It seemed like an immense privilege to her, compared to harvesting tomatoes, which is what her parents had made her do the previous summer, when she'd said she wanted to quit school. That had been vile work, spending the whole day in the sun and dust. She would return home at sundown, her body exhausted, her skin itchy and sunburnt, her back aching. The acrid smell of rotten tomatoes that emanated from the earth as soon as the sun got high made her feel like vomiting, she gathered San Marzano tomatoes with a handkerchief in front of her face and a fisherman's cap; to keep from losing her mind, she carried a portable radio with her, which she put in the breast pocket of her work overalls, she set it on Radio Castello, where her friend Tiberio worked, she listened between four and five, when Tiberio did the dedications hour, and always played a song for her, "Bollicine," by Vasco Rossi. Sometimes the radio didn't get good reception in the fields, and the batteries often died, but even when it was turned off, it was company.

Harvesting tomatoes wasn't a job for a girl, but her parents had insisted all the same, because Giovanna didn't want to go to school anymore, and she needed to understand that the alternative would not be better. Her pay arrived every night after the crates were counted. She got paid the same as Rachid, the Moroccan who only spoke French, she never figured out where he slept at night, maybe in an abandoned car, or in the shelter of a hunter's cabin in the woods. Giovanna shoved the money she got into her pockets without looking at it—it seemed dirty to her because every lira stood for a drop of sweat, and she didn't say that metaphorically. Her father would come by to pick her up, and she'd ask him if they could go to the beach so she could take a dip before they went home. Most of the time he said no, that Mamma was waiting and dinner was ready. When, however, he said yes, she'd run out of the car and fling herself into the water, the beach already partly empty. She'd float on her back; it was the only enjoyable moment in the day. She felt the coolness enter her head, carrying off the stench that hung in her nostrils, the weight of her body. She would have fallen asleep in the water if her father hadn't been in the car waiting for her for the pre-arranged ten minutes, after which time he would start honking the horn.

Her parents' lesson worked: Giovanna decided not to quit school. But the next June, she was held back in math, and her mother told her she would have to work to pay for tutoring. When she thought of the tomatoes, she felt like dying. But Adriana told her the countess was looking for a housemaid for the summer and that she could start at once. Even though she didn't know how to do housework, it seemed like incredible luck to her not to have to go back to the fields. Giovanna told Annamaria that the countess had always been really warm and friendly to her. She pardoned every mistake, she taught her everything, and when Giovanna made some blunder, she found a way to let her know about it without yelling at her. Rather than offend Giovanna, she would take responsibility for the mistake herself, "I didn't teach you well enough how to put away the glasses, I'll have to show you better." "I'm going to give you a nice wicker basket, and when you've finished you can take it home; in the meantime, you can use it to gather up whatever's left in the garden."

Giovanna was grateful to her almost to the point of worship; she talked about that job as if it were the luckiest thing in her life. She told Annamaria, "At home nobody had ever treated me that kindly, and I suspect at your place it's the same." Annamaria nodded, and every so often she'd ask, "Then what?" And Giovanna told her how she'd learned to clean and to keep the house in order, to serve at table, to polish the silver with Sidol, to set the table correctly, and to address strangers. The next summer the countess called again, but this time to entrust a more difficult task her. To cook and look after a lady, a Franco-American artist who would be staying in the area for a long time. She was a friend of the princess, Marella, and had been introduced to the princess's brothers, who had immediately fallen in love with her project, a garden of gigantic sculptures, and had given her a hillside where she could create it. She was a fascinating and persuasive woman, especially with men. But when she arrived, Giovanna had had a difficult time. Niki was extremely thin and was in an acute phase of her arthritis that made it hard for her to walk. Giovanna had to cook for her, and she wasn't able to; she had to act as her nurse, and she'd never done that before. The countess helped her this time, too. A Swiss luminary ordered Niki to gain weight. Little by little, Giovanna found herself charged with a task that brought great responsibility and satisfaction: to fatten up the artist, return her to form by cooking delicacies for her made with ingredients of the highest quality, of which there was no shortage in the countryside; she would go get cheeses from Porcu, cured meats from Torracchio, vegetables from the countess's garden, fish from Porto Santo Stefano. She cooked for Niki and nourished her as if she were a baby girl who had to grow, feeding her because her hands hurt too much to hold a fork; and day by day she saw her improve, always becoming more capricious, which Giovanna indulged with good grace. The artist would eat nothing that wasn't aesthetically beautiful; wouldn't touch a minestrone that had fewer than five different colors in it. Giovanna spoiled her, decorating the dishes with flowers gathered at the last minute, took her on walks by the sea, and tried to make her laugh.

"Then what?"

"Then she recovered and started working like a maniac."

"Then what?"

"It was truly a stroke of luck that I was there when she arrived. It was a stroke of luck that the countess was there. The nobility seem to feel at ease in so many different situations. We're afraid of going anywhere for fear of feeling lost, but they're afraid of staying in one place. They know languages, they don't seem to be attached to any one home, to any roots. It's like the world is full of castles just waiting for them, and every castle is their own. And basically, that's how it is. But in this case, with the whole world at her disposal, all the time she could want, all the people, the entire universe, she came to live here. Nothing in our lives could have led us to predict this encounter. But it happened. My work is contained within hers. And you can't imagine how much I've learned. Looking into her eyes is like seeing yourself reflected in those infinite mirrors, you don't know who you are anymore, yet, at the same time, you understand very well; being at her side, it's like you understand more. I learned to be patient, I didn't use to be at all, but she's given me that, like a gift. I understood that accepting her whims and her odd ideas, complying with her wishes, was helping me. When she calls me 'Giovanna, my angel,' I know that I'm an angel for real. I don't know if I'm explaining myself well. It's like she gave me the shape she wanted me to have, and I found myself embodying it perfectly, like one of her Nanas, those fat statues. And it works with other people, too, like that guy Rico, he was a cat. Niki manages to reveal people's true nature to them, to draw out the best that's inside them; she must have learned it from Jean, who did the same thing with her, or maybe it's one of her own gifts. Please don't think I'm crazy."

"I don't think you're crazy, it's wonderful what you're saying, even if I didn't understand all of it. Who knows, maybe one day I'll find someone who can show me who I am."

"You definitely will find that person. All you have to do is to be patient, and to keep your eyes out for all the mirrors that reflect you well."

11. STRENGTH
Energy. Courage. Creative Initiative.

The Wild Boar Festival was celebrated in the village on the first weekend of September. For years it had just been a gastronomical event, with long tables covered in waxed white canvas tablecloths, under neon lights strung up beneath a marquee above the old skating rink. The silverware, plates, and glasses were all made of plastic. The countrywomen did the cooking: for the first course, *acquacotta* stew or polenta with wild boar ragù; for the second course, wild boar *cacciatore*, grilled steak, or *mazzafegati* liver sausages, served with fried potatoes or tomato salad as side dishes; homemade dessert of only two kinds; and local wine in bulk. There were endless lines for tickets, and masses of people filled the tables. It was never clear why so many people wanted to go there, considering that if you went to the best restaurants in the area you generally could eat better and pay not much more for the same meal. But the festival offered more than the simple celebration of food. There was music, a fair, an unforced feeling of community. The scent of caramel floated amid the hawkers' stalls, which were illuminated at night, and were where everyone always spent too much money on bags of candy that didn't taste as good as they smelled; the rancid pralines would be thrown to the pigeons the next day, fake baby bottles filled with colored sprinkles that nobody would be brave enough to open. There was a jewelry stand, and a stall that sold knockoff designer handbags; the illusion of shopping in a place where there weren't any stores.

Furthermore, the Wild Boar Festival had a feeling of festive finale about it, because it came after all the other celebrations of the seasons of fertility and harvest: the festival of the strawberry; of the tortello; of the melon; and of the local fish known as *ficamaschia*—"manpussy"—whose popularity had never really taken off because everyone stole the signs to take to their homes in the city, and hung the "Manpussy Festival" banners in their kitchens. The Wild Boar Festival was the last burst of summer before school, before the season in which nature fell asleep, and with it all the activities attached to tourism, which for many meant the beginning of vacation.

That year Pro Loco, the local tourist board, had decided to add yet another festival: to invent a tradition and divide the village into different districts, called *contradas*, as in Siena, where the annual Palio horserace had taken place for centuries. But this part of the country had never had *contradas* in the middle ages, unlike Siena, so they took their names from streets outside the town walls, and from different housing developments. There would be four districts, four different flags, each with a different pair of colors on it. The villagers liked feeling that they were part of a historical tradition that had taken place near them, more or less, which lived on in the popular imagination. The cowboys' Palio would feature a demonstration of cattle skills: they would have to guide a calf into a corral; open and close a wooden gate without getting off their horses just by using the *mazzarella*, a long stick with a little cleft at the bottom and a hook at the top; then there'd be a high-speed gymkhana with a few hurdles and a sort of carousel, on which, while galloping on the horse, they'd have to pierce an iron ring with the *mazzarella*. All these exercises required great skill, but they were things every cowboy knew how to do.

The cowboys were randomly sorted into *contradas*. The deputy mayor, who had instigated the *contrada* committee, immediately invited Decimo, the oldest man in the community;

then Giovanni, the youngest, who was twenty; Bruno, the only one who still had wild cows; and obviously, Sauro, who was the first to decline the invitation, proposing his son Saverio for the spot. Saverio was out of practice as a cowboy, but you couldn't say he lacked physical strength, or the desire to show off.

He told him about it at Annamaria's birthday dinner. Saverio had shown up with a gift for his sister, an envelope with two hundred thousand lira in it. It was important that the girl open it in front of their father, to show him how much he could afford to give her, something he proudly called "a little keepsake."

Sauro made no comment; he confined himself to saying, "Savè, would you be willing to compete in the cowboys' Palio? You still up to the task?" and smiled at him. It had been a long time since he'd done that. For Saverio this was proof that what he'd told the tall man he'd almost run over was true. Your fathers love you if they respect you, your fathers love you if you succeed at something they would like to do, like making money.

Saverio started practicing early every morning. He rode the most obedient Maremma horse, Brigante, and in the riding arena he recreated the gymkhana course, the ring game. All he lacked was the animal to corral; he practiced with the dog Tiburzi, who was not useful, however, because he instantly obeyed. In the meantime, he practiced opening and closing the wooden gate without dismounting and without using his hands. Around eleven he would finish and go wash up and change clothes to start his rounds. Then Annamaria would arrive and take out Brigante; school hadn't started yet, and she thought it was fun to do the same game, the gymkhana, the ring, and opening the gate with the stick.

One morning at the end of August, when the air was clearer and cooler than usual and the colors of the countryside shone in high contrast, Annamaria noticed the presence of Lisa, sitting on the fence, watching her practice. She got off her horse and went up to her.

"You're really good," Lisa said, "you should compete in the Palio."

"But there's no such thing as female cowboys."

"There's you, so yes there is."

Annamaria smiled. She was a little sweaty, and her heart was pounding. She was ashamed that her T-shirt was stained under the arms.

"God it's hot out. We should go for a swim, right now."

"We could go to the pool at my place," Lisa said without much conviction; maybe she was hoping Annamaria would turn down the invitation.

Annamaria accepted, liberated the horse from his saddle and harness, and led him to the stable without taking him on a cooldown walk, without brushing him, duties she'd never skipped before. She got on her moped and made Lisa, who was very light, ride behind. She felt Lisa's chest against her back; it made her feel uneasy in a very pleasurable way. It felt more charged than on horseback, and she wished the trip would take as long as possible, but in ten minutes they were in the allée of cypresses that led to the Sanfilippis' place. It was a former farmhouse that retained of its rural heritage only the squat shape and the external brick staircase that characterized those historic buildings. They'd enlarged the ground floor, creating a veranda that dripped with wisteria, to which they'd matched the color of the blinds. They'd converted the pigsty into a guest house. Where once there had been a crude drinking trough, they had dug a pool, around which a terracotta deck held lounge chairs, sunbeds, and wicker armchairs covered in white cushions. There was almost nothing anymore that would distinguish this house from a villa in Provence or Liguria.

Giulia welcomed her happily. Annamaria was happy to see her, too: she was one of the few adults she could talk to, as opposed to just taking orders from. Giulia asked her how she was doing, what her favorite subjects at school were, and if she had a boyfriend, even though she knew the answer was no. Sometimes she brought her books from Rome, or little presents. She gave her compliments in front of the others, about what a good and willing worker she was. Annamaria found Giulia intelligent and affectionate, maybe a little too formal, constrained by the obligatory elegance of fine families, among whom she'd spent her life. Sometimes she wondered why she took such an interest in her, given that she already had a daughter to talk with, to give books or presents to. But Lisa seemed indifferent to the attention her mother gave Annamaria and treated her with contempt, if not outright disdain. Behavior that Annamaria was so familiar with that she almost took it as the most genuine substance of family ties.

Giulia invited her to stay for lunch, and she accepted. She asked to make a phone call home, and while she went to the phone in the corridor above an old cupboard, she seemed to perceive Lisa making some kind of muffled complaint to her mother. She turned and saw her with her eyes raised to the sky, her lips forming the words "What a drag!", screamed voicelessly. Acting like nothing had happened, she called home. Only her grandfather was there, who would probably forget what she was saying: "Tell Mamma that I'll be back at two thirty."

She went back to the kitchen and asked Lisa if she could lend her a swimsuit. "I'll get you one of my mother's because you won't fit in mine."

Annamaria was tempted to get on her moped and go. Once again Lisa was the girl who was *too good* to be her friend. If not too thin. And yet, the letters she wrote her. And above all, her compliments on her horsemanship. She heard Giulia say to her, "Come with me, I've got a small one I can give you," and appreciated the kindness of that lie, wanting Annamaria to think that her ass was smaller than Giulia's, when it wasn't true. Annamaria put on the pink bikini with a white lace border, which she never would have chosen for herself, but as she retied the bows on the bottoms to make them wide enough to fit her hips, she thanked her many times. Giulia remembered Sauro's fingers untying them and closed her eyelids for a second. Luca, Lisa's brother, was in the pool too, with a girl who was sunbathing and reading Isabel Allende's *Eva Luna*. Lisa entered the water probably just as she would have exited a scene onstage, almost without the others noticing her pass. Her slender body penetrated the teal surface of the pool through the fissure her joined hands had made. Annamaria watched her vanish under the water, without a splash.

Annamaria, who didn't know how to dive headfirst, only how to do a cannonball, decided to enter by the ladder. She swam underwater all the way to the other end of the pool. When she re-emerged, she heard Luca telling the girl next to him, "She's the daughter of Sauro, the horseman."

She got out to dry off. The contact of her cool feet on the hot tiles was intoxicating, the towel she was wrapped in was clean and soft. There were pleasures for all the senses. For the sight: Lisa herself, on an inflatable yellow lounger, in the middle of the azure of the pool; in the distance, fields of round, golden hay bales that only stopped when the hills of olive trees began. For the hearing: the keening of the cicadas, which all fell silent together at one stroke. For the smell: the aroma of tomato and basil sauce coming from the kitchen. Yet she felt ill at ease. From the French doors she heard music playing, the guitar riff of a famous song whose name she didn't know. She asked Lisa, who replied, raising her eyes skyward, "My god, it's 'Brothers in Arms,' by Dire Straits, you don't know the most fundamental things." Annamaria went to lie down on the hammock tied between an olive tree and a slat of the pergola. She wondered if she should have asked permission. She closed her eyes, tried to rock.

She wanted to convince herself that she felt fantastic. She felt like she was sliding into sleep, but suddenly she started, because she'd stopped breathing for a moment. Apnea. A thought had stuck in her subconscious. "The daughter of the horseman," "What a drag," "My god, you don't know the most fundamental things." What was she doing here? Her presence clashed, and she didn't feel welcome. She went in to get her clothes and told Giulia she had remembered she had to do something urgent for her father.

"Can I do it? What do you have to do for your father? In my opinion you shouldn't let yourself be treated like a servant. Are you really sure you can't stay a little longer? We'll have a quick lunch, it'll be ready in five minutes, and then I can drive you."

"Giulia, I'm sorry to have made you cook extra. But it's no use, I'm the one who forgot that I'd promised to do something for him, to write the menus out prettily by hand. I know it seems unlikely, but I've got beautiful calligraphy."

"You should just say 'calligraphy' or 'beautiful handwriting', beautiful calligraphy is redundant," Giulia said critically.

"I know, you're right. 'Calligraphy' comes from the Greek, *kállos* and *gráphein. Beautiful* and *write.* I know some Greek, too, I study Classics in school," she smiled, blushing. Giulia blushed too, ashamed of herself. Annamaria felt bad to be leaving, she felt bad for Giulia, even if, after all, she was a total bitch, always there with her red pen ready to correct you, and to show off how much more she knew; but she felt even worse about her badly brought-up children, who hadn't given her one glance, not one decent greeting, had treated her with contempt. Why had Lisa invited her if she was going to be annoyed by her presence and treat her this way? Lisa only realized what had happened when she heard the sound of the moped accelerating toward the gate, disappearing in the cloud of dust it had raised.

The day of the Palio arrived. It was the last Sunday before the start of school, one of those cool days when the melancholy of summer's end is as clear as the sky. In the grass playing field outside the village, everything had been set up for the challenge: a round corral made of wooden stakes; a kind of pitchfork that held up a chain from whose tip hung the ring that was to be pierced. There were hordes of people, villagers and tourists, everyone there to enjoy the show by the cowboys who had bested Buffalo Bill in the ring on his 1890 tour, when a cowboy from the Pontine Marshes named Augusto Imperiali, a cowboy who couldn't be thrown by even the wildest Appaloosa colt, had sent the American packing. The Maremmans were so proud of that story, it made everyone so happy to see the men with their animals, half of them horsemen, half of them herdsmen, prepared to translate the archaeology of their profession into spectacle.

The first to enter the field was Saverio, who was competing for the *contrada* of the Old Town. He was wearing the complete outfit of brown moleskin with leather trappings, but he hadn't taken into account that his bodybuilding had changed his physical shape. He was squeezed into the jacket, which gave him little freedom of movement, but he smiled smugly from beneath his black cap. He executed a perfect gymkhana, at a good pace, and pierced the ring on the first try, but he had difficulty making the calf enter the corral, the herding exercise. Saverio managed to open the gate handily, but then the calf took fright and started running. Saverio chased him from one end of the sports field to the other for a good ten minutes, while the timekeeper on the microphone limited his comments as much as possible ("Here's Biagini, attempting a save with the *mazzarella*") to avoid making the situation worse; the calf got more and more terrified, and would have run into the road if the other horsemen hadn't blocked him. As the minutes passed, Saverio became visibly irritated, shouted at the beast with no effect, and took off his jacket so he could be freer in his movements, but when his awareness of the disaster became too sharp, with all those eyes upon him, the echo of laughter landing in his ears, it made him want to give up the whole thing and shout: "Damn it, you assholes! Come out here yourselves and see if you can convince this demented calf!" When he'd finally stopped in the middle of the grounds with a defeated look, the calf, on its own, had gone into the corral. Saverio quickly rode off on Brigante and closed the gate with the *mazzarella*. Abundant applause followed, but he was shaking his head as he dismounted his horse.

Then the other cowboys took their turns, faring better with the animal, having understood the strategy. Saverio came in third all the same, because Decimo, the oldest cowboy, who didn't want to compete with his glasses on, missed the ring three times in a row and came in last. The awards ceremony took place amid a torrent of furious off-field arguments.

In the general chaos, Lisa went to the emcee and, when everything was over and people were beginning to get moving to go eat, she asked him, "Could you please let a girl have a try?" The presenter gave her a bewildered look and said, "No, you see, we don't have any unscheduled activities, and people are already leaving. I'm sorry. Besides, you girls do other things, and you'd be wonderful at the hurdles, but this is a different expertise."

"I didn't want to participate myself, I don't ride. But there's a cowgirl among you, and nobody knows it. It's Annamaria, Sauro's daughter. I'm telling you for the sake of the event, and for you personally—it will make a good impression, and my mother could write an article for *La Repubblica* about the little girl who challenged the cowboys."

Upon those words, he gave the matter no further thought. Turning the microphone back on, he shouted, "Annamaria Biagini is expected on the stage!" as if he were calling for a child who'd gotten lost. Then he asked everyone not to leave, because there was to be an unexpected, unscheduled event. Annamaria had come to the Palio on horseback, but she wasn't dressed as a cowboy, she didn't want to do the trial, she was ashamed, she hadn't trained, it would be better not to.

"But they've already announced you," Lisa said. "You can't turn back. Go out and win!" And unexpectedly, she gave her a kiss on the cheek.

Annamaria felt like she was on fire. She took Brigante's reins from her brother's hands. She felt her heart in her throat as she adjusted the straps. She thought it would be a disaster, that she would fall, that she'd never pierce the ring, that she would be forcing the crowd to stay till the end of time to watch the calf, who would run from one end of the field to the other, resolute in its disobedience. She could have cried at the disappointment she was about to give Lisa. She was convinced she was about to endure the greatest catastrophe of her life, but once she was on the horse, she stopped thinking. She heard her name announced over the loudspeakers but was deaf to the encouraging applause that had been requested, deaf to her brother's words, she didn't even understand what Lisa was saying.

She spurred the horse and took off, her head completely empty and her heart racing. She felt like a single unit with Brigante, her muscles effortlessly commanding the horse's feet. She felt like she was the horse itself. She completed the gymkhana without any errors. The moment came with the ring. She'd tried it before a thousand times, she missed it on the first try; on the second, she pierced it skillfully. She confronted the calf, opened the gate with the stick, then followed the animal, slowing Brigante, showed the calf the stick, while gently saying, "Come on boy, go in, be good," and she didn't know if it was that voice that calmed him, or just the fact that the animal now knew what it was supposed to do, but it trotted into the corral at once. Annamaria shut the gate and dismounted from her horse in one leap that ended in a bow.

The stands of the sports field resounded with applause that never ended. The emcee shouted into the microphone: "Exceptional! Exceptional! The best trial at the end, the shortest time of any of them, let's hear more applause for this girl who's shown that she's at the level of all the other outstanding cowboys!" Lisa, who was standing beside him the whole time, reproached him: "It's not that she's at their level, she was better than them. Say it! Say it! Better than the men!" The presenter didn't say it, but the audience's enthusiasm soared.

Sauro took his daughter in his arms and lifted her into the air. Saverio, not to be outdone, lifted Lisa, who laughed, shouting, "Put me down!" which sounded like it meant the opposite. It took Annamaria an hour to leave the sports field, shaking hands and thanking everyone. She was the star of the evening. When she got to the food stands, a new round of applause came from the long tables. Giovanna had come up to her and hugged her. She was holding her nephew by the hand, her brother's son, who had watched Annamaria with admiration, and said to her, "Is it true that we're kind of cousins? So now you're my famous cousin?" Annamaria had looked at Giovanna and said quietly to her, "I've got to talk to you later: I might have found my Niki, the person who's made me understand who I am." Giovanna had nodded as she went away. It still wasn't possible for the two of them to be seen in public so near each other. The rest of the night, Sauro had shown her off to all his important friends like a trophy, not realizing that Annamaria had served them all at the restaurant—they knew her already. Saverio looked proud and happy, and kept on telling everyone who congratulated him, "We raised this one well," taking part of the credit for himself. Before she went home, Lisa had hugged her a long time and said into her ear, "You're one of the great ones, stupid, don't you see that you've got to listen to me?" And Annamaria inhaled the scent of Lisa's conditioner and thought there could be nothing better in this life than listening to her.

*

She spent the night completely sleepless, listening to the owl. Half asleep, she wrote Lisa an imaginary letter.

Look what you've done for me. You made it so other people would notice me, but more than that, you made me see myself, convinced as I am that I don't amount to anything, that I don't know how to do anything. I think it's the first time in my life that this has happened. Still, what's kept me awake until now isn't the joy of having won, or of being appreciated by the village and in the midst of so many men, but the joy that you noticed me. The rest of the world means nothing to me. Your world, which seemed so out of reach to me and faraway; you, so different and so beautiful. All of a sudden you seemed closer to me. My frustration disappeared, for one instant the world had become fair. You gave me a kiss, and I won the contest for you. All the things I can't tell you are here, in these thoughts that keep racing through my head. I think only about you, care only about you; and whether a place for us has ever existed, and could continue to exist, a world in which both of us belong, and love each other.

There was nothing to do, sleep had not come, the crowing of the rooster and the birds had begun to build and then to blend with the noises of the house, of the countryside, the barking of the dogs. Annamaria got up and went to have breakfast. The air was cool, and the jujube tree she saw through her window was laden with fruit. It was the second-to-last day of vacation.

12. THE HANGED MAN
Pause. Hidden depths. Reversal.

A few days after the beginning of eleventh grade, Annamaria appeared in class with a copy of one of the major national daily papers, in which a little article about her appeared in the "Free time and vacation" section, titled "The Maremma Celebrates its Little Cowgirl." It was signed Giulia della Rovere. The article described the event, and spoke of the daughter of Sauro Biagini, "known as 'The King,' a cowboy in his own right and a noted local entrepreneur, enlivener of the Maremma nights," and of this "determined sixteen-year-old brunette, who in addition to being an Amazon and a model student, is capable of beating older, more experienced male colleagues in ability and speed." It ended: "The village is proud that its traditions can be carried forward by this courageous girl, the little cowgirl in skirts." Annamaria disliked the expression "cowgirl in skirts" so much, because for one thing, there hadn't been a skirt, and also, the photo that was published, among the ones taken by Tamara, was hideous, with her eyes half shut, and in a strange pose that made it look like she had no neck. From that day on, her classmates had started calling her "Cowgirl," which sounded even worse to her than Annamarì. She regretted having brought the newspaper to school. But all in all, she was very proud to have won that contest and to have ended up in the paper.

The article was kept in a glass frame that Miriam had hung in the kitchen. For Annamaria, everything that had happened—the gymkhana, the applause, the sudden popularity, the article in a major national newspaper, had only one meaning: Lisa. That she'd suddenly stood up for her, introduced her, encouraged her, had given her an official sign of approval, and a proof of friendship. Of all the possible forms of attention she'd always sought from her, that one had struck her as enormous and confusing. An unexpected act of love from a sea of indifference, amid so many small gestures that had made her feel snubbed, if not hurt. Lisa continued to be moody and hard to read, but Annamaria felt she was the key that could unlock the door to Lisa's most beautiful secret rooms. She began building a castle of her own around these rooms, rereading the letters from Cuba to add bricks and cornerstones.

Dearest Lisa,

I finally have time to respond to all the letters you sent me from Cuba. They are amazing and I think you should recycle them to get As on your next essays. You have such deep ideas, and every line is so full of meaning and so well written that now I'm almost ashamed to write to you with these banal thoughts and the details of my idiotic life that's always the same.

School has started again, and I wake up at six thirty, take the bus, work really hard, come back at two eat, rest a bit then go do my homework, which there's always so much of, and finish at supper time, watch television or read and then go to sleep, or try to, while Mamma and Grandpa watch taped episodes of the Indietro Tutta! *show at top volume. That way I hear it, too. It's great, do you watch it? Then the next day is the same. Thrilling, right?*

As for what's going on at my high school, there's one good thing and one bad one: the good one is, I don't have that hag from the last two years anymore; the bad one is, ever since my classmates read the article in the newspaper they call me Cowgirl, and that's not very nice, because obviously there's an offensive connotation (see, I know big words, too), since I'm from the country, a farmgirl, a peasant, while they're the children of lawyers, doctors, pharmacists from Orbetello.

But I have to say that I don't give a shit about them, as they say here.

They should shut their mouths until one of them ends up in the newspaper for doing something worthwhile.

I wanted to thank you again for making me do the cowboy Palio—if you hadn't spurred me on (that is: dug in with your spurs to force me on) I would never have had the guts, and you know how important a thing like that was for me, with my insecurity.

I think that only people who truly love you take your success to heart, and that, more than anything, is what filled me with joy: to know that you truly love me.

I hope that dance practice won't keep you too far from the village. You know I'm always waiting for you, I do nothing else, practically everything I do is to fill the time while I wait for you.

I love you,
Ciao

Ann

She had written that "ciao" in puffy letters with a special pen, and filled it in with all sorts of colors. She attributed the fact that she'd gotten no reply to that babyish handwriting. Lisa hadn't been back to the village. Annamaria always asked Sanfilippi, however, who came regularly every weekend, and he responded vaguely that she was studying, or had a test, or was doing something with her friends, or her boyfriend, and wanted to stay in Rome. "Give her my very best," Annamaria replied, sure that this would be forgotten. Various times she was tempted to ask Lisa's father for their telephone number, but she was ashamed; maybe Lisa wouldn't have been home, or maybe she wouldn't have known what to say to her. She wrote her another letter, first making two ugly drafts that she ripped into tiny pieces.

Dearest Lisa,

I am so sorry that I've gotten no reply. If it's due to the fact that I seem moronic to you because I signed off with colored letters like in middle school, I promise I won't do that anymore.

How are you?

I think you're doing well, because your father told me you have a whole lot going on, but I hope you'll find five minutes to respond to me. Even a postcard would be fine.

But hopefully you'll be free some Saturday to come out, so we can spend a little time together.

It would be wonderful to go back with you to the Monsters, oops, to the Tarot Garden—they've grown so much since last time. Now the fountain is entirely covered in a blue mosaic, and that tower that had a wheel sticking out of it sparkles all over with little mirrors. What a flash there was that day! It would be so wonderful to talk with the artist again.

That second cousin of mine who works there, Giovanna, has told me lots of things about her (she's her personal assistant, and she is truly a fantastic and magical person).

I'd like so much to know her better because, from what Giovanna has told me, from the little I've understood, it's as if she had a great fire inside her, which gives off light and shines on the people around her, not just on her work. I don't know if I'm getting the idea across.

But I don't want to go there alone, because I get shy and don't know what to say, whereas you're always in fine form, and know the names of artists and famous people. I'll wait for you and maybe we can go there on my moped or we can get Saverio to take us (he's been making a pile of money at the gym lately, and he gives me 50 bucks every week, it's so great).

I want to thank you again for the cowboy competition. It was incredibly important to me, this might have been the first time in my life that anybody helped me achieve a personal success. I don't think I'll ever be able to repay you given that you already know very well who you are, and given that you're surrounded by people who remind you every day how marvelous you are, including the mirror.

You will become the prima ballerina of the Opéra de Paris. Maybe I'll take you there one day on horseback, just think how cool it will be, we'll arrive, me dressed like a cowboy, you in your tutu.

You in your tutu makes me think of the tu-tu-tu-tu-tu-tu sound the telephone makes when you hang up: I'll leave you my number in case you want to call me instead of writing me, that would be faster: 0564 897617.

I love you so much and I miss you. Answer my letter, please.
Ciao.
Til soon.

Ann.

Annamaria put the period after her signature, in which she changed her name. She hadn't realized she was using so many periods. A capital letter. Next line. Another period. Next line. So much insecurity in this parataxis. And all that self-deprecation, and the compliments. The person who responded to her letter instantly picked up on that, and tried to reassure her with her reply.

Dearest Ann (you like to be called that, and not Cowgirl, right?)

Forgive me for not writing to you more often, but since school started and dance resumed, I haven't had a break. I wanted to apply to the Academy, because there, at least, they're more lenient about studying, but my father said no, he says I have to graduate from this school or I won't be well-prepared for college (which, moreover, I'm not sure I want to go to, either), so I think I can't get out of it. This year I've got the graduating exam, and the professors are already stressed out and filling us with anxiety. I don't

172 - LORENZA PIERI

know when I can come, I hope soon. I also saw Niki again, she's mythic. Her husband Jean was there, the sculptor who makes the wheels and the mechanisms that move, with scrap metal and the skulls of dead animals. I don't think I've ever seen a husband and wife who are so complicit, and so hard to explain. It's something you perceive in the way they look at each other. When other husbands and wives are among other people, it seems like they look at each other only to find fault. But these two do it to encourage one another, as if to say, "I like what you're saying, go on." You should get to know him, too. I think Jean did something major, for her, for years he's been giving her the thing I gave you only once, and in a small way: the encouragement, the stimulus, to make you recognize what you are very capable of doing, and the support to make you do it for yourself. The way men do it, without fear, with vanity; with ambition, and without shame. We girls have to learn to be ambitious and not to be ashamed of it. That's no small task, given that the greatest ambition that was pressed on our mothers was to marry "a good catch," and to achieve that, all that was necessary was to be beautiful and quietly educated. We've got a big job ahead of us.

In the meantime, straighten those shoulders that I can see you're hunching as you read.

A big hug, Ann, I hope I'll manage to see you at the end of October.

I love you too,

Lisa

Annamaria reread the letter countless times. She sniffed the fuchsia ink that retained a faint scent of strawberry and stroked the sign-off, "I love you too," indented in the paper, with a finger, closing her eyes. Beneath her fingertips was the most equivocal of caresses. How easy it is to find signs of love, when you're young and in love, and don't know anything yet.

13. Death

Change. Profound transformation. Rupture.

October came, bringing its shorter hours of daylight and the temptation to keep wearing shorts, to take a midday swim, and to get dressed immediately after, feeling salt between the skin and the cotton, hair bathed in the illusion of sunshine. Enchanted days, like all the days in the countryside that mark the passing of one season into another. The transition that brings new colors, and the thrill of standing on the threshold before taking the definitive step.

It was a long weekend, because of a general strike that was keeping most of the schools closed, so all the Sanfilippis were in the country by Friday afternoon. For Saturday morning they'd organized one of the usual horse rides with a stop at the Seaside Cowboy for lunch, the last day before it closed for the winter. Sauro had asked for maximum participation from the family: Filippo had brought a government minister with his wife and children. They wanted to buy a house in the area, so they needed to make them feel welcome, to make them see what a delight it would be to spend time there, to go horseback riding, to revel in the countryside, the sea, to spend time with prominent people and to always eat well, at tables with beautiful views and well-connected fellow diners.

Lisa didn't want to go on a ride, and Annamaria was upset that she couldn't be with her. Giulia came up with an alternative: she would take the girls to the Tarot Garden to meet the artist. Sauro had to accept, and he asked Saverio to accompany him, taking the riding group out on the horses. Given that he'd recently agreed to play cowboy, Saverio accepted again, but he made it clear to his father that he shouldn't count on him to entertain the guests, or to serve at table, and that this would be the last time.

Giulia had told Annamaria that she knew Niki, knew the owners of the property where the Garden was built, and that she had made an appointment with her for "a chat with promising young women." Niki had said yes, but not for more than half an hour. Annamaria was a little astonished that Giulia had taken the initiative. She had asked to go to the Garden with Lisa, not with her mother. The fact that Lisa had been considerate enough to have sought her mother's intervention seemed strange to her, all the more so because she seemed fairly uninterested in the trip. But for Annamaria, this was just part of her friend's strange moods, sometimes nice, sometimes bitchy, in the space of a few minutes.

Regardless, everything was working to perfection, and they would rejoin the others at the Seaside Cowboy for lunch.

Giulia and Lisa, along with the minister's daughter, who was ten and was called Maria Vittoria, Mavi to friends, came by around ten to pick up Annamaria in the car. She had put on her best outfit, a pair of pleated navy pants and a shirt with pink stripes that Saverio had given her when his hormone-puffed shoulders no longer allowed him to fit into it. She'd also dared some mascara, but all in all, it wasn't different from what she wore when she was in uniform serving tables. Seeing what the others were wearing, much more suitable for the occasion, she wondered why she'd chosen to dress as if she were going to mass. But Giulia complimented her: "You look good in pink, and the mascara heightens your femininity, too." Lisa hadn't even gotten out of the car, and had remained chilly when Annamaria had opened Lisa's door before taking a seat in the back, to give her a kiss and tell her how happy she was to be going back to the Monsters with her.

Only Guilia talked all the way to the Garden, preparing them for the visit with a few observations.

"Niki is an exceptional person, you've noticed, a fascinating and very charismatic woman. My friend told me that when she went to propose the project to the Caracciolo brothers, they immediately said yes, because they were persuaded by the idea, but most of all, because they fell in love with her on the spot. Beauty helps, girls, nothing can be done about that. It shouldn't, and mustn't, become a goal, but it certainly can spare you many unpleasant paths, it must be said. For that reason, you've got to try to hold onto it . . . without making it an obsession, but don't believe anyone who tells you it counts for nothing."

The road was increasingly winding. Giulia drove in bursts with lots of braking in between, and Annamaria felt a little nauseous, but she started talking anyway, to amuse Giulia, who responded to all of her comments with a Pavlovian laugh. Annamaria put on a Tuscan accent because she knew that worked even better.

"Yeah, but let's admit, it's just a question of asses. Some women have nice ones, some don't, like Lisa and me, for example. Nothing I can I do about it now. I'll use mine to hold tight to the saddle."

She had scored another laugh.

"But you're pretty Annamaria, and you're really nice, you've got a lively intelligence that shows at once in your eyes, those are all qualities that are part of beauty."

"Ah, OK, so the niceness makes up for the ass. Good to know. Can you also tell me how to make guys understand that?"

"I'm not putting you on, beauty is a complicated thing, it goes far beyond measurements."

Annamaria could feel Giulia's tension from the way she handled the steering wheel, even though she kept on giggling.

"And if I may make a personal observation, you're very well turned out today. I wanted to mention it to Lisa, for whom this is a sensitive topic. We discussed it earlier. She's taken to wearing crummy clothes from dance school, ripped jeans, ratty T-shirts, shapeless sweaters—she was going for *Flashdance*, but she looks like a gypsy."

Lisa emerged from the torpor she was stewing in.

"Oh, then obviously the 'you've got to hold onto it' bit was a generic formula for telling me I should dress the way you tell me to. You're so annoying!"

"Well, dressing well isn't simply a question of appearance, it's also a form of respect you show to the people you interact with. In my opinion, showing up in those ripped pants makes you come across as a badly brought-up, disrespectful girl."

"God, Mom, I know you would go there. To come across as badly brought-up. I beg you, take me back home before I destroy your image for your important girlfriends. I didn't even want to come, you know. And do you think you're presentable and respectful of others, just because you're wearing an Armani jacket? Have you ever seen yourself in your revolting little performances when you're dancing drunk on the beach? You're ashamed of me? Well, you should know that I'm ashamed of you, too. And I think the artist over there is much more open and intelligent than you are about not confusing appearance with identity."

Giulia clenched her knuckles even harder on the steering wheel, conscious of having managed at one stroke to offend both girls, and most of all, of having created a scene she would have preferred to avoid in front of Annamaria and the daughter of the cabinet minister.

Annamaria longed for the fight to end, and, as it turned out, there wasn't time to prolong the debate because they had arrived. Giulia only had time to retort, "That's enough. You've read two lines of Erich Fromm and you think you can preach to me about morals. And quit speaking in Roman dialect, which no one can understand; with all those truncated words you sound like a suburbanite from Centocelle."

Lisa wanted to have the last word: "Which you have just demonstrated. Spending your whole life trying not to seem like what you wouldn't want to be: a beggar, a gypsy, a suburbanite, in short, a poor person. You're so leftist, but you give speeches worthy of a neo-fascist like Assunta Almirante."

Giulia slammed the door of the car with too much force. It was clear that a scolding was called for, which she was sorry to postpone. She adjusted her linen shirt, which hung down over her white pants, redid her low ponytail, attaching a tortoise-shell clip that matched the color of her bangs, put on a pair of big sunglasses.

When the gate opened, the first person Annamaria saw was Giovanna, who was in her work coveralls, holding a bucket of fresh whitewash. The dragon at the entry was finished, and the entire Garden looked more colorful and even more majestic than it had the last time she'd seen it. Annamaria gave her a kiss.

"Don't kiss me, I'm sweaty. What are you doing here? I haven't seen you for a while."

"Since school started, I have too much homework. I came with them to meet the lady."

"Oh, the *lady,* how nicely you speak, and you're all glammed up, with that ironed shirt. Come on, I know she's waiting for you, she's inside the Sphinx. We just had tea with the workers. When you come back later on your own, I'll give you a personal introduction." And Giovanna went off with the whitewash.

The little entry door to the Empress was open. It still produced a strange effect, you had to stoop a bit to enter, and once inside, you found all that brilliant light reflected from the mirrors. Niki came downstairs from the bedroom in a short kimono jacket of blue silk, embroidered with red flowers, over loose pants of the same color. For Annamaria she once again appeared like a vision. Next to her, all other human beings vanished into ordinariness.

She asked her guests if they would like to take advantage of the beautiful morning to go outside, "to take a tour, a walk, if you like. Would you like some tea first? We still have some, I think."

Everyone said no, the impromptu walk was fine. They passed by the steps that descended from the mouth of the High Priestess, where a boy Annamaria recognized from the village was putting cement into the cracks between bricks of variegated shades of blue; it looked like a swimming pool bombarded by a hailstorm.

Niki sang the praises of her ceramicist, Venera. She explained her work at the building site, how every day she enriched the Garden with unique pieces made by hand and baked in the kiln, small bonded ceramic tiles, mosaics of mirrored glass. Niki had planned every inch and had seen her Tarot Garden take shape and come to life. She had already dedicated herself to it for ten years without pause. She said, "For a project like this one, there must be enthusiasm, but also obsession. If I hadn't been so determined, I would never have succeeded in finishing even the first statue. I can live with pain, with problems, but I can't live without my work. For me it is my life."

The four women passed through the archway of the Sun, above which an enormous bird perched, painted in acrylic varnish with its wings spread and its head adorned with a crest of radiating yellow spikes. "That's the symbol of the sun, I gave it the shape of a bird because that's the creature that comes closest to it. I drew from Native American deities and Mexican legends. It's the vital force." Everything that represented the Emperor was enclosed in a kind of village on the columned square they'd seen the previous time. It was the same structure where Annamaria had done her first welding when she was little. Now, the floor was protected by an enormous plastic tarpaulin and you couldn't go in, but the tower of Babel rose at one side, covered in mirrored glass and broken at the tip, from which an iron sculpture protruded like an object that had rained down from the sky to interrupt its sparkle, to crack its completeness. An oak emerged from the plastic, its leaves already brown. It seemed as though it had been put there on purpose, a height for contrast, nature still holding on to its space though surrounded by artifice.

Annamaria looked at the tower. She had the courage to ask the artist if it was just her impression, or if the tower hadn't been broken before. Niki responded that she was right, the tower had been too tall, and Jean had had it cut off; later he had added the mechanical structure that emerged from its open top. "I was against it, it seemed like a bad omen to break the tower, but Jean made fun of me for my superstition. All the same, a number of bad things happened after we broke it."

Annamaria would have liked to ask her what had happened. She also would have liked to ask her how she'd managed to get up every day for years and work this way, to monitor an immense work site, to build, to direct workers to create something wondrously useless.

They stopped at the bench in the wall built at the Empress's back. From there they could behold the rest of the monsters from on high, and the countryside, and the power station.

Giulia, surveying the panorama, turned back to Niki: "We're organizing another demonstration against Montalto. That power station is a scandal. Now, after the nuclear issue, they're trying to convert it to a multi-fuel plant. They want to create an enormous regasification terminal and enlarge the port of Montalto to admit ships full of fuel. That would transform this section of the coast into a chemical complex worse than Porto Marghera, outside of Venice. Do you want to come? We need to do everything we can to convince people that this idea is harmful and possibly even more dangerous than the nuclear reactor."

"I'll try to come. It's not easy for me to walk for long—as you know, I've suffered a lot from arthritis these last years. And *de toute façon*, I don't vote in Italy."

"That doesn't matter, your presence is important all the same. Whoever has the power to be heard should intervene. It would give us a way to make people listen to the need for intervention. And you've got a large following, and great importance here."

"Oh, far from it. I have no following and I'm very solitary. I don't see anyone, and I rarely participate in social events. Every now and then I leave this place to go walk with the dogs on the beach when nobody is there. Only the workers are here to listen to me, and sometimes even they pretend not to understand me. They're not used to taking orders from a woman. But I act like a mother, so it works. Mothers in Italy have the power to give orders." She laughed quickly, throwing her head back a little. "These girls, on the other hand, will they vote?"

"Next time, yes. Lisa will turn eighteen in three weeks. Speaking of which, Annamaria, you must come to the party, I would like it so much." At those words, Lisa grimaced.

"It would be wonderful if it were up to them to decide," Niki said. "Girls are the best energy we have. In Italy there's a lot of corruption, a lot of dishonesty."

"I'm sorry you've run into that."

"Oh, I'm not talking about my work, I'm speaking in general. My work I pay for myself. It hasn't been easy, but every piece I've sold, the gadgets, then the perfume, I've made to finance the Tarot Garden. And then I got that complaint about illegal construction, which was truly absurd."

"Ah, yes, unfortunately there's a fair amount of narrow-mindedness in this village. People can't seem to tell the difference between a building and a work of art. Then they make you do horrendous reconstruction, to comply with the planners' random building codes. It's a shame."

"It was complicated to reopen the site. This work doesn't fit into any building category. I got a complaint from a person I didn't even know existed, for a reason I didn't understand. Ruining the landscape without a license? As an artist, I'd never heard of such an offense. I was upset for a long time. I was afraid the city council would make me take everything down. And I'd already invested everything I had in it."

In a few seconds, Niki's expression changed; she seemed to have been overtaken by another thought that had darkened her mood. She said, "Now you must excuse me, but I must go to the atelier. Jean has built a semi-subterranean studio for me. I've become a sort of mole. You may continue the tour, stay and look around." Then she turned to the girls. "As for you, I suggest you think hard about what you want to do, don't do what others tell you."

Lisa looked at her mother with gleeful satisfaction.

Giulia didn't return the smile, she waved and thanked Niki for the splendid morning. The sky had gotten cloudy again, and a strong wind had arisen that was whipping up the earth and leaves around them.

"It looks like it's going to rain," Annamaria said. And it did.

Within a few minutes, big cold raindrops had started pounding them as they ran to the car. A storm burst that only an hour before seemed unimaginable.

On the way back they all remained in silence. The rain intensified, and Giulia concentrated on her driving; she had turned on the car radio with the De Gregori cassette. Annamaria, seated behind her, tracked the drops that ran down the window, playing at guessing which one would reach the bottom first. She felt strange, she couldn't identify the sensation that came from her gut as she remembered Lisa's expression when Giulia had invited her to the birthday. She saw her own face reflected among the raindrops, then looked at Lisa's in the window in front. How good it must feel to see yourself in the mirror when you looked like her, she thought. Mavi was catatonic; it seemed like nothing had interested her— she had stayed silent the whole time, and had looked at that magical place without evincing the slightest sign of wonder.

When they arrived at the Seaside Cowboy, no one was there. The meal had been moved to the Saddlery because of the rain. Sauro had changed locations because, with the storm, the restaurant on the beach couldn't provide the atmosphere that would have pleased his new guests. At the Saddlery he could start a fire and end with a calm after-dinner moment, with wine and desserts.

And that's how it went: it was an afternoon of endless bottles of red wine, biscotti, and chatter. All the daily papers, weekend supplements, and weekly papers were spread out on the tables. Nobody had ever played cards at the Saddlery. There was only an old chessboard, with pieces missing. Apart from that, the only games permitted were power games, tacit but also on display, like the economics of everyone's possessions, the politics of which friends had been invited, which people sat where, and which ones could be shown off. Sauro was the only one who focused on the continual verbal jousting, which revealed who was rising or falling in the hierarchy. The others were rivals, and not entirely aware of it; antagonists in an informal competition, at the end of which everyone would win, more or less, and everyone would get their quota of ephemeral guaranteed pleasure.

The old leather sofa that had been moved to the center of the room had attracted various nappers. There was always too much food. Everyone was in a state of continual satiety that stimulated more hunger. In the end, the downpour didn't last long, someone went out for a walk, or to pretend to hunt for mushrooms. Annamaria had served at table, and in the afternoon, when it was already dark, she was still there, uncorking bottles. She had learned to sniff the corks, which she then threw into an enormous green glass carafe in the corner between the kitchen and the bathrooms, which was now full. She couldn't wait to finish so she could talk a bit with Lisa, who certainly had gone home. Her eyes burned from the smoke of the cigars and the chimney. She decided to go out and get some air. Tiburzi was outside, and jumped up on her. His enthusiasm made her so happy, his crazy tail and his leaps, she felt like she was a celebration to him. She wanted to look for the tennis ball that was all battered and drooled on so she could play catch with him. She went into the barn; the main door was ajar. It was almost completely dark, but she could hear the breathing of the horses, the flicking of tails, the chewing, then other sounds, more human. A flickering light that came from the skylight up high fell on the pile of hay in the back, by the row of stalls where feed and tools were stocked. She recognized the silhouettes of two people perfectly, one on top of the other. Underneath was Lisa, above was her brother Saverio.

There was a concentrated, motionless moment in which frozen glances were exchanged. Annamaria left immediately, bashing her shoulder hard against the main door, which stayed open. Those dark shadows had exploded in her chest, and now she could no longer control her breathing and her thoughts. She ran toward the fountain and sat on its edge, her head spinning. She held her wrists under the gelid water. She stayed in the dark to catch her breath, her heart racing, Tiburzi beside her, still leaping, and hoping that she would throw him something. Time passed that she wouldn't have known how to quantify; it was a magma of pounding heartbeats, anguish, and

canine persistence, he'd mistaken her desperate flight for a game. Annamaria didn't stop. She stumbled and fell on her hands. The dog, surer than ever that the running was for his benefit, licked her tear-streaked face. She pushed him off with a violent kick to the stomach, the mutt fled whining into the distance, then gradually came back, not understanding what he had done to deserve the blow. In other circumstances Annamaria would have petted him to make up for it, but at that moment, she was blind with rage and humiliation. She ran on in the dark until she couldn't breathe anymore. She paused for breath, even though she would have liked her heart to definitively burst. She had to find a way to eradicate the memory, the feelings, the disgust she felt inside her. Lisa's face when she was saying, "You are pathetic." She arrived home, limping. She knew where her brother hid the boxes full of the pills he distributed. People took them to calm themselves and feel better, she knew. She popped a blister pack of pills and got into bed. A voice inside her head repeated infinitely *You are pathetic You are pathetic You are pathetic*. An infinity that lasted less than a quarter of an hour until her senses abandoned her.

When she woke up after her stomach had been pumped, she said to her mother, who was looking at her more with anger than sorrow, "I didn't want to die, I just wanted to sleep, so much."

Nobody ever spoke of a suicide attempt. It was "the night of the incident," and then a generic "after what happened," a premise that from that day forward took away a great deal of Annamaria's freedom. Miriam invented a justification and a solution. Poor Annamaria had been bullied at school, where they called her "Cowgirl," she had complexes about her appearance, she had suffered in silence at being made fun of, and that had resulted in an adolescent depression that was difficult to confide to her parents. They had her transferred to a teacher's training school, and began keeping her under observation and giving her brief interrogations whose sole object was to make themselves feel better. Annamaria accepted everything; the alibis suited her fine, the protection, the fictional reassurance, not having to go to a psychologist, not having to tell anyone the reason why she had wanted to die. The truth was heavy, for her and for her family. It was better to keep the stone on her heart, to let time erode it, to lock it up in a well-hidden place, hoping it would never get out.

Miriam and Sauro did not want to know Annamaria's version; Saverio's version was suffocated by another silence, somewhere between punitive and resigned. They told the medics at the hospital that the girl had collapsed and they didn't know why, maybe she'd taken the pills the doctor had prescribed for their grandfather when he couldn't sleep. The chief physician was a friend of Sauro's, and the question of whether or not the incident should be treated as an accident didn't come up, there was no reason to investigate. Annamaria recovered quickly and without physical after-effects.

Her grandfather had found her, lying on the ground with a stream of vomit by her face. He thought it had something to do with those female troubles that make women sick every month. Sometimes he'd come upon Alma when she had fainted from cramps. He had run to the restaurant to call for Miriam. "Sorry for bothering you, gentlemen," he had shouted as he entered the Saddlery, heading for the kitchen. Nobody understood if he hadn't wanted to involve Sauro, or if he thought that the sole person adapted to a situation like this was his daughter-in-law, but he didn't stop for one second by his son. Miriam was tending a wild boar stew she wasn't happy with; although it had marinated for a long time, it still tasted gamey, she said. Settimio said to her, "Think about how it tastes later, right now Annamaria is at the house, and I know she needs you. Run."

She threw off her apron and cap and fled, ahead of her

father-in-law's halting steps. Annamaria was never sick; Miriam was very worried. Sauro followed them, pissed off at having been ignored, totally ignorant of was going on, but sure in his heart that something terrible had happened.

Miriam stayed in the hospital overnight, and once she was home Sauro grabbed Saverio by the neck, the box of psychopharmaceutical drugs that he'd found on the floor in his other hand.

"What the hell is this shit you're bringing into my house? Throw it all away now and don't you ever set foot in here again, do you understand? Do you understand?" he screamed in his face. "I don't ever want to see you again, and if you come near us or Annamaria again, I swear I'll turn you in. And I will kill you. I don't give a damn if I go to jail."

When Sauro let go, Saverio kicked the door to avoid kicking his father.

"Babbo, as usual you don't know shit, you haven't understood shit, but you insist on putting all the blame on me? What matters to you now? To understand why your daughter wanted to kill herself and to try to help her? Do you want to know that Annamaria has problems? Are you going to figure out why she's sick? No, you're always looking for a scapegoat, it's enough for you to lay the blame on me, and you think you'll solve every problem by kicking me out of the family. Do what you want, Babbo, do what seems easiest for you, as you always do; just know that I love Annamaria and Mamma, and they love me. You can turn me in or kill me, I will always come back to them. I just wonder why those two poor women always have to be at your beck and call. I don't know how long it will last, Babbo. Annamaria is a good girl, but she's smart. I hope one day they will abandon you like a dog, that's what you deserve."

He took his gym bag from the closet, the one with the outfits and the drugs hidden in it, and left, giving a thump on the shoulder to his grandfather, who was sitting alone at the dinner table with his coat still on, an empty bottle in front of him, putting apple peels in a paper bag to put aside for the rabbits. An air of hopelessness. "Bye, Nonno, don't worry, Annamarì will be fine. Have a good time with your jackass of a son, who I can see cares a lot for you, as he does for all of us."

He went out into the night; smoke still came from the roof of the Saddlery. Saverio would have bet that the Romans had gone, leaving the lights on and the fireplace going, because nothing mattered to any of them.

To friends who heard about Annamaria, Sauro said it was nothing, a little meltdown; to the women he spoke of the pain of the monthly periods of virginal girls—a man who knew about things like that and who felt compassion for his daughter awakened their understanding and tenderness. The efforts of the following months were all channeled into an attempt to bury the story as soon as possible, in order to return to the equilibrium that had always existed. It wasn't clear whether it was the effect of the overdose of benzodiazepine or some form of repression, but Annamaria remembered next to no details of that night. The last images she retained were of Saverio and Lisa semi-naked in the barn, of the dog jumping up on her, then Lisa screaming in her face. Words she couldn't recall, but which she knew had wounded her.

She had started going to school again after a week. At the teacher's training school she studied less and got higher grades. To escape interference from her mother, who otherwise would have wanted to do her homework with her, she had pretended to need help with different programs and learning tools. She often went to the little country library where Lorenzo, the nearly blind librarian, helped her a little, knowing that she didn't need his help, but that she liked to stay there in silence, reading without being disturbed. Actually, nobody ever came into the library. It had been established through a legacy from a philosopher who had died not long before, and whose descendants frequently visited the area. A few years later, when Lorenzo died, he wasn't replaced; the place was sold and the books thrown into a cellar, inside boxes that were never opened again.

And so, Annamaria spent her afternoons with Lorenzo, who was perpetually bent over a book in his thick glasses, forehead leaning in so he could read, in a state of silence that was only interrupted when she asked him to listen when she read her lessons out loud. He told her she was terrific, but it was empty praise. He recommended other reading that might interest her—he had her check out *Bonjour Tristesse* by Françoise Sagan, not suspecting the distress it would inflict on her, in the form of the protagonist, Cécile, who was so much like Lisa in her thoughtless amorality. She brought the book back to Lorenzo two days later. He asked her if she'd liked it. Maybe he had hoped to spark a titillating conversation. She shut him down with a "Good book, shitty characters." She thought about Lisa every day. She tried to distract herself by keeping mind and body occupied: she studied, went riding, watched television. But every now and then, all of a sudden, Lisa came to mind, laughing at her, the tight hug after the cowboy competition. Her eyes. Images that were so powerful that she felt her stomach clench.

At the new school, nobody made fun of her, and the fact that almost everyone in class was female allowed her to test her doubts every day: whether it was Lisa, specifically, that she liked, or whether she liked women, not men, in general. She still didn't understand it. Even when the obsession and the rage had abated, she felt like she wouldn't ever be attracted to anyone but Lisa. She was totally uninterested in the relationships that couples had, thought she would never have a love like that. Her jealous reaction at Lisa's involvement with her brother had turned into a kind of lingering envy. Lucky him for getting to kiss her, touch her, penetrate her. How Lisa could be attracted to someone like Saverio was a question she could not answer. But there was an answer, and it was very simple: Lisa liked men, and women liked the men in Annamaria's family, including the lovely and refined ladies of the Sanfilippi family.

The anger of the first days was followed by a profound sense of disappointment at the thought of Giulia writing those letters to her, at the falseness that permeated all the ties that bound their two families, so apparently united and full of common interests, but which ultimately came down to two: food and sex, with nothing fairly divided; it was just a power game in which the Biaginis lost miserably. In both cases, her family gave the lion's share and the other family took, as they were used to doing. They paid with money, sometimes, but they didn't contribute in any other way. She'd begun to think the way Saverio did, that their interactions would always be hollow. She had lost the will to joke, she never felt like laughing or making anyone laugh. Her castle in the air had crumbled, and out of the rubble she had built a monastery, in which she cloistered herself to recite prayers of mistrust of the outside world.

From that night on, Lisa and Giulia had not returned to the village. But Filippo came back every week—there wasn't the slightest change in his routine. Annamaria had asked if she could keep helping out on Sundays with the horseback rides: that was something that always made her feel good. On horseback there wasn't time to think, she had to make decisions, give orders, and lead, and there were the paths, the low-hanging branches, the wind, the mud, the brackish lake, the sea. The time that passes month after month, which is the only cure for heartbreak.

One afternoon, instead of going to the library, she kept going straight and went all the way to the Tarot Garden on her moped. She hadn't planned it: she'd come to the stop sign and thought she didn't want to shut herself up in that silent room with that disturbing blind man who didn't bathe very much and whose T-shirts were covered in dandruff. The air was crystal clear and cold, she wanted to talk a bit with somebody, and realized it had been months since she'd gone to see Giovanna. She crossed the path in the bushes. The abandoned chapel had been transformed into a completely new structure. The arbutus was in fruit, and it looked so beautiful to her how the berries had ripened, they were like Christmas decorations, gracefully dispersed among the branches. She heard gunshots in the distance, the barking of dogs, the scent of the underbrush and mushrooms, a smoking chimney. All at once she felt something she hadn't felt for ages: like she was in the right place, comfortable in all five of her senses. She recognized that her land was a beautiful and comforting place, when it wasn't infested by alien presences.

Giovanna was busy when she found her. She'd had to cook at the last minute for two people who then became six; as usual she was knocking herself out to please Niki, who continually changed plans and had no idea what it meant to cook a meal.

Giovanna was glad to see her. She asked her to give her a hand with the dishes—she was curious to hear about Annamaria because she'd vanished for such a long time.

"Have you become a snob like your girlfriends, now that you've been in the newspaper?"

"Actually, I've been going through a really shitty time. It's in part because of those friends . . . that is, basically, it's hard to explain, but one night, I felt so bad that I swallowed half a box of sleeping pills."

"What in the hell are you saying, Annamarì?"

"No, no, calm down, I didn't want to die, I felt sorry for myself and I felt useless . . . I just wanted to sleep . . . that is, basically, to forget that I was alive." She giggled as she said it.

"You haven't lost your sense of humor. Now let's go out and smoke a cigarette and you can tell me more."

"The cigarette, OK, but talking, no. That's over. I'm fine

now, and I'm happy to see you. My mother's a little anxious these days. I changed schools. So that I won't always have her on my case, I go to a library to do my homework, but today I didn't feel like it, so I came here. Tell me about yourself, about her, and about that asshole we all know you'll never leave."

Giovanna did as her cousin had asked; she talked, without ever losing track of what she was doing. It was Annamaria's problems that she cared about. But she talked about her own, she spoke to her about Niki in a way that she knew might help her. When they'd finished their smoke, they went back into the Sphinx. Niki wasn't there. Annamaria's eye fell on a catalogue. It was a photo of the artist with a rifle in her hand, shooting a painting; she was wearing a fitted white jumpsuit, red hair. "Why on earth isn't this woman our undisputed idol, the Madonna that we pray to, seek advice from, take as our role model? Why don't we carry her in a procession through the village?" Annamaria asked.

Like a sympathetic schoolteacher, Giovanna kept on smiling at her. "Because she's too different from us. And there's nothing about her that could serve as a positive example for the women in the village." She continued, because she wanted the story to serve as a kind of lesson: "There's a strong destructive impulse at the root of Niki's creativity, too. I know this from her stories: she's always had a death wish, suicide fantasies. Her last attempt was only a few years ago. It was when she was in St. Moritz, right before she met Marella, she had planned an artistic suicide, she wanted to go to the hairdresser, do her makeup, put on a beautiful dress, and then get herself some caviar and champagne on ice, her favorite book of poems, the *Duino Elegies* by a certain Rilke—which she later gave me—then take herself off with a bottle of sleeping pills, so they would find her beautiful and frozen, like Sleeping Beauty. Does that seem like healthy thinking to you? Someone to emulate? And then, luckily, even if she says it was bad luck, two days before her "adventure" on ice, they took her to Bern in an ambulance because she had pneumonia. Dying in a hospital bed wasn't the way to go about it, that death would have been too inelegant for her, so she recovered, and a few days later, her casual get-together with the princess was her permanent salvation. She began the Garden project, and her thoughts of death were transformed into something else. The same thing was at work when she did the shooting paintings: she used art as a kind of pressure-release valve, she killed her own obsessions. She killed the canvases to keep from shooting herself or other people; men, her father. She shot them, and in the end that made her feel better, she felt vindicated in her own way, fulfilled. She had done something, rather than destroy someone. It's a very interesting thing."

"Cathartic acts. Aristotle talked about that, too. He thought that theater, through enacting tragedies, could help the spectators cleanse themselves. Something like that."

"Mamma mia, you know so much."

"Now that I'm going to the teacher-training school I'm forgetting the four scraps of Greek I learned at my old high school, and soon I'll be as ignorant as before, don't worry."

"Who's worried? The more you know, the better. It's just people in the village who think that knowing things only confuses people's ideas, and that being ignorant is the best way to keep in touch with the true things in life. That's idiotic. Staying ignorant is staying ignorant. Keeping in touch with the most primitive things, with no possibility of elevating yourself. Niki's always telling me, you've got to study, read, and travel."

"Yes, Giovà, but how can we take advice from a woman who's so different from us, who comes from such a privileged background compared to us? What does she know about what it is to be like us? A noble, incredibly rich artist, a model, half American and half French, who grew up in castles between two continents, without ever having to worry about having to work, to clean, to cook. What does she know about what our life means, country girls born to humble parents, without travel, without stimulation, with only the pressure to help Mamma and Babbo in the barns, at the restaurant, in the fields, to clean other people's houses?"

"Annamaria, you don't know her. But you have to have faith, if not in her, then in me. She knows very well what suffering is, it has nothing to do with money. Maybe the same thing that we feel, you and I, that all of us feel, the same thing that made you take the sleeping pills. If she tells you to try and perform some ritual, do it. If there's something that bothers you, a thought that obsesses you, free yourself of it by taking some action. Ghosts don't exist, but if you pretend to shoot them, they can die."

Giovanna had succeeded in saying what she wanted to say, without digging too deeply into the nature of her cousin's problem, as she'd been asked.

Annamaria left the Garden with the usual sensation that this place was magical, and that entering it had put her in contact with a truth, with a project to put into action.

And that's what she did. She returned home and took Giovanna's advice. She took the letters from Lisa/Giulia that she'd kept, because they were the most beautiful things she possessed, the things that had moved her the most, and which, reread after the fact, were even more wounding. She took them to the barn. Getting an empty can of peeled tomatoes, one of the big ones that they used first for making the sauces at the restaurant and then for watering the horses. She threw the letters into it, and with a Zippo she'd found on the bar counter, which had a Gothic capital A inscribed on it, and which she'd immediately kept as her own, she set fire to everything. She watched the flame of the letter that was written in pink ink make a blue peak. She repented her action. She felt her stomach clench. What a waste. Once everything was reduced to ashes, she took the can and emptied it into the straw in the middle of the barn, along with Pallino's shit, the horse that had made Lisa cry. And then she started laughing, all by herself, and felt better. It would have been marvelous to tell Lisa and Giulia what had become of their heartfelt testimonials. Thinking of the faces they would have made, she kept on smiling to herself, flicking the Zippo on and off as she went back to the house.

14. Temperance
Protection. Healing. Flow.

Before Christmas, Giulia, who in the meantime had made no contact with Sauro, Miriam, or Annamaria, went back to the country with her husband. She was dressed more carelessly than usual, her blond highlights showed a visible regrowth of grey, there were dark circles under her eyes. Without the guile she typically used in such circumstances, she asked Sauro if he could come see her alone because she needed to talk to him. "It doesn't have to be in private, as long as nobody can hear us," she specified. He told her that in public it might generate even more talk. They agreed to see each other at her place while Filippo was out riding on the notary's property.

They sat in the living room, where they had made love so many times. As soon as he walked in, Sauro threw off his jacket and put a hand on her shoulder, pulling her to him for a kiss.

"I've missed you," he told her.

She stepped back. "Please, don't touch me."

"Why? It's been so long since we've seen each other. Why did you stop coming?"

"I missed you, too. But let's not start over. This thing between us hasn't done anyone any good. And I, unlike you, put my heart into it, and the heart always goes off in uncontrollable directions."

"How do you know that I didn't put my heart into it? Because I'm a man, you think my heart doesn't work?"

"No, no," she smiled, "maybe it just works at a lower

register than mine. Lower consumption, lower engagement. It makes everything easier." She liked so much to speak in metaphors with him. She liked it when he made her talk while he was undressing her. Her words a bass line under their shared excitement. He liked it when she talked about politics, when she discussed complicated things. He would pretend to listen to her while he moved gently inside her, watching her. Giulia would get tired of continuing the speeches, he would ask her, "Explain it to me better," and then she would talk as long as she could between sighs, until the lectures dissolved into panting, and then into cries of pleasure. But this time she tried to control herself, to be concise and dry.

They sat down, she on the sofa and he in an armchair, at a distance they'd never preserved when they were alone together. He remembered the times when she had jumped on top of him when he was sitting there. He felt excited. Giulia lit a cigarette and asked him to listen without interrupting her.

"I have to tell you that what happened to Annamaria involved me."

He could not hold back: "Don't worry about it, it's water under the bridge. She's doing very well now. But still, you could have called. As for her, she was used to you bringing her books, maybe it's not good that you've showed no sign of life, but she hasn't said anything to me about it. I know now that I shouldn't expect anything from you. Annamaria is a strong girl, and she has plenty of resources, she doesn't need help or pity. It was just a moment of confusion. At that age that's how it is. They were making fun of her at school. They called her "the Cowgirl." A school of assholes, the Classical high school. Annamaria is not depressed and she does not want to die. Miriam and I are watching her closely, and she's made a great recovery. She likes her new school and keeps getting good grades. Thank you for your sympathy, but when you come down to it, my daughter is none of your business."

"Actually, she's more of my business than you think. I asked you please not to interrupt me. There are a lot of things you don't know about your daughter. And I think the school has nothing to do with what she tried to do. I love Annamaria as if she were my own daughter, it's true. To the point that I think that Lisa got jealous of her, of the attention that I was giving her. It seems to me that your daughter has an extraordinary intelligence, sense of humor, and potential—in a certain sense, I always thought it was a shame to see her talents wasted in waitressing and working in the stables."

Sauro pulled the half-cigar out of his mouth and leaned his back against the armchair; the color in his cheeks was darkening. It cost him great effort not to reply.

Giulia raised a hand to stop him and continued. As she spoke, she threw off her shoes and tucked her feet under the cushions. She buttoned an old moth-eaten cashmere cardigan of Filippo's over her chest.

"I understood that Annamaria had great admiration for Lisa. She wanted her company, her friendship, her approval. Maybe in some way she would have liked to be like her: I don't doubt that she envied her beauty. You know how easy it is to have complexes at that age."

Sauro clenched his jaw.

"I wanted them to be friends. I wanted it so much. Even more, I wanted them to feel like sisters, I wanted to be another mother to Annamaria, one who could give her more intellectually . . . than village life offers."

Sauro got up and went to pour himself a whiskey.

"Please listen to me, I absolutely don't mean to question you or Miriam as parents, I want that to be clear, I just want to tell you how things stand, and where our love for Annamaria led us. We went down a wrong path, and we didn't realize it."

"Who's included in your 'we'? Can I ask you that at least?"

"All of us who love her . . . because we've all made mistakes."

Sauro clamped the cigar between his teeth.

"In short, the fact is that at a certain point, Annamaria started writing letters to Lisa. Beautiful letters, full of confidence and affection. The correspondence seemed like a perfect way to cement their rapport, because they would forge an alliance, they would develop a habit of sharing, just from writing, from reflection. But Lisa never had time to respond . . . You know, with dance, and high school, and everything. So she asked me to do it, basically . . . I started to keep up the correspondence with Annamaria, writing in Lisa's place. It was nothing, you understand, simple stories about what she was doing, about her days, reflections on school and on boys, criticisms of us parents; I never made up anything, to be clear, these were all true things that she could very well have written herself. And I also tried to reassure Annamaria, to help her have faith in herself, all the advice that you might expect to get from a close friend a few years older. At first Lisa reread what I wrote before I sent it, then she said it was fine with her if I did it all myself. It seemed like such a perfect way to make them communicate. But I'm afraid these letters were written too well; that is, I can't help writing the way I write, I'm a journalist after all—they led Annamaria to exaggerate her admiration for Lisa and increased her desire for her attention. In short, Sauro, I'm afraid that Annamaria has developed a crush on my daughter."

Sauro broke in: "What the hell, Giulia! Apart from pointing out that we're giving her a shitty life out here, you're telling me that you made a fool of her, and because of that, my daughter has become a lesbian?"

She shifted to sit in a normal position and gestured for him to calm down.

"What are you thinking, Sauro! I repeat, I did not criticize you as parents, and I didn't say that Annamaria was a lesbian. Very simply, I think that her admiration for Lisa may have gone beyond the limits of simple friendship; at their age they're still figuring out their sexual identity. And all the same, my dear troglodyte, if it were to turn out that she was a lesbian, there would be nothing wrong with that."

"No, of course, there's nothing wrong with it—my daughter's a lesbian and yours is a slut, we're all progressive and modern, right? Nothing wrong with it. You're not offended, are you?"

"Sauro, how dare you? Leave Lisa out of it, please, we're talking about Annamaria. You can simply deny everything, but then how do you explain the fact that she took those pills right after she saw Lisa with Saverio?"

"Lisa with Saverio? Doing what?"

"My god, Sauro, is it possible that you're this out of it? That you're this naïve? What do you think Lisa and Saverio might have been doing to shock Annamaria to such an extent?"

"Well, what do you know about it? How in the hell would you know about what happened? These are all figments of your sick imagination, spinning dramas out of other people's lives. Giulia, you are dangerous!"

"Sauro, do whatever you think is best, feel free to not believe me. But Lisa told me, and I assure you that she was there. And she also tried to talk to Annamaria, after she came upon her with Saverio. That's how she found out that Annamaria was jealous of her, jealous enough to regard her encounter with Saverio as a true and serious betrayal. If you don't believe me, ask your son, given that he was there, too."

"All of you are sick in the head, Giulia. You most of all. You think you can come here and act like the boss lady, get yourself fucked but demean me, pretend to be my wife's friend, while you're a Judas, pretending to love my daughter while you're deceiving her, and trying to educate her because your own daughter is a bitch who doesn't listen to you? Not to mention Filippo . . . he's less interested in you than in the whinnying of his horse. And your son, who treats you like a dish rag. Obviously, he's better than mine, because he goes to university, while mine is a poor ignoramus who works in a gym. You didn't think about educating him a little, too? To give him some of those opportunities you wanted to give Annamaria that country life could not supply? To get Saverio a terrific internship at RAI, like you did for Luca, or a guaranteed spot in Parliament? You don't need a degree for that, right? It's enough to know the right people. But it looks like Lisa's taking care of his education, no? I guess that's all you people think we men from the village are good for. You women are top-notch, minds and thighs always wide open, all in the family. If your life is shit and your family exists in mutual indifference and falsehood, that's not my problem. And nobody asked you for anything, you got that? So, the less you meddle in our lives, the better. You know, I feel bad for Filippo, because he's really a great guy. But you, you . . . I have no words."

By then they were both on their feet, red with rage. Giulia screamed with a finger pointed at him, "Sauro, I knew you were crude, but not to this extent! You're offensive at an unacceptable level. You're preaching to me? You? Who betrays your wife right in front of her face with a hundred different women, who exploits your daughter as a stable girl and who are always putting down your son even though the two of you are the same, with your father who's dying of cirrhosis before your eyes, and you can't be bothered to bring it up with him? You say that Filippo's a great guy, your best friend even, but you had no qualms about taking up with me—and I'm the Judas? You speak to me of indifference when you're the prime example of someone who doesn't give a damn about anyone! Anyone! And you know why? You're silently ashamed of them because they're useful to you as servants, but you don't like having them as relatives. Because you like the rich and power-ful better, too, don't you?"

"Servants? Servants? You're the one who democratically despises and exploits servants and Filipinos, you and your ass-hole children who are even more badly brought up than you are, convinced that they can treat everyone however they like. In our family we work together."

"Attack me, but leave my children out of it, please. I do not permit you to judge them and even less to insult them."

"Oh no? And then why did you permit yourself to judge and insult mine? Maybe because you're the boss lady and you know more words than the peasant?"

"I didn't insult them! I told you that I loved Annamaria from the bottom of my heart, and my love for her has led to a misunderstanding."

"A misunderstanding? A misunderstanding? It very nearly killed someone, your misunderstanding! *I can't help it that I'm a journalist,*" he mocked her. "But what right did you have, goddammit? And can I tell you something, Giulia? Because this is what you came to tell me, right? Do you need to clear your conscience? Or am I the only person you aren't fake to? Did you think you would be embraced, and understood, and thanked, for taking on the burden of giving my daughter the education that her mother and I didn't know how to provide?"

Giulia was on the verge of tears.

Sauro continued: "Know that I believe Annamaria is a thousand times smarter, more mature, and more sensitive than your daughter, and that Miriam does not need to learn any-thing about being a mother."

"I told you because I thought it was important that you knew. And yes, I thought you could understand that my intention was generous and selfless, but instead, you don't understand dick, unfortunately."

"My role is to use my dick, not to understand it."

"You're pathetic."

"Don't you and Lisa ever dare come near my daughter again. Ever."

"You know what, Sauro? I really overestimated you. I think my husband did, too, these years, and that we've all overvalued this shitty place. We're good people, unlike you. You can be sure that I won't set foot here again. I feel bad for Annamaria; it's true, she deserves better. Lisa and I can go to a lot of places that are much nicer and more interesting than here."

"Go where you like, golden cunts. As far as I'm concerned you can go to hell."

"A true gentleman, there's nothing to say. You go to hell. You are nothing."

Losing all self-control and without thinking that he would only be confirming Giulia's opinion of him, Sauro spat on the floor and left.

She set to work cleaning, washing the glasses, and, even though it was cold, she opened the windows to disperse the stench of the cigar and Sauro's scent, which shamed her when she smelled them, for having indulged an obsession which now was transformed into fury. She let the air into that house, to which she vowed never to return, and went to take a shower.

At home, Sauro had found Saverio at the dinner table. He waited until the two of them were alone to speak him.

"Leave now, Saverio. This is no longer your home. I've already told you."

Saverio looked at him with a questioning air. "I just came to have dinner with Mamma," he replied, thinking, "here we go again," but not understanding why. "What's wrong, Babbo? Are you pissed off? I thought we'd gotten over that."

"I'm furious. Let's go outside please."

As soon as they were outside, Sauro took Saverio by the jacket. "What does that maggoty head of yours tell you, hey?

If you ever dare touch a minor again, I'll turn you in," he said to his son.

"What in the hell are you talking about?"

"I'm talking about Lisa Sanfilippi. You're a disgrace. Are you aware of what you risk if you're reported for fucking the daughter of a parliamentarian? And one who's my business partner, on top of it? Take it out on the girls at the gym, the girls on your rounds, with that pretty girl Tamara. You're out of control, Saverio. I don't understand where I went wrong with you, I'm ashamed of everything you do."

"Know that that shame goes two ways. Aside from the fact that she's eighteen years old, which is what she told me, I can tell you that the reality is far from what you think. She literally jumped on top of me. Her. What would happen if I said that you're fucking her mother? The wife of the parliamentarian who's also your business partner? Your dear, dear friend Filippo."

"What do you know? What are you saying?"

"Lisa knows all about it, she told me, I know that she found you out. I don't know why I don't tell. Mamma could finally leave you. There's a divorce lawyer who comes to our gym. Threaten me one more time and I'll give his number to Mamma. Then we'll see if you talk to me that way again. I will destroy you. And if Sanfilippi wants to destroy you, he has many more ways to do it than I do."

"Are you threatening me? Watch out, Saverio. Watch out, because I also know about you. I know that you're not just a trainer in the gym. And I'm not the only one who knows. In your position I would be very wary of saying 'I'll destroy you' to me. It's better you keep out of sight."

"The night I wanted to talk to you about Annamaria, you threw me out of the house. She was the one you should have been worried about. Instead you acted like an asshole to me, like now, like always."

"Get lost."

Saverio got into his car and drove off with a squeal of tires. When Sauro went back in, Miriam asked him what they had talked about, since Saverio had left without saying goodbye.

Sauro shrugged his shoulders and put his arms around her waist. "I'm tired, Miriam, let's go to bed."

Giulia ran off to Rome on a pretext. On Monday morning she got up early so she could be at the bank the moment it opened, retrieve her diary from the safe deposit box and go to the usual bar. All the mysterious actions she had performed hundreds of times were now coated in a patina of anger and duty. She needed to write a correction, to officially berate herself through the diary.

She sat at the table by the bathrooms, ordered tea with packaged cookies, and started writing with her head held low, like a Fury, her handwriting narrow and nervous.

I ask forgiveness, and I hope that one day I'll be able to pardon myself, even if that seems impossible right now. I tore out the pages in the diary before these ones because they were unbearable even for me. I want to erase that period as if it had been a bad dream. Besides, I've now understood that it was an unhealthy dependence, that I was intoxicated, not in love, but drugged. And yet, I felt so euphoric, so unpredictably full of life. A fictional happiness, indeed, like a heroin high. What happened? A midlife crisis, the longing to feel desired, physical needs repressed for too long? Probably. The fact is that Sauro understood my body's desires so well that I tricked myself, I believed that he'd also understood my soul, that, in all of his coarseness, he'd perceived the truest and most sincere part of me. But it was just a question of skin, something that responds to chemical and physical laws, the scaffolding on which we build castles of sentiment to give meaning to our emotions, or to relationships that seem unjustifiable to us. Is it only us women who do this? Maybe. At the same time, Sauro is right: I wanted to tell him the truth because he was the only person I permitted myself not to lie to. Even if it was a half-truth. I lied to him all the same; if I'd told him what I was truly feeling when I'd lost my mind I would have been humiliated, he would have thought I was crazy. Maybe he would have been right about that, too. I'm crazy, and my life is the quintessence of hypocrisy. Even if I'm right, I still think the same way he does about life. But he does it instinctively, without even knowing—knowledge isn't necessary for someone who isn't used to thinking and who acts on his own instincts. Good for him that he can stay laid-back and thoughtless, life will be easier for him. For people like him, who claim to believe in God while acting in the least ethical way possible, there's confession, absolution, forgiveness of sins, a merciful Madonna like his wife, who always pities your human weaknesses, and who is ready to erase them if you show enough remorse; and then you can start everything up all over again after a little while. Another great advantage that I unfortunately don't possess: faith. Nor the indulgence of my spouse.

I've felt terrible these last months. I struggled not to be consumed by a sense of guilt. I tried to work as hard as I could. I signed up for an aerobics class, I cried almost every night. I tapped all the reserves of my goodwill. I tried to tell myself that I'd always done everything I did with full awareness in my mind of the difference between right and wrong. But maybe in that confused moment, in which the principle that dominated was pleasure, I got confused. On the good side, everyone's first priority is "well-being." Pleasure and enjoying yourself are the imperatives of this era. It seems like they've found the formula, they've made it work. Always keeping in mind that life could end in one hour, tomorrow, in a week, has been enough to make us stop thinking about the future, about the consequences of our *choices, to avoid weighing lost opportunities, because we don't want to lose out on anything; so we do everything, and load each occasion onto the next without letting anything go to waste. It's as though suddenly we all have a hunger for life and for lightness that nobody had before. Maybe we want to make up for the sacrifices of the previous generation, maybe we're bored of politics, maybe we're more afraid of dying than the others had been, and certain that when we do die, we'll leave almost no trace, we surrender ourselves to the nearest, most ephemeral pleasure. We consume, we are consumed. Everything is going so well that we're sure either that we can pay for it, or that it's not that expensive. Maybe someone will pay for it who comes after us, but that doesn't seem very important to us. We're unable to look ahead to the future, we're really in no condition to worry about our children. We're superficial, and we lack any higher goals beyond the infantile satisfaction of our material desires. But it's useless to talk about what will happen to this generic 'us' (into which I can doubtless insert all the adults I know, my so-called friends), in the end, society does nothing more than provide us with an incredibly stupid alibi. In these months, I lost the will to live. My nights were plagued with nightmares, of Annamaria drowning, Sauro drowning, me drowning in the water in front of the Seaside Cowboy, and Filippo at a table, eating, not seeing, not hearing the shouting, not intervening. A dream so didactic that it made me think once again how useless my therapist is. Nobody in the family noticed how I was feeling. Nobody asked me if anything was wrong. Not that I expected my children to worry about me. But Filippo. My god how invisible I am to him. I think that, in the end, that's the sole certainty that remains to me. I don't exist for him. Sauro is right, he's less interested in me than in his horse. I hadn't admitted this, and I think that everything comes from this, my effort to make everything go smoothly, the equilibrium of unhappiness that we had covered over with feigned joy, now has turned on me. The loveless banality of everyday life that you have when you've been together for twenty years seemed to me to be compensated for by our household and all of our comfortable shared routines. Knowing certain people, appreciating sophistication, carving out an area of freedom while always keeping the children's needs in mind, ensuring that they lacked for nothing; that they would dress well and eat better, travel, get jobs that were essentially guaranteed, with a purpose—democracy, the environment, the correct information. It's so easy to look happy when you've got well-being. Still, it's enough to scratch this shiny surface for just one second to see the truth of what we are. People who are petty, egotistical, incapable of any pure, generous gesture, of any impulse that would demand a true sacrifice. I've watched Filippo over these months, while he wasn't watching me. I was transparent, and he was unrecognizable; who knows for how long I hadn't dignified him with real attention either. But now that I've opened my eyes it weighs on me so much. I needed his love, his support, I needed to tell him everything and to know that he was by my side, unconditionally; to know that my mistakes would be treated with the same leniency that I showed his. But I knew that nothing like that would have happened, that I'm just a useful person to run our household with, the children, the business, friends. And that, apart from my role as a support, as wife and mother, I'm nothing to him, nothing but a nuisance, who cries, and grows older. We're strangers to the people we live with. I don't know if I will have the patience to keep going, to keep putting up a good front amid this lovelessness. Over the years, I thought we were heading toward some kind of paradise, only now do I see that, instead, we were headed straight down opposite roads, our backs to each other. It's impossible to turn back now.*

I think I will ask for a divorce and move to another city. I think about all the people I have around me, and I have only one certainty: we are all monsters. Except for Annamaria, but she will also come to nothing, surrounded by so much human and emotional misery. We are all monsters.

* * *

Annamaria had started going secretly to the Garden at least one afternoon a week. She had recognized that talking with Giovanna was much more useful to her than the silence of the library, so she asked her when she could come by without causing trouble, because she'd understood that she might be in the way when the others were working, and above all she did not want to disturb the artist.

Once she had barged in during a meeting, when Niki was going over stock with her workmen. She had run away without saying hello. But later a funny thing happened that had changed everything. On another afternoon she was behind the Sphinx with Giovanna, who was cleaning. She had brought the Madonna cassette *True Blue*, and they had put it on the stereo at low volume. Annamaria had started sweeping and imitating a scene from the meeting between Madonna and her relatives from Abruzzo that had been broadcast on RAI Uno a couple of years earlier, when the singer had come to Torino for a concert, a media event that Annamaria had passionately followed. Annamaria, who would have given almost anything to go to that concert, had been captivated by the family from Aquila who were catapulted into the global pop star's dressing room on the first night, and displayed their ignorance to the entire country, demonstrating that Madonna's genius was a shocking victory over her genes. They were grandchildren of the same grandparents, but the one in front of the microphone was conquering the world, while the others couldn't form a sentence. Annamaria recited all the Abruzzo relatives' lines. She spoke as if she had no teeth. "My name izh Bambina, and I'm Madonna'zh

great aunt, I condradulade her sho sho much on the conshert."
Then she did Madonna, posing for the photo with her Italian
cousins. "How do you say? *Formaggia*?" Madonna wanted to
ask what to say instead of "cheese" to smile in the snapshot,
but they corrected her: "Noooo, *formaggio*."

Once again in an American accent, Annamaria imitated
Madonna inviting her little cousin to dance with her on stage,
then alternated the responses of the little boy and his mother
in different voices.

"Jaseppi, do you want to dance with me? Dance with me,
please, *per favori*?

"Dunno how ta dance."

"Please, come on, dance *con me*?"

"Nooo, dunno dance."

"It's not true, he knows how to dance, he knows how to
dance, when he's alone he puts on the Madonna cassette at top
volume and he dances like a demon around the room."

"No, Mamma, dunno dancin'.'"

Annamaria imitated Madonna who went along with it, saying "Okey-dokey," then followed it up with the interview with
the family, alternating the voices of the journalist and some of
the Abruzzo relatives.

"Amelia, how did you feel when you were face to face with
Madonna?"

"I hugged huh so hahd. I thawt I was dreamin'. She was
supah nice."

"And you Annalisa, which Madonna song do you like
best?"

"Umm. Dunno. They're all good."

"And your favorite, Giuseppe?"

"Umm. Same ones as my sister."

Giovanna was doubled over laughing. "Please, do the
whole scene again from the top, it's stupendous."

"'I thawt I was dreamin'.' That's how I feel when I'm with

Niki . . ." Annamaria said, not realizing that, while this was going on, Niki had walked in, had watched the performance of the whole scene and was highly amused.

"Could you do it again for me, too?" she asked.

Annamaria felt her face blazing; Niki insisted. At that point, Annamaria couldn't say no, and redid the sketch. Niki laughed so much that they all laughed together, then she said to Giovanna, taking her aside, "I beg you, ask this girl to come more often, she's good for my cure."

When the time came to leave, Giovanna took her cousin to the gate, and next to the moped, parked under a mimosa tree, explained: "I haven't ever told you that Niki is taking a laughing cure for her arthritis. It's an absurd thing, a kind of Indian therapy. She says that laughter produces a natural painkiller that works really well. So she makes the people around her laugh. Just like that, for no reason. She turns on a kind of cushion with batteries, which makes terrible artificial laughter, it sounds satanic. I'm incapable of fake laughing. And what's more, when she asks me, it just makes me think about how awful it is that the other cures don't work, which makes me feel even worse, and the worse I feel, the harder it is for me to laugh. For me it's torture. I beg you, come often, and tell her jokes, do your imitations, the things you know how to do, and they really do make people laugh, it would be such a relief for me and also for her . . ."

"Oh my god, but I don't know how to make people laugh on command."

"Yes you do, I'm sure you know how."

"I tell three dirty jokes, I do the imitation of Madonna's cousins, and my repertory is complete." Annamaria paused. "Of course, if the competition is just recorded laughter from a battery-operated pillow . . ."

"You see?"

They hugged. While she breathed in the fresh air on her

moped, Annamaria dedicated a thought of gratitude to Madonna Ciccone and to her relatives, who had a house similar to the one she was returning to, with doilies on the couches, and who gave her so many things to laugh about, including herself.

15. THE DEVIL
Passion. Money. Temptation.

It was spring again. The Seaside Cowboy had reopened on weekends. For the inaugural meal of the season, Sauro and Filippo had organized a giant table for the regulars. Only Giulia was missing, though only Sauro truly missed her: he thought of her much more often than he would have liked. The big table reflected the implicit hierarchy of the power structure. Where you were seated depended on the level of conversation you could maintain between the two heads of table, Sanfilippi and Sauro. To the right of Sanfilippi, Gianmaria Molteni; to his left, the CEO of the national television network, and from there on down were politicians, journalists, lawyers, photographers, screenwriters, filmmakers, until you got to the women, who generally all were to be found at Sauro's end of the table.

Annamaria had been exempted forever from working as a waitress. "That's not your kind of work," her father had said to her one day. "It's a waste of your time."

"Why is it a waste now when it wasn't a year ago?"

"Because you're better now than you were a year ago."

"In what sense?"

"You're older and there's not so much need."

The grandfather had interrupted. "The children of bosses have a seat at the table, and since your father has made himself a boss, sit down and let yourself be served, Annamarì."

In a clumsy attempt to learn something about his daughter, Sauro had also asked her during that conversation, "Is there a boy you like?"

She blushed. "No, I'm not interested in anyone. Besides, I'm sure that if I liked someone he wouldn't like me." Intending to reassure a jealous father, she achieved the opposite effect.

"What are you saying, Annamarì?"

"I'm ugly, Babbo, you can see that, too. You recognize beautiful women, I know. But it's not a problem, you know? I can make people laugh, I'll have a lot of friends."

"What does that have to do with anything. You're pretty, and you're still growing, at your age it doesn't mean anything. You'll see the woman you'll become."

"Babbo, at my age, it's very easy to see the woman I'll become. And I will become an ugly woman." She hadn't expected a response, and she went to her room; it was incongruous for her father to respond that way. He was a man with a very rudimentary understanding of emotional intelligence, and she was in a phase of life in which the heart's rules for what worked and what didn't changed continually. But she knew that in general everything her family said sounded wrong, simplistic, and consoling, if not humiliating. She wasn't her daddy's princess anymore; really, she never had been. She was the daughter he was ashamed of being ashamed of.

At lunch by the sea Sauro was less cheerful than usual. He remained silent while he waited for the meal, paying hardly any attention to the diners who were sitting beside him, who in any case weren't making any effort to involve him in the conversation. They were talking about Gorbachev's book, Gorbachev's mystique, the mark on Gorbachev's forehead as a portent of great global change, the pathetic quality of Raisa Gorbachev's wardrobe. Sauro tried instead to hear what was being said on the other side, having overheard Gianmaria Molteni, who was pontificating about diversity. With his rolling "r"s and a broad smile he was saying, "Not everyone experiences the present in the same way. Here, you not only run into two types of people, two classes, two cultures, two geographies—the country and the city—but above all, two different modes of existence. Here, they live in the past, while we in Rome already live in the future. It's an enormous opportunity for us, to see history up close, but it's an even greater opportunity for them, to stand beside us in the present and, through us, to see the future. They can see what awaits and what to aim for. It's strange that there hasn't been a showdown, or a war, but in a certain sense, they're all already our prisoners."

The others nodded. "If it's a war of words, I know they don't have a prayer, Gianmaria. You're a heavyweight. Nobody would dare get into the ring with you. In your presence we're all featherweights," said Sanfilippi.

Gianmaria responded, "Look who's talking, you're the alchemist who holds the philosopher's stone in your hand. With that, you have the power to transform any human relationship into the gold of classism, without anyone being the wiser."

They laughed together. From the other end of the table, Sauro called the waitress to bring the second course and poured wine for the lady on his right, Chiara, Giulia's best friend, a screenwriter of modest success, whom Sauro always introduced as a set designer. He turned the cigar in his mouth. He bit it. He felt ill at ease. "What the fuck," he thought. "All of these weaklings and fatsos in glasses, and not one of them would want to get into the ring *with me.*" He clenched a fist to flex one of his biceps in his jacket. He told himself that with this fist, the King had once knocked a horse to the ground, punching it on the forehead.

He turned his wrist to look at his stainless steel Patek Philippe. It was almost two o'clock, the sun still made you squint; the yellow paper placemat on the table, greasy with oil and torn at the corners, was scattered with crumbs of unsalted bread. Sauro remembered how Giulia would tear little strips from the placemats during every meal, rolling them into little coils. By the end of the meal she would have made dozens, and her place at the table was always recognizable. As he waited for his salt-crusted sea bream, Sauro felt a strange impatience, a sense of discomfort that he rarely felt and couldn't define. He got up abruptly to go join Miriam in the kitchen, where he found her giving orders in an aggressive manner. She turned toward him, sighing. "Teaching people to work is harder than working," she told him. The sous-chef turned toward her brusquely with an arch expression that looked like a go-to-hell, but since he said nothing there were no consequences, except for the certainty that afterwards he would do nothing but trash talk Miriam with all the others. She could already hear it: "If it weren't for Sauro, who's always nice and generous, it would be such a pain to work here." Sauro gave Miriam a hug, took her chef's hat off her head, and tenderly led her out of the kitchens. He needed to hear from someone who was on his side, he needed a benevolent assessment of himself, and knew he could only find it in his wife.

"What is it?" she asked.

"Nothing."

"What do you mean nothing? You call me from the kitchens for a 'nothing' when we have thirty-five second courses and their sides on order?"

He gave her a kiss on the forehead.

"I just wanted to tell you that you're still the most beautiful of them all."

She smiled.

"Have you been drinking or is there someone at the table who you like but not enough?"

"I like you."

She smiled, took the cap from his hand and stood up lightly on her tiptoes to kiss him on the mouth.

"Go sit down, go on, that's better." And she returned to the kitchen with her chest all warm and a childish contentment. She needed so little.

He took two more bottles of Morellino and uncorked them before returning to the table. One of the corks broke in half, and he pushed it regretfully into the wine.

Before dessert, Sauro, who was once again on his feet, wrangling bottles, saw a blue Fiat Uno police car in the distance, parking next to the Mercedes that belonged to Giuliani, the short, hairy lawyer who was always making speeches that were so old-fashioned and retrograde that Annamaria had nicknamed him Dirty Old World, which was what everyone now called him behind his back.

The marshal came out, alone.

This was not a good sign: it meant that this wasn't a passing patrol visit, as often occurred; he'd come for a particular purpose.

Sauro carried the bottles to the table and went up to meet him before he came onto the terrace. The police, what a nuisance and what a false note, their uniforms of linen and coarse silk. They knew each other well, they addressed each other informally.

Sauro gave the marshal his hand and with the other slapped him on the shoulder.

"Giuseppe, what are you doing in these parts? Everything's in order with our permits, right? We're not due for an inspection."

The marshal withdrew his hand and gave him a fake smile that was not necessary. He assumed a rigid and serious pose; he could control everything, but not his Neapolitan accent.

"Sauro, I don't want to disturb you, and I see that you have people here. But I need to tell you something important before you hear it from someone else. My colleagues in Albinia have arrested Saverio, your son."

Sauro turned pale.

"What the fuck did he do?"

"Barbiturates and other hard drugs. Significant quantities, for distribution, not for personal use."

"Thank you, Giuseppe, thanks so much for coming to tell me this in person. You'll see that they've made a mistake, we'll clear everything up."

"Sauro, they haven't made a mistake. There were three boxes in his car. And it's impossible that he didn't know what he was transporting because he had hidden it well, in the spare tire well. Don't count on error. Better for you to call a good lawyer as soon as you can."

Sauro went back to the table, his hands shaking. He looked at his fellow diners without hearing their words. He tried to smile, nodded, kept pouring wine and chewing on his cigar, inhaled. Time seemed to stand still, the courses continued to arrive on the table, Chiara had begun to write on her placemat, making strange notes around the grease spots. He saw Luca Sanfilippi, the same age as Saverio, next to a movie producer, his destiny already on the table. While talking with the producer, Luca was looking past him, because the CEO of RAI was behind him, with whom he would have been even more eager to chat. His eyes were always and only aimed at whoever could benefit him. A born opportunist. Whereas Saverio, on the other hand. It wouldn't have been such a bad thing either, his impending fate; he needed to become more diplomatic and to put in a certain amount of effort, to work on being nice to people, the way Sauro had done. His son was an asshole. He had raised an asshole without a scrap of gratitude. He couldn't wait for everyone to be gone, so he could tell Miriam, *they've arrested your son for dealing drugs, now try to tell me the poor kid is such a good boy*. Because it was clear, if there was anyone who had spoiled Saverio, sparing him any notion of effort and work, it was his mother. When the mascarpone mousse arrived at the table, Sauro had to raise his eyes and look at the sea, breathing deeply, to smell the brackishness in his nostrils, hoping the urge to vomit that was rising in his gorge would subside. He lowered his gaze, it fell again on Luca, in his light-blue shirt with the numbers on it, a salmon-colored sweater thrown over his shoulders, laughing at the jokes of the man beside him, repeating over and over, "You're a titan, you're a titan. And as the mythic Molteni says, life isn't worth living if you don't live it in the most extravagant luxury."

The screenwriter asked Sauro, "Do you feel all right? You look pale."

Sauro revived. "I have a slight headache. It must be all that sparkling water."

He closed his eyes and breathed. He tried to think of the last time he'd felt happy. It seemed to him that it had been a long time ago, in Giulia's arms, that bitch who was always right. His life and his family's life were even worse than she'd described them. She was bad luck. He began to think that Saverio's arrest was her fault, that maybe she'd been the one who reported him, to punish him. His mind was spinning out of control, he blamed it on the wine. It wasn't the first time he'd had obsessive thoughts when he was drunk. To distract himself he mentally said a Hail Mary.

While the diners were leaving, a few at a time, the sun was veiled with a mesh of orange clouds and then disappeared. After he'd said goodbye to everyone, Sauro rushed into the kitchen to Miriam. He called her outside and gave her the news, but as soon as she raised her voice, he turned his back on her. "We'll talk about it at home," he said, adding: "Come immediately. I don't want scenes in front of all the people."

Once they were home, they would be free to shout, to hurl mutual accusations at each other: a mother who had spoiled her son versus a father who had denigrated him, insulted him, diminished him, and left him on his own. The grandfather was drunk, he laughed and repeated his stock anecdote about his grandson. "Saverio? I've known it since he was little—that one hunts for death like an old snake. I would have put my hand in the fire when he was five years old and sworn that sooner or later he'd end up in jail!"

"As far as I'm concerned, it could only do him good to spend a year in there," Sauro added.

Miriam burst into tears: "You're a breed of men who have no heart, no heart, and no hope! How can you talk like that? We have to help him, and immediately." She shouted again: "And immediately means immediately!"

Annamaria, silent until that moment, had gone up to her mother and passed her a piece of paper with a phone number on it. She'd said that Saverio had called some time before, leaving it for her. He had warned her, "Give it to Mamma and to no one else."

Miriam had taken the number and called it without knowing who she would find at the other end of the line: police headquarters? The prison? The police? Andrea from the gym?

A female voice answered.

"Hello . . . I'm Saverio's mother."

"Who are you calling for?"

"I don't know . . . Saverio left me this number and said to call."

She learned that the girl on the other end of the line was named Barbara and was a lawyer.

The exchange was quick, Barbara knew everything, she'd also been able to talk briefly with Saverio. She knew that the quantity that was found was fairly substantial and risked a very high sentence. She was worried, even though Saverio was a first-time offender. She'd said that Saverio wanted her to be his lawyer. Miriam asked her how old she was, then hung up, after saying she would call her back very soon. She didn't. She was thirty years old. Too young.

She turned to Sauro, whose eyes were red and whose breathing was labored.

"I'm sorry, Sauro. Let's try to calm down. We lose our tempers over nothing, but we simply have to reflect and to take action; it makes sense that you would be angry and that I would be beside myself, but you know that as parents we want to be useful. This time, at least, we have to act for the best."

She tried to hug him; at first he drew back, but then he let himself be embraced. He stayed in her arms two seconds then raised his head. "Miriam, I think I'm going to throw up."

He went to the bathroom. When he came out, she called him into the kitchen for a cup of chamomile tea. Sauro said he was going to go lie down for a moment. She rejoined him in the bedroom with the tray and the cup and sat down on the side of the bed. His eyes were closed. They stayed like that for a minute, not moving.

Then Miriam resumed the discussion.

"You know, we can do something. What are all those important friends for if they can't help us at a time like this?"

"No fairy tales, Miriam, what kind of question is that?"

"The question is, what were we licking the asses of all those powerful people for if, when we need them, they won't give us a hand? Your partner is a deputy, thick as thieves with a load of magistrates. Can't we think about asking for his help at a difficult moment?"

Sauro sat up in bed.

"Who licked whose ass? Make me understand."

"You, we, have fawned over your parliamentary friends, lawyers, even judges, dozens and dozens of times. What for? Explain it to me, for what? Disinterested friendship? Maybe on their part, yes, given that they found themselves spoon-fed in a beautiful place like ours. But us? What have they done for us? What do we get from these people? I see how they look at me, you know? At most they feel a little pity for me."

"Pity? What are you saying? It's work, Miriam."

"Unpaid work is not work."

"Unpaid? What are you talking about?"

"About my work, of the hundreds of meals cooked *for the sake of friendship*, out of *love for you*."

"Again this talk of free meals! You might as well include the ones you cooked for the children, I suppose. Do you want us to tally those up, too? Of the baby food pureed and the diapers changed? Because if that's what you want, say so. There's no such thing as love, there's no such thing as friendship, unpaid work is all there is. But I can tell you, the reality is that the people you're talking about pay. And pay well, too."

"What in the hell does what I do for the children have to do with it? You know very well what I'm talking about. And let me tell you something: everything I do, I do for the children. And if you, on the other hand, are not interested in their lives or their futures, then tell me once and for all, and I'll deal with it on my own."

Sauro screamed, "You'll deal with it on your own, will you? To ask favors to save the ass of a delinquent son? A fine example of a mother you set. Know that they will never do a favor for you, because you don't count for shit, Miriam! You should go back to the kitchen before you really make me furious."

Miriam threw the tray with the chamomile tea to the floor. The cup shattered, and the boiling liquid spread across the tiles. She left the room with the keys of the minivan.

Sauro didn't stop her; he was sure she would go to Grosseto to try to find Saverio at the jailhouse.

Miriam breathed in the damp night air. She turned on the engine at once, but she lingered a while to collect herself. She needed to catch her breath. The night was very dark. She was going to Filippo Sanfilippi's house.

She found him there, surrounded by the accoutrements of a man who's enjoying the solitude of his country house: a fire in the fireplace, jazz on the turntable, an armchair, whiskey, a cigar.

Surprised by the visit, he made Miriam welcome and instantly brought her a glass of water, seeing that she was distraught. He was almost certain that it had to do with a discovery of infidelity; he would have to defend his friend and deny being in on whatever affair it was, which up to then he had always concealed without remorse.

"Excuse me for barging into your house like this, but I need to talk to you about something pretty urgent."

Filippo decided the best strategy would be to offer a solution before the problem was revealed. "If it's about Sauro, Miriam, I must tell you one thing. He loves you. A lot. There's no argument. He might have made mistakes, of course, he's not a perfect man, none of us is. He might be a dick sometimes, you know that better than I do, but I can assure you that he would never, never do you wrong, or . . ."

Miriam trembled; she no longer even tried to control her manner of speaking, as she'd always done in front of the Sanfilippis.

"Shut up, right now. The problem isn't how much he loves me. And I don't even care, sincerely. I've lost count of how many years it's been that I've known that he cheats on me . . . I don't even want to think about it. 'He loves you he loves you' . . . yeah, he loves me, that bastard. But the problem isn't me. The problem is that he doesn't love his son. Saverio is in a mess now and he doesn't want to help him, do you understand?"

"In a mess? Does he need money?"

"No, Filì, we've got money. He's been arrested. Something to do with medicine, illegal medicine, some kind of drugs."

"Dealing? But when?"

"We found out a few hours ago, I think it happened in the early afternoon."

"Shit, but what in hell was he thinking, with all the advantages he has here . . ."

"If only Sauro had given him a chance."

"It seems to me that he was the one who didn't want that."

"Filì, dammit, let's not have a trial now over who could do what, and who wanted what. I need your help, *now*."

"But in what sense?"

"In the sense that you know everyone, you know how to make things happen, you even go sailing with the police chief. I know that with one phone call from you, Saverio would find himself free and with a clean criminal record."

"Miriam, calm down, you're too agitated. Let's wait to find out the charges first, then I'll put you in contact with the lawyer Giuliani, he's the best, have you met him? That short guy . . . he's even got mafiosos acquitted, he'd be able to make Bokassa look innocent. Hopefully it wouldn't take much for him to sort out Saverio. I've heard that for first-time offenders there's some leniency. Now, try to stay calm and we'll talk to him in the morning."

"Filì, you haven't understood me. That Giuliani? That man will ruin us all; if we call him, in two hours even my aunt will know what happened. I don't want there to be a lawsuit, I want this gotten rid of and erased. And it should be clear that I'm ready to pay whatever is needed."

"Miriam, maybe you're forgetting the fact that I'm a politician, and putting pressure on a police chief is just not something I can do. At the very least that would be undue influence; if there's money involved, it's bribery. You know how much I care for you, and Sauro, and also for Saverio, but understand me. I can't. My position does not permit me." He lowered his eyelids and dragged deeply on his cigar. It was a moment in which he could flex his personal power, and it gave him enormous satisfaction.

"Listen, Filippo: in my opinion, you're making it more

complicated than it is. It seems to me that you can do much, much more than that."

"Darling, thank you for your high opinion of me, but I'm not a big shot, you know," he said with little conviction. "I've never done anything illegal, and to put my position and reputation at risk for the shit your son has gotten himself in would be bad for me in a lot of ways."

"Tell me you wouldn't do it for Luca."

"That's different, and Luca would never get into shit like this."

"Because he will never need to. Your son will always have a smooth path."

"Maybe because we raised him well?"

"Maybe because that was guaranteed from the moment his ass was born, let's say."

"Listen, Miriam, if you want a favor from me, it would be wise to ask me in a different manner, and not to make me feel like the privileged, unjust man that I am not. The last thing we need is for you to lecture me while you're asking me to corrupt someone."

Miriam lowered her eyes, more convinced than ever that the Sanfilippis were assholes. But it was clear to her that she was taking the wrong tack.

"Forgive me, Filì, forgive me. I'm very distraught. And I need to resolve this situation as soon as possible. In the meantime, the news of the arrest must not get out, OK? I know that the first thing journalists do is call police headquarters. This thing must not get into the papers. And that's also in your interest, if it gets out in a headline like they do, tomorrow at the newsstand we'll see: *Son of local noted businessman arrested for drug dealing*. And the name that will appear right after ours, as business partner, will be yours."

Miriam lit a cigarette. She leaned her head against the back of the armchair. The same one where Sauro had leaned back in desperation in front of Giulia. She had a disturbed and sensual air. Filippo had always found her attractive. He knew that at this moment he could have asked her anything. He chose the thing that interested him most.

He told her, "I'll call the editors of the local papers, *Il Tirreno* and *La Nazione*, I know them both very well. We'll invite the two of them to lunch, immediately," and disappeared into his study.

Miriam finished her cigarette. She was happy with what he was doing. She thought that, deep down, Sanfilippi was an idiot, too, and that she'd only have to push a little more on the subject of his reputation as a partner to get him to call the police chief, too.

Filippo knew he was in a strongly advantageous position. All he had to do in this game was to hide the fact that he had a knife up his sleeve. He had just needed to make Miriam understand how risky it was to brandish the blade that way.

He returned to her in ten minutes. Ten minutes in which Miriam had lit another cigarette and was standing and smoking it by the window.

"I've neutralized the papers, for the moment. Shit, Miriam, you don't know how much it cost me to make that call. And I hope that my phone here in the country isn't tapped, otherwise we're all in deep shit."

"Thank you, Filippo, I can't thank you enough. And I have an idea. Remember that fifty percent of the shares of the Seaside Cowboy are in my name, and I can do anything I want with them. If you can get the complaint against my son erased, if you do it cleanly, as if it had never happened, I'll give them to you. All of them. And Sauro doesn't even need to know."

"Miriam, no. I can't. You don't know what you're saying."

"I know very well what I'm saying. I know that you're taking a risk. And I'm prepared to pay you for it."

Filippo looked into her eyes. They were reddened, it made

the blue stand out even more. Miriam had the melancholy expression of all women who've been married for many years. He thought he should tell Lisa to never get married.

"Miriam, really. I want to help you, but you're suggesting something improper and dishonest. And I'm not saying this on my own behalf. I know that, as a politician, my reputation is already compromised, by definition. To the public we're all corrupt thieves, right? Regardless of our actions. But that's something I can't do, I consider Sauro one of my best friends. I can't make a decision like that without consulting him. First off, the restaurant is his. It was his idea."

"At the same time, that's not true, because, in fact, the restaurant is *ours*. And our son is his, too. And I can't bear the fact that a father wouldn't do something for the good of his child. I can put up with everything Sauro does, and you know very well how many things I close an eye to, not one eye but both eyes. I'm blind to him. But not when it comes to the children . . . I can accept that he isn't a good husband, but not that he isn't a good father."

She started crying again.

"Sauro *is* a good father," Filippo soothed her.

"I don't know how you can say that. He's a father who kicked his son out of the house."

"Pardon me, but actually this situation makes me think that he *is* a good father; he insists, fairly, that Saverio should pay for his mistakes. You, on the other hand, seem to me to be a loving mother, certainly, but maybe over-protective. Not only do you want your son to pay no price for his mistakes, but you're asking me to help you erase them."

Sanfilippi lowered his eyelids partway, feeling a satisfaction whose source he could not identify. If he'd been self-aware, he would have known that it came from self-congratulation for his ability to direct the game, his way of controlling every situation by placing himself in a position of unassailable reason.

"Filì, Saverio wouldn't have made those mistakes if his father had lent him a hand, if he had guided him, if he had made him work with us, if he hadn't criticized every one of his choices, only to kick him out of the house telling him he was a disgrace, an asshole, making him feel worthless. Saverio is only twenty years old, he's gotten into trouble because he listened to the wrong people, that moron, his friend at the gym. We are respectable people . . ." Her voice grew fainter, as if these words didn't really want to come out. "Nothing . . . nothing would have happened if Sauro had loved Saverio more . . . nothing would have happened."

Filippo embraced her. She let her head fall on his shoulder, as if she might fall asleep in that position. He held her there, putting up with the smell of the kitchen in her hair, putting up with the pity that she provoked in him, which made him want to push her away. He broke away after a few seconds that seemed interminable to him.

"Listen, Miriam, I want to help you. But this thing has a cost, do you understand? A cost that is very high for me, for the risk I'm running in getting involved, and a real cost to the people who'll find their jobs at risk, in turn. Don't think this is a cakewalk for anybody. I'll have to compensate the people involved, and well. Among them will be the chief of police, who in turn will have to ask the court clerk, or work out a solution with the cops who arrested him. To fake a procedural error, to rewrite the report. In which case, we'll have to implicate someone else in Saverio's place, which yes, we can do, but it will be hard. Don't think that a parliamentarian is omnipotent. Far from it. And judicial affairs are very complicated, they involve a lot of people, at various levels. To make testimony disappear, evidence that's already been collected . . . the stuff in his car will have been seized, and will already be registered and on the record, sent to the laboratory for analysis, kept in the court clerk's office. In short, we are getting into a real shitshow."

"I'm sorry, Filippo, I'm so sorry. Let's do this. Let's make it so you're not doing this for me, and not even for Sauro, or for Saverio, but for your son. Let's make it so that, once this has been done and settled, I sign over my shares of the restaurant to Luca. He will become your partner, you will sign over the remaining shares to him, for his future. The restaurant will become yours, Sauro and I will continue to work there, but you will be the bosses. Do you think we can do that?"

"I can do that for you only if Sauro agrees. And if I can leave him at least ten percent of the shares. The Seaside Cowboy is his baby."

"Saverio is his baby, too."

"I know. And I get you. I also get that you can't really talk with him about this, right? You've been arguing, I imagine."

"How did you guess?"

"So, Miriam, do something for me. Go home and try to calm him down. Make peace somehow. I will call the chief of police immediately and then I'll call Sauro, I'll tell him that you came here, I'll reason with him. You and I have a plan for the future of our children, that will be enough to make him understand, to make him agree with us. I'm sure that everything will go fine. You've just got to trust me."

"There's nobody I could trust more, Filì. Truly."

"Five million lira in cash would help, for a start."

"I'll bring it to you tomorrow morning."

"No later than seven thirty. I'll let you know what the chief of police and Sauro and I have talked about. Then we'll go forward. We'll deal with the notary calmly."

"And you have to trust me, too, I've given you my word on the shares."

"There's nobody I could trust more," he repeated to her, smiling.

Miriam put on her coat and scarf and left. A damp wind came from the sea. The dim lights from the house, the distant lamppost, filled her with infinite sadness, a sadness that was a prison.

She thought of Saverio—he must have been feeling that way, too. She quickly got into the car and prayed that the night would be over quickly, that everything would be over quickly, and there would be a new day.

Annamaria couldn't sleep all night, trying to understand how something like this could have happened; she had heard her parents fighting furiously, her father saying terrible things about Saverio, she'd realized that Saverio had gotten caught up in some kind of mess, but she couldn't figure out exactly what; Sauro had sent her to her room and shouted at her not to break his balls, that they'd already had enough trouble. She had found out about the arrest from her grandfather, who had told her about it, sniggering and repeating the joke that he'd been asking for it since he was a tyke, that he'd always known that sooner or later that good-for-nothing was bound for jail.

In the morning, when the alarm rang at six o'clock her eyes were already open. She got ready and went to the kitchen, where she found Miriam at the table smoking, her eyes swollen from crying.

"Mamma, everything will turn out all right, nobody's dead."

"Not quite. Your father says that Saverio is dead to him, can you believe it?"

"You know Babbo always exaggerates when he talks, but he's not a bad guy, really. It just takes him longer to digest things. And Saverio isn't a bad guy, either. They're both assholes, sort of, but look, you don't go to prison if you haven't done anything wrong. At the most they'll give him a little bit of house arrest, which means you'll be stuck with him here at home for a few months. That's not so terrible, is it?"

"He can't be under the same roof with Sauro. But why has

this happened to us? Why? We've always been upstanding people, respectable. We have a reputation in the village."

"In my opinion you're making too much of this. It's the gym that gave him the pills that's responsible, not him. He just has to prove it."

Miriam kept shaking her head. Annamaria poured milk into her cup and added some coffee from the coffeemaker that had already grown cold. She threw in a couple of biscotti and dug in with her spoon without looking at her mother, to whom, with her mouth full of a last bite of biscotti, she said, "Oh, I've got to get going or I'll miss the bus." She got no answer.

She grabbed her jacket, her backpack and started off on her moped for the bus stop, which should have taken her to school, but instead of stopping and locking her moped to the post with a chain as she usually did, she turned left and took the Aurelia in the opposite direction. She found herself in front of the gate to the Garden at 7 A.M.; the building site was closed, and motionless in the frost. Tools all over the place, cement mixers, plastic sheeting, and the sound of dogs barking seemed to have neutralized any magic. She wondered if it was only human presence that gave meaning and beauty to constructed places. Nature is full of significance all on its own. Artificial places, no; art needs someone to observe it. She wondered how long she would have to wait for Giovanna to arrive and to see Niki, and wondered if she would ever again find the magic that seemed to have disappeared behind the gate on this damp morning bereft of poetry. She had gotten so cold on the moped, and there was no place to sit down in the parking lot. She decided to go to the bar around the bend, where she had gone with Saverio the day of the accident. She was sure it would be open: shepherds, farmers, mushroom gatherers, and hunters always got up early even when hunting season was over. She knew she would have to explain her presence there, this bothered her, but she had no alternative.

She had just gone in when she met Decimo, the man who had baptized Sauro on his first hunt with the blood of the wild boar that had just been gutted. At home they had a photo in which you could see an enormous boar in the background, hanging by its trotters; in front were four hunters on their knees with a shotgun in one hand and dogs' leashes in the other. Sauro, sixteen, was standing in the middle with his face daubed with blood and with a smile that could not conceal his grimace of disgust. Annamaria was happy that the photo was in black and white so you couldn't see the real color of the stuff her father had on his face—it might have been mud. "Cavemen," she thought, as she greeted Decimo, his companion, and the barista, all of them dressed in military green.

Decimo did not let her get away without a scolding. "Shouldn't you be in school, young lady? What are you doing in these parts at this hour? I'll tell your father when I see him."

"Go ahead and tell him. I'm here because I have to do research on the Tarot Garden for my design class, and I have an appointment with the artist in a little while."

"What a pigsty. What do they have you studying at school? What are you going to do with that? If I were your mamma I'd teach you to cook and clean, and leave art to the artists."

Annamaria turned red and responded, "Where did you leave your club, Decimo?"

He didn't understand and answered, "My wife isn't named Clara, her name is Assunta, and she's where women should be, at home."

Annamaria suppressed a laugh and responded, "What home? In a cave, more like." But then she felt like an imbecile for having answered him at all. She asked for a tea with lemon, and sat down at the table farthest away, unaware that this was something Giulia would do, Giulia, who in her mind now was identified as "the traitor."

To keep anyone else from coming up to talk to her, she

pulled Dante's *Inferno* out of her backpack. It was the one in which he was badmouthing her region. Describing the forest of the suicides, Dante wanted to put across the idea of a place so inhospitable and wild that it was even worse than the Maremma.

> Not foliage green, but of a dusky color,
> Not branches smooth, but gnarled and intertangled,
> Not apple-trees were there, but thorns with poison.
>
> Such tangled thickets have not, nor so dense,
> Those savage wild-beasts, that in hatred hold
> 'Twixt Cecina and Corneto the tilled places.

She took her notebook and wrote: "There were no green fronds, they were dark in color, no straight branches but knotted and contorted, no fruit, but sticks with poisonous thorns. Even the wild beasts who take refuge far from cultivated land get stuck in the dense underbrush of the woods in the Maremma."

In the comment that she added to her paraphrase, she wrote something banal copied from the curator's note, even though what this canto brought to mind was a thought directed at those who did not know the place where she was born and raised. Did the people who came here on vacation ever realize that the Maremma was so horrifying that Dante used it to describe a forest in the *Inferno*? Who knew if the intelligentsia were aware that, almost seven hundred years after the brilliant Tuscan wrote his *Divine Comedy*, there were so many men like Decimo in this land, who didn't even speak proper Italian, and who flayed the wild boars they'd hunted, using their hot blood to baptize new hunters, making their wives who were waiting for them at home cook the meat. Had anything changed? They had beautified the land, but the inhabitants could still make the place evoke the *Inferno*.

She was filled with agonizing thoughts, and the stench of the cigars and the suspicious and judgmental looks of the old men drove her out into the open air. Even if Giovanna wasn't there yet, she would go sit on a rock in front of the Garden and cry over her own damned business. She watched the clouds passing swiftly and continued her string of reflections about herself, about the village she lived in, her father, her mother, her brother, the people who rode their horses. She wouldn't come to the rescue of anyone but the beasts, and maybe Giovanna and Niki, but who knew if they would rescue her. When Giovanna got out of her beat-up Panda, Annamaria recognized from her face that seeing her there had alarmed her. She hurried to tell her, "Nothing has happened, nothing serious," but as she was saying that, she could no longer hold back the tears that had made her pinch her nose the whole time she'd been at the bar.

Giovanna immediately let her in and took her straight to the belly of the Sphinx.

"What happened? Tell me."

"Nothing, and it's . . . another fight between my father and my brother. I hear that Saverio has screwed up again, I don't know. And then Babbo got enraged at him, and Mamma got enraged at Babbo, and I'm always in the middle, and I feel like nobody loves me, everyone expects me to be the peacemaker and that's it, but they don't know what's going on with me inside, and none of them cares at all."

Giovanna made her sit down and brought her a glass of water. Niki was coming down the mirrored steps.

"Oh, the laughing girl is crying today. Why?"

Giovanna hurried to answer her. "It's nothing, Niki, don't worry, a family crisis. Nothing serious . . . as a rule, parents get to an age when it would be better not to have them."

"Ah, I understood from the first that this girl sees in you a younger and more understanding mother, Giovanna," Niki said as she slowly descended the stairs to the bathroom.

Giovanna took advantage of her absence to say to Annamaria, "See what she's like? Incredible, she can't fry an egg, she would give blank checks to the first workman who passed, but she's got such incredible intuition. She always seems to be in the clouds, but she can see what's in people's hearts on the fly. She's crazy and magical."

Annamaria blew her nose, producing a tragic echo in the belly of the Sphinx that made her laugh.

When Niki came out of the bath, she told the girls that if they had a little time, she would tell them a story that would make them return to their fathers' houses thinking they were very fortunate daughters.

She adjusted her robe and asked Giovanna to make her some tea. Then she began.

"It was the summer of the snakes. I was eleven, but I had grown a lot over the last year. For summer vacation my parents had rented a pretty house in the country, in New England. It was me and my siblings, and other friends and cousins often came to see us. It was hot, and invisible, disturbing creatures lurked in the tall grass. All the same, this was still the open air. I went out early in the mornings and often went on my own up the paths beside the house, I liked to study the effect of the sun on things, to look at the shadows that changed shape and color depending on the hour of day. It was on one of those mornings, when it was getting late and the sun was already high, that I saw two snakes intertwined on a rock beside me. They were two black snakes, poisonous, which they had warned all of us about at the house. I was paralyzed, I could neither move nor breathe. For the first time, I was seeing death up close. The serpents were mating. What was this for them, a dance of death, or of life? Would it be death for me and life for them? I was enthralled. Everything was there. Perhaps my whole life in some way is contained in that moment, when two opposites took meaning in the form of a distillation of fear. There was movement, stasis, growth, sex, life, and death; life that reproduces itself, the dance and the terror.

"A few nights later I found one of those black snakes in my bed sheets. My brother John had hidden it there to scare me. I began to scream so loudly that my cousin Jean-Charles, who was twenty-two at the time, came in from the next room. He took the snake, which obviously was already dead, and threw it out the window. I was so scared that I asked him to let me sleep with him, and Jean-Charles let me stay in his bed all night. The next day my parents found out about it and were infuriated. I didn't understand why, they made me see wickedness where there hadn't been any. Their strict religiosity led them to see evil everywhere, and to suspect that I might already be a nasty girl, ready to jump into men's beds and tempt them. They made me feel dirty, when I had just been afraid and in need of protection. I looked older than my age, and they made me feel like that was a sin. Perhaps it was this incident that planted a sick thought in my father's head. I provoked his disapproval. His desire. And he had the absolute power of an adult over a child, of a father over a daughter.

"A few days later my father took me into the tool shed—he had asked me to come with him to look for the fishing pole. Once we were in the shed, his hands began to explore my body in a way they had never done before. That afternoon the aristocratic and ultra-religious banker André Marie Fal de Saint Phalle put his penis in my mouth. He told me not to move, but I was already completely paralyzed. That moment completely changed my life. From that point on, shame, anguish, and fear have never left me. The man who was supposed to protect me and love me had transformed into a monster who was violating me. I loved him and felt that he loved me too, I understood that this was something that was completely beyond his control, that it dominated him, but I could not distinguish the borders between feelings anymore. I knew nothing about sex, but I knew it was not right for me to learn it from him. That man destroyed everything, he transformed the love I felt for him to contempt. He destroyed my faith in human beings forever. He tied my physical pleasure to a sense of shame. My father left me to bear the whole burden of the incest on my own. The whole burden of something I didn't understand, but which I knew was wrong, and for which I felt responsible in some way. To survive a trauma of this kind at that age, the only thing I was capable of doing was to close off the episode in a corner of my memory and forget it. To delete it. Until, twelve years later, when I had just gotten out of a psychiatric clinic for a breakdown, my father wrote me a letter in which he asked for my forgiveness. My psychiatrist refused to believe that confession. I didn't speak to my father again, and now that he's dead, I suppose I've forgiven him, but the trauma has continued to work, ever since, and for always. Traumas cannot be erased. If you're strong you can hide them under a mask. A mask behind which at length you start to suffocate. All of my monsters were born in that moment. For years I had nervous tics. I kept on biting my lip, I did it until I bit it all the way through. My rebellious gestures. My nightmares. My capacity for isolating myself and living in an imaginary world, disconnected from the real. The magic box I played with by myself, alienating me from everything. The collapses. The obsessions. The time I got kicked out of school; the other time, when I was fourteen years old, when, still knowing nothing of sex, I wrote a pornographic story and circulated it among the girls at the high school. The weapons that I always carried with me. My suicidal impulses. My scattered studies, my rebellion against the nuns at the religious school, the marriage at nineteen, the rage at the works I created, shooting them, building enormous women . . . everything. Every one of my choices comes from that moment. My Nanas, which reassert feminine power at a size in which they can't be crushed . . . my autobiographical film *Daddy*, in which I killed my father seventeen times, my inability to be a good mother, all the way on to this inordinate ambition which has led me to build the largest sculptures a woman has ever created, sculptures that are also monsters . . . All, all of this is part of that, of the summer of the snakes."

At this point, Niki looked into Annamaria's eyes.

"I don't know why I'm telling you this; I told my daughter fifty years later, in a letter. Now I'm telling you, and not because I want to share lurid details, I'm sorry to upset you, but you're old enough to understand. And without knowing this, you cannot know anything about me, you cannot make sense of anything I tell you, but most of all, you cannot make sense of anything I've created. And I also want to tell you that the pain you feel now, the things that have hurt you so badly that you think they'll always hurt, maybe they will, but they are part of your story. You can transform them, reshape them, enlarge them, until they emerge from you to make something great, if you want. Because I'm certain that you can. It's something that's visible, you know? I know how to see things and people; I see that you feel that you are bad. But I know that you are not. Someone more grown up and more responsible than you has made mistakes, and it's not fair that you are paying for it. But you can try to defend yourself. You know how to make people laugh, and you know how to laugh at yourself; you can become an actress and laugh as you talk about all the things that hurt you. Transform the mistake into what you are, a marvel, unique in the world."

During the confession, Annamaria had barely breathed. Only when Niki fell silent, as if the silence had suddenly restored her vital functions, did she notice that her heart was beating wildly in her chest; she also felt it in her throat and her temples. She swallowed, and two tears fell on the table of mirrors with a noise of heavy drops. Her reflection, Giovanna's, and Niki's became unrecognizable, reassembled in a thousand fragments on the mirrored ceiling, as if pain had broken them into pieces and the light of truth had done what it could to put them back together, without succeeding. She felt overwhelmed yet also invaded by a strange, comforting heat. She was nestled in the belly of the Empress, and there and only there, with these two women beside her, she was sure that nothing bad could happen. Niki said to her, "Good for you for crying, tears are good for you, they wash away ugly things. But this is the last time, because you come here to laugh, don't forget."

She would never forget.

16. THE TOWER
Opening. Construction.
Emergence of that which is hidden.

A
nnamaria had returned home at the normal time for a school day. Nobody paid attention to her. There was a serving of lukewarm, overcooked pasta on the table, covered by a plate. She ate it distractedly and went straight to her room, eager to think over that morning, in which somebody else's anguish had been superimposed on hers. It felt like she was still marked by it: the deep circles under her eyes marking her face like wreaths left over from a celebration that had ended, her clumsiness accentuated, as if the burden of what she had learned were reflected in her uncoordinated steps. She felt like she needed to lie down on the ground and try to make sense of everything she was feeling. There was something new inside her. To passively experience someone else's pain and trauma, other people's sins, other people's fights, was to take part in them completely. She absorbed all of it. She wanted to find a way to become less permeable. Her most private thoughts about herself and her family, about Niki's story that had shaken her so much, were interrupted at intervals by the sounds of her grandfather, the toilet flushing, his house shoes clomping, hawking into his handkerchief. She had to break her train of thought to shout at him to turn down the television. It seemed to her that something comic, prosaic, and tangible always came along to disturb the roiling of her unquiet mind whenever she was trying to make sense of what was happening to her. Maybe that was part of her, too. She struggled for understanding, but she always ended up listening

to that grotesque voice that pushed her thoughts to the side, overlaying her pain with the irresistible urge to laugh at herself. A ridiculous girl, that's what she was.

Miriam wasn't there. After Annamaria had left, early in the morning, she had gotten dressed and returned to Sanfilippi's house. She thought he'd been born with a silver spoon in his mouth, and everything always went well for him, and it still would this time, when they needed to do *something for their sons.*

Things went so well that it was much easier than anticipated. Sanfilippi saw the chief of police around midday at Porto Ercole, where he'd gone out on his sailboat, docked next to Sanfilippi's boat *Granma.* The police chief said hurriedly, "I don't want to know anything, but take down this telephone number. It's the number of the court clerk. I'll see him tomorrow, I'll talk to him, you can call him after lunch. Then the two of you can come to an understanding, but you've got to give him a gift. He likes the sea. Fishing. Sometimes whole documents can disappear, even he doesn't know how that's possible, but whenever it does, it's a mess that he's got to hurry and clean up."

They exchanged slaps on the back, thanks, promises of mutual favors. Filippo called the court clerk from a public place. He knew that the telephones of the police chief's employees were monitored, so he made an appointment with him to meet at the Grosseto marina in the afternoon, to pick up "some fishing gear."

He took Miriam along with him; he had her come in his car for two reasons: so she could see how much he was doing for her, that it wasn't enough to "make a phone call," it was necessary to involve more than one contact, and to do so personally; and also because he wanted her to be there in person to hand over the bag with the five million lira in cash. In the event— unlikely but still possible—that someone tracked them down and nabbed them, he wouldn't be in the photograph.

It was a very humid day. The appointment was in front of a closed restaurant on the promenade by the sea. The court clerk was waiting for him in a metallic blue Fiat Regata parked under the pines. As soon as he saw them arrive, he got out of his car and lit a Marlboro. He was tall and bald and was wearing a life jacket that wasn't appropriate for the day. Sanfilippi stayed in the car and made Miriam get out. There was nobody in the area, there was no need to playact, even though the court clerk really did have fishing tackle in his trunk. Miriam hurried to deliver the duffel, a bag from the gym where Saverio worked; as she handed it to him she thought how stupid that was, and asked him for the bag back, but he said he would make it disappear. Miriam, agitated, repeated two times: "Saverio Biagini, Saverio Biagini, he's the one to save." She said it just like that, "to save," and felt ashamed. He made a grimace of impatience and quickly said goodbye, he wanted to get away as soon as possible.

On the way back, Miriam cried silently. The gray Aurelia extended along a sea of the same color. Miriam told Sanfilippi all her worries: "But what if he takes the money and doesn't do anything? And what was I doing, that was a bag from the gym, I just wasn't thinking."

Sanfilippi hesitated to reassure her. It would have reduced his power, diminished the risk and the significance of what he was doing.

"Miriam, what can I tell you, it's in God's hands. I've never bribed anyone, and I don't even know if this is how these things work. I don't know if this amount is sufficient, either; we'll definitely have to give the chief of police a sizable gift, too. As for the bag, that was unfortunate, to say the least, but a whole lot of people go to that gym, why would it necessarily be yours? Plus, he won't be stupid enough to let it be found. You've got to keep calm. I don't know what to expect now. Sometimes they make false records with wrong names. In that case, considering that they caught him in the act and there's written testimony from the two cops, either they pin it on someone else, which can be done—Grosseto is full of known heroin fiends—or they make the folder with the whole file just disappear, which would be better. It certainly won't be a cakewalk: these documents are registered and under key. It's not normal for them to disappear, and it's not guaranteed. But you have to admit that I've done everything I could, for you, for Saverio, for Sauro. I'm risking losing everything I have, my reputation, I hope you understand that."

"I understand it very well, and I don't know how to thank you. Even though you're also doing this for Luca."

"Yes, of course. On that subject, next week we have an appointment with the notary to transfer your shares in the restaurant to him. We have to agree on a symbolic figure that you'll give back to me later in cash—it shouldn't be a donation, but a sale, for all intents and purposes."

"But wouldn't it be better to wait a bit? Maybe something will come out that will show all the connections . . ."

Sanfilippi burst out laughing. "So you're Perry Mason now? Don't go there. We've said that everything would be concurrent regardless of the outcome. As you've seen, I did everything I was supposed to do, and I acted without hesitation. Now it's your turn. Stalling wasn't part of the deal."

"I'm not stalling, I just wanted things to be secure for you too, for all of you. Filippo, I'm truly sorry if you think you can't trust me. I put my son's life in your hands, and everything I had; I think we can rest assured on the question of trust, can't we? If you want, we can go to the notary tomorrow. I don't give a damn at this point."

She had altered her tone.

"Next week is fine," Sanfilippi said, turning serious.

Miriam gripped the steering wheel even harder. She was certain that she had only made mistakes in her life, and the idea that this was the worst of them all made her feel hollow inside.

She knew nothing of what Filippo and Sauro had said to each other that night. Sanfilippi had confined himself to saying that he'd persuaded Sauro, and they could go forward. She hadn't spoken to her husband since she'd thrown the cup of chamomile tea onto the floor.

She wanted to go home, she wanted to hear from him that everything was all right, she wanted a hug, but she didn't get one. The next day she hugged Saverio, and as she cried on his shoulder she told him that he was the ruin of their family. Sauro could not be found when their son arrived at home. He hadn't told anyone where he was going or when he would be coming back; Miriam was afraid he would never come back, that the last fight about Saverio had marked the end of their marriage. She didn't care. So they'd get divorced. She had Saverio, free and innocent again, in her arms. Annamaria could not bear her mother's complete surrender to this excessively loved son who made her lose her reason, her control, her dignity. In front of the giant that was her brother, Miriam looked like a little girl.

Annamaria felt like she was going to explode, she had too many things inside to risk letting them come out in the form of words. She took Saverio by the arm and said to him: "Listen, there's something we need to do. To not talk for a little while. Let's go out riding, you and me. We'll gallop until we're completely exhausted."

It seemed like a good idea to him, too. In silence they went to the stables, saddled the horses and were hardly off the asphalt when they broke into a gallop together, it was almost a competition, almost as if they were still little kids, and it was beautiful, the light of the spring and the cool evening, the scent of the humid earth, the first trees in flower, the sweated horses, the wind from the sea that blended with everything and awakened memories, erasing all their worries.

*

What had convinced Sauro, Miriam would never know. She had guessed that Sanfilippi had made Sauro feel at fault as a father in some way, putting evidence in front of him that he hadn't done enough to make his son feel loved, respected, heard. The night the two men saw each other, Sanfilippi had pulled out his best arts of persuasion. He spoke in a low voice, preceding each sentence with mellifluous affirmations, like, "You are my dearest friend, I would not do this for anyone else," "I'm talking to you with my heart in my hand," "You know how much trust there is between you and me, we've shared every kind of experience, we've always protected each other," "Other people are malicious, they're not like us," and then glasses of whiskey, and in between, the injection of a sense of guilt, and the repeated insinuation of his own agenda: "For once you should do as your wife says, maybe you owe her, this time." And so, to exonerate Saverio, Sauro had accepted everything, the bribery of the public official in exchange for their shares in the restaurant.

It was never clear to him how even the trade was. In the moment, he felt so wrongfooted in his interactions with everyone, and Filippo's magnanimity seemed to put him in a corner. He felt like a traitor. Filippo was someone who had never done anything wrong, and he wasn't doing anything wrong now, even as he was declaring himself ready to bribe and to be bribed. He, on the other hand, what had he done? He had betrayed him by taking his wife to bed. He hadn't raised Saverio well or protected him. He hadn't listened to Miriam's requests for help. He had ignored Annamaria's problems.

In front of Filippo, Sauro had bit his cigar, he had fidgeted on the armchair, gripped by a sense of nausea. Once again he found himself sitting in the same armchair in which he had fought with Giulia. The same one on which Miriam had despaired. He thought again about all the unlucky coincidences.

Maybe he deserved to be atoning for his sins while sitting right there, in front of the friend he had deceived. Filippo looked fresh, his clothes were impeccable, his frameless glasses made his blue eyes look smaller in a way that made him seem younger, as if no wrinkle could touch him.

"Listen, I see that you're sorry, and I understand. I don't want to take anything away from you, you are more the owner of the Seaside Cowboy than I am, the idea was more yours than mine; it's our baby . . . but you know very well what I'm risking. And I don't have a plan B, I don't have another restaurant, land, or horses. I only have my job as a burnt-out politician. Let's just say, I wouldn't take a risk like this for my brother, but for you I will, because you're practically like a brother to me, even more. You know what, Sauro, if we're really doing this for Saverio, let's give him ten percent and a real job. Have him be a waiter, the maître d', anything he wants, but he'll also be something like a boss; and it's clear that that's another thing entirely, he'll work in a different spirit, he'll put himself into it. What do you say? And at that point you'll leave him alone, you won't interfere, you'll just take care of the horses and the Saddlery. Because I know that working alongside each other isn't something either of you would want. We'll leave the boys to the sea, Luca and Saverio." To break the tension he made a joke. "With the two of them around, you know how much ass will turn up . . ." He laughed by himself and gave Sauro a pat on the back. Then he resumed his speech with his customary aplomb: "Seriously, we'll give Saverio an opportunity, we'll do something for everybody and even for you and Miriam, who need to return to being a tight-knit, solid couple. For the sake of the village, you need to stay together, you're an institution. The king and queen."

Sauro's stomach was continually seized by spasms, but he hadn't given up drinking whiskey. He needed indulgence. A Hail Mary set off in his head, as it did every time that he felt bad and didn't know what to think. His eye fell on the shelf where there was a framed photo of Giulia with the kids, her blond hair gathered in a clip, her broad smile with the little space between her front teeth, the same light in her eyes as when they had just made love. He laid a hand on his stomach.

When Filippo stopped talking, he nodded. "Thank you Filì, truly." No other words came from him, just two fat, silent tears. He stood up to go, and Filippo hugged him at the door. Once outside, he couldn't figure out what to make of this conversation with his business partner, this friend who was doing so much for him. He had feelings that were hard to define, other than alcoholic emotionality. He got into the car and turned on the radio. "La Bamba" was playing: "*Io no soy marinero, yo no soy marinero, soy capitàn, soy capitàn.*" I'm not a sailor, I'm the captain. He felt like a failure. Then he started once again going over images of Giulia in his mind, of the satisfaction of having held her in his hands, of having shown her how to surrender to her own desire. Satisfaction that seemed to him like revenge on both of them, on Filippo, because he was sure that he was better in bed and better endowed than he was; on her because, in Sauro's mind, fucking a woman was also a form of punishment.

When he got home he threw himself into bed without getting undressed, giving way to a hopeless sleep that began with a sigh of resignation, like someone who is dying after a long and painful illness. He didn't notice that Miriam wasn't there.

The night after Saverio returned home as a free and exonerated man, after the embrace in which his mother said to him through her tears, "You are the ruin of our family," after the horseback ride, Annamaria had witnessed the scene she had anticipated and had wanted to avoid: the longest and most thorough battle of recriminations and accusations of her life, in which she and her grandfather had participated as spectators, referees, peacemakers without hope.

There had been the moment when Saverio had screamed the truth: "You two have fucked up royally on my behalf, which nobody asked you to do, not only did I not need it, but you let yourself be screwed over like two idiots. Why in the fuck did you make a decision like that without talking to me? I was a first-time offender, I had a terrific lawyer, she would have gotten me off with nothing, two weeks' house arrest maximum, I was sticking to saying I didn't know what I was transporting, I had put all the blame on the distributor. I would have come out of it clean and with my head held high. By pulling off this major bribery shit you've put yourselves in the hands of that exploiter Sanfilippi, who'll have you under his thumb the rest of your lives, you've given him the restaurant! You're both morons. What did I do wrong, God, to end up with two parents this moronic?!"

Sauro started to lunge at his son, but the grandfather got in the way. Miriam sat crying at the table and shouted at him: "You're the moron! An ungrateful moron!" Saverio shouted: "I'm getting out of here, or this night will end badly!" and went straight to his own room and locked the door. Sauro kept on screaming insults at him, then went for Miriam: "If there's a huge moron in this family it's you: I'd told you that as far as I was concerned it would be fantastic if that piece of shit spent ten years in jail."

After the shouting and tears were over, everyone had gone to their own rooms, and Annamaria had pulled out the trundle bed under her bed so her mother could sleep there. Before going to sleep, she'd told her mother that maybe that was how things had to be before they could get better: that they had to tell each other everything, to tell each other the truth, everything they thought of each other, which was something you could only do with the people that you knew loved you; and that, all things considered, this is how things were in a family, in every family; they shouted the worst things so that afterwards they could promise themselves the best, taking account of what the others said about them to better themselves, or to discard harsh judgments that were only prejudices.

Miriam had taken her daughter's hand in the dark. "At least I have you, Annamarì, at least I have you, you're the only good thing I've done in my life. Men are all egotists, my daughter, all egotists and ingrates; think hard before you marry. It's good that you're studying: if you want to, you can leave this shitty village, I'll only be happy for you. I've made my mistakes already, but you still have time. But if one day you leave, I will come join you and . . ." She couldn't finish the sentence. Annamaria gripped her hand harder. It was so horrible to hear her mother cry, to hear all the discord in the house. She knew that what she had just said was not true, it was a false thought, and not very consoling, since she didn't believe it herself, for a start. She knew very well that, in her family, at least, no one was equipped to promise anything good to the ones they felt despised by, and that contempt, the sole tangible sentiment that had been expressed by each of them, was hard to transform into something positive: it ruins and destroys every kind of love.

She cried in the dark, too. She didn't want to be the only good thing. It was too big a responsibility, it meant that she was surrounded only by people who were worse than her, egotistical and stupid, who didn't know how to love, and this thought brought her down because she was just a little girl, and the only thing she wanted, like every girl her age, was to be appreciated and loved, not to appreciate and love.

you, but your father forbade me to reach out to you, and I respected that, understanding his state of mind and yours, the sense of betrayal that you both felt for something that was born completely out of good faith, in the frame of the pure affection I've always felt for you.

Since then, I've realized that good faith alone doesn't fix anything, that even if you have the best intentions in the world your behavior can be harmful, and that's what happened. Over the course of a few months, I laid waste to everything that was dearest to me, from myself, my peace of mind, and the equilibrium of my family to the joyful harmony of the time our families shared in the country and by the sea. I questioned everything. Intending to strengthen our ties, I tied knots that were too tight, that made the rope break. They broke something in me first, but my greatest regret is if by chance they also broke something in you. Apart from trusting in your capacity for forgiveness, your willingness to believe me, I also trust in your youth; everything that is happening to you now will be nothing but a step in your growth, something that can help you and be useful to you, and which you will have time either to forget or to process. I think I will take advantage of this destruction to build something new. That's one of the thoughts that have obsessed me here in Berlin. They sent me here to write a report on Germany after the fall of the Wall, and I noticed something extraordinary. My best thoughts, the best things I write—now that writing seems like the only good thing left in my life—are the things I write as if I were writing to you. I've sent you hundreds of mental letters these last months, drafted dozens of articles with the same fervor that I brought to the letters I wrote to you about Cuba, about life in Rome, about dance, about school as I saw it, putting myself in Lisa's place.

Here in Berlin it's been overwhelming, I've recognized that you're the primary audience for the stories I want to tell; and beyond that, I've understood that, in the end, my idea that I was undertaking that correspondence to cement the rapport between you and my daughter was just an excuse. There's something more. Now that everything seems foreign to me, I can see the exhausting hypocrisy of human interactions, the empty superficiality of everything that surrounds me, the ridiculous childishness; and the only person I feel I can talk to in a context of total purity is you. I saw you when I was standing on the remnants of the Wall, I took a piece for you as a souvenir. In every kid your age in East Berlin, I saw something of you. The power of something new being born, transforming itself, becoming aware of itself, after having been kept down by a suffocating reality that we, outside, had idealized, needs to be revealed to the world. We had regarded communism as immortal, but we didn't envy the lifestyle of the communist countries. Now we've come to envy the citizens of the East, who are undergoing a moment of change and liberation. We watch them entering the shops of West Berlin, and we feel emotion for their terrible clothes and their hunger to buy things. In only a moment that emotion will morph into disapproval or shame at the thoughtless way that they'll squander their liberty, which we've prepared for them, and which we have already spoiled. We would like for them to remain pure and communist, with no interest in material goods beyond having them available, even though we ourselves are lightyears away from that. I can already see my colleagues on the Left thumbing their noses, "The ex-communists are on the way to becoming the most rabid consumers of all!" I, however, am more focused on thinking about what we ourselves are; the lack of hardship that has defined our era has turned us into people who can no longer take pleasure in anything. We've cut ourselves off from reality and would like to trade places with the ones who are enjoying this opportunity for freedom that my generation hasn't experienced, or that we badly underappreciated. But I'm going off topic, and once again abusing your patience and your ability to listen. In spite of all the good things life has held in store for me, my fate now seems to need, to draw comfort from her presence, from her attention. In her letter, she was giving a sociopolitical lesson, knowing that Annamaria wouldn't understand it in depth, but she was lucky to be able to do that for her, so she could feel like someone who could make a person gape in admiration at what she was saying. A mild form of oppression.

Niki wasn't like that. If Niki needed something, she said so explicitly. She gave curt orders to Annamaria: "Make me laugh! Now go away." But when she told stories from her own life, it wasn't to get consolation, or to give facile encouragement, or to feel superior to or stronger than a village girl, or to someone uglier than herself. It wasn't ever so she could be pitied, either. It was just to give her the gift of her story, to give her true help, the example of something that had gone badly or had gone well for her, depending on how she'd worked through it, so that Annamaria could make something of it herself, so it could serve as an instrument of understanding, of rebellion, of growth, an opportunity to write another personal story, one of her own jokes. Niki was her mentor.

She put Giulia's letter back in the envelope and pulled out a box that she kept under the bed. She had put her most precious things inside it: a diary, Dante's *Inferno*, the Madonna cassette, leather bracelets. It was her magic box, like Niki's.

The artist had given her the idea in one of her personal stories.

"When I was born, I received as a gift, I never knew from whom, two tarot cards: the Magician, which is the card of creativity and energy; and the Hanged Man, which signifies sensitivity, receptivity, the ability to understand everything and everyone. I believe they were my symbols. I've always hated the injustices I saw around me. The racism that the nuns showed at Christmas when they gave donations to the poor families in Harlem; my aunt Gioia who came from Georgia, and who wouldn't let me sit next to colored people when I went out with her; the difference in the ways that the rich and poor were treated; the disparity between men and women. In the world I lived in, from the time I was little, I had nobody who understood my sense of unease. I learned to play on my own, to live in my own world, a magic world. I had a secret box under my bed. A box of precious wood, inlaid and enameled in intense colors. It was my spiritual refuge. The beginning of a life into which my parents could not enter, not them or anybody else. Nobody could see it. I kept my writings there, my projects, all the magical things that helped me create. I deposited my soul in that box. Since I couldn't manage to have a deep relationship with my family, I began talking to myself. This is where my need for solitude began, which is as necessary to me as air is to the lungs. You have not suffered my kind of solitude, Annamaria, I needed to isolate myself, to separate myself from the world around me. You have the privilege of having grown up amid all this beauty. I open it every night, that box. Maybe you could make one for yourself."

At that moment, Annamaria had wanted to tell her that she was a girl with no imagination, and that there weren't any magic boxes you could use to save yourself. That she had experienced the beatitude of solitude and the ultimate feeling of escape from her family only once, when she had taken the medicine that she thought would help her sleep better. That her childhood had been void of cultural stimulation, that her family had not accustomed her to beauty, elegance, travel, foreign languages, and fine literature. The nature that surrounded her didn't seem exceptional to her at all, it was a normal countryside, with manure, insects, the animals covered in ticks. She would have liked to tell Niki that in order to rebel, you have to be conscious of what you have and what you lack. If you lack everything, you also lack the courage to imagine what you would like. "It's easy for you," she had wanted to say. But she had confined herself to nodding and responding, "A magic box. What a nice idea." And then she made one.

She put Giulia's letter at the bottom of the box and never responded to it. To hell with the piece of the Wall, she told herself; and I forgive you, Giulia, there was no need to ask for my forgiveness, I know you didn't have bad intentions. But simply put, I don't want to listen to you anymore, I understand that, once again, what you have to tell me is just for your own benefit.

With more joy than usual she got on the moped and went to the Garden. As soon as she saw Giovanna she said to her, "I've got a couple of new jokes to tell Niki—they're both about Jesus, let's hope she doesn't take me for a blasphemer."

"Not to worry, blasphemy doesn't exist for her, she explained this beautiful thing to me, which is that her sense of the sacred isn't connected to religion. More than that, let's hope she gets the jokes—Tuscan humor is not in her bones."

"If she doesn't laugh, I'll redo the sketch with Madonna and her cousins. *Dunno dance*, and *I thawt I was dreamin'* still works."

It still worked, and Giovanna burst out laughing.

It went as she'd thought it would; the joke about Jesus mocking Judas at the Last Supper when he says, "Lord, Lord, is it I who will betray you?" fell flat. The one in which he asks Saint Peter to put him up on the Cross while centurions are violently attacking, so that he can get a better view of the landscape from up high, went over a little better, but the one that worked best was the joke about the three ascetics who go to a mountain to meditate. They remain silent for three years, then one of them says, "Look, a cloud." After three more years of silence, the second guy says, "Look, another cloud." Then, after three more years of silence, the third bursts out, "Guys, if you just came here to horse around, I'm leaving!"

Niki was overcome by a fit of laughter. This time Annamaria

made a decisive move: for the first time, she asked Niki to tell her another story in exchange for her joke. She had meant to ask her something about her relationship with her parents, how she had managed to liberate herself from them, instead she asked her why she'd stopped shooting at the canvases.

"I'm glad to hear you finally asking something, instead of saying you're sorry. I decided to stop with the shootings because I felt that the performances were becoming a drug: I had become dependent on the ritual, and after every session I felt empty. One of the last shootings, which was titled *King Kong*, was one of my favorites. There was a dinosaur attacking a city, two airplanes crashing onto skyscrapers, and masks of the faces of politicians from all over the world, while higher up, at the left, there was a woman in childbirth. I shot the last of the monsters that had been my favorite theme. That moment was a watershed: I started reflecting on women, on their roles. My anger had left, what remained was suffering. After a certain period of time, the suffering went away too, and I returned to the atelier to make joyous creatures that celebrated feminine power. It was as if at a certain point, after my death and destruction phase, all at once I had found serenity and a certain stability again. The thing I couldn't have foreseen is that I had found that stability by stopping pretending, by stopping believing that I could attain it in the ways that are normal for other people. Home, family, conjugal peace. I wasn't cut out for paradise. I had left paradise and followed the fire of hell. My north star was Jean, he showed me the way, telling me only that I had to stop pretending to be what I was not, to remove my mask and accomplish my projects, however freakish they might seem. We were the *enfants terribles* of the New Realists. I linked myself to somebody who breaks all chains—wasn't that a paradoxical stroke of good fortune?"

"If you say so! But tell me, when did you start making your

Nanas? Because those are really different from the bleeding paintings, wouldn't you say?"

"When they kicked us out of the Impasse Ronsin, Jean and I decided to buy a big property in Soisy-sur-École in the country about thirty miles south of Paris. It was called the Auberge du Cheval Blanc. It was an enormous place, strange and inspiring: it had been a cinema, a ballroom, a restaurant, a bordello. When we bought it, it was falling into a state of total disrepair, it was overrun by weeds, nettles, and scrap metal, which actually made Jean ecstatic. We renovated it, and I set up my atelier on the ground floor, in the old ballroom, where there were still signs that said "dancing" and "bar." After a while, the cold became unbearable, and I fought with Jean about putting in heating, but he didn't want to. We managed to create a stimulating atmosphere, friends came to see us from Paris, we had very long lunches, accompanied by interesting debates. Jean took notes, and I made sketches on sheets of paper. I began a series of collages, of mothers and brides. I stripped away the peaceful part of the sacred and serene image of maternity, the sweetness. Childbirth is an atrociously painful ordeal. My brides were tragic dolls, all dressed in lace, but disturbing; would they end up marrying monsters?"

"My god, the Nanas don't seem tragic to me, they seem like fat little dancing girls. Like me when I dance to Madonna's songs."

"You're so goofy. I was inspired very much by Clarice, a friend of mine who was pregnant at the time. I saw in her round, proud body the inspiring idea of a woman who was no longer dominated, who creates and rules the world. *Nana* is a word that means "girl" in slang, but I always liked the way the name sounded like "Inanna," the goddess who's the daughter of the moon, who can assume a thousand and one forms and embody all feminine roles. I liked it that they became big, bigger than men, and colorful. The first time I showed them, in

Paris, I took them wrapped in plastic to the Boulevard Saint-Germain, loading them into my convertible Deux Chevaux with the top down. The exhibition was called *Nana Power*. That happened more than twenty years ago, and I still see it as the portent of a new matriarchy, the only possible response. I replaced all the sad wives and the *mater dolorosa* with joyful, exaggerated, liberated generous mothers, proud of their rotundity, ready to dance. Of course, not everybody liked them: to a lot of people they had a terrifying aspect. My granddaughter Bloum even said they looked like an army, and as an army, they provoked fear. They've got small heads, and they're monstrous, creatures outside the ordinary. One of the first models for the Nanas was my sister Elisabeth, when she was pregnant. When she committed suicide, everyone in the family hid it from me for more than a year, telling me it had been an accident." Niki paused, looking into space. "How shocking to think that you could protect people with lies. When the truth comes out it's a thousand times worse to bear, because it adds to the betrayal."

Annamaria got distracted, thinking of those words, then asked, "What was your mother like?"

"She was more beautiful and elegant than me. From her I acquired my love of clothes, hats, music, fine food, art. She had a cabinet filled with colored glasses that I always adored, and I realized that I've used the same colors in this Garden. Her house was full of mirrors. Years later, I noticed that I'd filled the Garden with mirrors, I was even living in a house whose walls were made of mirrors, but in which I couldn't see myself all in one piece. Everything reflected me, but I can only see myself in shards. Doesn't that have to mean something?

"I loved my mother besottedly, I craved her attention, and at the same time I hid from it. I wouldn't have wanted to be her for anything in the world. I didn't want to end up with a life like hers: outwardly perfect, full of privilege, but in truth a trap of hypocrisy, devoid of choice. Her frustration served as a perpetual warning to me: I had to do everything I could to not become like her. She had no way of freely expressing herself, and that fact made her devour her own family. But I was at risk of following her path. When I recognized that, I made the decision to separate myself from my children. It was painful, but it was also the only way to not devour them in turn. My mother was a prisoner of rigid rules that could not be questioned. A woman pays for the well-being she acquires from a rich family with her own freedom. Only the men had freedom. I wanted to be a woman and to have the same power that men had, but without becoming a man. I've devoted my entire life to that, it has cost me enormous effort, and I don't even know if I've achieved it.

"You, Annamaria, need only to understand what you want, and to do everything you can to get it, without letting anyone tell you what you should be. Freedom is something you have to take: you can't wait for it to be handed to you. You must try to be true to yourself. We women can do everything, even if now you're looking like you don't believe me."

"Of course I don't believe you, Niki. Women like you are only born once a century, and I, in all modesty, was not born one of them. You can't understand this, it's like Totò, an actor from Naples, who was a member of the nobility like you but made people laugh."

"You see? Noble like me, but he can make people laugh like you. You and I have more in common than you think."

"Sure, hand me a trowel so I can build a palace shaped like a horse and live inside it. Actually, maybe the idea of living in a horse isn't so original . . . Can't you see that I'm not creative at all?"

"What does that matter, if you make me laugh. You can be an actor, like Totò."

"An actress? With this ass? Actresses are beautiful—have you even looked at me?"

"Was Totò good looking?"

"No."

"See?"

"What does that have to do with anything? He was a man. Men are forgiven for being ugly if they make people laugh; women, no."

"That's your own idea, you should get rid of it immediately."

"Fine, I can make people laugh, and I can ride horses. I'll invent a cabaret rodeo for myself. You know what I'll call it? "Cackles with the Cowgirl." "Unrein Your Laughter with Annamaria!" "The Ugly Cowgirl *Live*: A Gymkhana of Laughter!"

Niki couldn't remember the last time she'd laughed so hard. This girl was a gift.

Annamaria didn't remember when or how, but during the course of these afternoons, she had learned so much about Niki's life, and picked up so many insights. Partly from her stories, and partly from Giovanna's, which her cousin explained and interpreted for her.

"You see, Annamarì, that's how Niki is, you can't expect anything from her that you'd expect of a normal person. Sometimes she makes absurd requests, as if she were a child. She shouts orders, gets mad, acts up. She heads off someplace and wants me to sleep here, not knowing that I'm afraid to be in here on my own; I can't take a day off because she wants me to spend all my days cooking for her, she doesn't like what other people make for her . . . But she's an enchantress, she's generous, she understands everything. The other day a box arrived in the mail, samples of all the things she sells to finance the Garden—her perfume, the scarf with Nanas on it. She was behind me, and without even seeing that I was watching, she took the fuchsia scarf, and said, "You'll like this one, it has your favorite colors, I'm giving it to you." In other words, she had understood my desire even when I was behind her, you understand? Then again, sometimes she seems like a little girl; and other times I want her to be my mother. Once she got it into her head that she needed to use the lace the women around here use to stamp into the clay, to give a local identity to her High Priestess statue. She ordered me to go out and gather panties and other things made of lace, but think about it—who would want to give me that? I had a fit and made Rico go with her to personally visit the countrywomen and ask for their things. In the end, her haul was as meager as mine: the aunties she asked to take part in the project wanted to hold on to their doilies and lace.

"Obviously, she doesn't like Rossano, she says he's too jealous—that he has a negative influence on me, that he clips my wings and makes me feel like I'm always wrong. But when you come down to it, she has nothing to teach me about jealousy— just imagine, she told me that when she and Jean were in Paris, he made absurd scenes, like, when she went to visit her friend Clarice who lived near them, he fired shots in the air with his rifle to make her come home: he fired until she came back. She tells that story as if it were some kind of game they were playing, partly for themselves, partly for their friends, but all the same I know that she was incredibly jealous of Jean. Just think, he had a baby with someone else the year they got married. He's always been a major skirt-chaser, then he actually got back together with that other woman, and went to live with her in Switzerland. She's always had a weakness for that kind of man, *womanizers*, as she calls them in English. Even when she was married, she and her husband didn't ever think of acting like a normal couple, who either stay faithful or secretly cheat on each other. No, they said to each other, let's do it openly. They only had one rule, which was that if a potential lover truly bothered one of them, they would tell the other to avoid them.

For example, Niki's husband had said to her, 'Listen, among all those artists you hang out with, go with whoever you want, but please keep away from Jean Tinguely. That one seems dangerous to me.' And actually, he was right . . . you see how it's turned out."

"Gosh, even the husband was far-seeing. Excuse me, but what does Niki know about Rossano? That is, does she know him? Has he been here? Do you tell her things that even I don't know?"

"No, not really. He's never come. Every now and then I've mentioned his existence to her, every now and then he calls me here. But Niki knows and takes an interest, but in a rather strange way. She never gossips, she almost never talks about herself, and she only asks me questions occasionally, when we're alone. Actually, I'm pretty amazed that she's told you all these things, that she's revealed so much. With me, it's like she senses things, and knows what's happening with me. She knows Tiberio, because he's come a few times, I listen to him on the radio, so she knows who he is. When Tiberio calls, she notices immediately. She says that I respond cheerfully and instantly start laughing, and then she says to me: "See? That's the man for you. As soon as he starts talking you start laughing, he makes you feel good, he puts you in a good mood." I've told her so many times: "Niki, but we're just good friends, I'm not in love with him," and she tells me: "You'll see." If he calls and she picks up, he starts kidding around and telling her all the words he knows in French: *abat-jour, madame, consommé, vol-au-vent,* and she starts to laugh."

"Well, you know, it's obvious she has a weakness for people who make her laugh, it's part of her cure."

"Sure. But it's also obvious that Niki sees things that we don't."

Annamaria would remember that conversation on the day that Giovanna asked her to be a witness at her wedding to Tiberio, five years later.

18. THE MOON
Intuition. Femininity. Mystery.

When a stubborn woman gets it into her head to rearrange her life, there's no escape for anyone. Miriam decided that the best thing to do was to restore the necessary balance to make them at least look like a happy family. That wasn't easy, and it couldn't happen immediately, but during the months of armed peace that elapsed after Saverio's release, she tried to clean up dirty laundry at home and to keep her husband and son as far apart as possible throughout the course of that busy summer.

In the winter, when the Seaside Cowboy was closed, Miriam decided they should all go someplace together over the holidays, and made plans for spring, too. She and Sauro would return to looking after the Saddlery; as for Saverio, he would work as the manager of the Seaside Cowboy, because in her opinion he'd already learned everything. "You and Luca Sanfilippi are *both* the bosses, don't you forget it," she always told him, leaving out that his ten percent of the profits came to little more than a month's tips, and that he was far from being the boss.

Annamaria would help out wherever Miriam decided, according to which place she was needed to diffuse tension. She said this straightforwardly: "My daughter is like the dog in the stables, she brings peace, she's like the roses in the vine rows, she catches the grape blight first, so you can catch it before it spreads elsewhere." Miriam knew that Annamaria was the only one who was capable of dispersing the atmosphere of reciprocal condemnation that the men in her family created when they were together. But she didn't know that she herself had a neurosis that made her see the dark side of everything, that her motherly countenance bore an eternal expression of worry, imbued with implicit grievance and devouring anxiety.

Because of that, to placate her, her husband and son did not oppose her idea of going to the mountains at New Year's. To Sauro, the idea of leaving the Saddlery in the hands of the waitresses at New Year's seemed absurd, but he knew he owed Miriam some of the bourgeois normalcy he'd never given her. They had a Land Rover, and a reservation at Madonna di Campiglio, the hotel where the Sanfilippis usually went, but they'd been going to Cortina for a few years. Miriam had bought ski suits and Moon Boots, snow hats and gloves, a hairband of fuchsia wool trimmed in badger fur that brought out her highlights—she'd spent a fortune in the best-known sporting goods shop in Grosseto. Besides, even if they still had debts and had practically lost one of their restaurants, the flow of revenue had stayed high, they had rented out the old farmhouse under the table, and they kept practically no receipts for the horseback rides and the meals at the Saddlery. At that time, and in their region, money changed hands quickly, and in cash; it went out, came back, and even the farmers in a lot of places had started to have liquidity. You had the impression that almost everyone had money, and they attested to that with their clothes, cars, watches, second homes, exotic travel.

The truth was that it was only Miriam who wanted to take this vacation. She was ready to enjoy a week as a fine lady. Full board, a hotel with a sauna and hot tub, a shuttle bus to the slopes, and ski school already reserved for Annamaria. Not for Saverio, no, he would ski with Sauro, who got by because when he went to see his mother's relatives in Amiata they always did a little skiing. It might have been a good moment for the two of them to come together. She, on the other hand, would have basked in the sun holding a foil reflector, waited for the others in the armchairs at the outdoor bar at the top, read *The Name of the Rose* by Umberto Eco, which Annamaria had given her for Christmas, and she'd also have bought fashion and gossip magazines, maybe she might see the singer Mina Mazzini there— didn't she have a house in Madonna di Campiglio, Mina? She would have waited for the slopes to close so they could all drink hot chocolate with whipped cream together before going to shower and heading down to dinner. It was the second trip they had taken in their life together; the previous one had been a cruise to the Canary Islands for their fifteenth wedding anniversary. That hadn't gone too well: both she and Sauro had gotten food poisoning, probably from the shrimp cocktail in the buffet. They didn't have good memories of those days, spent in large part sitting on the toilet while their children were entertained by the cruise directors with amateur theatricals, in which Annamaria and Saverio played a magician and his dog.

The trip from the village to the Dolomites seemed endless to all of them. Saverio had brought cassettes of disco music, remixes that he'd been given by a friend who recorded in the afternoons at the New Line disco in Orbetello. But Sauro, who wanted to drive the whole time, had asked him for silence instead. As a compromise they had alternated a Zucchero cassette with a cassette by Bruce Springsteen, one after the other, side A, side B, four or five times, until, drunk and deadened by the repetition, they couldn't tell one song from another. When the road had narrowed, with snowbanks on both sides, and the cold had started penetrating the car, Sauro had turned off the car radio and nobody objected at all.

The hotel was very elegant, welcoming, and clean, just as Filippo had described it to Miriam. They'd taken two adjoining rooms, one for the parents, and one for the kids. There was a lot of snow, which, since they never got to see it, had a magical effect on them whose enchantment lingered. But Annamaria enjoyed that cold, soft silence more than any of them, she wasn't used to it, she caressed the mounds on the windowsills, left footprints on the pristine surfaces, rested her lips on the immaculate peaks atop the hedgerows, made snowballs, opened her mouth to catch the flakes that fell on her tongue.

The forecast wasn't favorable, nor was the mood of Miriam's travel companions. Annamaria suffered from the cold, and skiing seemed unnatural and not at all fun to her. As soon as she awoke the next morning, she realized with annoyance that was would have to put on tights and then the padded suit, which made her look even clumsier, and then rush through breakfast, when she would have gladly spent the whole morning spreading butter and strawberry jam on walnut bread, eating croissants and refilling the cup from the thermos of hot chocolate. Instead, she had to put on those extremely stiff boots, and the mittens, which would be soaked in an instant, then pick up skis and ski poles while trying not to hit anyone, and put on the wool cap that itched, and the snowsuit that kept sliding down, and the turd she felt pressing as soon as she left the hotel, but there wasn't time to go back; and the shuttle bus, and three interminable hours of cold during which she had to battle the ski lift, attempt the parallel curves which inevitably finished in a snow plough that would not work on the layer of ice; to fall, get back up, while the instructor, irritated and sarcastic, shouted at everyone as if he were the shepherd Porcu with his sheep, and didn't remember even one of their names, even at the end of the week. "Hey you, red snowsuit, yellow cap," that's what he called them. Annamaria did a hilarious imitation, it was the only good thing she got out of the whole course. Her father and brother didn't ski, because it was snowing. Annamaria didn't understand why, in the end, she was always the one who had to be the family's sacrificial lamb. "We've paid for the course . . . why did we bother coming here for winter break if nobody's going to ski?"

At night her legs hurt; during the descents and the climbs she used all of her muscles to avoid falling, but she knew her effort wouldn't help her learn to ski, the people who could ski were limber and light, and after a week, all she'd seemed to learn was how to fall less often. Every time she found herself on her ass on the ground she thought about Lisa, who surely was excellent, elegant, and slender even in in her padded snowsuit. She thought occasionally about what Lisa was doing. She felt a fierce dislike towards her, but not resentment. Sometimes she also thought about the times Lisa had been nice to her—they seemed like moments she hadn't given enough importance to at the time of her disappointment. She thought that maybe it had had nothing to do with Lisa, who, when it came down to it, hadn't promised her anything, hadn't shown her any intimacy. Everything had been born out of the misunderstanding over the letters, and everything that had grown in her heart came from the isolation of her own imagination. What could Annamaria do about it if she'd never gotten attention from anyone, if she'd grown up like a wild animal in a family in which everyone barely talked to each other; friendless, without anyone who'd ever explained to her how the world worked; and who, at the first slight attention from someone beautiful and privileged who showed a speck of interest in her—nothing personal, she had understood later—maybe just a little pity, had split open her heart like a ripe pomegranate? She was glad she didn't see Lisa anymore; most of all she was glad that Lisa couldn't see her in this obscene snowsuit, her skis crossed in the snow. She laughed at herself.

Her brother slept all morning then went to the hotel gym. Once again she envied him. He knocked himself out on the machines, he showed up at lunch but ate little: all that cheese, sausage, polenta, gnocchi, and greasy stew wasn't good for his physique. One time he made them bring him grilled chicken, and their mother reproached him because it wasn't on the menu, and they would have to pay extra, and besides, in a kitchen, she knew, special requests are a pain. He told her that they always accepted special requests, too, and that the customer was always right, and that now that she found herself on the other side, she should make the most of it, too. She snorted and told him that it was a question of showing respect to others. Every morning she asked him if he was going to ski. "Mamma, I'm no good at it, it's not the sport for me," he repeated until he stopped answering her entirely.

"At least today there's a little sun, you could try."

Sauro said nothing. He spent the mornings with the newspapers, went out to smoke his cigar, came back in, read a little more, told Miriam he wanted to go see Annamaria at the ski camp and take photos of her, but then he didn't do it. The third day he got a fever, he who never got sick, which gave him an excuse to stay in bed. In the afternoon he called Adan, the Albanian guy who helped him in the stables, to ask him if everything was going well, if the horses had eaten, if anyone had come to take them out and walk them, if they'd been well-saddled, if he'd groomed them afterwards. These were very short conversations, in which it became clear that Adan, at the other end of the line, was responding only yes or no. At night he called Settimio. Sometimes he had to let the phone ring a long, long time. His father kept the television on at top volume, then drank and fell asleep in front of it. One night he didn't pick up at all; they tried to call him until one in the morning, but nothing. They didn't worry much about it. Indeed, the next morning he picked up, and with his mouth full, let out a string of expletives that prompted the usual recommendations: "Don't drink, take your pills, don't eat too many sausages, I know you only eat sausage when you're alone, remember to turn off the fireplace at night, otherwise it smokes." Their grandfather only wanted to talk to Annamaria. He asked her how the snow was, if she was having fun. She feigned enthusiasm, told him that the village was beautiful, that it looked like it had been painted, that she'd learned to ski, and that she would send him a postcard. She raised her voice so she could be heard, and sometimes she had to repeat her words. "Grandpa, on the address, beneath the road and the number of the farm, I'm going to write 'Stinking Maremma,' so you'll know immediately that it's for you, OK?" He laughed with the cavernous echo his toothless mouth produced. Annamaria could sense that her grandfather loved her, that she missed him. But she also sensed that he missed her, which felt strange to her, because her grandfather was almost never affectionate, especially not on the telephone. But it was true that he only loved women, and that if there was any person in the world for whom he still felt a bit of the tenderness that had departed with Alma, that person was her.

Miriam got tired of concentrating on her book. She wasn't used to reading, she got bored. Sometimes she realized she'd gotten to the end of a page without having absorbed anything, then she would reread it, and once again, by the third line she would be overtaken by her thoughts, by tension, by frustration. "Why can't we get along? Why do we get so bored when we're together? Why don't the men of the house ever manage to speak to each other? Why do I have to feel guilty for having come here and for having spent all this money, when, despite the beauty of the place, the white snow, the food that's ready and cooked for us, they all can't wait until it's time to go back to our village?"

In the afternoon she gave some of her leisure time to Annamaria and took her to buy souvenirs. Annamaria picked out little pocketknives with horn handles, magnets, postcards, ashtrays with alpine stars embedded in the glass; one was for Giovanna, but she didn't tell her mother that. Miriam also bought her a pair of mirrored sunglasses that would be useful on the slopes, and a bulky Tyrolean sweater that she would never have worn at home. Annamaria indulged her mother's wishes—these things didn't matter to her, if it had been up to her, she would never have gone into the shops, she was annoyed by the shop girls' glances, their insistence on helping her. But she appreciated this time with her mother, she liked it when Miriam tried on clothes. She looked good in everything, weird glasses, fur hats, high-collared sweaters with baroque patterns. To Annamaria it seemed that her mother could make even ugly clothes look beautiful. As she watched her go in and out of the dressing rooms, she regretted that she didn't look like her, just as she regretted seeing her mother's sad face when Sauro and Saverio were next to her and nobody talked. It made her happy to know that their little outings served as consolation to Miriam for a life that had held so few moments like this for her. Her material needs were met, she'd always thought that would be enough, but harmony is a distant goal that lies at the end of a path of thin ice, and all of them had such heavy treads that it was impossible to think of even getting near it.

The vacation hadn't lived up to her expectations, yet it still might have been something to preserve among family memories, choosing only the best moments: the breakfasts and the meals, the afternoons in the shops with Annamaria, the mornings of sauna and massage. Had it not been for the New Year's Eve incident.

They had made a reservation for New Year's Eve dinner in a restaurant recommended by Filippo. They had shown up early, well-dressed, Miriam wearing a long-sleeved dress of black lace, something that was a little excessive, by her own standards, and given the cold. But she wore the fur over it that she'd bought herself the year before with her own money, and the diva aura that it conferred helped draw her out nicely, far away from the village where everything restricted her to her role in the kitchen, where she was ashamed of everything, where wearing anything original or expensive meant laying yourself open to ferocious and malevolent judgments. She was in an excellent mood; she immediately ordered a bottle of champagne and an Altesino white to follow, because, after all, wine was something she'd been forced to know about.

Their table was served by a very pretty girl, who was provocatively dressed. Full lips, prominent cheekbones, big eyes of a piercing color that looked artificial, her eyelashes too, probably all of it was fake. Two mischievous braids fell on her chest, which was exposed by her extremely tight white shirt, open all the way to the third button. She was friendly and smiling, and although they had all remained silent during the antipasto as she poured the champagne, the climate had warmed up after the second course. Sauro had asked her name, Saverio had begun asking her advice on the courses, exhibiting a level of interest in her tastes that is very rarely shown to a waiter. Miriam was so used to seeing her men flirt with girls that she paid no attention. Annamaria followed the girl with her eyes among the tables, saw her narrow waist in a wide black elastic belt, which was very fashionable that year; she watched how she moved with the platters in her hand, delicately and sinuously, her body seeming to float almost weightlessly.

They ordered a second bottle of wine and then a third. Miriam proposed a toast, Saverio took off his jacket. He was wearing a turtleneck with red and brown damask trim; you could see that he'd been sweating. Annamaria said to him, "Nice sweater, you look like you've got third-degree burns."

Saverio laughed, twisting his mouth. "Always sweet, aren't you?" He pushed his sleeves up and uncovered his arms, putting his biceps on display. He raised his glass and his voice. "To the end of this shitty year!" He wanted to clink glasses with every diner, and when the waitress approached he said to her, "Have a drink and share a toast with us, beautiful!" She smiled, and said pleasantly to him, "Maybe later, when I'm off-duty. I can't now," and she went away, called to another table. Again Annamaria followed her with her eyes, and Saverio turned to her with the same tipsy cheer. "You like her too, don't you? I'm with you, have you seen how hot she is?" The joke would have fallen into the void, into the heat of the night, into the fog of all that wine, if Annamaria, the only abstainer among them, had not replied in a shrill and offended voice, "Thanks for your sensitivity, Savè. If you were trying to get back at me for my compliment on your sweater, it didn't work." And if he had not retorted, still laughing, insolent, and drunk, "What? What's wrong with being a lesbian? I get you, women are much better than men." He hadn't even finished the sentence before Sauro's hand struck his face, launched by the memory of how he'd restrained himself when Giulia had made the same insinuation about Annamaria.

This took one second. Saverio grabbed his father's wrist and stood up, bringing his face right up to his father's, Sauro was still sitting down, and growled through his teeth, "You're not allowed to do that, Babbo, you don't know what the fuck you're doing, I'm not ten years old anymore." Miriam, as if she'd been stabbed in the chest, turned pale. Displaying her own lipstick-stained teeth in turn, she gritted them and ordered her son to sit back down. Annamaria got up and ran to the bathroom. Everyone at the other tables had turned in their direction. Saverio sat back down. The waitress approached, alarmed, exposing her full accent as she broadened her vowels. "Is everything all raaaght, sir, ma'am?" Miriam responded in an altered voice, "Nothing is remotely all right, but just go, darling, go, we don't need you."

The three of them remained in silence. Miriam looked at Saverio, shaking her head, disappointed in him all over again. She asked herself why her son always managed, one way or another, to ruin everything. She put all the blame on him, even though Sauro had been the first to raise his hand. "But no," Saverio thought, "I'm the one who gets the blame, and always will, for everything bad that happens in this family, it's always my fault." He leaned back against his chair and closed his eyes. Miriam got up to find Annamaria, who had locked herself inside the bathroom and would never have opened the door if her mother hadn't started furiously knocking. On Miriam's advice, for this special occasion she had applied black eyeliner under her eyes and brushed mascara on her lashes. Now all the makeup was running down her cheeks.

"Mamma, I'm not a lesbian, don't worry," she said, hugging her and trying to make herself smile.

"I know, my love, don't let it get to you. Saverio always likes to joke."

"It's a hell of a joke. Nobody's laughing."

"But nobody's crying, either. It's the usual stupidity, he likes to make jokes. Yours make people laugh, his don't. Wipe off that makeup, and let's go have dessert."

"I really don't feel like it."

"Come on, they even have meringue with melted chocolate."

"But why do you think Babbo got so angry? Apparently he thinks that I really am a lesbian."

"No, no, remember that it's Saverio who was being an asshole to you."

"Yes, but there was no need to slap him."

Miriam's chin began to tremble. "No, there was no need. Fucking Maremma."

Annamaria looked at her mother, and even though she understood perfectly that she was trying to control a profound feeling of despair, and felt sorry for her, she couldn't help seeing the absurdity of the moment: her ridiculous dress, her drunken expression, her attempt to cling to the last edge of sobriety, which had degenerated into curse words in dialect.

"Let's go back and act like nothing's happened. We'll start over from the toast, all right?"

Annamaria followed her, not before checking out her appearance in the mirror with fresh dismay. Her mother took a hand towel, dipped one corner into the water and passed it beneath her daughter's eyes. Annamaria let her do it. Miriam's heart ached for her daughter. But Annamaria felt the urge to laugh. Seeing the results in the mirror she said to herself, "Fantastic. I look like a cross between a panda and a clown overcome by nervous exhaustion."

When they got back to the table only Saverio was there. "Babbo left. He said his fever had come back." He said this calmly, or rather, with a certain relief. Saverio had totally resigned himself to his father's disregard. He seemed not to want to think about it or worry about it. He would have liked for his mother to feel the same way, but instead of reassuring her, instead of saying to her, "Don't worry, I'll be just fine without Babbo's love," he was irritated by the pain he saw in her, by the tension he felt in her yearning to bring them together. Miriam sat back down in her place, across from Sauro's empty chair. She understood that everything was ruined now, that the relationship between Saverio and Sauro was irretrievable, and that however hard she tried to bring them closer again, she would always fail. Anyway, maybe, she'd made a mistake from the start, when she'd decided to marry him. With Annamaria, for example, where had she gone wrong? Why was she a lesbian? Was her marriage so disastrous that the idea of having a boyfriend was unthinkable to her daughter? Maybe she'd made too much of the idea that all men were egotistical, and that she should never get married? Maybe she hadn't stressed femininity enough? Had she left her alone with her brother too much, in the riding arena with the horses? With her grandfather on the tractor? With her father, playing at welding? Maybe she should have bought her Barbie dolls, and skirts, and put more bows in her hair when she was little? Maybe she should have made her play more with other little girls? It wasn't her fault if her friends in the village all had sons Annamaria's age, not daughters. She thought of the package of pink baby clothes that Adriana had sent to her. Maybe the curse had come into effect when she turned sixteen, like it had for Sleeping Beauty.

While she interrogated herself, she felt a pain in her right temple, which she decided to treat with another swig of wine. It was clear that everyone was looking at her, that they felt sorry for her family, for this ruined feast, for the daughter with makeup running down her face, for the lace dress she was wearing for the husband who had left, who was clearly a violent grouch who victimized all three of them. Oh, if they'd only known how nice he could be. What did they know about her family, they should mind their own business. She smiled, raised her chin as if she were challenging everyone in the room, but in reality, the battle was taking place all in her head, with accusations, excuses, and justifications.

She turned to Annamaria: "My precious, what dessert have you decided on?"

She'd never called her "my precious" before.

While her mother was engaged in her solitary war against her sense of guilt and the patrons of the restaurant, the two siblings had smiled at each other.

"What's come over you, kid?"

"Nothing, *my precious*, everything's fine. You're just being an asshole, as usual."

"It was a joke, I didn't mean to offend you."

"It wasn't a very funny joke, in front of Babbo and Mamma."

"Not so funny, you have a point. But again, I repeat, there would be nothing wrong with it . . ."

"Knock it off, you're a moron."

"I'm joking, kiddo, I wanted to see if you were relapsing."

Saverio gave her a kiss on the forehead, and she felt unmoored all over again: she was surrounded by incomprehensible people who continually had to be forgiven. That must have been why she had become incomprehensible to herself, too.

"I don't know, either the tiramisù or the panna cotta," she said in a whisper; desserts always went so well with despair.

They waited for midnight, the three of them. Then Saverio went up to the lovely waitress, who was about to finish her shift, and asked her what there was to do around here, if there was anywhere you could go dancing. She said yes, there was a discotheque, and she'd be going there later with her boyfriend.

"That's a pity," he said, "I would have liked to take you."

She shrugged her shoulders and smiled at him.

"Tell me the name again?"

"It's called White Cat."

"Not the name of the disco, your name."

"Oh," she giggled. "My name is Katia, but if you want, you can call me Kat."

"Like 'cat' in English?"

"Exactly."

"And my name is Saverio, but you can call me '*Very*,' like 'very much,' in English."

They laughed. Saverio regretted the existence of that boyfriend. Before he left, he managed to steal a quick kiss and feel her breasts.

"All night I was imagining what it would be like to sample

that dessert. And I wasn't wrong. You taste delicious. Happy New Year," he said to her.

"Happy New Year to you, too," she responded, smiling at him before disappearing through the back doors.

Saverio returned to the table, where Miriam was signing the bill, and cast an eye at Annamaria, who understood at one glance what had happened. It was incredible to her how easy it was for her brother to attract women. "Who knows what they see in that mass of muscles," she thought. "It must be the blue eyes and the black hair; one day I'll buy myself some contact lenses, and then we'll see."

It was freezing outside. They heard booming sounds; in another valley they could see the luminous bursts of fireworks.

"Let's go to bed, tomorrow we have to leave early."

"What a shitty New Year's Eve," said Saverio. "Let's hope the rest of the year won't be this cruddy. To bed at 1 A.M., like children. I've got to hop around a little at the disco, I'm going to go do that."

"Suit yourself, I'll wake you tomorrow at seven."

"Let's hope that tomorrow I'm still awake at seven. Good night, and Happy New Year, ladies. Give my regards to Babbo. I promise that this year I'll be better, in so far as that's possible," he said, heading away from the hotel.

Miriam responded, "May you succeed." She and Annamaria continued on their own. On the snowy path they saw two dogs running off, spooked by the booming of the fireworks. They soon vanished; only a sliver of moonlight remained, illuminating the snow. Mother and daughter walked in silence, listening to the crunching under their boots. Their rhythmic steps seemed to say to Annamaria, *An-swer, an-swer, an-swer.*

Another year was beginning, and she didn't know how to answer. She didn't even know what the question was.

Meanwhile, with every step Miriam felt the chafing of the red synthetic underwear she'd bought for the occasion—the lace thong rode up between her buttocks, she couldn't wait to take it off. She had hoped Sauro would do that, had hoped at least that it might set off the propitiatory lovemaking that they'd always done on New Year's Eve, crude, quick, and drunken. Instead she found him already asleep in the room and very sweaty: it probably was true that he'd come down with a fever again. She thought it was better that way—indeed, she truly was tired and would have liked to sleep so long that she'd wake up and find out that it was already summer, with the apricots ripe on the tree in front of the house, and Annamaria gathering them. She took off her underwear and massaged her breasts a little, once they were freed from the elastic cage that had confined them. She put on her flannel nightgown and lay down next to Sauro without even taking off her makeup. She had drunk too much. She tried to fall asleep in the company of the apricot tree, even imagining she heard the hum of bees, but it was just buzzing in her ears from all the booze.

That same night, Giulia was at home with the flu. Filippo wanted her to go with him to the party of a filmmaker friend of his, an event full of people from the movie industry. She thought it would have been useful for her to be there, for the newspaper, for contacts, but she was seriously ill. She had a fever of 101°, a splitting headache and chills; even with all the good will she had promised to devote to her rising professional career, she couldn't manage it. She knew that much of the time Filippo didn't believe her when she made up excuses not to go out with him, often there was reason not to believe them, but her face, the crumpled tissues in her hands and her red nose convinced him much more than her words. He'd even asked her if he shouldn't stay home, too. She knew that this was only for show, that he would have killed her if she had ruined New Year's Eve. He'd been stranded by his friend Sauro, who had left for the mountains, leaving him behind in Rome. Giulia sat understood that he loved her, too; there could be no other explanation, her body had understood it before her mind had, her mind filled with paranoia, useless information, prejudices, rationalizations, analyses, and counter-analyses, criticisms, moral judgments, accusations of insensitivity and ignorance, guilt that was inflicted, endured, expiated. She lay down again, her body shaken by chills, put a hand between her legs and made love to him, remembering every time he had kissed her, remembering his neck, his scent, his tongue, the hands which, so many times, maddened by jealousy, she had imagined running over other bodies. In delirium she raved: "For you I lost myself, I was prepared to lose everything, I've already lost everything, you are my most exposed nerve, most buried, most exposed, most hidden. And you, you still love me? You *loved* me? That past tense killed me, it was wrong, more than wrong, it was monstrous. I think of you all the time. You're my blood that flows the opposite direction, my pleasure, my most intense trembling, my most immense pain. Don't look at me now, I'm ugly and sick, my hair is dirty and I'm sweaty and I would disgust you. I want to die, I want to die gripping your shoulders, don't look at me. I'm burning up."

Many times, she saw Sauro coming near her to kiss her, then going away without doing it. In the morning, when her fever had gone down, she woke with confused thoughts, her nightgown sticking to her body. Filippo told her that around one o'clock he had tried to call her, and because the line was always busy, he'd started to worry and had come home. He had found her wracked by chills, she was burning hot and was speaking nonsense; the only thing he could make out was "I want to die," and then he had given her a fever-reducer, standing at the ready to call an ambulance if he heard her talk that way again. In twenty years together she had never done this. Giulia was terrified, afraid she might have said Sauro's name, that she might have said compromising things. Poor Filippo, poor me, she thought; she remembered nothing of her husband's return to the house, nothing of what really happened, she didn't know if she'd ever received that phone call. She remembered only the things that she had repeated to herself in her mind. And it was still true that she wanted to die.

19. The Sun
Heat. New life. Success.

The fields had turned yellow with rapeseed very early, then made way for the green of the wheat and the red of the poppies. The landscapes striped with colors that looked made for postcards of Tuscany only lasted a short while. Long was the season of gold and brown, of fields for reaping, of crop stubble and freshly ploughed furrows.

Annamaria had finished school with honors, and they had bought her a Vespa. She had asked not to work, at least in July, and they had consented. Miriam was happy that she'd started to go to the village on her Vespa, to the games arcade, to the seaside with the kids she'd known forever, and with some who only came in summer. They weren't the same kids she'd known when they lived in the village. Some families had stopped coming because they could no longer afford the rents, but the kids she'd gone to middle school with, the sisters from Florence, Sara and Betta, who had a private house, were still there. At the horse yard, Adan's younger brother had come from Tirana to help as a stable hand for the summer. His name was Duran, and he was eighteen years old. They paid him very little, they gave him food and lodging and a weekly stipend—it was mostly a favor they were doing for Adan, who dreaded Albania, poverty, and unemployment for his little brother. To bring him here was an opportunity, even if after the summer season he would have to find work someplace else. He was a shy, handsome boy, very thin, he had big green eyes that always looked frightened. The grandfather Settimio, never having learned his name, once said, "Call that one over to me, the sad little boy who looks like a gate." After that, Annamaria couldn't look at him without thinking of the aptness of her grandfather's metaphor: Duran had the sadness of an abandoned gate. All the same, they'd connected at once. He had asked Annamaria to lend him books so he could learn Italian, she had given him her middle school grammar book and a textbook to read. He'd also asked her to correct him whenever he made a mistake, and she was glad to. She felt sorry for Duran, she was practically the only person he could speak Italian with. The others completely ignored him: once he'd put on a saddle or cleaned a horse he seemed to become invisible. She'd taken him to the village with her a few times, not without a certain embarrassment. She knew that being accompanied by an Albanian who was almost always dirty and wore weird clothes wasn't good for her reputation.

The other kids called him Duran Duran, and he was their favorite object of ridicule. If they wanted to make fun of someone for how they were dressed, they would say: "You're dressed like Duran Duran." If someone wanted to tell the others that he didn't have any lira on him, he'd turn his pockets inside out and say, "Tonight I'm broke, I'm worse than Duran Duran." At a certain point it was no longer necessary to add other words: when anything didn't go well, was inadequate or pathetic, you'd just say, "Duran Duran," and everybody understood.

Annamaria felt sorry for him, but often at night she slipped out furtively, knowing that otherwise he would have asked her to take him to town on her Vespa, and she preferred to go out secretly rather than tell him no. A few times he'd gone to the sea with the group. He had very pale skin and immediately got sunburned. He had a terrible swimsuit, one of those Speedo types that were hardly worn anymore, and he didn't know how to swim. Thanks to life in the country, he'd put on a little weight and become more muscular, but his appearance suggested poverty too strongly to be considered attractive. And still, one night, as he was standing at the bar leaning against the counter, his blond forelock washed for once, his suntanned face setting off his green eyes, and in better shape than usual from lifting bales of hay, moving equipment and eating Miriam's good food, Sara had poked Annamaria with her elbow and said to her: "We're used to seeing him one way, but take a look and just picture it: in better clothes, Duran Duran wouldn't be half bad."

Anamaria thought about it. If Sara could see it, maybe she could see it, too.

Duran spent all day in the horse yard and bunked with his brother in a trailer with a thatched roof that was parked behind the hayloft. To camouflage it, they'd grown vines all around the fence, and for a long time it had been almost invisible. There was no running water, and Annamaria knew that Adan and Duran bathed when they could with cold water from the watering can attached to the horse trough. They used the Saddlery's service bathroom. One day Annamaria had taken pants and T-shirts that her brother no longer wore from his wardrobe and given them to the two Albanians. When Saverio saw Duran in a salmon-colored T-shirt with a surfing shark on it he scowled at him. He immediately thought he'd gone into the house and stolen it from him. He grabbed him by the collar and asked him with an ugly expression: "And where in the hell did you get that? The boy turned red and answered, "Annamaria give to me, I sorry, sorry, I give back to you." Saverio let him go and said: "No need to give it back, go wash yourself, because you stink."

He brought it up with Annamaria, who should have asked his permission before she gave away his clothes. She responded, "I would give them my clothes, but then they'd look like fags. They're Albanians, they're poor, all they need is to look gay on top of that, you're already pretty racist as it is. You don't even wear those clothes anymore.

"I'm not racist."

"Noooo, of course you're not," said Annamaria, who these days almost always took a sarcastic tone with her brother, part of their continual game of scoring off each other.

In the late August holidays, the carnival came to town. They'd set up in the sports field where Annamaria had won the cowboy tournament. It was a miserable carnival, with only three "attractions": the bumper cars; a carousel with swing chairs called the Chair-O-Plane; and the punching-ball—the *puncibòl*, or iron fist. Lots of people came to the carnival from the countryside, not just little kids, even if the Chair-O-Plane was primarily for them. The bumper cars, on the other hand, were monopolized by the older boys, who amused themselves by making the game dangerous: they cornered the girls' cars and rammed them, so the recoil would jolt them out.

But the main attraction was the fist: with sounds and colored lights, it attested nonstop to the different levels of strength of the boys, who challenged each other and made bets until the carnival closed at night, until the big leather punching bag that received all the blows was covered with blood on the front. There was always a thick crowd gathered around the boys who were doing the punching: the thicker the crowd, the more violent the challenges. Occasionally women participated, too, just as a joke. They took on the challenge, but they weren't even able to hit the center of the bag. They would giggle at their physical weakness, almost flaunting it, as if it were a feminine accessory to display, when appropriate, like the white purses they carried when they went out at night. Almost all those country girls knew how to wring the neck of a chicken, to hack a lamb into pieces with a cleaver so it would fit in the freezer, yet still, landing a punch wasn't exactly something they would be proud of.

Among the principal contenders were Fabione and Sandro. The former ran a gas station with his father; he was a tall, big guy with a face ravaged by acne, his greasy black hair always tied in a ponytail. He had a tricked-out Vespa on which he'd put a fringed seat cover and a tall, skinny backrest. He could cover dozens of yards on one wheel, despite his bulk and the weight of the scooter. Nobody had ever seen anything like it in town. It was plain that he had an anger problem, and for anyone who looked at him, it was almost a relief to recognize how liberating it was for him to let off steam this way. Every punch he landed was followed by a kind of guttural scream, then by the *ching ching ching* of the highest score, which guaranteed him another punch for free. You weren't allowed to have more than three turns in a row, otherwise he would have stayed there all night, landing thousand-point punches again and again, just him alone. This way, the others got a turn. Sandro, his strongest challenger, came from a village in the province of Viterbo, something which in itself obviously constituted strong grounds for hatred. Like Fabione, Sandro scored a thousand points with every punch. After a while he hurt himself and started punching with his right fist, squeezing his wrist with his left hand. He was a bullock with prodigious biceps, probably less powerful than Fabione, but there wasn't a score higher than the maximum score, which lit up an image of the Incredible Hulk, to prove it. For that reason, Fabione got frustrated if he happened to bloody his knuckles. It was easy to think that, as he punched, he imagined he was slugging Sandro's face. Their competition was a kind of simulated boxing match between heavyweights. Fabione would have won in the ring, but at a certain point Sandro left with his sore wrist, something that on its own would have been a concession of defeat, except that he left taking a girl with him, his real victory over ugly Fabione.

One night, Adan had joined in; by then he'd been working in the village for four years and everyone knew him. Between him and Sandro the out-of-towner, it was the latter who was the one to hate, so nearly everyone rooted for Adan. The Albanian knew how to throw punches, but he didn't stay long, especially since he wanted to let his brother, who'd just barely achieved a status above wuss, have a turn. Adan didn't want people to make fun of Duran, so he took him to the bumper cars and gave him money so Annamaria could try out the vertical crane that picked up little toys from a box. Annamaria had money, but she accepted Duran's offer all the same, to make him feel important. She started to guide the crane, moving her whole body as she handled the joystick. The gripper snapped onto the ear of the blue rabbit that she pretended to be aiming for, but she didn't succeed in lifting it up.

They decided to go the Chair-O-Plane, where other kids were, including the sisters from Florence. There was always excitement surrounding that ride, from the first leap, with your arms grabbing onto the long chains, so you could take your place on the swinging seats, where you would sway until the ride got started. If you'd grown since the last year, you would notice if your toes finally could reach the ground, so you could make a little leap at the magical moment of takeoff, just before the ride started moving and the swings slowly, slowly began tilting outwards, and then the spinning kept getting faster, and meanwhile the angle between the chain and the earth widened, and you could feel the wind in your face, and the energy that you drew from the ride and from the music that came from the bumper cars, and they were the hits of the summer, with Rick Astley and Nick Kamen. There really was something that resembled happiness in that centrifugal flight, most of all if someone behind you gripped your seat at some stage, pulled it towards them, and then, just a moment before the curve where the prize tassel was, launched you firmly into the air, and you flew and grabbed those soft strands of artificial leather and knew that you'd won a free ride, thanks to your airborne feat.

Duran had tried many times to launch Sara, who was light and had touched the tassel every time without managing to grab it, so she insisted: "Please make me fly again, Duran Duran." Annamaria had felt a surge of jealousy: even though she was far from being truly interested in that boy, even though she wasn't in love with him, his attentions mustn't go elsewhere. He was the only male who had looked at her that way in her life, and she couldn't even define what "that way" meant, she couldn't recognize it as desire, but she had perceived that there was something nice about having it, she had never had that before, and she knew that that Sara could easily take it away from her.

Niki had said that to her once, that it was nice to have the male gaze upon you, the one that gave you the power to "turn them on," to trigger their desire. A power that Annamaria was sure she would never have, because she was ugly. Niki maintained that it actually didn't depend on her appearance, but on her will: "If men don't look at you it's because you don't desire to be looked at: there are many, many women with physical flaws in this world who are extremely attractive."

For the first time, Annamaria felt like she had a tiny bit of that power. She asked Duran to sit behind her and to try to launch her. He held onto her swing from the start, when they were still on the ground, gave himself a push backwards before it started and grabbed hold. They went around six times, and at the moment when they were at the highest, he pulled her swing back hard against him, then launched it forward with a thrust of his foot. Annamaria flew outside the orbit of the other swings. She felt like she was in space; she contracted her abdominal muscles and captured the tassel. It was a moment of joy that she hadn't felt for ages, she had flown, and she belted a song from the summer whose words she didn't know; somebody had done something for her to make her win. It was a beautiful feeling, one that she'd already felt one time before, and which was something like love. When the ride was over, she gave the tassel to Duran. The free ride was his. He accepted. They went on to win several more rides in a row. He held her firmly, then launched her, pushing her off with his foot; she raised her arm and always found the tassel at the right moment. She flew and screamed. Once they were on the ground, they gave each other high fives and cashed in their winnings. The others got annoyed and decided to go to the bumper cars. They did one last turn on their own. Annamaria didn't take the tassel, even though it grazed her; she didn't like winning when she didn't have an audience to do it for, and she didn't want to win for him, she wanted to beat Sara.

It had grown late. Duran had gotten a ride there with his brother, Annamaria asked him if he wanted to go back to the farmhouse with her. The boy accepted enthusiastically. She had parked the Vespa very close by. Once they'd left the village, as they were traveling the dark road that led home, the crickets going crazy in the stubble of the mown wheat, Duran clasped her waist and moved his hands toward her breasts. She distinctly felt something hard leaning against the base of her spine. She braked abruptly, the Vespa went into a skid, which Annamaria knew how to recover from as she did with horses that reared. She shouted at him, "What in hell are you doing?" He immediately removed his hands and apologized.

Annamaria kept going, she had the wind in her face, the sharp scent of tomatoes rotting in the fields pricked her nostrils. She felt cold, even if the crickets were insistently repeating that it was a summer night. Once they arrived, she moved to say good night, but he didn't give her time, he gripped her hand, pulled her to him like he'd done with the swing at the ride, and kissed her. Annamaria wasn't prepared, she felt Duran's damp tongue pass across her closed lips. So this disgustingness was kissing? She pulled back at once. She didn't know what to do. She didn't want to be rude.

She went back up to him. She kissed him, this time opening her mouth. Then she told him, "OK, let's go to sleep, that's a better idea." He remained motionless. Only his Adam's apple moved, in his neck. If she'd had all the words in her head at her disposal, she would have said something to him, but she knew too little, and it all seemed wrong. He let her go, watching her walk up the stairs, agitated, and from the doorway, give him a quick wave of the hand. When she disappeared from view, he headed to the trailer, his chest pounding with all the things that hadn't been said and hadn't been done, while she went to the bathroom to brush her teeth, spitting repeatedly into the sink.

Annamaria slept until noon, which never happened to her. There was something traumatic about waking up, which she continued putting off a few times, even when she understood that the sun was high, and when the noises coming from the horse yard told her that the eleven o'clock ride was setting out. It was her grandfather who pulled her out of bed, "Fucking Maremma, what do you think you're doing? Get up, there's breakfast dishes to do, and go gather the eggs, do you think it's normal to sleep until noon? At noon we close up for lunch after we've already worked six hours, stinking Maremma, thief of modern times!"

She jumped out of bed and put on shorts without even washing, wearing the shirt she'd slept in. She was hungry. Dodging her grandfather's curses, she went into the kitchen. On the table, next to the bag of cookies, there was a package wrapped in newspaper with writing on it in marker: "For Annamaria." She opened it. Inside was the blue rabbit from the carnival. And a square piece of notepaper on which was written, "It was wonderful fly you yesterday, and when you kiss me, I flying. Duran." Oh no, she thought, balling up the letter inside the newspaper.

She would have liked so much to take the Vespa and rush to Niki to make her laugh a little, and to confide to her that she'd finally found out what it was like to "turn on" a man, a bit, and that it was not for her. Niki, however, was away for the summer as always and would only return at the beginning of September. If she'd found her she would have made her tell her stories about her and Jean, about the fire that always seemed to be lit between the two of them without ever devouring them; about all the betrayals, the abandonments, the fights that had never turned into permanent rifts. In Annamaria's eyes, the two of them were Adam and Eve, who ate all the apples and, when they were kicked out of the garden of Eden, created another garden, still more beautiful; they were inventors of parallel and moveable worlds, who destroyed themselves in order to give life to other universes. She knew that she would never have a relationship like that, even if she had wanted one, or could have endured it, but she needed consolation from Niki, who had told her, "You'll see, it will happen to you, too, it's enough to want it. You just have to grow up, understand, and believe in yourself." She would have liked to hear again the story about the men who'd been brutal to Niki, including the ones she'd dealt with in her cultured, elegant social milieu whom she'd come to love.

"The men in my life, those beasts, have been my muses. For years my work has been fed by suffering and by desire for revenge." That's what she had told her. It would have made Annamaria happy, too, for those beasts to inspire something in her other than repulsion, an instinct for self-defense. She would have liked to tell Niki that Duran only inspired compassion in her, he didn't give her the fire to forge any sword—instead he seemed to sap her energy, transforming it into a pitying tenderness. Only once in her life had she felt as if an intense flame were setting alight all the energy she had inside her, illuminating all her hidden beauty. It was in the arms of a girl with unreadable thoughts, who had spurred her to achieve a great triumph, then had left her there, on the threshold of the door she had imagined was ajar, ready to be pushed open with one hearty shove, but which was in fact armored shut. When she had learned this, she'd wanted to die from the pain of the rejection, and, even more, from her awareness of her own naïveté. Annamaria was sure Niki would have understood, that she wouldn't have judged her harshly. She would have told her something beautiful: "Being a woman is a magnificent experience. You can be whatever you want."

She went to wash her face, and what she saw in the dull mirror didn't displease her as much as usual. She had learned how to apply makeup, and the eyeliner that she hadn't removed from her lids the previous night gave her something of a bad-girl aura, her messy curls accentuating a wildness that she liked. She wondered if it wasn't true, after all, that notion that it was having men look at them that made women attractive. For the first time, she had been looked at, touched, kissed; she had moved a boy, had even gotten a present. But from an Albanian loser. She couldn't help making fun of herself, and she started to sing Duran Duran's "Hungry Like the Wolf" at the top of her lungs. Outside, the bells of Porcu's flock served as backup.

20. JUDGMENT
New consciousness. Rebirth. Family.

After the night of the kiss with Duran, Annamaria asked to do as many shifts as possible at the Seaside Cowboy with her brother. It was a way to avoid dealing with the boy's attentions. She was more interested in doing that than in telling him clearly that she had no intention of getting involved with him. She didn't want him to be into her, but she still wanted to be desired. She was confused.

At home everyone had understood the situation, and teased her as if that would make her happy, as if it were the sign she'd been waiting for from them: that they all recognized that she wasn't a lesbian, that, on the contrary, she had a boy she was "sneaking around with," as Saverio said in front of their parents. It was as if he wanted his jokes to make up for the one at New Year's, and to serve in some way to reestablish the "normality" of his sister's sexual orientation.

Sauro had said more than once: "Better a son who does drugs than a son who's a fag." He was the only one who didn't know what to make of his daughter. Who had avoided every conversation on the subject, even after Giulia's confession. To him, Annamaria was an asexual being: he couldn't conceive that she could be desired, much less that she could ever desire anyone, and still less that she could ever desire another woman. And so, whenever he was troubled by an uncomfortable thought, he thought about that miserable Albanian, who—for God's sake, they were good boys those two brothers—but how could he think of pursuing someone so different;

different in the sense of richer, with a life better than his, how could he even think of coming near the boss's daughter? If he'd known that Annamaria had kissed Duran, he probably would have grabbed him and booted him out of that trailer, kicking his ass every step of the way. He restrained himself to giving Duran stern looks and ordering him around every time he saw him. It was clear that the boy was afraid of him, and that Sauro wanted him to be. Sauro didn't know how to relate to Annamaria. She wasn't his little girl anymore, he couldn't stand watching her grow up, he couldn't see her as a woman, and he never contemplated the thought that his daughter had wanted to kiss Lisa. He didn't know that this attachment had powerfully shaped his daughter's emotional life.

Sauro had lost control of everything. He'd lost his mother as a child, and with her, the affection of his father. Then he'd lost a son, with whom he had no ties beyond blood and resentment. He had a daughter who, as she grew older, was becoming increasingly less recognizable. He'd also had to say goodbye to his wife's submissiveness, even if Miriam was the only one who still seemed to be attached to him, if only for lack of alternatives. And still, with all of this, he only struggled internally with his one material loss: he'd lost the restaurant by the sea. And now he was trying to compensate for that, he used his power with anyone he could: the horses, the Albanians, the dogs, the friends from the village who still saw him as the King, the friends from outside the area who considered him the best among savages, the women who considered him the best in bed. It wasn't so little, but he couldn't count on anything, there was nobody he could stick his neck out for, because there was nobody who would stick their neck out for him. He was the king of an empty kingdom populated by horses, dogs, and unwitting subjects.

He'd seen Giulia again that summer. They'd greeted each other with hugs, full of indulgent smiles. The contact of their *written after New Year's, and once again I felt immensely sorry for myself. Every day, until June, I picked up the phone and dialed the number of the Saddlery, at the times when there was the greatest chance of finding Sauro there. Sometimes I stopped at the last digit, sometimes I let it ring just two times, sometimes I waited for the "hello" and hung up; most of the times Miriam, Annamaria, or Manuela answered, he only answered a couple of times, and I made him repeat "hello" two or three times before hanging up. If there's a god who protects women who've lost their minds, I thank him from the bottom of my heart for having stopped me, even if maybe I would curse him for bringing me to the edge of the abyss this way. I've walked along the precipice for an immeasurable length of time, in which I sabotaged my life and the lives of others with an unconscious obstinacy, all on my own. I chose an easy lover, it seemed like an escape without consequences; instead I found myself in a fatal trap. I let my body succumb to desire, and only after that did I make my heart follow, and even my head. I lost sleep, and health, and now I realize, looking back, that all that time, this story depended only on me. He contributed sex, which was no small part, considering the person he is, a man whose dick is his spiritual guide, but I built all the rest with a persistence worthy of Penelope, my fanciful mind worked on the tapestry with the thread of imagination, with feelings, with illusions, weaving a drama that had no connection to reality. I started to hear voices. What a moron. He didn't love me even for one moment. I'm sure he hasn't devoted even a thousandth of the thoughts I have devoted to him. Now I'm ashamed of what I wanted to do: to call him, tell him everything, confess my passion, propose to him that we start over, go away and live together somewhere, far from everything and everyone. Using the word passion makes me ashamed now: when we saw each other it was clear that mine was nothing but a gigantic illusion. He greeted me coldly. And despite that, I was bold enough to ask him if by chance he'd called me on New*

Year's Eve. With a certain sarcasm, he implied that I was a madwoman even to think he could have done that. He looked at me with contempt. The illusion, and all the humiliating wrong paths he led me on, suddenly became crystal clear. It's almost like I had an unforeseen eruption of pride, a feeling that I thought I'd almost forgotten. I retrieved a fantasy that Filippo and I had chased years ago, when we loved each other and believed we could also do good by adopting an African baby. How comfortable I felt back inside my dear, old hypocrisy about who's been raised to tell good from bad, according to a simple, automatic, redeeming rule. I was dead inside, and now I am finally reborn into my earlier life. A resurrection is still better than nothing.

The Seaside Cowboy had resumed activity after the April weekends, and would open permanently in May. Miriam had delegated all the management to Saverio; she had shadowed him, teaching him the trade for several months. Things had gone surprisingly well at the beginning—Saverio was extremely capable and demonstrated great determination. His mother thought that for once maybe she'd done the right thing: her son was keeping his New Year's promise. He listened to her patiently and let himself be scolded when he made mistakes. Often, at least in the first period, they went together to do the shopping and to speak to the wholesale suppliers, and together they had decided the weekly supplies, the menu, the rotations of the waiters' shifts, the selection of new wines. Saverio went personally to pick up the fresh fish and to buy the newspapers to spread out in the display rack every morning for the clientele, who were used to breakfasting with the day's headlines. He also took care of paying the bills, and made sure that the laundry service brought the clean tablecloths back in time. He had re-stained the woodwork by himself, choosing a sage green that was very fashionable that year, and remounted the photos of the VIPs at the opening party in art gallery-style frames. Luca had never interfered in the management, he'd only asked about the framed photos, which in his opinion gave the effect of a "pizza joint with TV celebrities on the wall," like the one near RAI in Piazza Mazzini.

Saverio worked, convinced by his mother that this place was his, that it represented his redemption and his future. Unfortunately, Luca arrived every now and then to remind him of the truth; in the end, he was the boss.

Filippo, without anything truly having been agreed upon with his son, had decided to hand him the reins. When he arrived at the village on weekends—practically all of them—he spent his time at the farmhouse, on horseback, or at the Saddlery with Sauro. Not that he'd given up networking; he'd simply diverted it from the Seaside Cowboy to his own home. He'd hired a new Filipino couple, Màlia and José (rebaptized Malìa and Giusè), who lived in the annex of the farmhouse, in front of which he'd placed a table of raw wood that seated twenty-four, with an outdoor oven set in brickwork near it. When the Sanfilippis arrived with their friends, all summer long, the couple was not granted any days off. Màlia knew how to cook very well, especially Roman dishes she'd learned from the lady she worked for before. When the lady had died, she had been left without savings and without any of the things the old lady had promised her when she was alive, which the heirs had refused to recognize ("The mink coat? I mean, can you imagine? Besides, what can she do with it, she's under five feet tall!" the granddaughter, one of Giulia's best friends, had said to her), and she had returned to the Philippines. For long enough to marry José and have a son, and then they had moved back to Rome, finding work with the Sanfilippis.

"They hit the jackpot with us!" Giulia thought to herself every time she paid them their salary at the end of the month. At the beginning she'd thought it might have been nice to let them bring their child, too, who had stayed back in Manila with his grandmother, but soon she took care not to propose that; it seemed to her that she was already doing too much for them. If the whole family were brought over, who would ever have been able to pry them out?

That summer, the beautiful allée of cypresses that led to the Sanfilippis' farmhouse was trod by the choicest leather loafers. The outdoor oven was perfect for lavish fish dinners, consumed in the shade of the olive trees, amid the droning of the cicadas, where there would be digestifs after dinner based on limoncello that had been made in the house, where the guests would throw off their elegant linens and do battle with watermelons in their bathing suits, finishing with a swim in the pool. Glasses clinked around Filippo, forging tacit alliances. Endless arguments went on, often about food, the best wines, and private access to the sea, which allowed you to be on the beach with nobody else around, even to go nude. There was always someone among them who occupied one of the twenty estates in the region with more than twenty-four hundred acres, which had been bought by Milanese businessmen in the twenties who had privatized everything in the area between the countryside and the sea. They were happy to find themselves among their own kind, just them. Filippo liked to teach everyone how to make the best salmoriglio marinade for the sea bream: to warm the oil in a bain-marie, not to use too much grated garlic, to add parsley and oregano in place of rosemary, which he considered banal. Only occasionally were there political debates, usually empty battles over principle, which Filippo liked very much and knew how to lead without getting into too much hot water. His manner of shutting down arguments, with a cutting, "Let's talk about this again when you know more about it," slowly lowering his eyelids and inhaling on his cigar, often irritated some of his guests, usually women or men who were younger than him, who had renamed these evenings "the Communist Lunch Salons." Later the expression was abbreviated, and when Giulia's friends ran into her in Rome they would ask her, "When are you giving the next C.L.S.?" A young Milanese fashion photographer had had his assistant make audiocassettes, which he had distributed to every couple at one of the lunches: Side A, titled "C.L.S.," were songs written by Italians: De Gregori, De André, Dalla; Side B, titled "Communists Just Want to Have Fun," had dance tracks.

Even if the members of the Sanfilippi entourage kept on going to the Seaside Cowboy for the beach and the sun umbrellas, the regular patrons of the restaurant, especially the night crowd, had gradually changed since Sauro and Filippo had left the management to their sons. There were younger patrons, mostly friends of Luca's, but also friends of Saverio's, who didn't shy away from the bar or the company of the waitresses, all of them local girls, to whom he gave brusque orders, alternated with occasional treats, like the fifty thousand lira Saverio tucked into the back pockets of the prettiest ones, at the end of one of the nights when the earnings had been high, and, as a result, so had his spirits.

The first month after school was out, things had gone really well at the place, in part because of the idea, which the fathers had criticized fiercely as an unacceptable loss of tone—of putting a big television on the veranda so people could watch sporting events. The profits were still high, and Saverio was sure he was doing the right thing, that he would pay his mother back for all the moral and material debts he owed her, even if—he repeated this as often as possible—he certainly hadn't asked her to take them on.

The greatest effort Saverio had to make to perform his job, reassuring himself and the others that this truly was the right path for him, had nothing to do with hard work. The greatest effort was hiding the hatred he felt for Luca. Unlike his father, who had found in Filippo a friend he could envy but also admire, and whose reflected status he enjoyed, perfectly at ease in the light that fell on foot of his pedestal, Saverio saw in Luca everything he'd always hated: the arrogant way he emphasized the differences between them, his ill-concealed braggart's manner of waving in Saverio's face all the things he would never be able to have. Even though he was definitely more buff than his Roman contemporary; even though he'd learned to dress like him—Levi's 501s, Timberland deck shoes (no more cowboy boots, not even in winter), solid-color shirts, strictly linen, rolled up to the middle of the arm (never T-shirts, those were just for sleeping), a steel Rolex Submariner watch (which had replaced his more vulgar gold version from the gym days); even though he had given up his mullet haircut, he remained less desirable, nonetheless. Of the two, the alpha male was indisputably young Sanfilippi.

Luca arrived from Rome with groups of friends who belonged to families like his, well-dressed, with big cars; students who were taking a few extra years to finish law school, or who would eventually get PhDs in literature, all of them destined to be called "Doctor" one day. For years they had completely ignored Saverio. Then, when he started running the restaurant, they'd become almost too friendly, with a succession of pats on the back, and "Terrific!" and "Well done" and "Hey handsome, how are you?" Luca never showed up with the same girlfriend three times in succession. He never let anyone at his table pay: they were "my guests," it went without saying. Saverio never protested, confining himself to putting aside all the orders and the related bills, which he totted up on a printing calculator, his method of avoiding tax receipts. Then he would staple Luca's bills together, intending to show them to the accountant when the time came to sum up the expenses and earnings. Saverio had a salary, and he also pocketed a few banknotes under the table every day, which made a difference at the end of the month. It seemed to him like he deserved it, given how much he had to put up with. All July, Luca had done nothing but show up with hordes of friends and give them free lunches and dinners in *his* restaurant. After all, he already had another job; for a year he'd been the personal assistant to a government minister, the same one who was a fixture at the dinners at their country place, and who'd given Luca a small statue by Pino Pascali for his graduation, which Giulia had installed in the former pigsty that had become a winter garden.

Saverio attempted a weak smile; it cost him enormous effort to remain patient and smiling every time Luca arrived with his plethora of pals, who always spoke loudly in Roman dialect, not because they were badly brought up, but out of their habit of letting everyone hear their brilliant pronouncements. "Savè, today there are only seven of us, bring us a coupla bottles right away, and some of those good antipasti your mom makes, the hot ones, with fish," Luca said to him, pointing to the kitchen with his hand, as if Saverio were his Filipino, as if he were incapable of going to get those "coupla" bottles himself. But Saverio kept his temper.

Before the decisive break, there were two episodes that brought them one step away from a fight.

Every June, a dozen little kids from a group home came to spend their vacation in a residence run by nuns, a mile away from the restaurant. The house, which belonged to the diocese, was big but was in a state of semi-neglect. Uninhabited for most of the year, it had big dormitories with windows that had no blinds, and bunkbeds for the children; a room with cots for the nuns; a living room with plastic tables and chairs of the lowest quality whose legs continually broke; and a kitchen with two broken-down cabinets, a recycled stove, and a stone sink covered in ineradicable mold. As there was only one bathroom for twelve children, the nuns only bathed four of them a day, since there was only enough hot water for a few showers; and there was a rule that you could spend no more than three minutes in the toilet. The courtyard of the home had been invaded by underbrush, which the sisters would clear away little by little with the children, while year after year they attempted to revive the vegetable garden. The nuns and the older guests made sandwiches in the morning, and then they all headed off to the beach on foot. They set out two beach umbrellas there, beneath which the nuns sat, all dressed in white, to pray as they sweated and watched the children play in the sand and in the waves, without ever losing sight of them, and shouting at them if they went too far away. The group went to the Seaside Cowboy every day to use the bathroom, but every other day, the nuns bought ice cream for the children. Every time he saw them arriving, Saverio raised his eyes to the heavens: "Here they come again, the procession of snot-nosed kids." He never gave them a hard time, but one day, when the bathroom line was very long, and his favorite customer, a young mother divorced from a semi-famous film director, had complained, he went to chase them away, and told the nuns that this was not a public restroom.

"No offense, but when they're all here together they make a mess, they leave the place dirty, they bother the customers. What do you think we are, the Salvation Army?"

The nun apologized and called the children to order. By chance, the scene was overheard by Francesca, the girl Luca had brought, a young staffer for the newspaper *Manifesto*, who reported the scene indignantly to her boyfriend, who was beyond distracted, checking her out in her bathing suit. Luca jumped at this opportunity. He got up from the table, found the nun, and, in a loud voice, looking at Saverio, not at her, said theatrically: "Sister, pay him no mind. There are some people here who don't know the meaning of the word compassion. But don't you worry, we're not all like that. I am the owner. Consider this place your home. If the children want ice cream, they can have it whenever they like. In fact, starting tomorrow, the children can come here for lunch, as my guests. Is it all right if we make pasta *al pomodoro* and cutlets for them? If you tell me how many days you'll be staying here, we can see to the menu; I'll let you speak to our cook, who's excellent."

Saverio swore softly. As Luca approached, he said, "It's easy to be generous with other people's work, isn't it? You're the guy who made the grand gesture, but who will cook, who will serve at table, who will clean up? The nice boss has come to save the day, here he is. Why don't you go and clean the bathroom after fifteen of them have been in there? I'll show you what they leave behind." Luca remained impassive behind his sunglasses, picked up the bundle of newspapers the girl had left on the table, and left with her.

The next day, Luca and Francesca returned to Rome, and the children appeared reliably after that for a whole week. Saverio seated them at noon, and even though he didn't give them more than half an hour to eat, they got into everything. Really, he was perfectly happy to feed them, but they got overconfident. One of them in particular, a little boy of twelve, black as pitch, acquired the habit of going to the ice cream freezer and serving himself on his own—getting ice creams for himself and the others. The third time, Saverio came up to him and said in his ear, "Listen, blackie, that's stealing, and your nun didn't teach you that, right? If I catch you one more time with your hands in that freezer, I'll cut them off like they do in your country. You got that?"

The little boy nodded yes. He was alarmed by all the muscles, but he could tell that Saverio wouldn't have done anything to him. The times after that, he showed up with a smile, in a faded swimsuit and multi-colored flip-flops, asking, "May I take an ice cream cone?" Saverio raised his head. "Take it and get lost."

A few days later an article come out in *Manifesto* describing the generous act at the Seaside Cowboy—refreshment from the "Little Athens" of the Maremma, which was a place of great compassion, and offered warm meals to the orphans of Sant'Eusebio.

That was the last summer for the nuns and the little kids. The next year, the diocese's farmhouse was bought for a laughable sum, and elegantly renovated by the brother of the government minister Luca worked for as a personal assistant.

One other event over the course of that summer tested the rapport between Saverio and Luca, and it involved a dog. One night, Saverio was coming back from the restaurant Da Vinicio di Ansedonia. The manager was his friend, and was the only one who could get a couple of boxes of Capsula Viola chardonnay for him, which the Seaside Cowboy had unexpectedly run out of. It was already almost three in the morning, and he was on the road near the archeological site of Cosa, when Saverio had suddenly seen a dark shape emerge from a ditch and stop in the middle of the road. There were a lot of roe deer in this area, that went in and out of the pine forest of Feniglia, but upon braking and seeing it in his head-lights, Saverio realized that the creature that had appeared was not a deer but a very big dog, a beautiful Irish setter, the biggest one he'd ever seen. He got out of the car, approached, and saw that he had a collar but no tag. He said to him, "Come on, handsome," and stroked his head behind his ears. The animal let him do it, wagging his tail, just a little bit wary. Saverio carried him to the car and put him into the back without meeting any resistance. He was too beautiful to leave there, he would have ended up on the Aurelia, and besides, he surely was worth a lot of money. At his family's farm, they would give him something to eat and drink, then they would set him up in an empty stall in the stable. After two days the area was filled with signs with photographs of the lost setter, who answered to the name Kubrick. A reward was promised to anyone who had found or seen him. The telephone number corresponded to Vinicio's. Saverio called, but his friend wasn't there; he left his name with someone, and said he would keep the dog at the Seaside Cowboy all day, in case anyone wanted to come pick him up. That afternoon, a foreign lady arrived, middle-aged, maybe German, who thanked him profusely and took back the dog, but to Saverio's great disappointment did not give him a reward. The next day a call came from a man who spoke English; by complete chance Luca was around, and Saverio asked him to take the call, because he didn't understand a word. The man introduced himself, it was Stanley Kubrick, and he wanted to personally thank him for having found his dog, and also to compliment him on their fresh ice cream, he'd come by the place once to get some (he probably didn't even know which restaurant it was, given that the Seaside Cowboy didn't serve homemade ice cream). He said goodbye and hung up without giving Luca time to say anything but, "Thank you, sir."

Luca, once he'd established that the director was in fact on vacation in a villa in Ansedonia, spent the rest of the summer telling everyone the anecdote, bragging that he'd "saved" Kubrick's dog, letting it be known that the master had called him, overflowing with gratitude, and that they'd spoken at length, like old friends, and that he'd even come to eat at Seaside Cowboy, albeit on a day when he wasn't there. Saverio let him do it, shaking his head at his nerve, without giving any more thought to how much of the glory of this success he was taking from him. He was only sorry that he'd given back the dog without even getting a tip; he didn't even know who he

was, this Kubrick. When they explained it to him, he remembered having seen *2001: A Space Odyssey* on video with
Tamara. He'd thought it was deadly dull, he'd probably slept
through the whole movie because he didn't remember a thing
about it.

But it was another incident that brought about the definitive rupture between Saverio and Luca. For the full moon at
the beginning of September, the Seaside Cowboy organized a
Night of the Full Moon celebration. It was one of the events
that Sauro and Filippo had inaugurated, but much bigger,
because Luca and Saverio were able to attract people of all
kinds. Before it started, they held a big, private dinner for the
Biagini family, along with the Sanfilippi men and some of their
friends, for Settimio's birthday. Nobody ever thought about
the old man, but he'd always been there, from the times of the
first horse rides to the rise of the Saddlery. He had attended
every meal, gone to every barbecue, raised his glass with his
calloused hands from the nook where he sat at every drinks
gathering. And when you came down to it, everyone was fond
of him. The idea had come from Luca, who wanted to do
something nice for Francesca, with whom he was infatuated.
"Tonight, we celebrate a true man of the soil, a true communist," he'd told her.

Settimio was moved. Nobody had ever done anything for his
birthday. Miriam ironed his good pants for him, Sauro lent him
a light-blue shirt, Annamaria helped him shave himself with the
straight razor, which she knew how to use with precision and
skill. Once he was shaven and rinsed, she kissed him on the
cheeks, and Settimio felt his chest fill with tenderness for this
granddaughter who caressed him with her soft hands, which
looked like those of his poor Alma. The birthday meal was to
be followed by a party with local DJs, the speakers cranked to
maximum volume from the terrace facing the sea, the dance

floor set out on the beach with plastic pallets positioned under-neath to keep it from sinking into the sand, the bar fully stocked with rum, gin, vodka, and tequila, which Saverio had known to do, having foreseen what was in store: he knew his people, their desire to get flaming drunk on a hot night at the end of summer, with the full moon and the dance floor.

The dinner was cheerful and pleasant. Despite his daugh-ter-in-law's recommendations, Settimio had started drinking immediately. Sauro and Luca sat next to him, one on his right, the other on his left. Luca refilled his glass for him, Sauro emp-tied half of it into his own, and Luca topped it up. Before dessert all three of them were drunk.

At a certain point, Luca tapped his knife on his glass to attract the attention of the onlookers. When he got it, he stood up and said, "I'd like to make a toast to this man, who is a great example of work and strength. Congratulations to Settimio, farmer, great drinker, and above all, a tremendous commu-nist!" Applause broke out, Francesca sang the old Partisan anthem 'Bella Ciao', which nobody joined in on, and she stopped at the word "invader," as the others shouted, "Speech, speech!' at Settimio. Confused, and drunk enough to have completely lost the power of speech, the grandfather unex-pectedly spoke while seated, the capillaries in his cheeks aflame with wine and emotion: "Don't ask me to give speeches, because I don't know how. And I wasn't even a communist, my wife taught me to be a communist. Before her, I would have gone to war to stop working in the fields. I never understood much about politics. I did it for her, made pork chops for the Unità festivals, and she was happy. For her father the miner, who was killed by the Fascists at Niccioleta. Don't you know about the massacre? They wiped out ninety people, all at once. I can only tell you that when you people act like communists you make me laugh, it's true. Because you don't know shit, fucking Maremma. I know you people by now, you could never truly be communists because you don't know what hunger is, what war is, what it is to battle with the earth every day. You don't know what it means to have a boss because you are the bosses, fucking Maremma. And you don't want to be equal to the servants or to the farmers because it's worse to be workers than to be bosses, and you know it, it's useless for you to pretend, damned Maremma. You don't even want us to become like you, because not everyone can be bosses. You want us at the table with you, but only sometimes, to make the gesture. For me this is the first time, and it's also the last. You've cleared your consciences, I've celebrated, and I'm content, and everything's in order. You know what I'll tell you? I don't understand a fucking thing, because I'm old and senile, but you don't look like communists to me. When I look at you, I know that you've ruined communism, and that's that. Because you're not interested in changing your situation, in fact. You're interested in keeping it the way it is. Communists are people who fight for change, and the only person who fights is someone who wants to change for the better, who wants to be better than he is. You're already fine. You were born comfortable, and sitting down, and what you're interested in is staying seated, eating and drinking. You're lucky, you're not communists. And you're worse than the fascists, because fascists you can recognize, they're enemies, but *you* people act like friends. And as my poor father used to say, who believed in God, unlike me, who doesn't believe anymore, 'God, protect me from my friends, I can protect myself from my enemies!'"

Luca had stiffened, he was poised to protest and retort, but Francesca applauded and shouted, "We should take him to Parliament! He's right!" And everyone started laughing and toasting, and people came out with the cakes. Settimio blew out the candles, extinguishing himself in the process, because he'd never given such a long speech in his life. All at once, he

21. THE WORLD
Plenitude. Attainment. Salvation.

T he air was charged with erotic tension. The DJs had arrived right at the moment of the cake. They'd turned on the inside speakers at eleven, when people were still coming in. To start, they'd mixed a row of the latest R&B releases that made the knees go weak and the hips loosen; Lisa Stansfield, Soul II Soul, voices that whispered sensually that this was the night to touch each other, to find someone to make love to, to keep moving, to come to life, to take a spin around the world.

Everyone was looking forward to the party: it was the collective culmination of the carefree mood that had accompanied the summers of recent years. There was the kind of ageless happiness of having a taut, suntanned body, of being able to move, and to enjoy every movement. There was emotion, exaltation. But there was also the hatred that the country boys felt for the *Romanetti*, the "little Romans," which is what they called them, wanting to express their contempt by using that diminutive, rather than the more common word for Romans, *Romanacci*, which meant something completely different. The expression "little Romans" connoted wealth and idleness, which to the country boys were offensive symbols of homosexuality. On the Romans' side, however, there was contempt for the provincials, who seemed to want to keep their distance, but in truth tried desperately to imitate them or to join them, and when they failed to succeed, revealed all their intrinsic and invincible inferiority. In the exaltation of that night, there was also a desire for fistfights, which presented itself as an alternative to the desire to have sex.

Unexpectedly, after more than a year's absence, Lisa had had also shown up. More beautiful than ever, slender, blonde, in a dress of extremely sheer linen without a bra underneath, flat leather sandals, no makeup, new glasses that looked fake. Even Fabione was there, in his torn jeans, a black shirt with a double collar in two different colors, Nikes with a phosphorescent swoosh, his knuckles primed to deliver all the punches he hadn't thrown.

Normally Annamaria would have been working at the bar, but she'd let it be known that after midnight she didn't want to hear about it, she was going to go dance, like everyone else. When she'd seen Lisa again, her heart had leapt into her throat and the blood had rushed to her extremities as if it all wanted to flee at once. She had paused for a moment, but felt her head turning, then, in fact, it really did turn away to avoid greeting her. Lisa had also pretended not to see her, flinging herself blatantly into the arms of someone who probably was her new boyfriend, a guy older than her, who affected the phony air of misery of a philosophy student. After midnight, when Annamaria was heading to take off her waitress uniform, she'd bumped into her as she was leaving the bathroom and there was no way to avoid it. Lisa had said "Hi" in an undertone, and had hurried to get away; Annamaria, jeans and tank top in hand, had raised her head with a jerk that was meant to be a greeting, but her voice hadn't allowed the words to escape.

She'd spent the whole night like that, her heart racing, hating herself for still reacting so strongly to the sight of Lisa, when so much time had passed, when she'd felt the conviction that she'd grown up, become more in control, more knowledgeable. She had changed quickly, looking at herself distractedly in the mirror to take off a ribbon that held a half-ponytail on her head, she had refreshed her curls, and drawn a double line of kohl under her eyelids. She was happy with the way the tank top looked on her—she had small breasts, but if she stood straight you could see her broad shoulders and her firm abs. Plus, her ass wasn't visible in the mirror.

She hurried to go, making her way with a certain weariness through the people at the bar. Francesca, who Luca now regarded as his girlfriend, was behind the bar; as the boss's girl-friend she was entitled to be on the other side. She mixed cocktails, giggling as her knife slipped on the peel of a lemon she wasn't managing to cut. "My god, I'm begging you, I'm totally useless, you do it," she said to some boy she'd invited to serve himself. Annamaria passed her by without saying any-thing. Her shift was over, and she just wanted to go dance.

The dance floor was full. People moved their hips and twirled their sweaty arms as Jill Jones asked, "*Tu vuole la mia bocca?*" It was great to see them from up high. She might never have seen so many people together at one time. She stopped at the fence to single out her friends, Sara and Betta, Duran. She couldn't find them. Luca Sanfilippi was next to her. He was also watching the people dance, looking the same direction as Annamaria, at the part occupied by the "locals." How ugly their girls were! As they bobbed around, flaunting their asses, he thought they looked like a bunch of monkeys. All those hideous women and all those stupid men, those two boastful sexes. He found himself regretting these thoughts, telling himself that, even if he was more intelligent, more attractive, certainly more cultured, and surrounded by more beautiful women, he needed to show solidarity with these people, because they were all cut from the same cloth, when you came down to it. After having formulated these thoughts he had decided to go home. Annamaria, for her part, had spotted Lisa, who, on the right side of the floor, was dancing sinuously, surrounded by an adoring throng. She couldn't stop looking at her. She felt paralyzed by the magnetism of her long neck, which rose to her tiny little ears, a loose strand of her blond hair. Annamaria wasn't aware that she was near the speakers, she felt the bass rumbling inside her; heat spread from the center of her chest and made her ribcage pound. She was still in love, fucking Maremma, and she couldn't deny it anymore. She looked at Lisa and thought she would have loved her forever, that she would have loved only her, because she was the only creature on earth who could be loved, her body was nothing but the obvious symbol of that unique possibility, which held her hostage. She didn't know whether it was anger or love that was making her stomach seize. And yet, if at that moment she had been told, "Press this button and you will completely forget about Lisa, you will erase her from your life and your memory forever," she wouldn't have done it, even though her love was not returned. Silently and with frustration she had shielded her heart from any form of happiness, because she didn't want to give up on that creature and the invisible weapons of fate she had once received in her arms, she didn't want to stop looking at her, or to stop remembering that one day when she had used her legs, her lips, her hands, her voice, to do something nice for her.

The reserved tables were behind Annamaria. Director's chairs, and bottles of champagne inside buckets loaded with ice. Luca was at the nearest table with his group of friends. "My god it's insane here in the village! The girls are all sluts . . . you won't find a thirteen-year-old among them who's a virgin." Then it was on to the waitresses: the tall, horse-faced one had a brown bush; the blonde one was totally hairless. "Can you understand what impression that makes? She looked like a little girl, I asked myself, am I committing a crime?" The other one, Sonia, had "a champion clit," you know, that half-Romanian one from last year—I must say, she was cute, but she didn't bathe, I had to drop her."

"And that one?" said his friend Marco, pointing at Tamara, who was a little ways away.

"I see that one all the time, but she doesn't work here and she's hot stuff, but maybe she's frigid, I haven't done her yet. She's sleeping with Saverio."

"But that one works here," Marco went on, pointing at Annamaria, who had her back turned to them. "Isn't she the one who was serving tonight?"

"Oh yeah, her, she's Saverio's sister, and she's improved a lot, but every time she moves, I keep expecting to see her scratch her balls."

Everyone burst out raucously laughing. Luca hadn't realized that standing behind him, an inch from his seat, were Fabione and Saverio, who said in a thundering voice, "I'm going to kill him." Fabione, who expected no less, though he hadn't fully understood the situation, raised the stakes: "Fucking Maremma, let me do it, I'll smash his head in with one punch." He had already drawn back his arm when Tamara, who had seen the movement, let out a scream that made everyone turn around. Fabione, who by then couldn't hold it back, discharged his fist on the table in front of Luca, breaking it in two, and sending glasses, bottles and ice flying. The young people sitting at the table instantly got up and formed a circle around Luca, who, drenched in champagne and water, took a second to realize that the situation might degenerate into one of those legendary brawls between the Romans and the locals that raged across different areas of the Argentario, and which he'd always kept his distance from.

"What in the fuck are you doing?" he shouted, turning to Fabione. "Are you looking for a fight? You're insane, get out of here right now, I'm calling the cops, and they will arrest you! You'll pay me for the table. Who the fuck is this psycho?" He looked at Saverio with a perplexed air, who, as he was being held by the shirt by the terrified Tamara, stuck his arm out in front of Fabione and said, "He's a friend of mine, he just heard what you said about my girlfriend and my sister."

"Why, what did he say about me?" said Annamaria, who had turned around when the commotion at the table had drowned out the music, and had stayed motionless, watching the scene.

"Nothing, let it go. Everyone, go dance, go right now, before I get angry. I'll clear away this stuff now, and the party will go on." Saverio broke off, taking Luca by the arm as if to accompany him.

"Yes, but let go of me, what the fuck! I'll take care of it myself. And Savè, make sure that that guy pays me," said Luca, detaching himself and rejoining his friends. "Now let's go dance: when you bust their balls these peasants get danger-ous," he said with a forced smile, unbuttoning his sweaty shirt. Saverio, Annamaria, Fabione, and Tamara started picking up the pieces of the table and quickly cleared everything away.

With her stomach in knots, and still not knowing the nasty thing that had been said about her, Annamaria hurried down to the dance floor, where she rejoined her little group. She drank a little bit of Cuba Libre from Duran's glass, but there was a boulder between her heart and the pit of her stomach that kept her not only from dancing but from breathing well.

She made herself act like there was nothing wrong for a lit-tle while, then went back to the bar. She went behind the counter, which was packed with strangers, and made herself a very strong gin and lemon. She drank enough to put herself in no condition to drive the Vespa, but not enough to forget the reasons that had tempted her to drink herself into a stupor. When Duran grabbed her waist on the dance floor, she let him do it, and even when he took her by the hand and led her toward a dark place where the beach joined the bushes she didn't say anything. She was eighteen years old now, and she was sure that she was the only virgin of that age in the village. Maybe it was time, maybe this was how she would grow up, and understand herself, and fall in love, by letting things happen. Maybe making love with someone who loved her would do it.

They lay down on the sand and started kissing; she let him undo her pants and put a hand between her thighs. But when he started to pant into her ear, "Beautiful, gorgeous," she realized she did not want to feel like his prey. Duran's breath in her ear, the smell of his saliva, disgusted her. When he was on top of her and tried to enter her, it hurt, she pulled back and shoved him off, he was already starting to come, he stained her jeans, tilting his head back and saying he was sorry. She got to her feet quickly, rubbed a handful of sand on the spot, trying to clean herself off as best she could. Her head was spinning. She said to him, "Let's forget about it, nothing happened. I just drank too much. I'm going to go now, and don't you dare follow me." And she started running toward the bar. When Betta asked her where Duran was, she shrugged her shoulders. "What happened, did you do it?" her friend instantly asked, as if it had been written all over her, with her smeared makeup, the sand on her clothes. "What in the hell are you talking about, Betta!" She kept on dancing, with uncoordinated moves and a grim look on her face. Her heart was still racing, she felt sick to her stomach. She saw Lisa at the back of the dance floor, the philosopher had one hand on her back while he spoke into her ear, she turned to kiss him, Annamaria saw her tongue. She closed her eyes and sighed.

She was the last one to leave the party, along with Saverio. They closed the place somehow or other, piling all the bags of garbage into a corner while the DJs played the last song, 'Africa', by Toto.

Saverio was drunker than his sister, but she asked him to drive her home on the Vespa because she would need it the next morning; she didn't say what for. She went up to him, resting her head against his shirt, which got soaked down the back with tears and eyeliner during their journey, while he talked to her, following the stream of his own thoughts: "Annamarì, keep your arms off me, it's so cold, cover yourself, get ahold of yourself, fucking Maremma, what are you doing in a tank top, where did you put your sweatshirt? what in hell did you drink to get in this state, I'm going to slap you when we get home, you don't have to get obliterated like we do, Annamaria, you're still young and you have other possibilities, fuck, even if I know you don't believe me, that you don't want to believe anybody anymore, that you learned too early that there's no justice in this world, and that innocence doesn't protect you from anything; but I pride myself on knowing you better than anyone else, because I've known you from the first day, the day you were born, from the moment they put you in my arms, and you had a tuft of black hair sticking up on top of your head that made you look like a monkey, and Mamma put on a hair elastic to keep it down, and I asked if I could lick you, because I was little and it seemed like tasting you was the best way to know you; from that moment I've known everything about you, I knew to tell Mamma why you were crying, "can't you see that she's thirsty?" "look, how tired she is," and I knew when your eyebrows turned pink it meant you were about to cry, but that when your ears turned pink it meant you had told a lie; there will never be anyone, Annamarì, who knows you the way I do, because nobody else will have shared that first part of your life with you, the most important part, from when you were a little girl, every day, from the time you started to become yourself, we rode together on horseback, we hurt each other, we fought, we defended ourselves, we invented a thousand games to play, alone, with the dogs, with the colts, with the chickens, at night we would count our bruises, and we would push all around them to see how much they hurt, what color they would turn when they had stopped hurting, green and purple hurt, but when they were grey it didn't hurt anymore, I always wanted you on my back, I didn't go anywhere without my monkey, you defended me to Babbo a thousand times, trying to take the blame for things you hadn't done, you defended me to Mamma, too, to Nonno, you and I always liked the same things, until finally, we also liked the same girl, and though she chose badly, it's obvious that that cretin doesn't understand anything; fair enough, everyone has their own tastes, but fucking Maremma, couldn't you have at least told me? you could have told me, we would have laughed about it together and I would have kept away from that one, totally, you'll see, she meant nothing to me, I think it's insane that she acts like she's such hot shit, why don't you ever talk to me? why do you always pretend everything's OK? you've always been good and I never was, and now you're paying for it. In the end I always did what seemed right to me, I've gotten a beating for it so many times, but I've never put up with a choice I didn't make voluntarily, maybe in these last few months, but that's finished now, Annamarì, I'm not going to be a good boy who does what his parents tell him anymore; you've always obeyed, you've always done what they asked you to do, and had the right answer to every question, to everything they expected from you; you're a great person and they want you to be beautiful; you're well-behaved and they want you to be rebellious; you're intelligent and they want you to be brilliant; you're open and they want you to be sly; you're nice and they want you to be sexy; you're strong and they want you to be feminine, poor Annamarì, so much pretending; I've always been a disappointment, they've never expected anything good from me, that's been my salvation, you, on the other hand, have started to suffer, stuck in this trench between what everyone else wants you to be and what you are, in fact you've helped them dig it deeper, and now the fear of not pleasing anyone is paralyzing you, making you lose the will to live; I know this time, too, Annamarì, the reason why you're crying, but I want to help you because I love you, because I understood it, I understood it at the hospital when they pumped your stomach, you're the only person in the whole world that I care about, I love Mamma, but she's already made her choice, she's already made her mistakes, she's a grown-up and knows what she's doing, she wasted herself on Babbo, but she's happy that way, but you still have your whole life ahead of you and I want to see you happy, because you deserve it, because if you're not happy, I'm not happy either, because you're the best person I know, and I'm not saying this because I'm your brother, or maybe I am, who the fuck knows; I'm saying this because I know so many people, and I have never found anyone who's better than you; when I thought you might die, I said, *what the fuck will I do now*—it's a good thing you can't hear me back there, with the wind, and this fucking little Vespa with its broken muffler, and the crickets out here, and the ones in that buggy head of yours, it's ridiculous how moronic you are, I don't give a damn if you're a lesbian, but then you waste yourself on an Albanian piece of shit, because you think you have to prove it's not true? but we're still in time you know, to save you from this village, from this family, from this mentality that wants to force everyone into a life like their parents', like they were happy, but you know what a shitty example they set, here nobody learns from you, except maybe me, and you can't learn from anyone, you need to be with people who are better than us and better than those rich outsiders, you need to be with people who think differently, who don't look down on everything that other people do, you need to be with people who can bring out the best in you, the freedom to be what you want and to be accepted as you are, people who make you feel happy, fuck, happy like when I used to push you really hard on the swing, and this time I want to be behind you, I want to be the one to launch you into the world, my sister, when you jump from the highest point; but not now, don't fall now, hold on harder to my back, stinking, fucking Maremma, it's cold as hell, and here you are, moron, in a tank top."

The next day, a very slow day, started late for everyone. Saverio didn't go to the restaurant. He woke up with a great sense of calm, forgot about the appointment with the meat supplier, didn't go pick up the tablecloths at the cleaners, which couldn't make deliveries because their van was broken, didn't go into the village to buy newspapers. He made himself a caffè mocha and went out on to the terrace. He looked down; his sister's Vespa was leaned against the jujube tree, without its kickstand. His headache made the buzzing of the flies and the stench of the stables even more unbearable, magnified by the heat. He sat down on the rush-bottomed chair that was his grandfather's spot. He closed his eyes and tried to think of nothing, listened to the crickets, the sun burned his skin. He opened his eyes again. He tried to focus on the things that had made this place so special, the olive trees, the sea that could be glimpsed from upstairs, beyond the fields gilded with stubble. He lingered a brief moment, immobile. He went straight down to the Saddlery. He found his mother, who'd already been at the stoves for a while.

Miriam turned toward him, her glasses covered in steam, her hair in the cap, the usual gentle smile spreading across her features when she saw him.

"Hey, what are you doing in here? Is it true that Fabione broke a table last night? What on earth happened? I also heard that some people's Timberlands disappeared while they were dancing barefoot in the sand."

"Mamma, listen, I need to tell you something important, can you come out for a moment?"

She wiped her hands on her apron, her shoulders slumped. "Have you screwed up again?"

They sat down at a table in the corner—in the summer the Saddlery always had very few patrons at lunchtime.

"I haven't screwed up, I promised not to do that anymore. But I almost did. It was incredibly close, but I managed to control myself. It's something even I wouldn't have thought I was capable of doing. You should be proud of me, Mamma. Because, under other circumstances, last night, someone like Luca, I would have punched his face in. If Fabione had done it I would have been glad, but he would have killed him, and I prevented that, get it? And do you know who I did that for? For you. For Babbo. For Annamaria. What I wanted to say is, yesterday I managed to restrain myself, but the next time, I don't think I could do it. I can't work for someone who, every time I see him, every time he opens his mouth, every time he arrives with someone, I have to hold myself back from punching him. I've got to quit the Seaside Cowboy, Mamma. This is not a whim. You know I've put all my goodwill into it, that I made things go smoothly, that I didn't miss one day—shit, the butcher was coming this morning, OK, I'll call him later—but I won't do this, truly. I won't do this anymore. He's the boss and I'm the sidekick, he makes me feel that every second, and look, I'd already made peace with that, but the problem is that . . ."

Miriam was listening to him with apprehension.

". . . is that he truly is a dickhead, he thinks he's better than everyone and hotter than everyone, he thinks he can judge everyone from the height of the position where he was installed without ever having had to move a finger. Because that's who he is, he's my boss, he gives the orders. And I can't stay there."

"But look, you're partners, nobody's anybody's boss."

"Don't take me for a fool, Mamma, he's got ninety percent of the place. Please, talk about it with Babbo and explain it to him. If I stay at the Seaside Cowboy I'm running a huge risk, because, one time or another, I'm going to crack, and I'll beat him to a pulp. I know myself. And to go to jail for a couple of pills would have been alright, but to go to jail for roughing up a politician's kid is something I don't want to risk. Please, tell me you understand me. Ask Babbo if he wants to return there to run the place; in my opinion he'd be fine with that. Or go there yourself, you're fantastic. We'll find a solution. I'll find another job. And I'll go back immediately to live in the mansard apartment. I can't stay here. Here we're all in service to the Sanfilippis. I'd rather do manual labor, a thousand times over, a million times, I'd rather break my back than spend one more day being ordered around by that little Roman sack of shit."

Miriam tried to vent her disappointment in a few requests for clarification: what had happened exactly, why was he acting like a child?

"But Savè, at your age, why are you still unable to think of your own good, why don't you understand that restraining yourself is a duty, not a sacrifice that's impossible to bear? Why fight like schoolboys in third grade? What can he have said that was so terrible?"

He tried to explain to her that Luca had truly gone too far, that he had insulted and offended his women.

"But can't you see that when you make certain kinds of jokes, it's fine, but when other people make them, it's unacceptable to you? On what grounds? I think you hate him because you want to be like him, you'd like to have his life. But he has studied, he has the right contacts, he doesn't get into the messes that you do, he's a good boy, he's always been very nice to us. He even organized the birthday party for Nonno, have you thought of that?"

"Very nice, and fake, like everyone else in his family. I would rather be dead than be him."

"But what will we tell him? What will we do? It's the beginning of September. We'll be open for at least another month."

"You go, and put Manuela here."

"Sure, why not, we're all at your disposal. You decide and we take care of everything. Who do you think you are? Look, take this up with your father. I'm done fighting for you."

She was shouting, but she knew her point hadn't hit home.

"Fine, Mamma. I'll talk to Babbo. I'll take the people out riding if he goes to the restaurant. I'll do it gladly, I'll make him understand that his important connections will be maintained—that's all that matters to him, not me."

"Savè, that's not true. Nothing can be done with you. It's pointless for you to say you tried hard. It's not true. You didn't even give it fifty percent. Look, I'm going back to the kitchen. You stir up nothing but bad blood for me. Nobody ever thinks about me, right? There's a problem? Miriam will solve it. You guys are incapable of the slightest compromise. I'm always the one left to clean up the mess!"

To talk to his father, Saverio had to wait for Sauro to come into the stable before the horseback ride. He'd chosen a moment that he knew wouldn't last long, because the clients would be arriving. Sauro was saddling up Pallino. He was sweaty, the horse was snorting, continually trying to swat flies with his tail. The heat was unbearable, and though Duran kept the place cleaner than it had ever been in previous years, the stench stung the nostrils, the need for fresh air was immediate, once you went inside.

When he saw his son, the first thing Sauro did was tighten the horse's girth strap very firmly. Saverio told him what had happened, from the offenses he'd endured and the impossibility of tolerating them, to the miracle of having succeeded in not raising his hand. Sauro had thrown his cigar to the ground, spat, and sworn: "Savè, do you know what I have to say? I thought this would happen before now. Really, I'm stunned you lasted this long. I'm sorry, because for once you seemed happy, and I'd even fooled myself into thinking you were made to run a restaurant. I couldn't believe it, but you know how to do something when you set your mind to it. But it's been a long time since I had any faith in you . . . and, actually, Luca told Filippo that he doesn't want to see you at the restaurant any more. He fired you. He got there first."

"What a moron. I'm the one who left."

"No, you're the one who screwed up, and you're the one who'll pay. He's banished you. I don't want to give you a lecture, it's no use anymore. But I don't want you underfoot. And this time I'm saying this for real. I've forgiven you too many times. You've already ruined the family. Forget about staying here and ruining my relationships with my partners, my friends, my clients. Find another place, go to the Feniglia and be a barista, go and do valet parking, do whatever you want, but I don't want you around here, I want you to stop disappointing your mother, who doesn't deserve it, truly. Every time, she hopes."

"I'm not the one who disappoints Mamma."

"Then there are two of us. But since she loves you more, the disappointment stings her more."

"Ask her about that. Ask her if she likes being the Sanfilippis' servant. Ask her if she'll be as happy working for Luca instead of me."

"Will you stop with this talk of servants? The only one who will end up a servant is you, we'd given you a chance with them. To be a boss. You can't do it, and you blame others. You can't stand to be around people who are helping you. I'm sorry, but I understand, it's hard to be around people who are better than you without feeling resentful. They continually remind you that you're a failure. Get out of here. The best thing for you would be a job at the garden center. You could manage to get along with plants, maybe. But I don't think they're looking for staff."

Saverio told his father to go to hell and kicked a metal barrel, which overturned clangorously, spilling soapy water onto the stable's cement floor.

"Look at that, now what if someone slips and gets hurt! Imbecile!"

Saverio took a handful of straw and threw it onto the slick. Then he left, intending to never see his father, the horses, or this place, again. At the exit of the Saddlery, his grandfather watched him and called out one of his adages: "Where are you going in such a hurry, Savè? Still hunting for death, like the old snake?" Saverio went straight to the house. He went up the steps two by two, pulled his duffel out from under the bed, and put his clean pants in it, the clothes that had been dried and not yet ironed, his flip-flops, his swimsuits, until there was no more room. Certain that he was alone, he turned the stereo on at top volume. Annamaria burst out of her room.

"You idiot, turn it doooooowwn."

"Oh, I didn't know you were in the house, what are you doing here? You're not at the restaurant?"

"No, I have a headache. And you know what? If you're not going there, I'm not going to go there either."

"And what do you know about me?"

"Gossip travels fast."

"So, do you want to go work together somewhere else? Mamma and Babbo would be happy."

"I want to be on vacation. I don't want to work anymore, it's not fair. School is starting soon and I'm tired."

"Good for you, you said it. In the meantime I'll move to Tamara's, and next week I'll rent the mansard apartment or something near Chiarone. They won't see me at home anymore. What liberation, Annamarì."

He picked up his bag, but Annamaria stopped him.

"Listen, if you're looking for a job in a beautiful and unusual place, I know where to take you. But you have to trust me, and you have to be reliable."

"I trust you, and I'm up for anything. At the moment, I'd be fine with picking tomatoes."

"Drop that bag and come with me."

When Annamaria took the keys of the Vespa, Tiburzi came up leaping with a stick in his mouth. He seemed excited to see the two of them together, almost confused. He kept sticking his muzzle between the legs of both the siblings, unsure of which one to focus his joy on. Saverio threw the stick far away for him, and the two of them took advantage of his run to get on the motorbike and drive off. The dog was already coming back with his stick and, stubborn and disappointed, followed the Vespa until his little heart and his short mutt's legs couldn't keep up. Annamaria was kind enough to give him a wave, something in between a goodbye and a suggestion to turn around. She would have liked to wait for him, to scratch his belly and tell him, "Look, we'll be right back," but for a while she'd been trying to stop being so accommodating to others all the time, and the effort required to quit indulging other people's expectations was minimal compared with waving off a devoted pet.

The morning was muggy, and a whitish and monotonous sky was the backdrop to the gray road, which was flanked on one side by dark-green woods, glistening with humidity, and on the other by dusty fields of stubble; in the distance, the olive trees stood in their regular rows, beyond which rose the sea's horizon.

There was a grace in this space and in these colors that Saverio and Annamaria were not fully aware of. It had always belonged to their gaze, it was as if, over the years, the landscape had imparted to them a substance that they had in their blood, a melancholy beauty they did not know they possessed, but which they could recognize as a kind of family trait. They kept silent; despite the anger of the last hours they felt a strange inner peace. They knew they had nothing to prove, which was the most reassuring feeling they could have felt. But maybe there was also something else, in that short trip together through their land, from home to the Tarot Garden. There was the expectation of something new for both of them.

They had skipped lunch, but they weren't hungry. They passed by the fields, made sharp turns, surrounded by the arid vegetation of summer, arrived at the village with its tower and its crows where they'd lived when they were little. They knew they were running away from home, and that this time they would succeed, even if they were only a couple miles away from everything they wanted to leave behind. They were still unsure whether they were going away from something or towards something.

They passed the cemetery where the bandit Tiburzi was buried, half outside and half in; the tree that Saverio had crashed into to avoid running over a prominent man and his dog; the old ironworks; the bar with the curtain of colored plastic strips and the old men outside it playing with greasy cards, Decimo at the door; the field with the grazing sheep; and again, olive trees and sea, all the way to the fork in the road on the right, the unpaved square, the green gate. After they had parked, they lingered for a moment by the Vespa, their helmets in hand. The sky was white, it hurt the eyes.

"You know the artist, right?" Saverio had said.

"Yes. And this will seem strange to you, but I think she may be the person I know best in the world, I know so many things about her life. And above all, she knows me."

"Better than I do? Impossible."

"In a way that you would dream to. In a magical and profound way. She sees the future, and the potential in people. She brings out the best in everyone, and if she can, she uses it."

"Oh my god, she'll never hire me. If she sees my soul, she'll understand that there's nothing good in there."

"The important thing is that you want to work—the only thing she can't stand is slackers. And besides, she won't care at all about looking inside you, she'll look at what's outside. You're young and handsome. And she has a weakness for young men who are handsome and strong."

"Anyway, Giovanna will introduce me, right?"

"I'll introduce you."

Saverio suddenly seemed to have lost all his bluster. Annamaria saw again for a moment the same frightened eyes that he'd had when they'd fallen off the horse, the eyes of someone who didn't know what to do but went ahead and did something all the same. A look that, nonetheless, was entirely his own, full of mistakes, and of courage. Her brother's look.

Saverio had stopped in front of the locked gate. Annamaria knew where to open it without making a sound. "Let's go," she told him.

To pass through the gate was to cross the threshold to another world. That day everything was intensely colorful and stupefying. The statues looked bigger, shining. The Dragon at the entrance, like the ones that guarded castles in fables, had been entirely covered in tiles of green mirrored glass, and there were other colors on the broad, shining wings that made you want to sit down and stay motionless, to look, protected by the big white teeth of that enchanted creature. The Emperor was enormous too, sparkling all over with sky-blue mirrors, with an open mouth from which descended a tongue of enameled steps. The swimming pool where the tongue rested had no water in it, but was ornamented with a sculpture of black metallic wheels, which she understood came from Jean's hand. She also saw a cement path that hadn't been there before. There was writing inscribed in the cement, about the meaning of life and the game of tarot. "If life is a game of cards, we are born without knowing the rules. All the same, we must each play our own hand."

"Read, Saverio!"

Then Annamaria guided him to the Tree of Life, which, in place of branches, had the heads of fat snakes. The trunk was hollow and covered in mirrors; inside was a two-dimensional statue, like a blue and yellow metal skeleton, with a flame of blond hair, falling from an upside-down head.

"This is the Hanged Man," she told him.

"I see," Saverio said. "So, these monsters must be figures from tarot cards."

"Yes, but they've also been completely reinterpreted. Some of them are enormous and others are small—they don't all have the same importance. It depends on how she sees them."

Annamaria had fixed upon the trunk of the Tree of Life, half of it colored in tiles in primary colors, half in white majolica tiles with blue drawings on them. There was also an inlay of fifty small square tiles, the only ones with right angles in the whole Garden. It was a long love letter, titled, "MY LOVE." Each square tile held a drawing and writing in round, childish characters. Annamaria tried to translate the captions from English.

"Where shall we make love?" asked the first tile. "On top of the sun, in a field of flowers?"

"Where shall we make love?" repeated the second tile, with other little drawings. "In a bathtub? Under the stars? In the jungle with lions and crocodiles?"

"What do you like the most about me?" asked the next tile.

"My lips? My breasts? My silly nose? Do you like my hips?" said the writing above a drawing of two turned-out thighs colored with pastel horizontal stripes, with a red heart at the junction.

"Do you like my brain?" asked a little tile with the head of a woman on it that had snakes coming out of it, and wheels, like the ones in Tinguely's sculptures.

"A flower for you."

"*You are my star.*"

A white tile with no design recited a silent affirmation. "A child with you."

"Walking on the beach together."

"Dyed my hair and bought false eyelashes."

"Do you like my new outfit?"

"I fell asleep under a beautiful tree."

"I dreamt about the monster again."

"Tea with you."

"Your hand."

"Remember your 300$ phone call?"

FLOWERS

LOVE LETTERS My love, you are my love, my crocodile, my sunflower, my violet, my idiot, a big kiss from your rosebud who loves you, a little? Yes. A lot? Yes. Forever? Yes.

You are my star.

Here I am.

I would like to give you EVERYTHING. My mouth, My heart, My money, My breasts, My imagination, My time, My terrific cooking (a drawing of purple mushrooms, duck). My everything.

Every morning you brought me breakfast in bed.

Our house.

The trips we took (Africa. A camel.)

The dress you bought me for my birthday.

CLOUDSCLOUDS

TEARS

Timetimetimetimetimetimetimetimetimetimetimetime-timetimetimetimetimetimetimetimetimetimetimetimetime

Grey tile

(An enormous question mark.)

Grey tile.

TEARS

What shall I do now that you've left me?

Will I cry a million tears.

Will I die? (Coffin.)

Will I take to drink?

Take a trip?

Will I consult the stars and a crystal ball on how to win you back?

Will we stay friends?

Will I fall in love again?

Our love was a beautiful flower. It grew and grew, the sun helped it grow.

The rain helped it grow (watering can).

Winter came and the petals started to fall

And then the flower died.

I took the petals and put them in a box (box).

And I locked the box in my heart (box of eternal love).

THE END

"You see, Savè, what true love is like? Niki has something different from anyone else we know. She's like a crazy, brilliant child, with the power of a thousand women put together. And that man with the mustache and the thick eyebrows is the one who left her, but he has built the Garden with her. The ceramic love letter is for him, and Niki has a box with petals of their love locked in her heart."

Saverio looked at her strangely. Annamaria would have said that his eyes were shining. They walked toward the Sphinx. In front of the door Annamaria pressed her brother's hand for a moment and looked at him sternly. "I advise you to do as I do. Don't touch anything."

"What, you think I'm seven years old?"

"I meant that more broadly. You must not break anything here, I've built something precious and delicate with this person."

"You're scaring me."

She smiled at him.

Annamaria knocked softly on the door and, without waiting for a response, asked, "May I come in?" Niki was at the table with the ceramicist. Giovanna was sorting through documents. Niki had a hand-knotted red scarf in her hair and was wearing a long tunic with pink flowers that went all the way to her calves, tied at the waist with an electric blue sash. The reflection multiplied in the room, radiating her figure, which was small, but magnificent in every other respect. She was working on the model of a kinetic sculpture. She raised her eyes toward the newcomers and said, "It seems like lately I only work to decorate the tombs of people I loved. After the cat sculpture for Rico, damned AIDS, and now . . ." She interrupted herself as she realized too late that she was thinking out loud, and invited the guests to come in.

It seemed as if she was having trouble breathing—between one sentence and the next she would inhale, filling her chest.

Saverio had never before felt such awe in front of a woman. For the first time, he was faced with a creature whose intentions he did not understand, and whom he struggled to see as related to his own species. Should he introduce himself? Should he wait until she did it? Or get Annamaria to do it?

Giovanna got it out of the way. "This is Saverio, Annamaria's brother."

He held out his hand, she didn't. "Excuse me, it's because of my arthritis, some people don't know and they grip too hard, and you seem like one of those, and I have atrocious pain."

"I'm sorry."

"Why are you here?'

Annamaria interrupted. "He's looking for work. Can he work with you at the Garden? He's strong and skilled."

"Can he speak, or do the two of you do that for him?"

Niki looked restless, she wasn't smiling. She asked everyone to leave, she wanted to speak to him alone. Annamaria asked if something was wrong. Giovanna told her that it had been a sad period for her, and said that, on top of that, she'd started taking cortisone again, and that made her anxious, but that she wasn't really having an issue with anyone in particular.

Saverio hadn't expected a private interview. He was terrified but had only said the truth. That he wanted to work there, that he needed to work there, that he would have done anything at all to do that.

"Have you ever been a builder?"

"No, but I'll learn. I lived in the countryside. I learned manual labor when I was little."

"Do you know how to make ceramics? Have you ever worked with clay?"

"In middle school I worked with Das. You know, that modeling clay that hardens. I made a trivet for Mother's Day. Once I made a pipe, to smoke. With a hole, and the decorations and everything. It came out perfect."

She smiled. "Good. That seems like something already to me. Do you smoke?"

"Only once in a while."

"I'll tell you right now that it's forbidden to smoke here. Or outside. I have pulmonary insufficiency, and I can't tolerate smoke."

"No problem. Drinking is allowed, I hope."

"Water, tea, or coffee. Come here to me to get that. Have you had problems with your father?"

"Who told you that?"

"Annamaria told me you didn't get along very well."

"It's a little more complicated than that, but it doesn't matter. Or does it?"

"The problems that you have are more important than your abilities. And it's by confronting them that a person understands what he truly knows how to do."

"I know how to attract them, problems. But now I'm also learning how to get out of them. I need to do something different, and above all, with different people than I was obliged to associate with before."

"You're right. You're young and strong. There's a lot to do here for someone like you. The salary isn't very high, but I've always found a way to make sure that everyone gets fairly paid. Finding money for all of you is another one of my talents, and it's not easy. The work here is back-breaking and requires patience and dedication. Don't expect it to be a fairy garden. Everything you see here looks like it's the fruit of magic, but it's made with muscles and sweat and hours and hours of baking ceramic tiles, cutting them, and gluing them together. With welding, reinforced concrete, whitewash. I'm getting older, my arthritis and my lungs are slowing me down too much, but I want to see this place completed. The workmen are fundamental, without them I could never have done it. Do you know how to weld?"

"No, but I'll learn. It might be easier for Annamaria. Did you know that welding was her passion when she was little?"

"I didn't know, but your sister can do everything. She just needs to free herself a little from fear. You must never tell her what to do anymore, all right?"

"I'm still her brother, but all right."

"If you want to be here you've got to promise me. Are you as nice as she is? Do you know how to make people laugh?"

"No, Annamaria has a gift I don't have. I'm the good-looking one, she's the one who's intelligent and nice. At home they divided the assets and gave the best ones to her."

"Fine, at any rate, you're here for the construction site. They will teach you. They've all learned how to weld and how to make cement. But now there's greater need for knowing how to cut the ceramic tiles and glue them. To keep the workshop clean. And that isn't hard, it's just tiring."

"When can I start?"

"Guido will show you what needs doing. Do you know him? The former mailman?"

"Of course."

"We don't waste time here, work is sacred. You'll do two practice days and if that goes well, we'll sort out the insurance and everything else."

"Thank you. I also want to thank you for my sister. I know you're doing a lot for her. She adores this place. She's totally in awe of you. And your myth. I think she considers you to be a kind of queen, a sorceress, a goddess. She's been having a few problems, too, lately."

"I know."

"Growing up isn't easy for a girl here. Also, Annamaria's a little unusual. She acts tough but she's fragile. She doesn't feel pretty, she doesn't feel feminine. The thing that's missing the most for us kids around here is someone to teach us something about the world. Here, all they expect from us is to obey orders and to repeat everything they did before us, they want us to think like they do. As if there were only one path, one solitary destiny for all of us who are born in the countryside. Here, it's the same place, but it's so different."

"In reality it's Annamaria who's helping me. I am only teaching her to be disobedient. Call her in for a moment."

Saverio went out and came back with his sister.

"Now, leave us alone. Giovanna will take you to talk with Guido. You can start at once."

Annamaria felt her heart speed up. She sat at the table of mirrors.

"How was your summer?"

"So-so. A boy fell in love with me, but I don't like him."

"But you fell in love with someone, I can see."

"Yes, but with someone impossible."

"Nobody is impossible."

"Some people, yes."

"In that case you have to liberate yourself from them."

"I will try."

"You will succeed."

"How do you learn not to care about other people?"

"You learn to listen only to what makes you happy. Almost nothing that other people say is important. You need to listen to yourself. But listening to yourself requires a lot of strength and patience. We say complicated and contradictory things. It's a continual struggle to pay attention to yourself. I don't know if you understand what I'm saying. I'll read your tarot for you, that's easier. They tell us what we need to say."

She took a pack from a box that was in a drawer and shuffled the cards. They were ones she had designed herself.

"Now, pick one. We will ask this one who you are."

Annamaria wavered, confronted with the backs of the cards that were spread out on the table. They were all the same, with an irregular black and white mosaic pattern.

She was afraid. She touched one, then with a sure movement picked another.

Niki turned it over. Her lips stretched into an unreadable expression. Was it a smile? A worried look?

Under a roman numeral was the drawing of a Nana, who was dancing with two rods in her hand atop a big egg surrounded by a colored snake, which in turn was perched on a machine with black wheels, similar to the kind Jean built. At the base of the drawing was a text in Niki's goofy handwriting, half in block capitals, half in cursive, that said "The World."

"Oh God, what does it mean? Am I going to be disgraced? Is it bad?"

"No, it's marvelous. It's you. It's everything you want."

Niki slid her the card of The World.

Acknowledgments

This book owes debts to other books, other people, and other places.

All of the volumes that have permitted me to reconstruct the character of Niki to represent the person she was as faithfully as possible are precious to me: her autobiographical texts *Mon Secret* (La Différence, 1994); *Traces: An Autobiography: Remembering 1930–1949* (Acatos, 1999); *Harry and Me: The Family Years* (Benteli, 2006); the biographies by Bernadette Costa-Prades, *Niki de Saint Phalle* (Libretto, 2014), and Marco Ongaro, *Psicovita di Niki de Saint Phalle* (Historica, 2015); the graphic novel by Dominique Osuch and Sandrine Martin, *Niki de Saint Phalle: The Garden of Secrets* (Casterman, 2014); the catalogues *Niki de Saint Phalle 1930–2002,* edited by Bloum Cardenas and Camille Morineau (La Fábrica/Guggenheim Museum Bilbao, 2015); and above all *Niki de Saint Phalle e il Giardino dei Tarocchi* by Jill Johnston, Marella Caracciolo Chia, and Giulio Pietromarchi (Benteli, 2010), for the precious testimonials and photographs of the birth of the "Monsters."

I am grateful to Gemma Pacini and her firsthand accounts: almost all that I learned about Niki that did not come from books came from the direct source of her memories. Thank you to the Fondazione Giardino dei Tarocchi, and in particular to Bloum Cardenas, for her kindness and for her dedication to her grandmother's artistic legacy.

And my thanks also go to Marcello Serra for Kubrick's dog; Tiziana Lo Porto (and Alejandro Jodorowsky) for the books on tarot; Grazia Bessi for the legal and equine advice, and for everything we have shared, of which there are continual traces in this novel.

To Michela Volante, first editor and godmother of all my paper children.

To Sandro, Sandra, and Eva Ferri, to Claudio Ceciarelli, to the entire editorial house of E/O + Europa Editions for their work, and for having believed in us again, more than ever.

To distant friends, to the *babbie*, to my sister Simona, to the early readers who, after having read my book, sent me beautiful messages which I woke up to in this part of the world.

To my parents Franca and Italo, who chose the most incredible places to live, and to whom I will always be grateful: nostalgia for a place is the perfect starting point to write from.

To Mattia, Anita, and Tobia, the *beautiful monsters* in my life, who bring me happiness beyond words every day.

And finally, to the places: I would like to thank the Civitella Ranieri Foundation for the artistic residency in the castle of Civitella in Umbria, during which part of this novel was written, in the best possible setting. And obviously, I thank Capalbio, the unnameable, and all those I spent time with when I lived there: this book is also a love letter to our village, and to the way we were.

About the Author

Lorenza Pieri was born in Romagna but spent her childhood and teenage years in the small island of Giglio, off the coast of Tuscany. She studied in Siena and Paris and worked in publishing for fifteen years. In 2014 she moved to the United States, where she works as an author, journalist, and literary translator. *Isole minori*, her award-winning debut novel, was published in Italy in 2016 and has been translated in five languages. *The Garden of Monsters* is her first book to appear in English.